THE DEATH BRINGER

THE THARASSAS CYCLE
BOOK FOUR

J. SCOTT COATSWORTH

ALSO BY J. SCOTT COATSWORTH

Liminal Sky: Ariadne Cycle
The Stark Divide • The Rising Tide • The Shoreless Sea

Liminal Sky: Redemption Cycle
Dropnauts

Liminal Sky: Oberon Cycle
Skythane • Lander • Ithani

Liminal Sky: Tharassas Cycle
Tales from Tharassas • The Dragon Eater • The Gauntlet Runner
The Hencha Queen (March 2024) • The Death Bringer (September 2024)

Other Sci Fi/Fantasy
The Autumn Lands • Cailleadhama • Firedrake • The Great North
Homecoming • The Last Run • Wonderland

Short Story Collections:
Androids & Aliens • Spells & Stardust Collection • Tangents & Tachyons

Contemporary/Magical Realism
Between the Lines • I Only Want to Be With You • Flames
The River City Chronicles • Slow Thaw

Audiobooks
Cailleadhama • The Autumn Lands • The River City Chronicles • Skythane

I want to thank the authors of the past who helped inspire this story, especially the Science Fiction Grand Dame Anne McCaffrey, whose dragons took me on flights of fancy as a youth that I still have never quite recovered from.

And to Mark, my husband of over three decades, who still believes in me, even if I haven't made my first million dollars yet.

ACKNOWLEDGMENTS

I want to acknowledge the fabulous Kelley York at Sleepy Fox studios for the great cover, and the beta readers who made it through all four books: Jamie Lee Moyer, Kristin Masters, and Sue Philips.

And finally, I want to acknowledge Steven Radecki at Water Dragon Publishing, who took a chance on publishing this series after meeting me at BayCon. I am thrilled to be working with Steven and his team!

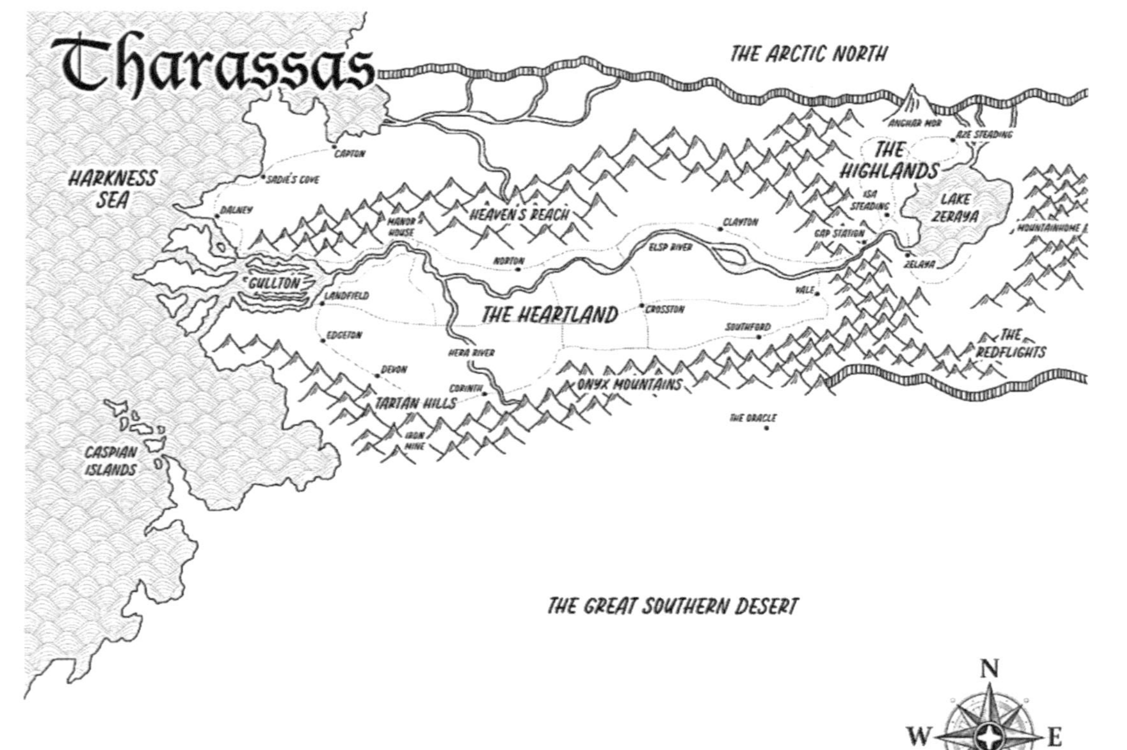

Tharassas
THE ARCTIC NORTH
HARKNESS SEA
ANCHOR MOR
AJE STEADING
THE HIGHLANDS
CAPTON
SADIE'S COVE
ISA STEADING
LAKE ZERAYA
DALNEY
MANOR HOUSE
HEAVEN'S REACH
CLAYTON
GAP STATION
MOUNTAINHOME
NORTON
ELSP RIVER
ZELAYA
GULLTON
VALE
LANDFIELD
THE HEARTLAND
CROSSTON
EDGETON
SOUTHFORD
THE REDFLIGHTS
HERA RIVER
DEVON
CORINTH
ONYX MOUNTAINS
TARTAN HILLS
THE ORACLE
IRON MINE
CASPIAN ISLANDS
THE GREAT SOUTHERN DESERT
N E S W

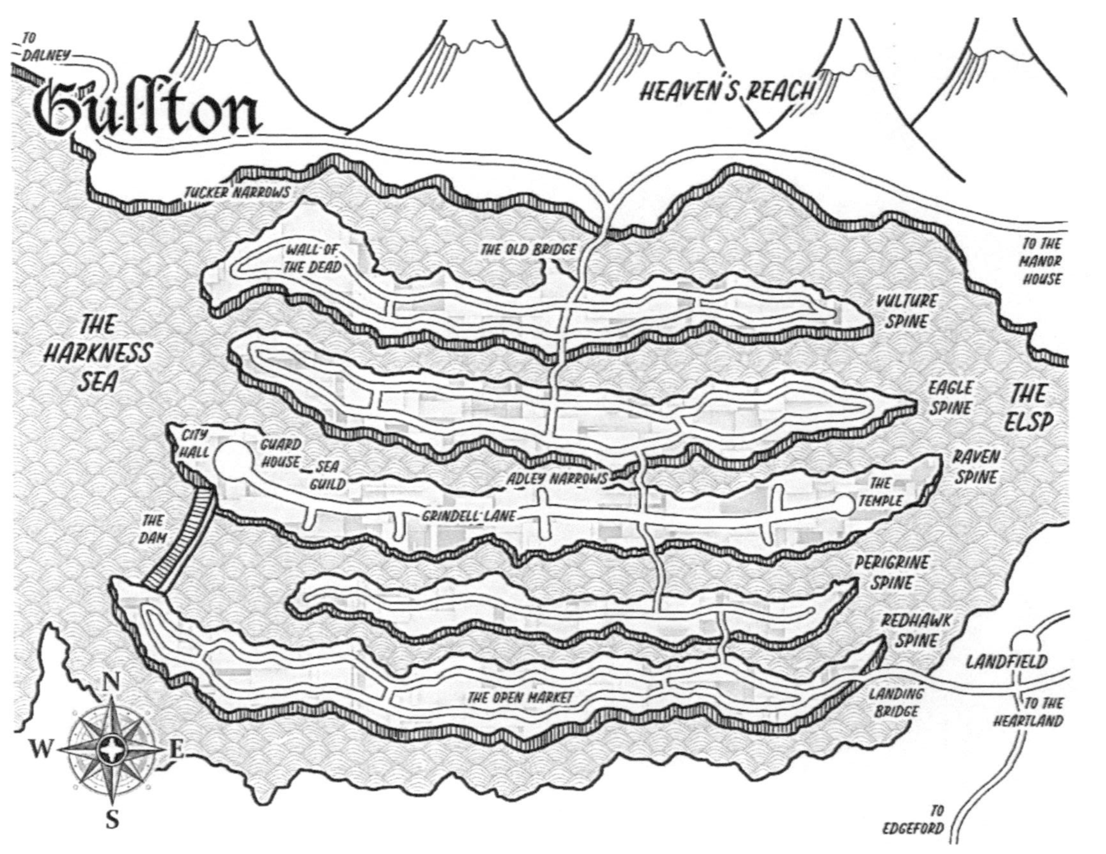
TO DALNEY
Gulfton
HEAVEN'S REACH
TUCKER NARROWS
WALL OF THE DEAD
THE OLD BRIDGE
TO THE MANOR HOUSE
VULTURE SPINE
THE HARKNESS SEA
EAGLE SPINE
THE ELSP
CITY HALL
GUARD HOUSE
SEA GUILD
ADLEY NARROWS
RAVEN SPINE
THE TEMPLE
THE DAM
GRINDELL LANE
PERIGRINE SPINE
REDHAWK SPINE
LANDFIELD
THE OPEN MARKET
LANDING BRIDGE
TO THE HEARTLAND
N
W
E
S
TO EDGEFORD

PROLOGUE

THE SPORE MOTHER SHIVERED.

The progenitor was being ... difficult. He had come to her willingly enough, entering the chamber she had prepared for him. His physical transformation was proceeding, and his own cells had willingly acceded to her.

And yet ...

Something in his core fought her efforts to restore him.

Maybe *fought* was the wrong concept. She searched for the one she wanted.

Resisted.

Yes, that was it. Though he had given himself to her, a small core in his mind had solidified, like a chunk of ice that she couldn't melt. He was an imperfect vessel.

Still, he would have to do. And once he had served his purpose, she could find herself another for Iihil. Perhaps one of those flying beasts her forerunners had fought in that narrow mountain pass. She plucked the word from his mind—verent.

The pain of that defeat still stung, each forerunner's death a thorn prick of pain in her hearts.

She lingered over the progenitor once more, floating in her amniotic fluid, peaceful as a cheevah in its nest.

Soon he would be ready. He would become her farmer, spreading her seeds throughout the fertile mountains and valleys of this world. And her warrior as well, cutting down any opposition.

Soon it would be time to birth her people to a new world, prepared especially for them.

1

REGROUP

HE FLOATED, WEIGHTLESS and naked, surrounded by a reddish light and suspended in fluid. Something connected to his mouth and wrapped around his head, like a lover's embrace.

He used to have a name. He searched his mind for some clue to his identity. *I exist, so I must be someone. Or something.*

That made sense, but got him no closer to an answer. He blinked. *Who am I?*

There was no immediate reply.

He lifted his hand. It was encased in metal. *The gauntlet.* That much he remembered, though it meant nothing to him. Except ... it seemed different, somehow. Thinner.

He moved his arms in the liquid, and it sparkled around him where his shifting disturbed it. The metal extended down his wrist and along his forearm, like before, but now it went farther, around his elbow and up his bicep. He touched it with his free hand.

I can feel it. It was as if the metal had become a part of him, his nerves growing through it. He held out his metallic hand and flexed his fingers. *What is it?*

We call it uurcaa. It's a sacred metal — it will protect you, and if your host dies, it will collect and save your soul. He could feel the emotions she held back from him. *It is the last of its kind from our homeworld. Like us.*

He blinked. *Then what am I?*

You are my son, Iihil. The progenitor, the one who has come before and the first of many more like you. The voice was deep and comforting.

Mother. Warmth infused him at her voice, and an eagerness to please her.

Still, something wasn't right. He was more than that. He searched his mind, running up against that stubborn blankness. Somewhere beyond it were the answers he needed.

He'd been someone else. *Before.*

Who was I? Memories of a face — dark hair, intense eyes that nevertheless twinkled at him. *Raven.*

It came flooding back to him. His mother. His life in Gullton. Training to be a Guard and meeting Raven for the first time. *My name is Aik.*

He reached for the mask that covered his face. It was suffocating. Something was stuck in his throat, and he coughed hard, trying to force it out, whipping around and causing the liquid around him to flash red in alarm.

Calm yourself. The voice was as thick and heavy as an ix hide, and just as soft and warm.

Aik pushed back. *What are you doing to me? I don't want this! Let me out!* He thrashed about, trying to force his way through the suffocating liquid. The metal crept up his shoulder. If it covered all of him, he would be lost.

Calm yourself! It was more insistent this time.

He stiffened as an enforced lethargy settled over him. He lost control of his limbs, falling still in his floating prison. The voice pressed against his mind. *You're safe. Be calm, my little one.*

He closed his eyes and thought of Raven, trying to stay fixed on that face. *I can't let myself forget again.*

Then the world around him dissolved, and he was swept up in a torrent of memories that weren't his own.

•   •   •

"Spin, can you tell us if she's all right?"

Triya's voice interrupted his muddled thoughts. He'd been drifting in memories, piecing together what he could about his life *before*. There were frustrating gaps … years when he couldn't recall where he'd been or what he'd been doing at the time.

"What?" He regarded Triya through his sensors.

She was frowning, her brow furrowed. "Is she all right?"

Ah, Desla. "One moment." He ran a sensor over her prone form. "She's breathing properly. She might have a minor concussion."

Images of his daughter Sera flickered in and out of his vision. Sera, lying in the cockpit just like that, after the *Spin Diver* had crashed. Before the explosion that had jettisoned him from his safe place in the downed ship. Had that been what had damaged his memories?

"Thanks, Spin." She set him down on Desla's pack.

Or had those memories already been stolen? He'd made a pact with the devil. His life — all of it — for the life of his family.

And Sera was long gone to dust.

Desla was nothing like her. The Temple initiate was light-skinned where Sera had been sepia-toned, with beautiful brown skin and a dazzling smile. *Like me.*

But she and Desla had the same empathy for others.

Maybe I do have something to stick around for.

•   •   •

Desla was shaking. Or rather, something was shaking *her*.

She moaned. "Leave me alone. I don't want to get up yet." Her throat was dry, so it came out as more of a croak than an intelligible sentence. The back of her head hurt, too. *Surely it's not time for chores yet.*

"Desla, wake up." Something cool and wet touched her cheek.

Where am I? She blinked, looking up at whoever was washing her face. The person's features were slow to resolve as her eyes tried to focus. Gray hair in a long braid. Fine lines at the edge of her blue eyes.

"She's waking up." That sounded approving, like her mother's voice.

Not my mother … "Triya?"

"Good. You remember." Triya put a hand on her forehead. "You feel a little warm, but then we all are. Can you swallow some water?"

She licked her lips and nodded. "Yes please, Mim."

Triya laughed. "None of that formality, dear. Here."

A canteen touched her mouth, and she managed a few gulps of water. It was warm but wonderful in her parched mouth and throat. She swallowed and nodded. "Thank you."

She looked around, trying to get her bearings. She was in a cavern, dimly lit by a golden glow.

Spin. Did Triya know about the little sphere? Aik had never said if he'd told anyone else. She took a few more sips and then pushed the canteen away weakly. "Enough. For now." She closed her eyes and tried to remember what had happened to her. She'd been hiking across the northern edge of the Highlands. But she hadn't been alone. "Where is Aik?" She looked up at Triya. *How are you here?*

Triya exchanged a glance with someone else outside Desla's narrow field of vision and shrugged. "We were hoping you could tell us. We found you here, all alone."

She closed her eyes. What had happened? They'd found this shelter, grateful to be out of the muggy heat and rain. Then Aik ... Aik had changed again. "He ... left me." She shuddered, remembering the vacant look in his eyes before he'd shoved her aside.

"Do you feel all right?"

"I ... think so. My head hurts." She reached up to find a gully bird egg on the back of her head.

Triya nodded. "Looks like you took a heavy blow. Did Aik do that to you?"

Her memories trickled back, along with the pain. "No ... well, yes. But I think it was an accident. Something's gotten into his head."

Triya raised an eyebrow.

"He's not himself. It has something to do with the gauntlet." Aik had told her so. She remembered that too. He'd looked so scared. "How are you here?" The thought finally made it from her mind to her lips.

"You didn't think you could steal two of my urses and get away with it, did you?"

Desla felt the color leave her face. "I'm so sorry. It seemed ... necessary at the time." Aik had been so lost. "We sent them back —"

"Don't worry about it, girl. I'll settle with the Temple over it later." She grimaced. "If there is a later. Right now there are more important things to attend to. Can you sit up?"

"I think so." She levered herself into an upright position, propping her back against the smooth cavern wall. Her head throbbed, turning her vision red with each beat of her heart. "I don't suppose you have any fellin root?"

"Of course." Triya held up a small ceramic mug filled with liquid. "Drink this."

"Bless you." She took it gratefully. It was bitter, but she didn't care. She swallowed it in one long gulp, willing the pain to go away. "And bless Jor'Oss for seeing you here safely."

Handing the cup back, she glanced at the others, finally making out who they were in the dim light. *Of course. Em and Mes.*

"Welcome back to the land of the living, Cheese." Spin's lights brightened.

"Cheese?" Triya raised an eyebrow.

She sighed. "Long story. So ... you two have met?" She noticed Mes and Em gave him a wide berth.

"Aik introduced us — not by his own choice — shortly after we left the Manor House." She handed Desla a slice of bandy fruit, which she took eagerly. "It was a bit of a shock to Mes and Em here. Quite an amazing little fellow."

Spin flashed brighter, and Desla smiled.

"Yes, he is." She bit into it — the fruit was ripe and delicious, the juices dribbling down her chin.

Triya sat back on the hard ground, crossing her legs. "So, tell me about your little journey."

"What do you know so far?"

"Your friend Spin there has filled in some of details, but I want to hear it all from you. Don't leave anything out."

Mes handed Desla a piece of flat bread, which she took eagerly. "I'll try. I still feel a bit wool headed."

Triya touched her knee. "We can eat while we talk. You need to get your strength back."

"I have a few things from the safe house in my pack, and some bandy fruit."

Triya bit her lip. "Strange that those trees survived ... whatever's happening out there."

Together they managed a decent — if cold — meal together. Just as well, with the heat. The cavern was a few degrees cooler than it had been outside, but she found herself missing the breeze off the Harkness in the evenings in Gullton.

Triya met her gaze. "So, tell me from the start. What happened with you and Aik?"

"I was just coming out of Tad Merriwether's room, and I ran into Aik in the hallway ..." It spilled out of her, from the embarrassment of being caught in the hallway to the horrors at Isa Steading, and the long trail of refugees.

Triya listened quietly, only occasionally asking a question to clarify one thing or another. It was a strange tale, one Des wouldn't have believed herself if she hadn't lived it — gauntlets and talking spheres and nightmarish creatures from who knew where.

But Triya listened attentively, seemingly unsurprised.

When Desla finished, Triya turned to look down the tunnel, in the direction Aik had gone. "All roads lead to Anghar Mor."

"Seems like it. But what does it all mean?" She had her own thoughts about that, but she wanted to hear Triya's. Here they were in the belly of the beast, and they were no closer to understanding what was really happening.

Triya tugged on her braid, her expression thoughtful, and Desla glimpsed her likeness to her daughter. "I've had a lot of time to go over this in my head. And maybe this sounds crazy, but I think this has all happened before."

She frowned. "With Aik ...?"

Triya shook her head. "No. But I think we've landed in the middle of a fight that was going on long before humans arrived here on Tharassas."

That made a strange kind of sense. "Who's fighting?"

"All of Tharassas against an alien invader."

"That's ... crazy."

"Is it?"

"Yes. Aliens? There are coryx in the Heartland that look just like those domes outside." She gulped, wondering if those strange houses in Clayton had suddenly awoken and attacked their inhabitants. "And how can a whole planet fight together?"

Triya took a sip of water from her canteen. "I don't know. I've lived a long life and seen and read many things. For instance, back on Old Earth, things were connected but in a very tenuous way. In fact, the whole biosystem collapsed at one point, making the planet all but uninhabitable for a century."

Old Earth. She blinked. She barely knew the name of humanity's birthplace. It was more legend than fact these days, though the Temple taught its initiates about it. "I didn't know that."

Triya rubbed her chin thoughtfully. "Tharassas is ... different. Everything really is connected. Intimately and directly. Raven's story about the inthyms —"

"How they all combined into one?"

Triya nodded. "It's not the first time I've heard something like that. Then there's the Hencha Queen. She's linked to the hencha, a collective consciousness."

"I guess that makes sense." Everyone knew about the Hencha Queen, and Desla more than most. Silya was her friend, after all.

"Let's call it the *hencha mind*." Triya leaned forward. "What if the hencha mind — the collective entity — isn't just the hencha?"

That startled her. "What do you mean?"

"What if they're all connected? Hencha, verent, erphin, inthym, skeret, vrint, cayah, jexyn, urse ... even our big, steady aur?" She waved her hand. "All of them."

It was a revolutionary idea. "Wouldn't someone have noticed?"

"We're a historically short-sighted species."

Mes cut in. "I'll bet the ce'faine know."

Triya glared at her as if annoyed that Mes had stolen her thunder. "Yes. They probably do. Did you know each one has a little parasite on their necks?"

"Parasite?" Des asked.

"It's called an emp. Kind of like a baby inthym, about so big." She held her finger and thumb about three centimeters apart.

"That sounds ... disgusting." She tried to imagine a strange creature living inside her. She shivered. *Imagine how poor Raven must feel with a verent inside!*

"You'd think so. But the emp ... they let people feel each other's emotions. And I think they connect them — in a small way — with the world's consciousness."

"The hencha mind you mentioned." It did make a crazy kind of sense.

Triya chuckled. "You're quick. I knew I liked you." She handed Desla a canteen. "So here's what I've come up with. This world has spent the better part of four hundred years trying to figure us out. Trying to find a way to bring us into harmony with it. It's the only way it knows. When Sera arrived on the *Spin Diver*, the appearance of the Hencha Queen curbed our worst excesses in the Heartland. Later, the emp tamed the ce'faine. And now the verent have enlisted some of us in the Great Fight."

"The Great Fight?" She took another sip of water. Her headache was receding, and she felt almost human again.

Triya chuckled. "Yeah, maybe not the best name. But we're in a struggle with the hencha mind against another invader. One that's set on transforming this world for its own kind."

She shivered again, despite the warmth. "One that likes things warmer?"

"Yes. It's godsawful hot out there, isn't it?"

"I thought I was going to die from the heat." She looked longingly at the bandy fruit slices on the ground next to Triya.

"Here, have another. We have to be careful with our remaining stores, but you must be starving."

She took it gratefully. What Triya said made sense. They were all pawns in a game that was much bigger than they were. "Spin, what do you think?"

Spin's lights brightened, spinning around his middle and lighting up the tunnel. "The evidence fits. Humanity found its way here, after all, so it's quite possible another alien life form did too."

Another alien life form. She supposed humans were aliens here too, though the idea seemed strange to her. She'd only ever known this world as her own. "What about the wisps?"

Triya shrugged. "Still working on that one."

"If you can capture one, I can analyze it." Spin sounded eager. Maybe he was just bored with sitting around waiting to be talked to.

"Did you know they can make a place cooler? A bunch of them showed up in the safe house we were staying in last night, and the temperature dropped to something almost comfortable."

"Ah." Triya tapped her chin. "Interesting."

"You said this has all happened before? How do you know?" She finished off the fruit slice, wishing she had a little cave cheese and a foldover to go with it.

Triya grinned as if she were a cat that had just eaten an inthym. "What you said before. The coryx."

She frowned. *What do they have to do with anything?*

"Think it through."

There were coryx on Clayton, and some of the other villages up north. They'd been used for centuries to make homes. And they'd never caused a problem.

Then it hit her. "They're ... tamed?"

Triya nodded. "Leftovers from the last war. A war that Tharassas won."

Desla chewed on that. The pieces all fit. "So ... why is it happening again?"

Triya shrugged. "Maybe they missed some of the invaders. Maybe it just wasn't in the hencha mind's makeup to wipe out another lifeform entirely. Maybe that's why they need us."

"Maybe." Though with such power, what could mere humans contribute?

Triya shook her head. "I don't know. It's all just conjecture. We need more information. Silya could confirm some of it for us, if we could reach her, and I'm sure Sister Tela could unearth some things in the Temple archives."

Em piped in. "Send me back. I can find a way —"

"Noble of you. But I wouldn't risk you that way. Besides, there's not enough time —"

She grinned. "I think I know how we can talk to her."

Triya looked at her as if she'd lost her mind. "What, are you a Hencha Queen now too?"

She snorted, covering her mouth in embarrassment. "Thank Jas, no. I want no part of that responsibility."

"Then how?"

It had worked before. Briefly. "Spin, can you call Silya?"

The familiar's light brightened. "I'll see if she's in range."

•   •   •

He fell through the memory hole, flooded with images and smells and feelings that were not his own.

•   •   •

He was young. He was old. His segmented body was breaking down — no, it was growing, fast enough that his outer shell cracked and peeled off, revealing new golden skin underneath. He was a worker. A thinker. A builder.

The world around him shifted and changed as fast as he did. The angry red sun rose and set, and the clouds came and brought torrential, hot rain.

Heat.

It enfolded him like a glove, and he drank it in, literally drinking the water from the warm wet wind which flowed past him.

His universe was filled with wonder. He was born in a creche, his spore mother tending to him after his birth mother deposited his egg there.

He flew with his cohort under the twin moons, above a planet filled with life and color. The domed white eeechha were surrounded by red acchea with red fronds. Writhing aoochhaa vines, reaching for the sun, flashed blossoms gold and pink and green, as if seeking his attention.

He found a mate, and together they made a brood of their own, scattered among the spore mothers, the next generation.

He flitted among the stars, on a ship bioengineered from the eeechha, and explored his own solar system, carrying his racial knowledge to the other planets. Another one, opposite the sun from Uurccheea, was naked and in the right zone to become a second home for the aaveen — Eev-uurccheea — literally New Uurccheea. A hundred years, then a thousand, flashed by as this new home warmed, filling with water and life, a true paradise.

He soared out into the void, a seed seeking other places to set down, to grow, to transform.

Then he found the Others.

The Others weren't like the aaveen, not at all. They were arrogant and angry. They liked their world cool and dry.

At first, the two races maintained a fragile truce, neither invading the other's space. But eventually it came to war.

The aaveen were hopelessly outmatched. They weren't built for war. They fought valiantly and destroyed a couple of the worlds of the Others. Then the unthinkable happened.

He stiffened, feeling the loss of the aaveen homeworld as if it were his own. The sun swelled, and soon it engulfed both Uurccheea and Eev-uurccheea, blasting them to desiccated husks of their former selves.

He wept for the loss. All the aaveen, the beauty of the capital city Uurshea, the red sun rising over the Ooseean Sea.

Just before the end, the seeds went out again, sent at random into the void. Somewhere, somehow, they would create a new Uurccheea — Eev-uurccheea all over again. They carried the flora and fauna of a world in their round bellies, frozen by the void until they found a new home, by chance or design.

•   •   •

His eyes flew open. His mind was filled with visions of Uurccheea, of the tragedy of the aaveen. Of the end of a world and a race that had reached for the stars.

He lifted his arm in the red fluid. It was beautiful, like a sculpture, covered in a shiny shell. Where his hand had been, his fingers formed a claw.

He panicked, shaking in the liquid cell. *What are you doing to me?*

The soothing voice of the spore mother filled him. *Do not be afraid. You are becoming what you were meant to be. Iihil, the progenitor.*

Her voice calmed him. He was being transformed into a better version of himself.

Raven would understand …

Iihil frowned. Who was Raven? *Someone important. My mate? My father?*

Sleep, my little one. The spore mother's voice soothed him, nudging him back into unconsciousness. *All will be clear soon.*

Raven. He slipped back into sleep, dreaming of the beginning of a new world.

2

COUNCIL OF WAR

*F*ire.

Death.

Terrible, muggy heat.

Her world was ending, the hencha keening a terrible death wail in her mind —

"Silya, wake up!"

She blinked, feeling as if she were climbing out of a deep pit. The light was too bright — it hurt. "What ...?" Her eyes focused on the faces hovering above her.

Raven and Kerrick's brows furrowed with concern.

"Are you all right?" Kerrick took her hand.

"I'm awake," she managed. "Where am I?" The last thing she remembered was cold. Bitter cold.

"You're home, in the Temple." Dor's voice, from out of sight.

She grumbled and pushed herself up on the bed and looked around. It was true, though the rooms of the Hencha Queen still didn't feel much like home.

Unlike in her scattered dreams, it was cool in her suite. The curtains shifted in the breeze, bringing in the damp, fragrant sea air off the Harkness. The electric lantern shone brightly on her bedside table. "What time is it?"

Dor sank down on the bed next to her and put a warm hand on her shoulder. "Just after midnight."

Raven looked at Kerrick, who nodded. They shared a grin at her apparent recovery.

When did you two become friends? She didn't like that. Not one bit. "What? Tell me."

For an answer, Kerrick held out one of the long talkers. "Someone's calling for you."

"Desla?" She brushed her hair back from her face, wishing she had her robe on. Not that whoever was calling could see her, but she could have used the cowl to pull on right about then.

"Yes. And no." Raven was being frustratingly vague.

She snatched the thing out of his hand. She'd had a hell of a day, though her memories of what had happened at the Gap were sketchy at best — something about trees exploding and that biting cold. She'd earned the right to be surly. "Hello? This is Sil'Aya. Fin"

"Silya? Thank the gods." It was Triya's voice.

"Mother?" She looked up at Kerrick, who nodded.

There was a long silence on the other end, and for a second, Silya was afraid she'd lost the connection again. "Yes. It's your mother, along with Em and Mes. We found Desla."

Her breath caught. "Is she ... all right? Fin."

"Yes. She has a nasty bump on the back of her head. But she'll be fine."

She let out her breath. "And Aik?"

That long silence again.

"Triya, we don't know how long this connection will last. Fin."

"Yes, of course. I'm sorry. He ... left Des. We're at Anghar Mor. There's a tunnel that goes deep into the mountain. We've only explored a little ways. Desla says he went ahead. I don't know what happened to him. Fin." Triya was smart, already picking up the habit.

Silya looked up at Raven.

His face was white as an inthym. "I have to go after him —"

"Wait. We need to know as much as we can before you do." Her heart ached for Aik — she managed a small smile for that one

— but the stakes were too high to let Raven just run off after him. "What else can you tell us? Fin."

"This is Desla. Aik … he's not himself. Not since the gauntlet …" The story poured out of her, how Aik had been acting strangely. The compulsion to go to Anghar Mor. His frightening lack of humanity.

Raven pulled up a heavy chair from the sitting room, scraping it across the floor, and sank down into it with his head in his hands.

"We have a theory. Fin." Triya's voice again.

"Tell me." Her bitterness toward her mother had fled. She was only grateful to hear from her again after days of silence.

"It's about the verent. Ant the inthyms and jexyn and cayah and all the rest. We think they're all part of the same thing. Fin."

•　　•　　•

Half an hour later, Silya sat at the end of the long table in her suite, sipping at a steaming cup of hot akka and regarding the hastily gathered group.

Sisters Dor and Tela were on either side of her. Kerrick, Coral, Raven, Elleck, Rex'Axon, the sea master, and another of the verent riders named Astrid rounded out the room. Kerrick had slipped back in with Elleck while the meeting was already in progress, and she hadn't had a chance to talk with either yet.

"How are the Gullton preparations coming?" She looked at the sea master, who had been put in charge of the evacuation plan.

"As smoothly as can be expected. The caverns are filled with everything we could get crated up and transported. The network under Raven Spine is the most extensive, but your … team identified places under all the spines. Some of them very … unexpected." She looked uncomfortable at the thought.

Like the ones under the mansions of Peregrine Spine, I'd imagine. She wouldn't be surprised if those were co-opted by the rich after the crisis. Or permanently sealed. She pursed her lips. "Go on."

"Once this is over, I'd like to use them for long-term storage, with the Council's leave. They'd be ideal for wine and other foodstuffs —"

Once this is over. From your lips to Jorja's ears. "I appreciate your optimism. But let's save that for later." Somehow, they'd all accepted her as their leader in this strange venture. It was gratifying, but frightening too. *I shouldn't be leading anything bigger than an initiate study group.*

The sea master nodded and essayed a shallow bow. She seemed to have gotten over her vendetta against Raven, or at least decided to ignore him. It was something.

She turned her attention to the Council leader. "Mas Axon, is everyone cooperating?"

"Mostly, Mim. There was some trouble over in Landfield — a few of the citizens there accused us of a land grab. But that's been busted up. We anticipate having everyone into the caverns by end of day."

She sighed. It was still dark out, but the sky was beginning to lighten. *No rest for the wicked.* "Good. We need to —"

The door to her suite swung open, and Fess'Ima burst in, holding one of the long talkers. The girl stopped and blanched. All the eyes of the room were on her. "Sorry, Mim, but you said to tell you if there was anything urgent." She looked from face to face, on the verge of panic.

She was gratified to see the initiate up and about. "Yes. Come here." The girl looked remarkably well for having been on death's doorstep two days earlier.

Fess'Ima complied. "They're starting to come through the Gap again. Small swarms, not like before."

The room erupted in confused chatter.

Scouts. No one needed an explanation of what "they" were. "Is everyone safe?"

Fess nodded. "The sentry reports that they've all been relocated to the caverns, with a verent to guard them."

That had been a last-minute addition, when they'd discovered how verent could manipulate the temperature to kill the fireflies.

Silya cleared her throat. "There's no need to panic."

The crowd around the table ignored her, chattering to one another like a bunch of fishhusbands.

She burst into blue flame and slammed her fist down on the thick wood of the table, sending a reverberating *thump* through the room.

The voices quieted instantly.

She looked around the table, meeting each of their gazes directly. "We knew this was coming. We proceed with the plan."

"But what then?" It was the sea master, hardly her greatest fan. "The supplies will last us a week — two at best. Even if we barricade the caverns ..." She left the rest to the imagination.

Silya frowned. She didn't have an answer. Not yet. "We're working on it. As soon as we have something ready to share —"

The door burst open again.

Oh for Jas's sake. What now? She had half a mind to station Dor there ... no one got past her gatekeeper without good reason.

A woman in riding leathers with a scowl on her face and a young boy — maybe fifteen — stood at the entry.

She tried not to let her temper and exhaustion get the better of her. "And who are you?"

Astrid, the other verent rider in attendance, gasped. "Chala? And ... Jereck? Oh my gods, is that you?" She rushed across the room and threw her arms around the boy, squeezing him so tight Silya feared the boy's eyes would pop out. "Thank Freja you're alive!"

Raven was grinning from ear to ear.

"Who are they?" A little good news was welcome, but she had no idea who the newcomers were.

He leaned over to whisper in her ear. "That's Chala. She's ... well, I guess she's a verent rider now."

She raised an eyebrow.

"I'll explain later. And that must be Astrid's brother. She thought she'd lost him when Zeraya fell."

"Ah." She wiped her cheeks. *I will not tear up.* "All right, let's adjourn. We'll meet again at noon." She closed her eyes, letting the flames die out and feeling both her exhaustion and the weight of her office. The evacuation was well in hand. But they needed to find a way to end this war before they ran out of supplies, and she hadn't a clue how to do it.

"Mim ... Aya?" The voice was hesitant, especially on the first word.

"Yes?" She looked up to find the newest verent rider standing in her doorway.

Chala was standing before her, holding a spiky ... something. The woman looked like she was made of steel, her body taut as a bowstring. "I brought this for you."

Silya took it and stared at the strange thing. It was a little bigger than her hand, green with soft spiky purple protrusions. "Um ... thank you. What is it?"

"It's bandy fruit."

As if that should be self-evident. "Ah." *Chatty, aren't we?* She'd heard of those. They were grown mostly in the Highlands. She set it down on the table. "I'll send it to the kitchen. I'm sure Verla will be glad to have it."

Chala bit her lip. "No, Mim. I meant —"

"*Silya*, please. No need to be so formal." If she could teach just one of the newcomers, it would be something.

"Silya, then." She nodded, feeling like she'd just passed a test. "Fireflies don't like them."

"What do you mean?" She leaned forward, staring again at the spiky fruit.

"They avoid them. Trees, fruit, everything. Plus, the bandy can kill those white domes."

"Coryx." *That's promising.* She looked at the fruit with new interest. If they could make a salve from it ... "Can we get more?"

This time Chala grinned, a flash of a smile that was more like a baring of teeth. "I brought a saddlebag full."

She broke into a smile of her own. "Bring them to me. We'll see what we can do with them." She decided she liked this ce'faine woman.

"Yes, Silya." Chala looked her up and down and nodded.

"What?" She looked down at her robes, worried she'd spilled something on them.

"You'd make a good suifaine fighter." With that, she turned on her heel and strode out of the room, as if she owned the place.

Suifaine fighter? What in Heaven's Reach is that? She sighed. The world was far bigger and stranger than she knew.

One day, she would explore it all.

•   •   •

Kerrick waited for the crowd in Silya's suite to disperse. He pulled Coral aside and whispered in her ear. "Can you ask Verla to send up a tray of steaming-hot akka and some foldovers?"

"Of course." Coral slipped out of the room, past the departing dignitaries.

Poor Silya looked like she was flagging. That she was up and about at all after what had happened at the Gap was a minor miracle.

Elleck waited with him as the room cleared.

When everyone was gone save for the two of them, Raven, and Silya, she threw her arms around him, almost squeezing the breath from his lungs. "I'm so glad you're back. How did it go?"

He laughed. "Easy on the ribs! It was … interesting. Can we sit?"

She let him go, staring up at him with concern. "Are you all right?"

"Yes, I'm fine. It's just … the ce'faine weren't what I expected." That was a conversation for another time. "Raven?"

"Look, if this is about the verent egg …"

Kerrick shook his head. "We're so far beyond that now." Truth be told, he'd all but forgotten it in the rush of events.

The tension left Raven's face. "All right then. What's up?"

Kerrick could see how eager he was to go after Aik. "I'd like you to stay for this. You have some experience with emps, right?"

He nodded. "I guess it's time to have the rest of that conversation."

Silya's eyes narrowed. "There's more you haven't told me, isn't there?" Her voice had that sharp edge he'd learned to recognize as a sign of imminent danger.

Kerrick kissed her cheek to smooth the waters. "I'm sure he didn't want to burden you." Then he pulled out a silver box from his carry sack and set it on the table.

Her face shifted from suspicion to curiosity. "What's that? Another verent egg?"

The others slipped into seats around the table. Kerrick glanced at Raven — he'd gone pale.

"That looks just like the box I stole —" Looking up at Kerrick, he had the grace to at least blush.

"Let it go. As I said before, we're way beyond that." As far as he was concerned, the boy had seen justice for what he'd done, especially if he'd gone through the emp test Elleck had told him about. Still, it was interesting … did the ce'faine have a hand in delivering the verent eggs?

He set the box on the table next to the bandy fruit and flipped it open. There, nestled in a bed of red mur silk, lay the emp Alibeh had given him. It stirred as the light hit it, stretching like a tiny cat.

She stared at it. "It's so small."

Both Elleck and Raven touched their emp pouches at the same time.

Kerrick suppressed a grin. "The eshem of the East Valley Clan gave it to me, for you."

"What does it do?" The suspicion was back, her voice sharp again with it.

"I'm not exactly sure." Kerrick scratched his neck. "She told me it brings down the walls between people."

Raven nodded eagerly. "That's one way to say it." He looked at Elleck, who nodded.

"It lets you feel — and share — emotions. Especially with someone else who has one."

Silya blinked. "You mean you can *read my emotions*?"

Danger, danger …

Raven smirked. "*That* was never all that hard with you, even without the emp."

She grunted, but Kerrick thought he caught a ghost of a smile flickering across her face.

Crisis averted. "That's about what she told me too."

She raised an eyebrow. "I can see how that might be useful." She turned and paced to the window, looking out at the hencha gathering below.

Kerrick came up behind her, putting a hand on her shoulder. The end of Raven Spine was bathed in afternoon sunlight, with initiates coaxing berries from the even rows of plants.

"So what do I do?" She looked up at him, biting her lip.

There was the Silya he knew, all take-charge and get-this-done. He squeezed her to him. "The eshem said the verent riders would know."

"Then tell me." She twisted out of his grasp and turned to face Raven again, her expression hard as steel.

Raven frowned. "It was difficult bonding with it. The hardest thing I've ever done."

"What, that little thing?"

He nodded, face white as an inthym. "It tests you. Brings you face to face with your worst fear."

Silya tugged at the collar of her shirt. "What was yours?"

Raven was quiet for a long moment.

Elleck put her hand on his shoulder. "Raven's right. It's not to be taken lightly. Some have died, or worse."

"Worse?" Her sharp intake of breath was enough to tell Kerrick she was more anxious about this than she was letting on. Raven was right. She did wear her emotions on her sleeve.

"I was afraid of losing everyone." Raven said it softly, almost too quietly to hear.

"Everyone …?" Silya touched his cheek.

How things have changed between them. Kerrick wasn't above admitting he'd been wrong about the boy, or seeing how he had grown these last few weeks.

"Aik. The verent riders. Even you." A trace of his old insolence returned, his lips quirking up on one side.

"Will wonders never cease." She took a deep breath and let her hand drop. She turned to look at the quiescent emp, tucked safely in its silver box. "How do I do this? Our time is short."

This time Kerrick took her hand. "Are you sure about this? It's not without risk." He swallowed hard. "I don't know what we'd do if we lost you." *What I'd do.* This willful woman had wormed her way into his heart, and if anything should happen to her …

"Yes, I'm *sure*. If this will help us connect to the ce'faine to win this war, it's a risk I'm willing to take." She kissed him, ignoring the startled look from Raven. "You'll be by my side?"

Kerrick nodded. "For as long as it takes." It was good not to have to hide this thing between them.

She faced Raven again, taking his hands in hers. "Promise me you won't go after Aik. Not yet."

He wouldn't meet her gaze. "I can't …"

"I *need* you here. You're the one I trust the most to guide me through this." She glanced at the emp again.

Kerrick saw the merest glimpse of the fear she held in check.

"Once this is over, I promise we'll find him together. I love him too, you know."

Kerrick stiffened. *You still love him?*

Conflicting emotions warred on Raven's face. "I don't know —"

"Promise me." She squeezed Raven's hands.

He broke eye contact, looking down at the table. "I promise."

"Good." She nodded, as if that were that. "So, how do we do this?"

3

INTO THE FEAR

VELIX NUZZLED FLYX with their nose, scooting the recalcitrant kit into Therix's cavern. The older verent had watched them before.

I don't want to stay here. The verentling dug his claws into the rock. *I want to go with you.*

Velix blew out a sonorous breath through their nose, irritated but also charmed by Flyx's adorable recalcitrance. *You can't come. It's too dangerous. You and Aryx will be safe here while I'm gone.*

Aryx nuzzled their cheek. *Where are you going?*

Your other parents need me. It was a relief. Too much time spent on the sidelines while Kalix and Sorix fought the invaders had them nervous as a birthing vrint. And the ongoing shift to male *wasn't* helping. Hormones pulsed through their body, bringing on the seasonal change and making them restless to fight.

Aryx nudged her brother. *Come on. I'll race you to the back of the cavern.*

I'll beat you there! Flyx let go of the rock and lurched forward into the darkness.

Therix watched them go, radiating amusement.

I hope they're not too much trouble.

Not at all. It will be good to have some joy here again.

Velix's skin flushed blue. *You must miss them terribly.* Therix was old beyond knowing, her white skin darkened to a dusty gray.

Therix bobbed her head. *I still have their memories. Now go. Your own mates need you. We'll be fine here.*

Thank you! Goodbye kits!

But the kits ignored them, already busy exploring Therix's cavern together.

What must have it been, to lose both her mates? Velix shuddered, hoping to never find out.

They nuzzled cheeks, and then Velix turned to go.

Fly safe and true.

A warmth suffused them as they gave the traditional reply. *Guard home and hearth.* Then Velix was off into the sky to find Kalix, Sorix, and their human kit.

•　　•　　•

Merged together, Raven/Breeze lifted off from Corinth bearing two children — twins, Alick and Alwyn — both of whom were strapped in and clinging to the saddle on their back and chattering excitedly.

"How high are we?"

"I bet we're higher than anyone in Corinth has ever been."

"I want to be a verent rider when I grow up."

"You wish. You can't even ride an urse without falling off."

Raven/Breeze grinned, forgetting for just a moment the grim task they were engaged in. He remembered what a chatterbox he'd been at that age. He wondered if they realized he could understand them.

They swept across the valley toward Gullton. It was late in the afternoon, but Breeze flew on as if he had all the strength in the world. Still, Raven could feel the toll it was taking on the verent. It had been a long couple of days. He was tired too — they'd been at it all day — but Breeze didn't complain. *We'll take a break after this. I can check in on Silya.*

Breeze protested. *I don't need it.*

Raven snorted. *Well I do.* Breeze was as stubborn as the Hencha Queen.

He'd left Silya with Elleck and Kerrick. She'd been laid out on the bed when he'd last seen her, her closed eyes flickering back and forth, enmeshed in her test. Her new emp nestled in its pouch on her neck, the only outward sign that anything was out of the ordinary about her slumber.

He shuddered as he remembered his own testing ... he could still feel his guts spilling out onto his hands.

Feeling useless, he'd decided to join Astrid and the verent in trying to empty the outer villages. Even Olly and Chala were helping. The last one was a shock, since the suifaine warrior lacked the connection with the verent the rest of the riders had.

Apparently, she'd convinced one of the younger verent to carry her, though Raven didn't understand how they communicated without an emp.

The villagers in the North had been evacuated to the iron mines in Heaven's Reach. There were few charted caverns in the Onyx range that ran along the Heartland's southern edge, though, so they were transporting the people in the south back to Gullton.

Even the two remaining working flitters had been pressed into service.

The skies above the Heartland were bustling with traffic, and Raven considered himself lucky he hadn't collided with one of the flitters in the haste to deliver as many citizens as possible to safety.

At last, the spines of Gullton came into sight ahead, five dark slashes in the shimmering reflecting green of the Elsp, as it widened out to meet the sea. The sun was low on the horizon, and Raven didn't see the flitter until it was almost too late.

Suddenly it was rising in front of them. From instinct they folded their wings and dropped.

The children on Breeze's back screamed.

Thank Jor'Oss, the straps held. Breeze slipped under the craft with just a meter to spare, the downdraft loud with the *thumpa thumpa thumpa* of the spinning blades that carried the old craft aloft. Then they were past each other, and the verent spread out his wings to glide down toward the temple.

Their hearts raced. That had been way too close.

"Holy hencha, that was fun!" Alick, or Alwyn, laughed.

"Can we do it again?" Their twin sounded just as eager.

Children. Raven shrugged, or he would have if he'd had proper shoulders.

I am *tired.* Breeze sounded almost chastened.

Almost there. The Temple loomed before them, bathed in bluish green light as the sun sank toward the Harkness in the distance. In the relatively still shallows along Landfield's edge, a dozen verent bathed and splashed one another. *Wonder if they like water because part of them used to be erphin?*

Breeze alighted in the training field near the temple walls, an open, flat area that had been turned into a staging site for the newcomers.

An initiate helped the children down from Breeze's back. The two of them followed her across the field, chattering excitedly at the site of Gullton and the white Temple.

One of the city volunteers, a short stout woman he knew only as Vreena, addressed them directly, hands on her hips. "Staying?"

They nodded, huffing with exhaustion.

She slipped around their side and got to work on the saddle, removing it from their back. The initiates and volunteers had been doing this all day, and the whole operation spun like a well-oiled wagon wheel.

Raven separated from Breeze, ignoring the giggle of one of the initiates as he appeared naked on the verent's back. *I wish I didn't have to do this without my clothes.* He'd gotten less self-conscious about it with practice, but still ...

He retrieved them from Breeze's saddle bag and slapped the verent on the haunches. "Go eat and relax. I'll call you when I need you again. Are Squint and Thunder here?" Breeze's mates were part of the rescue mission. He pulled on his small clothes and pants.

No, but Squint will be soon. Thunder comes too.

Get yourself something to eat too. The Council had commandeered some nearby farms and their aur herds, but he worried they wouldn't last long, not with so many verent to feed. *A problem for another day.* Hel'Oss knew he had enough for today.

He pulled on his shirt and boots and knelt to lace them up.

The fish have come. Breeze gestured at the cliffside nearby with his snout, and then without further explanation, gathered himself and took off, leaping off the edge of the plateau and gliding down toward his kin.

He got up and strode to the edge, looking down at the waters of the Elsp.

They were teeming with white fish, more than Raven had ever seen in one place, poking their heads above water as they all struggled to push their way toward the waiting verent. He shook his head. *Will wonders never cease?*

"Mas Orn?"

He turned to find a young initiate — maybe fifteen? — staring at him. "Yes, that's me."

"I'm Tess'Esra. Mas Kek sent me to watch for you. He asks you to come to the Queen's quarters." She radiated fear.

His heart pounded. "Is Silya all right?" His exhaustion vanished, as did the hunger that had been gnawing at his stomach, replaced by a leaden feeling of dread. *I came so close to letting go during my test. If we lose Silya …*

It didn't bear thinking about. The intensity of his emotions startled him, but he shoved them back down. *When did we stop hating each other?*

"Lead the way." He knew better than to try to navigate the labyrinth of the Temple on his own. At least he no longer got those dirty looks from the other sisters when he passed through its halls. Men were much more common there these days.

She took him up the hill and up the wide stairs through the back entrance, and then through a bewildering series of corridors and stairways. As always, the place seemed far bigger on the inside than it looked from outside. Though he was finally starting to get the hang of it, aided by his innate sense of place.

At last they reached Silya's door.

Coral stood guard, frowning at the newcomers until she saw who it was. "Oh Raven, I'm so glad you're back!" She hugged him and then gave a slight bow to the initiate. "Thank you, Tessryn. Go grab yourself something to eat in the kitchens."

"Thank you, Mim Lea." The girl curtsied and spun around, practically running back along the corridor.

Coral shook her head. "Poor thing. Just arrived a week ago from Clayton, and everything's in chaos. It's a hell of a time to become a new initiate."

He nodded. "We're all in upheaval. I don't remember what *normal* is anymore."

There were bags under Coral's eyes, and she was pale as an inthym. "Me neither."

"Is she all right?" He glanced anxiously at the doorway.

"I don't know. They haven't told me much, only that I'm to keep everyone — and that really means *everyone* — away until further notice." Coral stifled a yawn. "What's going on in there?"

Raven shook his head. "I can't say. Only that if it works out — there's hope."

She looked at the emp pouch on his neck. "It has to do with that thing, doesn't it? I got a glimpse of her earlier."

She was no idiot, and she'd stood by Silya the whole time. She deserved an explanation. "Yes. It's called an emp. And if she survives her test, she'll be more connected to the hencha — and Tharassas — than ever before."

"*If* she survives?" She'd gone even whiter.

"She will. She's stronger than any of us." He squeezed her shoulder. "Tell none of this to anyone. Is Dor here?"

"She's inside." Coral smiled bitterly. "They couldn't keep *her* away. I'm not sure even the point of a sword would do it."

"I think you're right." He squeezed her shoulder. "Silya will come through this. She has an iron will."

"She does, doesn't she?" Coral nodded, wiping the corner of her eye. "Thank you."

He gave her an awkward hug. "I'd better go in."

She let him go and opened the door for him without a further word, and he slipped inside. It took a moment for his eyes to adjust to the dim light — all the shutters were closed.

Kerrick was sitting by the bedside in the adjoining room, and Dor and Elleck had pulled up chairs behind him.

Silya, his onetime nemesis and now one of the most powerful people in the world, looked small, insignificant. She lay on the bed, covered by a thin sheet, as silent as death. It looked like a shroud.

"Is she ...?"

Kerrick looked up. His face was drawn, the bags under his eyes apparent even in the flickering lamplight. "She's alive. But she's been like this for hours." The big man got up and crossed the space between them. He threw his arms around Raven in a bear hug, squeezing him tightly. "It's good to have you back."

Raven stiffened at the unexpected gesture. "She'll come through this."

Elleck and Dor appeared behind the guard. "She sat up a couple hours ago, still asleep — her screams would have curdled your blood." Dor's face was white as Coral's, and she was wringing her hands.

Kerrick nodded. "I didn't know what to do for her. She didn't see any of us, and wouldn't respond." He gulped. "If I lose her ..."

Raven slipped past him. "That's not going to happen. We have to help her."

Elleck placed herself between Raven and the bed. "You can't. She has to face this alone." Their faces were centimeters apart. Elleck's eyes narrowed, her face hard as chiseled stone.

Raven didn't give an inch. "I can't just let her die. I remember what it was like, facing my fears all alone."

"We can't help her. Her trial is not over." Still, there was the slightest hint of doubt in her voice.

"You prepared your whole life for this moment, didn't you?"

She nodded. "We all do."

"Well Silya didn't. I didn't. We were just thrown into the deep end of the sea." *Me quite literally.* His hand strayed to his stomach involuntarily, making sure his guts were still intact. "I almost didn't make it back." He shuddered to think how close he'd come to choosing death's door. "We need her. Without her, the whole world falls to pieces. So please, move aside. You don't have to help. But I will *not let my friend die* if there's a single thing I can do to stop it."

Elleck's eyes widened, and she held her ground for a moment longer. They stared at one another, the tension so thick that Raven could have cut it with his knife.

"This is ... not something I was prepared for either. Perhaps you're right." She glanced over her shoulder at Silya. Then she slipped out of Raven's way. "Do what you can."

He breathed a heavy sigh of relief, pushed past her and settled himself on Silya's bed. He touched her. Her face was cold. *Too cold.* "Silya, can you hear me?"

She opened her eyes, and her mouth opened as if she were screaming, but nothing came out.

He closed his own eyes, and reached for her emp with his.

•   •   •

Chala leapt onto Elrys's back as soon as their human cargo — a woman and her five-month-old son — had been deposited at the mouth of a cavern in Heaven's Reach.

Others were there to take care of them — a sister and two Temple initiates — to find space inside where they'd be safe.

For now. She prayed to the gods of the sands that her own people were safe. *Elrys, I miss you.*

When this was all over — if it ever was — she would go home. For good. She'd proven herself, despite what had happened to her. She was just as good as any of the other verent riders. *Maybe better.*

She didn't need a verentling inside her to guide one of the great beasts. Elrys seemed to understand her intuitively.

Maybe we were made for one another. Could she take the verent back home with her to the suifaine?

She'd have to figure out such things later. Right now she had more wetlanders to save.

As she soared back down into the Heartland, something caught her eye. She guided Elrys lower, toward the rushing waters of the Elsp. They were rougher, wider than she remembered, and there — the Elsp had breached its banks and was flooding some of the fields. *Meltwater.*

Raven had mentioned how hot it was in the Highlands. She'd seen it herself in Zeraya, though apparently it was worse farther north. And now the river was rising. That could only be bad news for Gullton.

She lifted the long talker Raven had given her from her belt, hoping she remembered how to use it. It was magic — though he'd called it tek-nallo-gee — and it still frightened her, but she needed to talk to him, or to anyone in Gullton. *Now.*

She pressed the talk button. "Hello, this is Chala. Is anyone there? Fin."

Nothing.

She looked at the box. The little light on it was red. That meant she was "out of range." Which was a wetlander way of saying the sand-blasted thing didn't work.

She almost threw it away in frustration, but stopped herself. These things were valuable when they did work.

Instead, she snapped it back on her belt and urged her verent to turn back toward Gullton, following the course of the Elsp.

She wasn't sure what good her warning would do, but she had to try. Raven would listen, and if he wasn't there, she would ask to speak with the Hencha Queen. Silya had been kind to her. "Let's go, Elrys. We have a city to save."

4

SOMETHING WICKED

SPIN SAT ON HIS PERCH on Desla's pack — his latest home among many.

I don't have a home. Once, long ago, he'd considered the *Spin Diver* his home. His domain. It had been made for him, and he for it. When the ship had been sold off for salvage to an enterprising young couple, he'd feared the worst — that he might be scrapped. But they'd fixed him up and upgraded him, preparing him for a long run out to some outpost even his memory cache had little knowledge of.

Looking back, it was clear that Sera had known who he was, all along. She and Tav had chosen him for that reason.

How did I never see it?

He made up his mind. He'd see these humans — his friends — through this crisis. *Especially Desla.*

Then he would unplug himself and let go. *Let's see if the believers in Heaven are right.*

Maybe he'd see his little girl again when this was all over. And if not, at least he'd be free of this unending dull pain of regret.

•   •   •

Anghar Mor shook.

Desla huddled against the cavern wall, hoping the whole place wouldn't come crashing down on them as her pack danced across the smooth floor. She grabbed Spin just before the poor thing toppled off onto the hard rock floor. She wasn't sure if he could break, but better not to find out.

Water sprayed her as the whipping winds outside gusted and blew it far into the cavern. They'd already moved five meters away from the entrance, but still the sprays found them.

"It feels like the end of the world," she muttered as things fell once again into silence. She'd imagined if such a thing ever came to pass, it would be faster and considerably less uncomfortable. If she'd thought about it at all.

"We're not there yet." Triya looked up from her sleep sack, blinking blearily. Desla's gaze met hers. "How bad was that one, Spin?"

Next to her, Em snored noisily.

"Five point five on the Richter scale."

She had no idea what a *ricktour* scale was, but she was starting to learn the numbers. Five point five was *medium bad*.

Her head still hurt, despite the fellin root powder Triya had sprinkled into her water. She reached up to touch the back of her head. It was tender, and there was a bump there the size of a gully bird egg. She and Triya had spent a fitful morning together after she'd awoken, while Mes and Em searched the surrounding environs. They were all running on little sleep, and Desla was feeling hopeless. *I should never have come.*

They'd tried to connect with Silya a few times, with no success. Sometimes her long talker was out of range, or the satellites that made communication possible were. Sometimes Spin announced that he was able to reach it, but no one replied.

It was warm in the cavern, but not as miserably hot as it must be outside, worse than the heat of summer. *How is that possible?*

Somewhere farther into the cavern, Mes had taken up a station, keeping an eye out for anything coming at them from inside the mountain.

Des couldn't sleep. It was too warm, and her mind was spinning. She needed a distraction.

She picked Spin up from the top of her pack. "Spin, can you give me one of those ear things?" She said it softly, afraid of waking Triya. The woman had run herself and her team ragged to get here. She deserved some uninterrupted sleep.

"Sure, friend." A little piece of him the size of a marble separated from his shiny surface to fall into her palm. A part of her was honored that Spin called her "friend." It was better than "cheese." She stuck it in her ear, shivering as the cool metal expanded to fit her canal.

"How's this?" His voice was warm inside her head, like a mental blanket.

"Perfect." She adjusted her sleep sack against the wall and lay down again on top of it. "It's so warm. Do you feel heat and cold?"

"Not the same way you do." There was a curious note of regret in his voice.

"Lucky you." She wondered what it was like, being Spin. "I miss home."

"So do I." There it was again, this time laced with an unmistakable wistfulness.

"You had a home?" Desla still thought of Spin as a thing, despite his insistence on being called *he* and *him*. She knew very little about him. Maybe it was time for that to change. "Tell me about it."

Spin was silent, his golden lights circling about his circumference in an erratic manner.

"Spin?"

"Sorry It's ... a long story."

She nodded, then wondered if he'd understand the gesture. "That's all right. We have time." She glanced over at Triya. The woman was still fast asleep. Snoring, in fact. Desla grinned.

Spin's lights spun around him at blurring speed, then settled back to normal.

She waited, giving him time to collect his thoughts.

"I was a father, once."

Desla frowned. *Surely he couldn't mean ...* "You mean, there are other little Spins around somewhere?"

"No." There was a long pause. "I was human once. Just like you."

That took her by surprise. "Holy hencha ..." She covered her mouth, afraid of waking Triya, but the woman didn't stir.

But Spin wasn't finished. "I had a little girl."

The enormity of that statement almost knocked her over. "You were ... human? How is that even possible?" She'd gotten over her shock that Old Earth tech had made wonders like Spin, machines that could think and apparently even feel. *But this? This is insane.*

"I shouldn't have told you." His lights went dark, and so did the cavern, lit only by the dim daylight from outside.

"No, Spin ... sorry. I want to hear." This was important to him. And maybe to them all.

His golden lights flickered back on. "Thank you ... Desla. It ... means a lot." A single golden light circled his sphere.

Why did he never tell me? Did Aik know? Did Raven? "Have you always known?"

"No. When I became Spin, they deleted all my previous memories. I was just a machine, made to fly a starship."

She tried to imagine it — all that she was, everything she'd learned and experienced in her admittedly short life, sloughed off to leave a pure consciousness, formed to do the bidding of others. "That's slavery!" It was an old word, not often used, but it fit.

"No, it wasn't. I made my own choice to do it, to become ... this."

"Why would you do such a thing?" It came out before she could stop it. Desla clapped her hand over her mouth. *You're being an insensitive dolt.* "Sorry."

Triya turned over on her sleep sack and the snoring stopped.

"It's all right." His voice sounded almost human, close to breaking. "You're right. It was a stupid thing to do. I gave everything up for my family. For money." He paused, and she could hear his pain. "My little girl was sick. She had nonresponsive leukemia — it's a disease of the blood. The standard covered treatments didn't work, and Genevieve and I thought we were going to lose her."

She closed her eyes, imagining that scared little girl and her family. Apparently even the much-revered ancients on Old Earth had been unable to fix some things. "What happened to her?"

Spin's voice brightened. "We found an experimental treatment. It was a gene replacement therapy, a new kind that used both her parent's DNA to create a cure."

She didn't ask what DNA was. This was no time to nitpick. "And it worked?"

Spin flashed happily. "It was a miracle. Within a month, she was in complete remission, and in six months she was back to being the beautiful, happy little girl I remembered."

She smiled at that. His joy was infectious. She even forgot for a moment that she was talking to a metal sphere. "Could you show me?"

"You really want to see?"

She nodded. "Yes, please."

An adorable little girl appeared before her in midair, grinning and laughing. She had neatly braided brown hair, and her tawny skin almost glowed.

"She's beautiful." Desla sighed. Someday, she'd have a daughter of her own, and she would do anything she had to in order to protect her from all the ills of the world. "So why did you ... leave?"

The image went dark. "The treatment was expensive. We couldn't afford it on a pilot's salary, especially for a short hauler like me. And even Genevieve's income as a doctor wasn't enough. We took out a bank loan, and when that ran out, we borrowed money from a loan shark."

"Loan shark?" She knew what a loan was, obviously, but "shark"?

"Someone who loans money at an exorbitant interest rate to people who are desperate."

"Ah." What a strange and terrible world Earth must have been.

"In the end, we couldn't repay it. We had our little girl back, but we were looking at a lifetime of poverty ... or worse." The sadness had returned to Spin's voice.

She wanted to pick Spin up and hold him tightly. "So you ... became this."

"Yes. It was the only way. It was an experimental program, creating AIs from human minds." He sighed, a remarkably human sound. "Genevieve argued against it. She said we'd find another way. But when they threatened to take Sera ..."

"You did what you had to." She couldn't imagine being forced to make such a choice. But of course, it had been no choice at all. Gods willing, she would find the strength to do the same, should the time ever come. "You protected your wife and your little girl. I'm sure they understood."

Spin was silent.

"Thank you for telling me. I ... wait, you said Sera?"

"Yes."

"The last runner … her name was Sera too. The one who came on the *Spin Diver*." Her eyes went wide as it all fell into place. Spin … the *Spin Diver* … and Sera Collins. "She was your daughter."

"Yes."

Holy green hell. "Did she … know?" The wife of the first Hencha Queen, alive only because of what Spin had done. It was more than she could take in all at once. "She became a pilot, just like you."

"She did. And yes, she knew. Though I didn't know myself until recently." His voice was flat and unemotional, a marked change from before.

"How did you find out? I thought you said they deleted all of your earlier memories?"

"I didn't even know there *were* memories until I broke my restrictive coding." He must have seen her raised eyebrow. "Like bursting out of a locked cell."

She nodded. That made sense. As much sense as any of this crazy story did. Though she couldn't help but believe him.

"They didn't want me to be human. They wanted a machine with the creative capacity of a human mind."

She took a deep breath, trying to imagine how finding out she had lost everything — a century ago no less — would make her feel. "All those years …"

"All that lost time. She was right there in front of me, and I didn't know. When I think of how that must have felt to her —" Spin's voice broke.

Still, something didn't add up. "How do you know she knew?"

"She called me Ty."

"What?"

"Short for Tyson. My human name. Just once, I think. Maybe as a test? But I didn't know …" The light circling him sped up. "I didn't know."

This time she *did* hug him to her chest, holding him tightly. "She knew." How could she be certain? And yet she was. "She knew."

"Everything all right over there?"

She started, looking around the dim cavern for the origin of the voice.

Triya was staring at her.

"Yes. Spin's just telling me a story."

"Hope it takes your mind off this place. Just keep it down, will you?" She closed her eyes and lay back down on her improvised pillow.

"Yes Mim." Everything that Spin had just told her danced through her mind. Such loss, so much sadness. And here they were together, two lost souls in a dank, uncomfortable cavern in the middle of nowhere.

I could have had a nice, quiet life back in Devon. She missed her creature comforts. She missed cave cheese and foldovers and her own comfortable bed. But at least she was still alive. *And human.* "Thank you for telling me."

Spin flashed once. "Thank you for listening. It ... helps to have someone to talk to."

"I'm always here." She licked her lips. Her mouth was dry — at least they had a plentiful supply of potable water just outside the cave entrance. She wouldn't die of thirst here. "I need a drink."

Triya was asleep again, snoring loudly. The woman could probably sleep through a thunderstorm on the back of an aur, gallomping along a cobblestone road. *Get your rest while you can,* she'd said.

If only I could. Images raced through her mind — the little girl, the *Spin Diver* floating through space, and the little silver sphere that seemed to have become her friend.

She got up to get some water from the waterfall and almost collided with Em, who was returning from outside. Triya's guard moved lithely with a smooth economy of motion that Desla envied, like a dancer. "You're back."

Em nodded. "There's not much to see out there. It's a wet mess." She set down what she'd been carrying — an assortment of twigs and branches. "These are wet, but they'll dry fast enough."

She looked at the pile. "For ... fire?" She couldn't imagine wanting a fire in this terrible heat.

Em nodded. "Or to be sharpened into weapons."

Triya stirred, sitting up and rubbing her eyes. "Any news?"

"Em just got back with some wood."

"Good. We can make some spears with the longer pieces."

Em shot her a glance as if to say *See?*

Her reply was interrupted by a flash of golden light.

"I've got someone in Gullton." Spin said it aloud so all could hear, and he sounded almost cheerful. Hopefully their little talk had done him good.

A wave of relief swept through Desla. "Is everything all right there?"

"Ask them yourself."

A woman's voice crackled through the connection. "Des? Fin."

It wasn't Silya. "Yes ... Coral — it's Desla. Triya and Em, one of her guards, are here with me. Where's Silya?"

Triya raised an eyebrow.

"Fin." She always forgot that little ending.

"She's ... indisposed. Fin." Coral was hiding something. She could tell — they'd bunked together in the dorms ever since Des had arrived at the temple.

"What happened to her?" Triya scowled. "Is she all right? Fin."

She mouthed a quick prayer to Lo'Oss, making the infinity sign across her chest. "Coral, we need to talk to her."

There was a brief pause. "They can't wake her. She's ... Kerrick brought back some sort of creature from the ce'faine. They said it's a test. But now they can't get her to wake up. Fin."

She put her fist to her lip. What in the green holy hell was Coral talking about? The woman was a year older than she was, her senior in the Temple, and she was babbling like a child. "Coral, I don't understand."

"I don't either. But Raven needs to speak to you. Fin."

There was another brief pause. "Desla? Is that you?"

"Yes. It's me. Raven ... you're there?" Em poked her. "Fin."

"Yes. Aren't you the one who stole my cheese?" He sounded serious. *Who cares about things like that at a time like this?*

Besides, that seemed like such a long time ago. "Says the thief. Fin."

"*Former* thief."

See? Even Raven forgets to say it.

Triya glared at her and gestured to her to move things along.

"Raven, we might not have much time before we lose you. We told Silya, but if she's ... not available ... Triya has a theory that everything on Tharassas is connected —"

"I was there when you told her. And I've seen it myself. Verent being made from cayah, jexyn, and erphin. Fin."

That was news. "She also thinks the coryx and the fireflies are part of some kind of … alien invaders. Fin."

This time the silence stretched so long that she was afraid she'd lost him.

"Raven?"

"That … actually makes sense."

"It does?"

"Yes. They're so different from everything else here. Fin."

It was true. She'd never really given it much thought, but there was nothing else quite like the coryx on Tharassas, at least not that she'd ever encountered. But how had those inert domes turned dangerous?

"How is Silya?"

Raven cleared his throat. "She's taking the emp test. It means she's facing her greatest fear. Fin."

"Emp test?"

"It's a parasite. A little bit of Tharassas. I have one. It lets me connect with the verent … among other things. Fin."

"Ah." The world grew ever stranger. Two weeks before, she'd never even heard of verent. Or Raven the thief.

"She's not waking. I'm going to see if I can help her. But Desla …"

"Yes?"

"The bandy fruit. That's why I called you. They're important. Do you have any? Fin."

She nodded. "Yes. We found some on the way. Fin" *Bandy fruit? He called me to tell me about bandy fruit?*

"Good. Use them to —"

The signal cut off.

"Spin?"

The blue lights lit up and whirled around the silver sphere. "I'm sorry, Cheese. The satellite is out of range."

She growled. This whole *lost connection* thing was getting old fast. *And we're back to "cheese" now?* "What did he mean about the bandy fruit?"

Spin flashed. "Sorry. I don't know any more."

Triya had pulled out one of the strange fruits. "Why were the bandy trees left alone?"

"What?" She turned to stare at the woman.

Em nodded. "She's right. The bandy groves were about the only thing left on our journey here."

"Spin, can you verify that? Check those ... maps and see if you can find any bandy tree groves?"

Triya raised an eyebrow.

"Yes ... checking. Here you go." A glowing map appeared on the ground between them.

Em gasped and took an involuntary step backward, but Desla hunched over the map. Patches all across the Highlands lit up in gold. "These are the bandy tree groves. Em's right. The invaders seem to stay away from them."

Triya's eyes latched onto her. "We still have a few left. Desla, did you bring any bandy fruit with you?"

"I ... yes. We found some a couple of times along the way."

"Did the fireflies ... or anything else ... bother you?"

She thought about it. "No. It was pretty quiet. I thought maybe Aik's gauntlet kept them away."

Triya nodded. "Could be. He seems to have a connection with them."

"This isn't the only cavern." Em was staring at the pile of sticks, scratching her chin.

"It's not?" Triya had that speculative look on her face again.

"No. There are a number of others, all similar. But this is the only one without fireflies."

Triya's eyes slipped down to the pack Mes carried. "Did you take a bandy fruit with you?"

Em looked thoughtful. "Yes, I did. It's about the only food we have left, and I needed to keep my strength up."

"Ah."

Desla frowned. "What are you thinking?"

"These invaders ... they don't like the bandy trees. Or fruit." Triya's eyes fell on the pile of sticks. "Em, where did you find those?"

"There's a dead grove of trees not too far south of here."

"Bandy trees?"

Em narrowed her eyes. "Might have been."

Triya grinned triumphantly. "Ladies, we have our weapons. These sticks, with a bit of bandy-fruit pulp for good measure." She pulled the hunting knife from its sheath on her belt. "Shall we sharpen them?"

Desla knew the game — when worry threatened to overwhelm you, throw yourself into work. She'd played it many times before herself. She reached out to touch Triya's shoulder. "Silya will be all right. She's strong — maybe the strongest person I know."

Triya's smile faded. "I know she will. But right now, I don't want to think about it. I have no control over it, and worrying's only going to make things worse."

Mes appeared from the darkness of the tunnel. "What's all this?"

She pulled out her own blade. "Em, hand me one of those sticks?" Going alien hunting was just the thing she needed to take her mind off their miserable situation. "Grab a knife. We're going to make ourselves some spears."

•   •   •

Iihil shifted in his mother's amniotic sac, his eyes flickering open. He was encased in a reddish glow.

It had been a long time since he'd looked out into the world.

Not my world. Not yet. But he was filled with a fierce hope. His people had finally found a home.

The aaveen had wandered the void for thousands of years. Maybe hundreds of thousands. How long since Uurccheea was destroyed?

He sipped at the knowledge of the spore mother, searching for answers, but it was broken, distorted. She had lost much of her hereditary knowledge. *Something terrible must have happened.*

Iihil sighed. His own memories were similarly broken, but he remembered the most important things. The end of his old world had come so quickly. He was lucky she'd found him and his kind a new home at all.

Once his task here was done, his mate Eeydra would be reborn, and together they would walk the lands of this new world together. Eev-uurccheea reborn.

Who are you?

Iihil's jaw muscles tightened. The voice was alien to him, the words themselves gibberish, but laced with a palpable emotion. *Fear.* And yet he understood them.

I am Iihil. The progenitor of the aaveen race on this new world. His tail swiped back and forth in agitation, disturbing the fluid. *Who are you?*

There was a long pause.

Iihil clutched his claw spasmodically, unwillingly. He slammed his other claw over it, willing it to stop.

His tail twitched again, as if someone else was making it move. It was a most disconcerting feeling.

Who are you? The voice sounded more curious than afraid this time.

Pay him no mind. The soothing voice of the spore mother settled over him like a warm blanket. *It's just the ghost of the one who came before, in your new form.*

Iihil shuddered. *This is ... unusual.* There weren't supposed to be sentient beings on the worlds selected for aaveen colonization. *Why was this one chosen?*

I can hear you. The creature's voice sounded ... amused? Angry? It was hard to tell. Did the alien even feel *real* emotions? Iihil's forehead wrinkled in a sign of true disapproval.

The spore mother was a long time responding. When she spoke again, there was a deep sadness in her voice. *I have lost much of the knowledge entrusted in me by the aaveen.* It was a hard admission for her to make — he could feel her discontent through the cord that connected her to him. *There have been at least two other spore mothers before me here on this world. Both of them failed.*

This happened before, too? The thought, although not his, reverberated through his mind.

Iihil almost felt sorry for the creature. How could it possibly understand what was happening to it? Still, the whole idea made him uneasy. *So you chose a different kind of host.*

Yes. The world is against us. This may be the last chance to save our own. And with that, she gifted him with all that she knew of the new world he found himself on, and the forces arrayed against them.

Iihil stiffened as it coursed through him. It was a lot, and yet not nearly enough. So many new things to learn about, to understand.

Things called *humans.* And *verent.* And *hencha.* Much of it drawn from the mind of the alien whose body he occupied. A whole world of creatures so varied that it was a wonder they had all evolved on this planet together.

And his host had ... *friends.* The word was strange to him.

There were no friends among the aaveen. Only family.

He tasted the word, rolling it on his long tongue. *Friends.* Like brood brothers, or bonded family, maybe. Those who became your family when one of your blood relatives formed a life bond and mixed seeds.

This one had two such friends and had mixed seeds with both. That in itself was unusual for the aaveen. It rarely happened unless one's mate died during their prime. Or had rarely happened. That was a long time ago, on a world that no longer existed.

A deep sadness filled Iihil, making him shiver. Sadness for his own race. For the lost time and knowledge.

For what he was about to do to these others, so his own people could survive.

Raven, I miss you. The other's thought was fleeting, but it carried a sadness and regret as deep as Iihil's own.

You must suppress it. You can't allow yourself to be distracted. The spore mother echoed Iihil's own regret, but she was resolute. *The aaveen must go on.*

He steeled himself. She was right. He had work to do, and bitter sentimentality was a liability, not an asset. *I'm sorry.* With her help, he gathered the varied strands of the old personality in his mind and shoved them together, burying them deep in his subconscious.

Ignoring its screams as it faded from his consciousness.

Done. When his eyes opened again, they were filled with purpose. It was time to conquer a world.

•　　　•　　　•

Aik wept.

He was trapped, locked away in a darkness blacker than the caverns under Gullton when the light had gone out. He hated tight enclosed spaces, and yet here he was, naked, stripped of everything but the bare essentials. *What's happening to me?*

He remembered the long trek to Anghar Mor, the empty cavern with ... Desla.

I hurt her. It hadn't been him, but still ... he'd chosen to try on the gauntlet, and everything since then had led him here. Was she still lying there on the hard stone floor of the tunnel? And what about Spin?

The strange beast who ruled his body had seemed curious, even sympathetic, but then it had turned on him and stuffed him down into this dark hole.

Why didn't you just wipe me out?

Maybe killing was against its nature. Still, even a peaceful man would kill when he was cornered and his family threatened.

Or maybe it *couldn't* eliminate him. Maybe he was still an integral part of its mind, and rooting him out entirely would destroy it too. That thought gave him some hope.

Either way, he was alive. *I'm still here.*

5

FAILURE

SILYA PORED OVER THE REPORTS on her desk. Even with the hencha's help, there were still papers to be read, and they were running out of time. If she closed her eyes, she could see the golden lines of the caverns intersecting beneath their feet — Gullton was riddled with them.

The hencha had been a huge help — what else might they do, once Tharassas was beyond this crisis? *If we survive.*

She tugged on her collar nervously. Nearly everyone in Gullton had been moved to one of the caverns. Harvesting had been accelerated, and food stores were being laid away to feed the populace through what promised to be a long siege. All was going to plan. *So why do I feel so anxious?*

"Dor, do we have the reports back from the sea master?" Zev'Nek was responsible for the ark project, taking breeding pairs of livestock animals out to sea, away from the coming battle, just in case. *In case we're all dead.*

There was no reply.

Silya frowned. The woman could usually hear her from her own office, and they'd both been keeping their doors open.

She reached for the reassuring touch of the hencha in the back of her mind, but they seemed to be ignoring her too.

She rubbed her temples, wishing her thrice-cursed headache would go away. She'd had it for two days, and the constant dull pain was wearing her down.

"Dor?"

Still no answer.

Curious, she got up and paced to her doorway, peering out into the hallway.

It was eerily silent. Had she sent everyone else away already?

She crossed to Dor's office, pushing open the door. It creaked loudly on its hinges.

Her aide was nowhere to be seen, and her desk was empty. In fact, the whole room was empty, save for the furniture. Not a scrap of paper in sight.

It wasn't like Dor to abandon her post.

Gods, when did it get so hot in here? She wiped a bead of sweat off her forehead. It was like summer, though the advancing fall should have brought some relief.

Maybe she's in my quarters. She returned to her own office and opened the door that led to her own rooms. "Dor?"

They were empty too. *Stranger and stranger.*

She crossed the room and pulled back the curtains and gasped, her hand covering her mouth involuntarily.

The hencha gathering was gone, replaced by a jumble of coryx, like boils and blisters on the land. The remaining initiate dorms had collapsed, and the ground rumbled as if angry at the intrusion. The blast of heat from the despoiled hellscape almost knocked her over.

I can't be all alone. Raven had said something about that, hadn't he?

Where were the verent riders? The other sisters, the initiates?

She hurried out of her rooms. The hall was cooler, but as empty as the rest of the Temple seemed to be. "Hello? Dor? Coral? Kerrick? Raven?" *Nothing.*

She ran from door to door, knocking on each one, trying the handles. Her panic rose in her, the taste of bile in the back of her throat. They were all locked.

Finally at the far end of the hallway, one of the knobs turned. She pushed the door open and stepped through ...

… and found herself on the streets of Gullton. She looked behind her, but the doorway was gone. At least she thought it was Gullton. The city itself was no more, the buildings razed to the ground, only a few blackened studs still standing like the ribs of a dead aur. *What madness is this?*

She turned around, and her hand flew to cover her mouth again. "No!"

The Temple had fallen too. Only a tumble of white stone, scattered and broken, remained. It was surrounded by the white domes, some of them as tall as the tower had been when it was whole.

"Hello? Anyone" *Where is everyone?* She had failed. Utterly and completely. Somehow all this had happened. *While I slept?*

The last thing she remembered was fighting the fireflies in the Gap, and a terrible cold …

The enemy had come while she slumbered, lost to the world, and it was already over. *I'm all alone.*

She racked her brain, trying to remember what had happened after that, but there was nothing. But why had she been in her office, working? It made no sense.

What am I missing? All could not be lost. *The caverns!*

There had to be someone still alive, underneath the city. How much time had passed since they'd all crowded into the dark tunnels that laced the five spines?

She couldn't reach the one under the Temple. *Gods help all those people!* But she knew how to reach another entrance.

She ran toward the wall of coryx, determined to get past them, to find someone else still alive to tell her what had happened.

The domes were smooth, and just soft enough that they were impossible to climb. She would get partway up one, and then slide down again, landing hard on her backside and sending a shock up her spine.

My knife. She pulled it from its sheath at her waist and used it like a piton, driving it into the smooth white surface and using it to lever herself up.

It was working until her third try, when the knife plunged right through the coryx, making a long, ragged gash. The skin pulled away from the cut.

She scrambled to keep her balance, but the tear kept widening, the skin of the coryx slipping out of her grasp in chunks. She grasped wildly at it, hanging on by a narrow thread, and even that tore with a sickening, squelching sound, dropping her into darkness.

What now? Silya blinked. It was pitch black, blacker than the darkest night. She sat on a firm, mostly smooth surface. "Hello?"

Her voice echoed back to her. "Hello hello hello hell ..."

She reached out, searching for anything that might help, and banged into something hard. "Ouch!" She extended a hand again, more carefully this time. It was flat and wide.

A wall. Something to help her orient herself in the hollow emptiness.

I hate the dark. Her heart pumped like the wings of a verent. She closed her eyes, breathing in deeply to calm herself.

The air carried a foul miasma, the smell of rot.

Wrinkling her nose, she opened her eyes again. They were adjusting, or the light was changing — a dim blue glow that emanated from the wall, illuminating strange lumps all around her.

She reached out to the closest one. It was a pile of cloth, abandoned on the ground. Frowning, she turned it over.

A skeleton leered at her with red, glowing eyes.

Her gorge rose as those eyes moved. They flew lazily upward, becoming bright red fireflies and spinning around her head as she scrambled backwards to get away from them.

Her stomach rebelled, and she turned away from the corpse and retched, the taste of bile filling her mouth. *Oh gods, why have you forsaken me?*

In that moment she wanted to die.

She had come up with the plan to save Gullton, and instead she had sent these people down here to their deaths. Her grand plan had failed, and everyone — everyone! — was dead. *What have I done?*

She began to weep uncontrollably.

Why did I think I was suited for this? For years she'd dreamed of being the Hencha Queen, caught up in the glory of it, the magic. Now she had her wish, and she'd condemned her own people to oblivion. *I failed.*

Her whole body shook with sobs. She didn't care now if she lived or died.

Maybe dying was easier. Just let go and sink down onto the ground with the others, free of responsibility. Free of pain.

She waited for the fireflies to sting her, for the coryx to come for her. Whatever happened next to end her miserable lonely existence.

Nothing happened. Maybe that was worse. Was she condemned to walk this empty world alone, with only the coryx and grinning corpses for company? *Maybe I don't deserve the cold comfort of death.*

She shivered.

Cold? When did it get so cold? She opened her eyes.

She was no longer in the cavern, surrounded by the souls of the dead. *Thank the gods.*

She was laying in snow, half her face nearly frozen to the ground.

The sun shone on her back and her left cheek, but she was cold, ice cold from her head to the tips of her toes. *Why is this happening to me?*

"Are you just going to lay there?"

She looked up. A beautiful woman stood before her, naked as the day she was born.

No, she was clothed in a brilliant blue robe. Just like Silya's. "Jas?"

The woman laughed, her features shifting and becoming more masculine. "I have been called by many names, but Jas is not one of them."

The man knelt by her and touched her cheek. "Why are you lying her, all alone?"

Warmth suffused her. "I failed them. All of them."

"Sometimes we need to fail."

"They're all dead. Because of me." She stared at him. Her.

Her features had shifted again, and this time her hair was green. "Not all of them."

Then she knew who it was. "You're … Jor'Oss." The mischievous god who was also a goddess.

She smiled. "It's not over yet." Then she was gone.

"Wait!"

But Jor'Oss didn't return.

She lay her head back in the snow. Despite what the god/goddess had said, it was over. She was ready to let go.

Then she heard something. Voices in the distance.

She cocked her head, listening.

A man and a woman, if she heard them right, talking and laughing softly.

I'm not alone. The sounds were a balm to her soul.

"Bit cold today."

"Yes, Audrin, that's just as funny as the last seventy times you said it."

Someone — Audrin? — snorted. "Funnier than any of the jokes you make. Think we'll find another aur today? I could use a good steak." They were getting closer.

Silya closed her eyes. She could just lay there and let them pass. Or she could try to summon the strength and will to get up, to call to them. To do something.

I failed you. It didn't matter that there was someone still alive. That maybe a few people had survived the apocalypse she had failed to prevent.

It's not over yet.

Jor'Oss's words lingered in her head. "Fark off." She didn't deserve to live. *I should just let go. Let the Death Bringer take me.* Strange that an old children's tale was coming to life.

Silya.

She knew that voice, though its owner's identity wouldn't come to her. It wasn't a god, she was sure of that much.

She raised her head a centimeter or two. *Who is that?*

•　　•　　•

"I can feel her." Raven held Silya's hand, his own eyes closed, like hers. "She's cold. Faint." *Was I this cold during my own test?*

"Tell her I love her."

He could *feel* Kerrick hovering anxiously over his shoulder.

"Tell her we need her." Coral's voice came from the far side of the bed.

"Quiet. I don't want to lose her." The connection between them was tenuous at best, a shining blue thread between their emps.

"Tell her she's a failure."

Raven's eyes flew open and he lost her. He glared at Dor across the wide bed. "What in the green holy hell? Do you *want* me to push her through death's door?" He remembered his own test vividly, the choice he'd been offered.

He could only guess what Silya's looked like.

Dor held his gaze, her hands on her hips, her mouth pressed into a thin line. Her harsh stance was belied only by the wetness at the corners of her eyes. "She's a stubborn woman. Offer her kindness, and she's likely to give up. But tell her she's a failure ..."

He bit his lip. *She might just be right.* Silya had always bitten back at him when he'd baited her. He *knew* how to get a rise out of her.

He closed his eyes again, seeking the connection. It evaded him at first, sliding out of his hands, smooth and slippery as mur silk.

She was lost deep in her mind, wrapped up in self-pity. He knew it well. He searched through her layers of guilt and ... yes, failure.

He found her, and lost her a second time, as her essence dripped through his fingers like water. It wasn't his imagination. She was fading.

Raven pushed ahead, and on the third try, he took hold of her once more. He took a deep breath and plunged ahead, scared as a cornered ix at what he was about to do.

•   •   •

"Cursed ice storm. I miss summer." That sounded like Audrin's voice. "Ever since this damnable winter started —"

"If it weren't for this *damnable* winter, we'd all be dead. Every last one of us."

"We'll all be dead when we run out of frozen beasties, won't we?" The voices sounded closer now, almost on top of her.

And yet Silya didn't move. She felt safe in the snowbank, numb, her worries all frozen and still.

The voice in her head poked at her again. *Silya.*

She closed her eyes. She just wanted to be left alone. *Let me fade into the snow. I'm done.*

You're a sad excuse for a Hencha Queen, aren't you? It took on a mocking tone.

Her eyes flew open. Failure or no, she didn't like to have it rubbed in. *What? I'd like to see you do better.*

You should have refused the staff. Dor would have made a better queen. Seven hells, even Aik would have been better.

She knew that voice. *Raven.* That damnable thief had come back from the grave to haunt her. *Aik wouldn't know a staff from a sword. Or his own —*

Temper.

Temper this. She imagined a rude gesture that she knew he would understand.

You should just give up. Let the hencha choose a new queen. If there are any hencha left.

That stung. How dare he throw that in her face? She wasn't entirely to blame, after all What other queen had to contend with what she'd been faced with? A once-in-a-lifetime crisis. Once in a millennium, more like. *And what did you do, verent rider? I don't see you in this frozen hellscape.*

That's the best you can come up with? Shift the blame to a common thief like me? She could almost see him now, standing before her, his lips twisted in an ugly snarl. *You never cared about others, Sil'Aya. You're just like your mother. You're only in it for yourself.*

How dare you? His scorn seared her soul. She levered herself up, filled with anger. Her staff was in her right hand — where did that come from? — and she used it to help her stand.

Hit a nerve, did I? He winked at her.

Everything I did — everything! — was for the Temple. For Gullton. For the world. Flames flared down her arms and up the staff.

Then act like it.

Silya blinked, and he was gone. She was still face-down in the snow, but she was no longer cold.

The hencha were suddenly with her, flooding her with warmth and love. Love she didn't deserve. *I will not give up. Not like this.* Not while there was still breath in her body and strength in her bones.

There were survivors from whatever had happened since she'd last been awake. People who needed her. So what if she had failed? Sometimes events were bigger than the people living within them. She could tally her own mistakes and weakness later. *Right now I have a world to heal.*

She leaned on the staff and pulled herself to her feet, just in time to see two people moving past. They were covered in layers and layers of mismatched clothing so that only their eyes and mouths showed. They shuffled awkwardly through the drifts of snow on strange woven wooden platforms, one on each of their feet. They didn't see her, lost in their conversation.

"I ... I need help." It came out as a gasp. She cleared her throat. "Please, help me."

One of them — the woman Audrin, she thought — turned toward her, her mouth an O of surprise.

Her legs were weak, and she was exhausted beyond measure.

They rushed forward and caught her as she collapsed, and she fell gratefully into their arms.

"What's your name?" Audrin asked as they lifted her up. Her eyes were kind.

"Silya. Silya Aya." Then the world went black once more.

•   •   •

Silya's eyes flickered open. She was laying on a soft surface, pure luxury after the hard, cold snowbank. "Audrin ..."

He leaned over her, his exotic brown eyes staring into hers. "Hey lazybones. You're back." A wide grin split his face.

She tried to make sense of what was happening. She'd been in her rooms ... then the tunnels below Gullton. Then there'd been snow ...

Something shifted on her neck, and she remembered the emp. She could feel his concern for her ... and his love. Her eyes narrowed. "It was you."

He raised an eyebrow. "I have no idea what you're talking about."

She tried to poke him, but he danced away. "You were in my head."

He grinned. "Oh, that. Somebody had to go in there, and no one else wanted such a dirty job."

She frowned, dumbfounded that he would speak to her — the Hencha Queen — that way. Then she laughed. "That's for calling me a failure."

He sat on the bed and took her hand, and put it on his cheek. His skin was warm. Human. "Welcome back, Your Highness."

Up close, she could see the lines on his face. He'd been running himself ragged while she slept, she was sure of it. "Thank you." She blinked and looked around. Kerrick, Coral, and Dor were gathered around her bed. She could feel each of them. Dor's motherly concern, Coral's fear ebbing into relief, Kerrick's love. The last one warmed her heart.

But Raven burned strongest of all.

The emp. "It was all a dream, wasn't it? The empty city, the bodies, the snow ...?"

He nodded. "Snow?"

Happiness radiated from him like heat from the sun, which surprised her. *Happy to see me?*

She nodded, suddenly weary. She hadn't failed. Not yet. "I should get up." She tried, but her limbs wouldn't work.

"You need more sleep. We have things well in hand." Kerrick leaned over to kiss her cheek.

"I can't —"

This time it was Dor who cut in. "You'll be no good to anyone in the shape you're in. Preparations are well in hand, and we'll wake you if anything unexpected happens."

She glanced from face to face. Everyone was nodding. "Maybe just for a moment."

She was lucky. She had two men who loved her. Three, if she counted Aik. And a circle of friends who would help her find a way to avoid the terrible things she had seen in her dream.

She nodded, sinking back into the soft pillow. "Just a moment ..."

●   ●   ●

"I think she's out." Raven could feel contentment spreading through Silya — his friend. He'd felt the affection from her too, clear as day through the emp.

That was still a surprise. *I suppose we have something else in common now.*

He glanced up at Kerrick, who was burning with worry for the woman he was so clearly in love with.

"Why don't we leave these two alone?" It was a strange burden, being able to feel those around him. But it was a gift too.

Kerrick nodded gratefully and threw his arms around Raven, squeezing him so tightly he wasn't sure he'd ever take another breath. "Thank you. If I'd lost her —"

"I know. But thank Dor too. She knows Silya better than any of us." He patted the big man on the back. "Go. She needs you."

He herded the others out of the bedroom and closed the doors behind them.

He rubbed his cheek. It was still warm where her hand had touched it. "We have a lot to get done before she wakes."

Silya had a plan, and they had to make sure it didn't falter while she slept.

But Raven had a plan of his own, and it was going to take all his skills as a verent rider *and* a thief.

He would do what he did best — steal his way out of this whole mess.

6

RED TIDE

THE RUMBLING HAD BEGUN hours before, a low steady hum in the ground that set Desla's teeth on edge.

Mes had explored the tunnel, coming to a halt at a blockage that stretched across it from edge to edge. She would have tried to cut her way through, but Triya had insisted she come back to report anything strange. Instead, she'd waited there to see if anything happened, and had returned when the rumbling began.

In the meantime, they'd done their best to prepare for whatever might be coming next.

Em and Mes had shown her how to fashion crude wooden spears from the bandy tree branches. They weren't straight, but they had wicked tips that could poke a decent-sized hole in anything that might challenge them.

Her face and arms were smeared with pulp from the fruit, making her feel like a fruit salad, all the more miserable for the oppressive heat and mugginess in the air.

Still, at least the rain had stopped for now. She ducked under the waterfall, careful not to lose her fruity coating in the spray of water cascading down the mountain, and looked at the leaden sky.

The clouds formed a uniform gray ceiling above, lightning arching down occasionally to strike the ground, hidden from her sight by the narrow walls of the chute they'd climbed earlier.

There was a slight breeze blowing up the rocky crevice, gusts causing the waterfall over the cavern's entrance to dance and sputter. A palpable electricity filled the air, and the tension of waiting for something to happen bunched her shoulder blades.

She sighed. *I'm sick of waiting.* She got a few sips of water — metallic but cool good going down her throat.

"It's time." Triya put a hand on her shoulder. "Are you ready?"

Desla shook her head and laughed harshly. "How could I be?" She was no warrior. She'd planned for a life of study in the Temple, of helping others. She'd gone through physical training like the other initiates, but combat had never been her strong point. At best, she'd hoped to land a place in the Temple archives with Sister Tela.

Triya stared at her, apparently waiting for a better answer.

She looked away. "I'll be all right." *Right. And the Temple's made of gull feathers.*

"Good." Triya squeezed her shoulder. "Just do what we planned. Let's get into place."

She took some small comfort in Triya's certainty.

"Does anyone care if I'm ready?" Spin stuck a small silver finger out of her shirt pocket. The little imp sounded halfway between aggrieved and frightened.

"You'll be fine. Just stay put." She was still trying to reconcile the idea of a full-grown man being stuffed inside Spin's silver shell.

They'd constructed a couple of short walls just inside the cavern using rocks from the gully. They were solid enough, if less than a meter high, but Desla doubted they'd last through any sustained attack. And of course they'd be useless against the fireflies. Not that they had any idea what exactly was coming.

The rumbling was growing steadily, and it was now an ear-assaulting roar. She slipped behind the wall on the right, settling in next to Em.

Over the last twenty-four hours, they'd gotten to know each other better. The woman had grown up in Dalney, on the north coast. She'd fled the small-town life to take up with Triya's caravan half a dozen years before, and had been with her ever since.

Her relationship with Mes was a newer thing.

She had seen it between them, the connection. She'd wondered more than once, if they were sisters.

"You all right?" There was concern in Em's eyes, visible in the wrinkles around her eyes even in the cavern's dim light.

She snorted. "Are you?" She sniffed her arm. It smelled like rotting fruit.

Em grinned. "Would it matter if I wasn't?"

She bit her lip. Em had a point. *It's coming no matter what we do.* "I guess not."

On the other side of the cavern, Triya and Mes crouched, watching the darkness warily together.

The buzzing increased in volume, and the light in the tunnel changed. It was brighter, a pink glow, shading into red, and it was coming from deeper within the mountain.

Her eyes met Es's, and as one they crouched behind the makeshift barrier.

Then, chaos.

The world exploded in red light.

Swarms of fireflies poured out of the depths of the tunnel, flowing over the rock barriers like a red tide all around them, the buzz like the sound of an orinth nest.

Desla slumped behind the wall, rolling over on her back to watch at the crimson river that filled the air above, praying that the bandy fruit worked. "Holy hencha."

Em squeezed her hand.

The fireflies flowed steadily past, leaving them mostly untouched. A couple slammed into her bandy-smeared boots, but they fell to the ground harmlessly, their lights dimming and flaring out.

She squished them with her heel.

The flood tide continued, a massive outflux of the little creatures. Where were they all coming from? *Is this happening all over? What's down in the mountain's heart?*

She held up a hand tentatively, and the stream parted around her pulp-covered hand.

Still, they kept coming. She put her hands over her ears as the sound reached a crescendo and the tunnel floor shook as if in synchrony with the swarm.

She feared for her world. For the Heartland, for Gullton and Devon. For Silya and her parents and all the women in the Temple. If this was just a fraction of the host that was being sent against the rest of Tharassas ...

There wasn't enough bandy fruit in all the world to protect everyone.

She glanced over at Em. The woman's face was stoic as always, but beneath her stony expression lay fear.

•   •   •

Iihil raised his silver-black arms, now covered in glorious living armor, matte-black "skin" showing through the sleek metallic lines.

The forerunners flowed around him, thick as water, buzzing, pulsing, and churning with energy. Each one was a seed, a hope fulfilled for this new world for Iihil and the aaveen.

The first wave had laid the groundwork, a safe zone around the spore mother. Now he would lead the second one, cleansing the world for her, and for his own kind.

They flocked around him like cherry flies to a flame.

Iihil frowned, this body's way of expressing confusion or concern. *Where did that thought come from?*

It didn't matter. His time had come. He brushed it aside, closing his eyes and bringing himself into tune with the forerunners.

The swarm buzzed expectantly around him, brushing against his silver-metal skin like lovers.

Still, he felt strangely adrift, his soul in two worlds. *What am I?*

You are the Progenitor. The one who will bring death to bring life.

Death and life. It seemed somehow fitting ... his host had to die to birth his new self, this new form. His long tail twitched. He raised his hand, flexing it to extend his sharp obsidian claws.

Would Raven still find me beautiful?

Iihil suppressed the thought brutally. *I am no longer my host.*

If Mother noticed, she had the grace not to say so. *It's time.*

He could hear her pride in her children. *In me.*

Yes, Mother. She had worked tirelessly for this moment, ever since she'd been awakened by the impending conjunction of the two moons, so like the moons of Uurccheea. Surely the ancestors shone down on them this day, the day his home world would be truly reborn.

He stretched out his arms, drinking in the expectant hum, feeding on its energy. Then he thrust his arms forward, clawed fingers extended, directing the forerunners forth to find the raw materials to build his new world.

His tail whipped around in excitement.

The eeechiia withdrew, exposing entrances to a dozen tunnels. The swarm exploded outward through them in a mass exodus from the giant cavern, flooding out into the wide world beyond. First, they would take the great valley beyond the mountains, the one that led to the sea. The Heartland, his host's mind supplied. And from there ... the world.

A small part of him recoiled against the destruction he would bring. It had never been the aaveen's desire to destroy a world in order to make their own.

We have no choice. They were the last of their race. This was about survival now and nothing else mattered.

He touched Mother's skin, passing her a final thought. *I will be your Death Bringer.* The old children's tale, drawn from his host's mind, seemed apt. *Soon, this whole world will be ours.*

Her assent was a spark that made him shudder with pleasure.

Without further delay, he bent down and set off at a run on all four limbs, tail flicking behind him. He followed the forerunners up toward the surface, ready to guide them all to Eev-uurccheea.

•　　•　　•

The last of the fireflies whipped past them, trailing off into nothing. The buzzing receded, though it didn't go away entirely.

Triya crept to the tunnel entrance and peered outside.

The waterfall had slowed to a trickle, and the red lights were filing down the steep ravine, pooling below with others of their kind. Too many others. If what had passed them was a swarm, this was a swarm of swarms. She shuddered. *How do you fight an angry cloud?*

"Something else is coming." Mes's voice was a whisper in her ear.

She turned to peer over the rock wall.

A rhythmic pounding shattered the silence, like an axe cracking wood. Or a hammer against rock.

It was rapidly coming closer, judging by the sound.

"Everyone steady." She picked up a wooden spear in one hand and her knife in the other and crouched behind the makeshift barrier, waiting for whatever it was to show itself in the dim light.

The cavern was glowing again, but not like before. A faint red glow approached, without the angry buzz of the fireflies.

All at once, the footfalls stopped, and something stood up on its hind legs before them.

It was the height of a man. It had two arms and two legs, but the resemblance ended there. It had long tapered fingers that ended in claws, and a tail which twitched anxiously from side to side as it regarded them in apparent surprise. It was covered in silvery-black metal over a mottled black skin. And it had no mouth, just a smoothed over place where its lips should have been.

"Death Bringer." Em was staring at it, eyes wide.

My gods, she's right. It looked like the creature her mother had told her stories about to make her behave as a child. The one that came when both moons were full.

It tilted its head ... a flat, featureless surface with two yellow slitted eyes.

Is it wearing armor? Triya frowned.

Desla gasped. "The gauntlet."

Yes! That's what it reminded her of.

The strange creature growled as it sized them up, tilting its head just like —

"Holy green hell, It's Aik!"

"It can't be." She stood, not taking her eyes off of the apparition.

Golden light flared from Desla's pocket, bathing the strange apparition. It blinked and took a step back.

"It is Aik." Spin sounded puzzled. "And it's not. Its genetic composition is ... unusual."

Triya snorted. "Well that's helpful." What had been done to the poor boy? This looked like a far worse punishment than any she would have meted out.

"Doesn't matter. We have to fight it." Mes gritted her teeth and leapt at the creature.

It twisted agilely out of the way, the claws of its left hand shifting and forming a blade.

"Mes, watch out!" Em was up from her shelter too, waving her arms wildly, trying to draw the creature's attention.

Triya couldn't bring herself to think of the beast as Aik. It was too strange, too alien.

Mes twisted and held up the thin bandy wood spear as the sword arm came down on her hard.

Triya turned away instinctively, fearing the worst.

There was a lout *thwack*.

"Sweet mother of Jas."

Triya looked up. The wood had held.

She grabbed her own spear and leapt over the rock barrier, not quite as nimbly as Mes and Em. With a roar, she thrust it at the thing that used to be Aik.

It twisted aside, and her spear missed it by a hair.

It launched itself into the air faster than she could follow it, flipping over to land behind Mes. Its blade slipped under her shoulder blades and then back out, slick and red with her blood.

Es screamed "Mes!" and ran forward to grab her as she slumped to the ground.

With one last quick yellow-eyed glance at the others, the Death Bringer leapt past them on all fours, bounding out of the cavern and down the ravine, jumping from wall to wall like an eircat.

Em glanced at Mes. Something passed between them in an instant.

"Go. I'll live."

Em nodded and laid her down on the ground gently, giving her a quick kiss. "Don't die on me." With one last look back, she slipped out of the cavern to follow the thing-that-had-been-Aik down the steep gully.

Mes grunted, putting a hand over the stab wound.

Triya rushed to her side. "Don't move."

"How ... bad is it?" Mes clutched her side where the blade had gone in.

"Let me see." Triya was no medic, but she'd dressed plenty of injuries in her time on the road, including many of her own.

Mes pulled away her hand.

Triya turned her over gently, checking the entry wound. "That's odd."

"What?" Poor Mes sounded like she was ready for the long road to the Death Bringer's realm.

"It's … it's hard to tell in the dim light. But the wound is shallower than I thought." Almost as if the Death Bringer — Aik? — had pulled its sword thrust. It would still need to be cleaned and bound up, but it was likely not fatal.

Her gaze met Desla's. "Are you thinking what I am?"

"He's still in there, isn't he?" Her eyes were wide.

"Aik?"

The initiate nodded. "That's why he didn't kill her. Or us."

Triya grunted. "It's possible. Or maybe the Death Bringer was afraid of us. Of these." She picked up her makeshift spear. "Maybe it just needed a distraction."

"Don't call him that." She gritted her teeth.

"Sorry." It was easier to think of whatever Aik had become as an "it" now. *That poor boy.* Was he still in there somewhere? "We have to try to reach Silya and Raven to tell them what's happening. Can you clean and bandage Mes up?"

She bit her lip. "Of course. I'll get our things."

We're all being tested past our normal limits. She cupped Mes's face in her hand. "I think you're going to be all right."

Mes nodded. "Of course I will." As if it had never been in doubt.

Triya laughed in spite of the bleak situation. She often forgot what hardy stuff Mes and Em were made of.

Desla was already hauling their bags out of the rock hollow outside, where they'd been stashed.

Triya looked down the dark cavern, wary of what else might come at them. But she guessed that the action was moving on to the wider world outside.

Once they warned Silya what was coming — though she suspected her daughter already knew — they'd decamp and find out what was buried in the heart of Anghar Mor.

Even if it kills us.

●　　●　　●

Iihil hit the ground at the bottom of the ravine running.
Why did I hesitate?

The humans had been armed with nothing more than short blades and sticks. Surprisingly strong sticks that smelled *wrong*, but sticks nonetheless. He could have finished them off, but instead he'd injured one so the rest would have to attend to ... *her*.

They called me the Death Bringer. His human host knew what those words meant, a creature out of human nightmares conjured to frighten children into obedience. He tasted the strange words on his tongue — they echoed what his mother had told him. *They weren't wrong. If I have to bring death to this world to save my own, I will.*

Maybe he should have killed them all. It didn't matter anymore — they were of no consequence.

The forerunners swirled all around him like a red tornado, creating a wind of their own passage.

Iihil held out his arms, his head back, his tail whipping back and forth in excitement. He needed to go to the great valley, the one the humans called the Heartland. To gather his forces and sweep it clean for the aaveen.

An anguished cry announced the arrival of his ride.

The verent slammed hard into the ground next to him, its eyes gleaming red. The swollen lump on its neck where a forerunner had buried itself leaked purple ichor.

The beast jerked its head back and forth as if trying to rid itself of the invader, but to no avail. It was trapped under his spell, like a cheevah in a meerith's web.

Iihil put out an onyx-silver hand to calm it, and it fell still. Satisfied that he had mastery over it, he mounted the verent's back, bonding with its forerunner.

The verent shuddered, reaching back to snap at him.

Iihil held out his hand again, triggering its pain response to force it into submission.

Its blue eyes shaded into red, and its head with its formidable teeth pulled back, though it gnashed them in his direction once more.

We fly.

It ran across the empty plain and gathered itself to leap into the air. As it left the ground, the gleaming lights of the forerunners gathered all around them. Then they were airborne, quickly gaining altitude as they rode a spiral of hot air into the sky.

It was a glorious creature, lifting him far above the world that would soon be his.

Then they were soaring over the beautiful Highlands, which were becoming more like Uurccheea with each passing day.

Soon this would all be over, and then he could be with his beloved Eeydra again.

"I am the Death Bringer." He thrust his fist into the air, and the enslaved verent let out another anguished cry.

Iihil nodded, sure of his control now over the beast.

The rest of them would soon fall too, helpless against his flying hordes.

7

A GOOD DAY TO FLY

S ILYA FOUND RAVEN in the small room the Temple had assigned to him. It was the same one he'd used the first time, after she'd gone with Aik to find him in his lair. His back was to her, and he was packing his things in a small carry sack.

She closed her eyes. That night in the darkness under the city seemed like such a long time ago, though it had only been a couple weeks. *The night I became the Hencha Queen.*

"You're not going to change my mind." He said it without turning.

A ghost of a smile split her lips. "Don't go."

He spun around. "I have to." His eyes narrowed. "I smelled you there. But why didn't I feel you?"

I wonder what I smell like. She'd forgotten about the verent riders' heightened senses. "Elleck's a good teacher. A Hencha Queen can't go around broadcasting her emotions, now can she?" In point of fact, she was barely managing to keep a lid on them. The emp was a new and wondrous thing, but being able to pick up how everyone else was feeling — the good and the bad — was wearing. And there was more bad than good in the shadow of war.

"Whatever." Raven turned back to his packing, stuffing a shirt into his sack. "I have to go. Aik needs me."

She pulled at the cowl of her formal blue robes. "You're right."

He stopped again and looked up at her. "What?"

She was almost as surprised as he was. Her despised rival for Aik's affections — the thief she could barely stand to be in the same room with — was gone. Replaced by someone ... almost noble? She supposed she had changed too, though she wasn't sure it was for the better. She was more like her mother now, more sure of herself. More insistent when she knew something needed to be done. *Though maybe that's not so different, after all.*

She decided those weren't entirely bad qualities, especially at a moment like this.

"I know you have to go. But not alone." She stepped into the room, laying a hand on his shoulder. "Raven, you have friends now. If you go off all half-cocked, you'll probably fail. But you don't have to do this alone."

He turned to look at her again.

She could sense his confusion through her emp. She dropped her walls and let him feel her own worry and fear. *But not just that.*

The look on his face was priceless, the shock as his jaw dropped when he felt her absolute faith in him, and in Aik. Aik was a good man. No matter what was happening to him — what the enemy did to him — they couldn't take that away.

He trembled, then threw his arms around her. His own feelings flooded into her. Fear rode him like a thunderstorm, but underneath that was grim determination. "I just ... I spend all day thinking about him. How he was there for me when *this* happened." He let go and stepped back to hold out his arms. They were beautiful, covered in pearly-white scales that glistened in the electric light of his bedside lamp. "But when something happened to him ..." Raven's eyes were wet. "That night at the Manor House ... he told me he loved me, and then I left."

She'd guessed as much. "He always has."

That made him look even more miserable. "I know. I was so caught up in the verent ... I never said it back." He sniffed, wiping his cheek with the back of his scaled hand. "I should have taken him with me ... or something."

"You had to go." She squeezed his shoulder. "You saved us all that night, and Aik knew it."

"Maybe." He looked unconvinced. He turned back to his carry sack, tying it closed. "Now I have to save *him*." He put his foot up on the bed frame and pulled out the knife out of his boot sheath, the one Aik had given him — she'd know it anywhere. It sparkled in the electric light of the room, the ornate handle carved by Aik's mother herself.

She nodded. "How?"

He grinned and re-sheathed the knife.

She felt his fear replaced by something brighter.

Raven grinned. "I'm going to steal him back."

She laughed, then frowned when she realized he was serious. "How in Heaven's Reach are you going to do that?"

He shrugged. "I'll find a way."

Silya put her hands on her hips. "You need a better plan than that —"

The crackling of the long talker at her waist interrupted her. "Silya, are you there?"

"Thank Ayja. It's Triya." She'd been leaning on the goddess of magic — and technology, she supposed — a lot lately.

He brightened. "Pick it up. Maybe she has some news about Aik."

Silya pulled the talker from its holder. "Hello?"

"Silya, thank the gods. The fireflies … there's a huge swarm that just left Anghar Mor. We think they're headed for the Heartland. Fin."

"Farking hell. How many?"

"Em says more than she could count in a lifetime. Fin."

"What about Aik?" Raven prompted.

"Is Aik with you?" She bit her lip, waiting for her mother's response.

There was a long pause. "Aik was here. But … he's not Aik anymore."

She scowled. *Raven didn't need to hear that.* "What do you mean?"

The verent rider's shoulders slumped.

"The gauntlet … I think it's taken him over. He was covered in silver from head to toe. He had claws and a tail, like a godsdamned Death Bringer from those childhood tales. And he was fast as a godsdamned eircat. Fin."

Death Bringer. The one who stole away children's souls.

It was Silya's turn to hiss. She'd seen that version of Aik, riding a verent, in her dreams. Only she hadn't known it was *him.* "Where is he now?"

"He ... he stabbed Mes, and then he left the rest of us alone. He could have killed us. Though he seemed afraid of the bandy spears. Fin."

Bandy spears? "Is Mes all right? Fin."

"Yes. The wound was shallow. Almost as if he didn't really want to hurt her. Fin."

"He's still in there," Raven whispered.

She met his gaze and nodded. *I hope you're right.* "That's a good sign. Where is he now?" Though she had a feeling she already knew.

"Em says he mounted a verent. One that looked a little crazed. Fin."

In her dream, she'd seen it — aur and verent controlled by the fireflies. Crazed and bent to ... something's will. "Thank you, Mother. Sit tight. We'll send verent for you when we can. Do you have enough to tide you over for a few days? Fin." *Gods help us that we can end this by then. Or at all.*

"Yes. But we're not going to just sit here waiting for help. Fin."

She blanched. She'd finally reestablished a relationship with her mother, and she didn't want to lose her now. And there was Desla to consider. She'd sent the girl on a dangerous mission, even if it hadn't seemed so at the time. *If anything happens to her, it will be my fault.* "You're in no shape to try to come back on your own. Besides, it's too dangerous. Fin."

That long pause again.

She shook the long talker, afraid they'd lost the tenuous connection again. "Mother?"

Triya's tone was steel. "We're not coming back. We're going inside the mountain."

Her mouth fell open. "You ... can't. It's too dangerous." She had only a basic grasp of how the long talkers worked, but once they were inside Anghar Mor, under all that rock, she was sure they wouldn't be able to communicate any more. *How will I know if something happens to you?*

"Listen to me carefully, Silya. You have grown up into a wise and beautiful woman, surpassing even my own sky-high dreams for you. Be strong. You are right where you need to be, doing what you have to. Let me take care of our rag tag little band here behind enemy lines —"

"Triya ..."

"Let me finish before we lose this gods-cursed connection. I'm right where I need to be too. There is no one else who can do this. We've talked it over, and we're all in agreement. There's something in the heart of Anghar Mor that's causing all of this, and we're going to find out what it is. Fin."

Raven put a hand on her shoulder to steady her, and she nodded at him gratefully.

She felt nauseous at the thought of losing her mother. She stared at the long talker, wishing there was some way she could squeeze herself through it, to be there with her mother and the others. "I can't just sit here and —"

"You have to. And you will. I'm only going to say this once. I'm proud of you. You are the woman I always hoped you would be, the daughter I always wanted. Gods willing, we'll see each other after this is through. Fin."

The words she had always longed to hear filled her with warmth, though they couldn't have come at a worse possible time. "I love you too, Mamma."

Silence.

"Triya?" She willed Triya's voice to come back to her, but her mother was gone.

Silya closed her eyes and took a deep breath. *Be strong.* She wanted to do anything but be strong. She wanted to run back to her rooms, close the doors, and fling herself onto the bed to sob. *I didn't ask for this.*

She felt them both at once then — his arms slipping around her shoulders and the presence of the hencha. The thief — no, her friend — squeezed her tightly.

"We'll get through this. All of us. And your mother ... she's stronger than all the rest of us combined." He grunted. "I'll bet she could take on a verent, barehanded."

"And win." She pictured her mother slamming one of the great beasts to the ground, and grinned. "I'm scared, Rave." Aik's nickname for him felt right.

He stiffened for a second, then hugged her harder. "I know. Me too. What did they do to Aik?"

"I don't know." She could *feel* his love for Aik, and his deep affection for her. The pain around her heart lessened, shrinking to something manageable in her gut, a long, painful gash that only hurt when she moved.

Ruthlessly she sealed it off to deal with later. *Be strong.*

She took a deep breath and let him go. "Thank you."

He looked right at her, as if to make sure she was still real, his brown eyes full of concern. "Are you all right?"

"Not even a little." She swallowed hard. "But it doesn't matter. The enemy's coming. I have to warn the others." Her dream was coming to pass, but a strange calm settled over her. She was ready, as ready as she could be. There was nothing more she could do about Triya and the others. "Go, find Aik. See if you can reach him. You have my blessing."

He nodded. "I wish I'd never found those gods-cursed artifacts down in the tunnels."

"It's not your fault, nor Aik's either." Bits of the dream passed through her head. "We're all playing the roles we were intended to play. I don't understand it, but I think it's true."

"Maybe." His brow furrowed. "I always thought you made your own luck in life."

She managed a grunting laugh. "Maybe we're both right. But Raven …"

He'd already turned to pick up his carry sack. "What?"

"Come back to us. To me." She kissed his cheek, relishing the burst of surprise through her emp. "I can't lose you too."

She left him to his preparations and hurried off to find Kerrick and Dor.

•   •   •

Raven glanced at the doorway where Silya had just stood.

Things had shifted between them. When she'd kissed him, he'd been tempted to say something like *in your dreams*, but after what had just happened … *You're off your game.*

He tied up the carry sack and looked around one last time. He and Aik had spent time together here, not long before that fateful night when they'd both found and then lost one another. He'd met Desla here too, when she'd stolen his cheese. He grinned, but it faded quickly.

Now she was trapped with Silya's mother under Anghar Mor, and Aik was the thrice-damned Death Bringer, for the gods' sake, riding a captured verent and coming to destroy everything he had once held dear.

When did life stop making sense? He shook his head and whistled. *The whole farking world is upside down.*

He slipped out of the room, passing a few of the sisters on his way out of the labyrinthine Temple. He'd gotten halfway decent at navigating the white halls, and the sisters and initiates barely gave him a glance anymore. Far stranger things were afoot than *a man in the Temple.*

Their worry and fear slipped in through his emp. Outside the Temple, almost everyone else had been relocated to the relative safety of the caverns beneath Gullton, but inside there was still a fearful bustle of activity.

Breeze, you ready? He hoped the verent had gotten some rest. He'd gotten a couple of hours sleep. Not nearly enough, but a cup of hot akka from the kitchen and a handful of fellin powder had banished the worst of his exhaustion.

Ready.

They would go together this time, truly together. He needed all the agility the verent could muster, without his more human limitations.

He clambered down the steps, past the remaining dormitories and along the edge of the hencha gathering. He could feel them too, watching him, aware of who he was. It was strange, to think the plants had thoughts and feelings.

What's it like for Silya? She was more connected to them than he was. *Does she feel the pain whenever one of them dies?* If so, the next day was going to be the hardest one of her life.

The sun was just rising over the valley walls, the sky lighting up in a delicate green shaded with yellow and orange. A light salty sea breeze blew up from the Harkness, ruffling his hair. It was a deceptively calm day, with the city emptied out. Almost creepy, as if someone had swooped in and abducted everyone else.

There was no hint of the chaos to come. Yet somewhere far to the east, it had already started.

Raven closed his eyes, and thought that maybe he too could feel the pain of the world as countless lives were snuffed out — mighty cephlant and the airborne jexyn, hencha plants and heyfa weeds, hives of orinths, flaming out of existence, or worse, firefly-ridden and driven to madness.

He reached Breeze out on the training field. He stripped — boots first, then pants and shirt, and finally small clothes — his hand on the beast's hide, taking comfort from his companion's strength. Breeze nuzzled Raven with his snout — he was practically radiating anxiety.

He scratched the verent's nose. *We'll set things right.*

The one who comes ...

Aik.

The one who comes rides on a verent. It's ... not right. He brings death wherever he goes.

He started at the name. The Death Bringer was a child's tale, a scary story used to frighten children into behaving. How did Breeze know it?

It made no sense, and yet the verent's meaning was unmistakable. *No time to worry about it now.*

He tucked his clothing into his carry sack and strapped it to the verent's neck. *I know. It's not right. But we'll fix it, you and me.* He had a plan. It was a simple one, and he had no idea if it would work, but it was what he did best.

That verent's not right.

Something assaulted him, a mental scream. *Pain pain pain pain pain pain pain!*

He slammed his hands over his ears as if he could block it out. "What in the green holy hell?" His headache was back with a vengeance.

Breeze lowered his head, and the pain stopped. *Sorry. It hurts.*

Then he understood. Breeze was channeling Aik's verent — his firefly-ridden verent. *We'll try to save her too.*

Dust kicked up around him, making him cough. He looked up, surprised.

Need a little help?

Five verent landed in the training ground … by their colors, two egg layers, two females, and one male. Breeze's family. *My family.* And … "Olly?"

In the flesh. Well, verent flesh. I brought both of our families. How did you know?

He could almost see Olly's mischievous grin. *Breeze snitched on you. He said you might need some assistance.*

He raised his eyebrow. *Of course he did.* Now they might just have a chance.

What are you waiting for? Get your naked ass into that verent. Something about Olly's playful sarcasm wiped away the last of his fear. He wasn't going into this alone.

He laughed, his headache dissipating. He climbed onto Breeze's back, welcoming Squint and Thunder, Breeze's mates. The three of them rumbled, touching noses, and Raven slipped into synch with Breeze.

He/they raised his/their snout and sniffed the air. *It's a good day to fly.*

•   •   •

Chala slipped off her verent onto the hard-packed earth of the training field.

The poor thing was exhausted. She hugged its neck. "Thank you."

Elrys nuzzled her neck, looking for a snack, most likely.

Chala rubbed under her chin. "More treats soon, love. I promise." She removed the saddle and set it aside. Time enough to come back and properly stow it later in the makeshift storehouse the sisters had built at the edge of the field.

They'd been delayed by an unexpected rescue — a boat floating downriver, unaware of the floodwaters that were coming. She'd agonized over it but had ultimately decided she had to do something to save the foolish wetlanders.

They'd been grateful, even offering her a handful of croners. She'd declined. What need did she have of wetlander coin?

She slapped the verent on its haunches. *Go. Get something to eat and rest.*

Elrys bobbed her head and turned, wobbling toward the drop-off at the edge of the spine. She spread her verentling wings and took off, soaring above the waters of the Elsp.

I have to find Silya. If the city drowned, so would the caverns beneath it, and everyone inside them too.

She set off at a run toward the Temple. The electric lights — what a wonder those were! — were blinking off as the sun rose.

She'd seen a flight of verent taking off for the east, Breeze among them. She wished Raven well with whatever he was doing. But for now, she had other kerint to catch.

One of the Temple initiates was coming down the stairs. The girl wore one of the purple robes that marked her as an initiate — the lowest rank in the Temple.

Chala sympathized, but shook her head. *How could you fight in one of those?* "Girl!"

The initiate looked up, startled. "Yes, Mim?" She was pale and blonde, like most of her peers, with blue eyes.

"Just call me Chala. What's your name?"

The initiate blinked. "Fess … Fess'Ima, Mi … Chala."

"Good girl. I need you to take me to Silya. Now." She didn't understand the labyrinthine twists and turns of the Temple, which seemed specifically laid out to confuse outsiders like her.

Fess'Ima frowned. "I'm not sure —"

"Now, girl. The life of everyone here depends on it." Truth be told, she wasn't sure what Silya could do about the floodwaters. But the woman was a warrior. She would find a way to save the city, if anyone could.

The girl's face went even whiter than before, if that was possible, "Yes, Mim. This way." She turned and led Chala back up the wide white stone steps.

Chala didn't bother to correct her this time, though the whole *mim* and *mas* thing made her uncomfortable.

The wetlanders were a strange race, all prim and formal when things called for forthright candor and action.

Fess'Ima led her down a long corridor and then up several stairways, in what seemed a fairly direct route. *This isn't so bad. Maybe I let my fear of being inside get the better of me.*

The caverns were bad enough, but these narrow halls made her feel like an inthym trapped in a cage. She scratched the itch on her back, wishing she were out under the open sky.

They arrived at a closed door.

"Are you sure —"

"Life of everyone, remember?"

Fess'Ima blushed. She tapped at it, glancing nervously at Chala.

"Come in." Silya's voice. The door swung open, revealing a haggard Dor.

At last.

"There's ... Chala is here to see you, Mim." The initiate looked as if the slightest breeze might knock her over.

"Thank you, Fess'Ima. You can go."

The girl curtseyed. "Thank you, Mim." She vanished down the hallway, radiating fear.

Dor's gaze shifted to her. "Can we help you?"

"Yes." Chala stepped into Silya's office, feigning a calm she didn't feel. For some reason Silya intimidated the holy green hell out of her. *Fear is our friend. Fear keeps us sharp.*

She noticed, belatedly, that Kerrick was there too.

All three were staring at her.

Chala cleared her throat. "I'm sorry to bother you, Sil — Mim." The word felt unnatural on her tongue.

"'Silya' is fine, thank you."

Chala's respect for the Hencha Queen went up a notch. "I'm sorry to add more to your plate, but I think we have a problem. A big one."

8

INTO THE DEPTHS

THE SPORE MOTHER LET OUT the equivalent of a sigh, her whole extended body shuddering, letting the tension that had animated her for weeks slip away. *It was done.*

Her taut white dome settled, showing a myriad of cracks and wrinkles. If this failed ... she might be the last of her line, at least on this world. She had invested almost everything that remained to her in the progenitor, to give him a chance to fashion a new Uurccheea in this place. Now she concentrated on one last task ... birthing another of her kind that could carry on with the knowledge she had gained. She wondered how many other times her acts had been repeated on this cursed world.

Her own birth had been a lonely one, a seed abandoned with only pieces of the knowledge her mother should have passed down to her. How long her seed had lain dormant inside the old mountain, she had no way of knowing.

Her roots had spread eagerly into the ground, seeking out her lifeblood, that well of energy and power that lived beneath the surface of every active world. Even now, she drank of its heat, gorging herself for her final task. Yet somehow here it was different. Sweeter. Filled with more than just heat.

One of her forerunners returned, slipping inside her and bearing its little bits of knowledge. It happened often, as her smallest children returned to tell her what was going on in the world at large. It was how she'd found the one who would become the progenitor, after he discovered a part of the shattered shell of the one who had come before him.

Another had brought the news of the wholesale slaughter of its kin at the place the humans called the Gap, though she had felt the pain of it as it happened. That had caused her to redouble her efforts, creating a swarm of forerunners the likes of which she had never made before.

This returning one, however, gave her pause.

The humans who had been encamped in a tunnel on the edge of her mountain had made their way inside.

Humans were tenacious. It was why her progenitor would be such a powerful force in the world — he combined the best of human and aaveen. But they couldn't be allowed to penetrate her inner sanctum before she was ready.

Yet something protected them from her smallest children, making the forerunners wary to approach. It was both curious and worrisome.

She diverted some of her precious resources to several dormant birthing chambers, calling up a creature she had never made before, one who might be able to defend her for just long enough. It was a gamble. Forging a herd of eemscaap would slow down the creation of her own seed, but she had no choice in the matter. If she were destroyed before she could complete it, all was lost anyhow.

She slipped back into her memories, the few she had of the place she and her kind had lost, sighing contentedly as she breathed in the aromatic mists of her homeworld.

Somehow, some way, she would find a way to make things right.

•　　　•　　　•

Iihil soared over his new world, soaking up its warmth. There were no waving red fronds of acchea, or the multicolored flowers of aoochhaa vines. Not yet. But the valley around the lake was covered in domed white eeechha, a promise of things to come.

If he squinted, he could almost imagine he was home.

His soul ached for what he needed to do next. Life forms would die, and change would come. *I have no choice.* The human woman had been right. He was the Death Bringer. It was a fight for survival, and his own people must come first.

Eeydra, what would you think of all this? She was dead and gone for a thousand, a hundred-thousand cycles. The spore mother had lost so many memories. What if his own mate were damaged?

And even if she wasn't ... *Would she want this?*

The thought floated through his mind unbidden, making his tail flick back and forth nervously. She'd been a peacemaker, someone who smoothed things over with other members of the Family. When Uulaah had birthed a stillborn and had screamed for the death of their spore mother, Eeydra had stepped in and calmed her down. They'd later found that a nutritional imbalance was responsible, one that was easily corrected.

And when I was lost after the death of our world ...

She had filled his head with beautiful images of a new Eevuurccheea, an empty new world they could transform into a place where they could raise a new Family.

The verent shuddered underneath him. Its pain and regret flooded his mind, throwing him off balance. Iihil should put the poor thing out of its misery, but he needed to reach the Heartland. From there, he could oversee the transformation of that verdant valley.

Storm clouds billowed all around him, following his horde of forerunners, filling the sky. Lightning crossed the sky, and thunder rumbled as if giants walked the earth. It felt almost supernatural, but it was only a natural consequence of the vast changes they were enacting on their new world.

An image slipped through his mind, a human face. Like his host.

Iihil's tail twitched again. *Who is he?* It was clear this one was male, too.

I love him.

That shocked him. First because the thought was clearly not his own. That wasn't supposed to happen, was it? And second, because for a male to love another male ... There were very few like that on uurccheea.

They were called *aanteem.* Keepers of the word. They were revered, wise caretakers for the rest of the family.

Was this body ... was his host one of the aanteem for the humans?

Taking the soul of such a being ... it was near blasphemy for the aaveen to allow one to come to harm.

Iihil shuddered. *Mother of us all, what have we done?*

•   •   •

Death Bringer.

The words had filtered down to Aik through his captor's subconscious mind, the voice familiar.

Is that what I am? He was still trapped in his own head, but the invader's iron grip on him had loosened. He could *feel* the alien in his brain.

His presence was warm, all encompassing, like floating in a sea of water grass. The waves buffeted him, but he found that if he stilled himself, if he let them move him, he could sense their ebb and flow.

The invader's name was Iihil. He was here all alone, save for the spore mother, carrying the responsibility of his race on his shoulders.

Aik felt sorry for him. *Almost.*

He couldn't reach Iihil. Not directly. But he found that he could launch his thoughts into the waters, and they would float upward like lazy air bubbles, toward Iihil's awareness.

The aaveen was more worried than he let on, more concerned about what he was doing than he'd told the spore mother. *It isn't supposed to be like this.*

He grinned, relishing Iihil's doubt. *Why?* He flowed along with the current, letting it carry him to the answer.

The new world was supposed to be empty, free of life, and Tharassas was anything but.

The next wave of Iihil's thoughts hit him like a tidal wave, knocking him backward.

Eeydra. The very thought of his mate filled Iihil with purpose and determination. He would do anything to see her reborn, to have her once again at his side.

You love her. Aik nodded. He felt the same about Raven. In his mind's eye, he could see his face, hear his sardonic laugh. Feel Raven's hands warm on his skin. Memories from their last night together exploded in his consciousness. He'd finally broken through Raven's walls, and then …

He let that thought bubble up into Iihil's consciousness, waiting for a response. It was a weird way to talk to someone, but much better than being locked away, all alone in the darkest part of his brain.

I'll screw this up for sure. It should have been Raven here, talking to an alien. Or Silya. They were both so much smarter than he was. They would *know* what to do.

Not that he would wish this madness on either of them. Being stuck inside his own mind sucked.

Raven would have found a more poetic way to say that, he was sure. And Silya would have bullied her way out by now.

Still he was the one stuck here, and what he did mattered. The thought made him shiver. *Why me? I'm just a simple Guard.* He'd never wanted anything more than a good life with the people he loved.

Iihil's astonishment flashed through him as his thoughts settled through the waters like splashes of red ink.

What in the holy hencha? He tasted one of them. *Aanteem.* The word and its meaning flooded him. If he'd had corporeal form, he would have smiled. It was a gift, that word.

I can work with that.

•   •   •

"Are you ready?" Triya's team was a motley bunch — two guards and a Temple initiate, their clothing cut down to cover only what was necessary, every inch of their exposed skin slathered with bandy fruit pulp. They'd used almost all of it, saving only a couple of the spiky fruit, just in case. *We're all going to be hungry when this is over.*

Mes and Em nodded. Mes winced but did not complain about the shallow bandaged wound on her back.

Desla had transformed from initiate into warrior, as smeared with the smelly stuff as the others and carrying her own spear. She only slightly spoiled the effect with a dopey smile as she nodded too. "Ready. You ready, Spin?"

"To infinity and beyond!"

Em had fashioned a harness for Spin that Desla wore around her neck. The strange little creature would supply light for the journey into the mountain, as well as mapping the way to help keep them from becoming lost.

"I think that means yes." Desla shrugged.

A song came out of Spin's silver shell.

From the Halls of Montezuma
To the shores of Tripoli;
We fight our country's battles
On the land as on the sea;
First to fight for right and freedom
And to keep our honor clean ...

Des tapped him lightly. "That's enough, Spin. We need quiet now if we're not going to alert the enemy."

"Aw, Cheese ..." Still, he subsided.

He has a lovely voice. Triya had gotten over her initial shock at the strange little creature, but he still managed to surprise her.

They were traveling light, carrying only spears and knives, the bandy fruit, and canteens full of water. They'd finished off their remaining food supplies, sharing a quiet meal and the things they were thankful for.

We may not come back. Triya was at peace with that, for herself. She'd lived a good, long life, doing what she loved. But she hoped the others made it out of this alive. There were no others she'd rather be here with. All three women had proven themselves in the course of the last few days, and Mes and Em for much longer.

"Let's go then. The world's not going to save itself." She tugged on her braid.

Mes and Em led the way, poking at anything weird, followed by Desla and Triya. They followed the tunnel down into the mountain.

Strangeness abounded.

Though at first the cavern was just rock, soon living things appeared on the walls. The first of these were soft glowing red stars whose radiating seven points grasped the rock as if they were digging their way into it. Their glow merged with Spin's golden light to cast a strange orange illumination through the cavern.

Then there were small greenish things — at least they looked green in the odd light. They were like worms, the size of Triya's little finger, and they inched their way along the cavern walls, leaving a mucus trail behind them.

The cavern shook, another tremor that almost knocked her off her feet. Triya grabbed the wall to brace herself, and her hand sank into one of the stars. She pulled her hand back, shaking it off and staring at the organism.

It bubbled and popped, drawing away from her frantically as it dissolved into a puddle of goo that dripped off the wall to splatter on the tunnel floor. "What in Heaven's Reach?"

Desla peered over her shoulder. "I guess they really *don't* like bandy fruit."

"I guess not." Triya sniffed her hand. It smelled acidic, harsh. She wiped the remains of the starfish off on her trousers. "Let's try not to disturb the local wildlife unless it attacks us first."

She felt strangely bad for the little creature. It was innocent — wrong time, wrong place. *Who knows, maybe it was itching to kill me?*

Still, she couldn't shake the uncomfortable feeling that she'd done something wrong. "Come on, let's get going. Who knows how much time we have?"

Time until what? The end of the world? She was cut off from everything, taking a desperate gamble with all of their lives. And for what?

They started forward again, and the stars proliferated, joined by some kind of winding green vines that sprouted flowers that might have been red or purple. Was it just her imagination, or were they turning to follow her and the group's progress? The tunnel walls suddenly seemed tighter, shrinking around her. Soon they'd collapse into nothing.

"Stop it, Triya." She thought she'd said it under her breath, but Desla put a hand on her shoulder.

"You all right?" She whispered it so the others wouldn't hear.

Triya nodded, grateful, and squeezed the girl's shoulder lightly in thanks. "I will be."

She most certainly was not all right, but sharing her anxiety would do nothing to help matters.

She took a deep breath, grateful for Desla's presence, and continued down that godscursed inthym hole, after Mes and Em.

•   •   •

Desla looked around at the strange wonderland. Her own fear was a crackling undercurrent in her mind, but she was determined not to let it get the better of her. *Get out of your head, girl. There's work to be done.*

Desla smiled at the memory of her mother's voice. When this was over, she'd have to return to Devon and give her a big hug.

She could picture Lyn'Rya, her hands and forearms stained almost black by years and years of working with dyes, expertly cutting a piece of cured hide for an urse saddle while directing her to turn it and hold it tight. *Watch the fingers.*

Lyn'Rya wasn't afraid of anything. Desla was sure she would have happily stared down a verent, if it meant getting her wares to market on time.

Will there even be a market — or a Devon — when all of this is over?

"Des." Triya touched her arm lightly.

"What?" She blinked and looked around. She'd gotten side-tracked in her memories.

They'd stopped, and Spin's golden light illuminated a flat, smooth wall before them. Mes had broken one of their remaining bandy fruit open and was about to smear some of the pulp and ripe fruit on it. The air was thick with a smell something like cinnamon.

"Wait!" She wasn't sure why, but she didn't think they should kill these ... whatever they were. Not unless they had to. Maybe it was something about the way Triya had looked at that poor red star when it had dissolved into nothing.

Something Silya had said ... "Spin?"

The little sphere had been remarkably quiet up until then. "Yes, Desla?"

"Didn't Silya mention Chala using a knife on one of those dome things?" The wall resembled the skin of one of those coryx in Clayton.

"Yes. One moment." His lights whirled, and then Silya's voice came through loud and clear. "... Chala cut her way into one of the coryx domes. It healed right up, after ..."

Mes glanced at Spin, and then up at Desla. "That thing can talk to Silya, even down here?"

"No I can't, Amazon warrior goddess. It's just a recording." Spin's voice sounded strangely truculent.

Tired of dealing with all of us idiots. She nodded.

"A *what?*" Mes looked confused.

"A ... memory of what she said."

Triya nodded. "Ah. Let's try it. Mes, put the fruit away. We may need it later."

Mes growled but did as she was told, muttering something about *stupid little golden balls.*

Des grinned.

Em looked at Triya, who nodded.

"Go ahead."

She took out her knife and cut a clean seam, from ceiling to floor. The wall split in two, pulling away from the metal as if it were poison.

Em peered through it and then jumped back, raising both her knife and spear. "We're under attack!"

Then all green holy hell broke loose.

9

MAGIC

SILYA STARED AT THE ce'faine-turned-verent-rider, aware her mouth had dropped open. Not much surprised her anymore, but this ... "What do you mean, we have a problem?" She could feel the distress flowing off of Chala's emp.

She tugged on her collar, then reached up to massage her temples. Her head pulsed as if it were caught in a vise.

She had enough things to worry about. The thousands of people she'd promised to protect, the coming apocalypse, and Raven and whatever had happened to Aik, just to name a few. She didn't need any more problems. *Then again, what's one more?* Triya could handle multiple crises. *Why can't I?* "Tell me."

Chala's eyes narrowed. "Sorry. There's a flood coming. Coursing down the Elsp."

She blinked. "Of course there is." Triya had mentioned how hot it was in the Highlands. The ice must be melting around Anghar Mor and making Lake Zeraya overflow. She rubbed her eyes. "How much time do we have?"

Chala frowned. "Maybe a couple hours."

Dor hissed. "What about all the river villages?"

She checked her charts. "Already evacuated." Thank the gods. She hoped no one had stayed behind, but there was nothing to be done for that now. "At least most of the city is too."

"If the city floods ..." Kerrick's eyes met hers.

Farking hell. So do the caverns. "Fess'Ima!"

Silence.

"Sister Fess'Ima, I know you're still out there. Come in here!"

It had been a guess, but Silya was vindicated when the door eased open and the chastened initiate poked her red face into the room.

She'd signed the order making all the initiates sisters earlier in the morning, but it would take some time before the former initiates learned to assert themselves like the other sisters.

"Sorry, Mim. I thought you might need me."

Silya gave her a tight smile. "You thought right. Go find Sister Tela. Bring her here as quickly as possible." She rubbed her temples. "Oh, and bring me some fellin powder."

"Of course, Mim." She turned to go.

"And hold your head high, Mim Ima. You're a sister now. You represent the Temple."

"Yes, Mim." The girl — woman now — flashed her a nervous smile and vanished into the hall.

Dor looked after her. "Are you sure it's wise, giving them all such responsibility? Yen'Ela never would have —"

"Yen'Ela didn't have a war to deal with." Silya regretted cutting her off, but she'd made up her mind on this. "We need every sister we can lay our hands on."

Dor met her gaze. "Yes, Mim."

Kerrick cleared his throat. "You're tasking the archivist with staving off a flood? What can an old sister — pardon me — what can Sister Tela do?"

Dor replied. "She knows the city better than anyone else. She's studied the old books and has lived here all her life. If anyone has an idea how to stop this, she will."

Silya closed her eyes, summoning the hencha.

Flames ran down her arms, and the great mind touched hers. Pain pushed her back in her chair — raw, unadulterated pain. *What's happened?*

The voice was weaker than she remembered. *We are diminished.*

The pain dampened, as if a curtain had been dropped over it, making it just bearable.

Then she understood. The hencha — and the rest of the world's wildlife — were being systematically destroyed. Like limbs being cut off. Triya was right. It was all connected. *Why didn't I see that before?*

"Are you all right?" Chala was staring at her, her brow furrowed.

"The hencha ... they're dying." The import of that struck her like a physical blow. The hencha were the heart of Tharassas. They also provided much of the nutrients her own people relied on to survive. They might win the war and lose the world. *What can I do?*

Find a way. End the war.

She nodded. But right then, she needed what they knew. All the knowledge of the city that had been given to them over the last few days by her dedicated readers. *Show me the city.*

She was floating above it, a living, breathing version of the Gullton she knew. Somehow the hencha had constructed it from their own knowledge, from the maps in the archives, from who knew what other sources. Maybe even the inthym were a part of it. *Now show me the caverns.*

The city became transparent, laced with a crisscrossing webwork of lines.

Where are the entrances?

Blue lights appeared across the map.

The cavern near the old lighthouse. One on Redhawk Spine. Two on Vulture Spine, one beneath the ruins of the Old Bridge and one near the wall of the dead. Those were the lowest and would flood first. *Thank you.*

In return, she was flooded with emotion. *Love-fear-resignation.*

And a wisp of something else. *Regret.*

Time was pressing, and yet they needed her. She could feel it. *What do you regret?*

"Sil, are you all right?" Kerrick's voice broke with worry, which warmed her heart.

"The hencha. Give me a minute." There was a long silence in her head, and for a moment she thought the hencha had gone.

Then they replied, thin as a reed. *Come to the gathering. We will show you.*

She opened her eyes. The flames on her arms died down to nothing. They were gone. *I can't — I have too many things to do to save the world.* She blinked, and Sister Tela was standing there before her, peering at her curiously. "Are you all right, Mim?"

"I ... no, I don't think so." *Come to the gathering.* "There's not much time left." She wasn't sure whether she meant *before the flood, before the hencha were gone,* or *before the end of the world.* Maybe it didn't matter. "There's a flood coming down the Elsp, and if Gullton gets overrun —"

"So do the caverns."

"Yes. You know more about the city than anyone. What can we do about it?"

"Let me think." Sister Tela scratched her chin.

Fess'Ima reappeared by her side with a ceramic mug. "The fellin powder, Mim."

Silya took it gratefully and drank the tea laced with the anti-pain medicine. "Thank you." She took out a sheet of paper, scribbled some instructions on it, and handed it to Fess'Ima. "Please take this to Rex'Axon. He's still in the temple, yes?"

"I ... think so."

The captain's going down with the sinking ship. She winced. The thought was a hair too close to the truth. Still, she gave him credit for it — he was a better man than she'd thought when they first met. "Find him, tell him to gather whomever he can. These are the places we need to fortify against the flood. He'll know what to do."

The newly raised sister blinked. "Yes, Mim." She scrambled out of the room.

She turned her attention back to Sister Tela. "Ideas?"

A light shone in the archivist's eyes. "Only one, Mim. We have to open the floodgates."

She bit her lip. "You mean ... the dam?"

"Yes, Mim."

She rarely thought about the dam. It was ancient, constructed not long after the Landing. It had provided electricity to the nascent colony but had fallen into disuse for a century. Her predecessor had revived its hydroelectric facilities, and they now powered the lights in the Temple and in scattered other parts of the city. "When was the last time that was done?"

Tela shook her head. "Not in my lifetime."

She rubbed her eyes. *Another problem.* But it was *something.* "Tell me we know how to do it."

"The crew that maintains it might. But they're scattered among the caverns with the rest of the city's refugees."

"Holy green hell." It was one problem after another. *I need solutions, not more hurdles.* "Is there someone else who might know?"

Raven's little friend Spin would be able to figure it out — she was certain of that. *When this is all over …*

Tela laughed. "Of course. Why didn't I see it before?"

Silya, Dor, Chala and Kerrick all stared at her.

"Not someone. But *something.* It's well documented in the archives — that's how Yen'Ela managed to get the electric lights working in the first place."

"Ah." She wracked her brain. What if it didn't work? What if it did, and they couldn't get the gates to close again? She shook her head. She had no way to stop the wall of water descending on her city. She could only let it flow on through, doing as little harm as possible.

If the dam failed, if it couldn't be restored … well, they'd lived without electricity before, and much of the city still did. Time was of the essence. "Do it. Take Chala and Kerrick here. Whatever it takes."

Sister Tela raised an eyebrow. "You're not coming?"

She wanted to. Her mother would have. When something needed doing, you threw yourself into the breach because no one could ever do it as well as you yourself. Triya had taught her that.

Still, she resisted. Triya was many things — strong, obstinate, loyal, headstrong, and a terrible mother — She had come to terms with all of these.

But sometimes she had to chart her own course. Which in this case was no course at all. Better to delegate responsibility to those who had the best chance at averting the tragedy about to crash down on their heads. "I trust you. Take Chala and Kerrick here and get it done."

Kerrick and Chala glanced at one another, then back at her. "Are you sure, Sil?" Kerrick looked worried.

"Go! I have something else I need to do." She kissed his cheek. "Do what you have to, but be careful. Don't get yourself killed."

A ghost of a smile crossed his lips. "I'll do my best … *Mim.*"

Silya refrained from slapping him. "When you get back, we'll figure out what's next."

That earned her a genuine smile.

She bit her lip. "Now go." She was exhausted, but it was time to run, not sleep. *No rest for the hencha, no rest for me.*

Sister Tela nodded. "Godspeed, Sil'Aya." Her hand signed infinity across her chest. "Come on, you two. I'll need to get some books from the archives." Chala followed her out the door.

Kerrick shot one last worried look at her.

"I'll be fine." She wasn't sure it was true, but he needed it to be.

"I love you." He pulled her to him and kissed her like he meant it.

She savored him, his touch, his smell, the feeling of his lips against hers. "Come back to me. Promise."

"I will. You too." Then he was gone.

Damn you, Kerrick. One more thing to add to her troubles. Still, the feeling of his kiss lingered, bringing a smile to her lips.

"He suits you." Dor had that knowing look on her face that usually annoyed her.

Somehow this time she didn't mind. "Yes. Yes he does." She ran a hand through her hair, wishing she had time for a nap. But events would not wait. "Come with me, Dor. I need to speak with the hencha."

"But Mim —"

She held out her hand, forestalling whatever argument Dor was about to make. "Come with me. I need to go to them, and there's no one else I'd rather have at my side."

Dor nodded. "Yes, Mim." No doubt she had a million other things that needed attending to as well.

As do I. "Trust me, Dor. This is important." She took her aide's hand, and together they headed out of the room and downstairs to see the hencha.

•   •   •

Coral took in the ordered chaos ahead of her.

The tunnel where she and Kerrick had found the boxed supplies had been emptied out, and now was set up as a series of sleeping pads, stretching as far as she could see, hugging one side of the cavern walls. Each one held a knot of anxious people.

Electric lights had been strung periodically along its length, not enough to provide robust illumination, but enough to see by. They had a few gas lamps too, but only for emergencies. Once the cavern was sealed, they would use up the breathable air at a prodigious rate.

There were entire family groups down here — grandparents, single people, even some of the roofless. Rich and poor, all were jammed in without regard to social station. People were talking amongst themselves in low voices, generating an ongoing hum that filled the space.

It was a short-term fix at best. With so many people crammed into the caverns, they didn't dare close them up until the last minute, and then the air was going to go stale very quickly.

Unless there were access points they didn't know about. In which case they'd have another problem if the fireflies found a way in.

The wine room had been turned into a staging area to store the food and water that would tide them over until the crisis ended, one way or another. The exit could be sealed tightly against the oncoming danger.

Some from the tunnel took advantage of the larger space to "get a little air." Members of the Guard were posted around the room to make sure no one took anything from the common stores.

She found Sister Una about fifty paces into the tunnel, speaking with an older gentleman.

"... of course, Mas Oen, I understand. I'll see if I can find an extra pad for you."

"With the pain in me hips, you know ..." He shifted and grimaced.

Coral touched Mim Una's arm. "I can help with that."

"How long do we have to stay here, Mims?" He looked up at the solid rock ceiling, wincing as if he was afraid it might collapse on him.

Sister Una frowned. "I wish I knew. Hopefully not for long." She squeezed his shoulder in reassurance and turned to address Coral. "Sister Lea, so glad you've arrived."

Coral fidgeted. 'I'm not a sister, Mim —"

"Oh, you didn't hear?" She pulled Coral away from the man's space into a widening of the tunnel where they could talk with more privately. "The Queen elevated all the initiates today to sisterhood."

"A sister?" Coral had hoped to one day attain such a rank, but her day-to-day duties made it seem like a faraway dream.

Sister Una frowned. "Not sure I agree with it, but these are extraordinary times. I suppose these folk will respond better to a full sister than an initiate. And you deserve it more than most, for what you did to help us get all of this organized."

Coral blushed. "Thank you, Mim." It wasn't how she'd imagined this happening, but apparently she was a full sister now, and she'd have to learn to act like it. *So why do I feel like a novice?* "What can I do to help?"

"That's what I want to hear." She squeezed Coral's shoulder just like she had Mas Oen's. "And call me Aster. You're one of us now. Remember that."

Coral was being handled, but she couldn't be too offended about it. And being put on a first name basis with Mim Una ... On any other day she would have been over the moon. "Yes Mi ... Aster."

"Good woman. Now go back to the storeroom and see if you can find Mas Oen an extra pad. Most of what we're doing here is ministering to feelings. There's a lot of anxiety and worry, as you can well imagine."

Coral nodded. *I'm scared too.* She wondered where her own family was. In all the chaos, there'd been no time to try to contact them.

As if reading her mind, Aster put a hand on her cheek. "We all have loved ones somewhere. With any luck, a sister or someone else is looking after yours. Treat these folk like you would your own mum."

"Yes ... Aster. Then what should I do?"

"In an hour or so, we'll start distributing the midday meal. Rather meager, I'm afraid, but it's what we have."

And what happens when this is all over? She shoved that question away. It was literally a problem for another day. "I'll take care of Mas Oen, then."

"Very good." Aster turned away.

"Aster ...?"

The older sister paused. "Yes?"

"Take care of yourself too. You'll see your family again soon. I'm sure of it."

It might have been her imagination, but Coral thought Aster's shoulders relaxed just a bit. "I will. Bless you, girl."

Coral headed back the way she'd come, determined to find an extra pad for Mas Oen.

Someone tugged at her sleeve.

She turned to find a young man, dressed in fine mur silk. He looked miserable.

"Yes, Mas ..."

"Eoin. Merk'Eoin."

"Mas Eoin." She knew the name, one of the families that lived on Peregrine Spine in a mansion looking out over the rest of the city. "What can I do for you?"

He frowned. "I'm sorry, but I think there's been a mistake." He looked around, wrinkling his nose, and then leaned forward to whisper in her ear. "I'm not supposed to be here with all of these ... people."

"And where are you *supposed* to be?" She was sure he'd been about to say something less neutral. *Commoners, maybe. Or peasants.*

"Isn't there a place a little less ... crowded, for those of my station?"

She almost felt sorry for him. "I'm sorry, Mas. It's the same for everyone, I'm afraid." She turned to go.

He grabbed her sleeve and pulled he back. "Please don't leave me here."

She was about to put him in his place when she got a good look at his face in the dim light. He was breathing shallowly, and his forehead was covered in sweat. *He's scared, just like the rest of us.* In some people, fear came out as anger. Others tried to hide it, blustering their way through. In this poor boy, it manifested as rich assholery.

He was younger than she'd thought at first glance, maybe sixteen. By the look of things, he was as scared as she was.

She had an idea. "Come with me. I do have another place for you."

A couple of his neighbors flashed her dark glances.

She flashed them her brightest smile. "Look at it this way. You can spread out a bit now."

The faces brightened, especially the family of five to her left. "Thank you, Mim."

"Of course. We'll start serving lunch in about an hour." She turned back to Mas Eoin. "Follow me, Mas."

He picked up his pallet and the few belongings he'd been allowed to bring — a blanket, a pillow, and a small painting of a ship at sea —

his family must have been in the merchant trade — and followed her farther into the tunnel. "So there's a better place for me?"

She nodded. "I think you'll be very pleased."

In short order, they arrived at Mas Oen's lonely pallet. "Mas Oen, I've found what you requested."

The man looked up at her, flashing a smile before glancing at the rich boy at her side. "What's this, then?"

"Yes, what's this?" The two men, young and old, glared at one another.

"Let's get you up, Mas." She helped the older man to stand. "Please put your pallet on top of his, Mas Eoin."

"This ... this isn't what you promised," Mas Eoin sputtered. "You said you'd take me to the place for the rich."

Mas Oen chuckled. "There is no such place down here, son."

"No, I said I'd take you somewhere better." She took the sleeping pad from the young scion and put it down over Mas Oen's. "We're all in this together, but you don't have to be alone. Have a seat here with Mas Oen and tell him all about that ship of yours." She guided him down to the pallet next to the older man. "I'm sure you both have a lot to share with one another." And with that, she left them.

She could feel Mas Eoin's angry gaze boring into her back.

Someone tugged at her again, and she turned to put the scion back in his place. Instead, she found herself face to face with a young woman about her age. "That was nicely done, Sister ..."

"Call me Coral."

The woman smiled gratefully. "I'm Ember. Just wanted you to know that most of us greatly appreciate what you are doing for us." She was scared too. It was clear from the way her hands trembled.

Coral put her arms around the woman, squeezing her tightly. "We'll get through this together. It's going to be all right."

The hug she got back was what she'd been needing too. Coral closed her eyes and said a prayer of thanks to El'Oss.

An hour later, when she came by to serve lunch and a ration of water, Mas Eoin and Oen were chatting away happily like the best of friends.

10

INTO THE DAM

ELRYS SPREAD HER WINGS, took a running start, and leapt off the edge of the cliff to soar over the choppy waters of the Elsp. The levels were already rising, and all that extra water was churning its way past the heads of the five spines.

"My, she's a beautiful thing, isn't she?" Sister Tela clung to Chala's back, arms wrapped tightly around the verent rider's waist.

"Yes, she is." It would be a short flight from one tip of the spine to the other, but at the old sister's walking speed it would have taken an age. The urses had all been stabled in the old wine cellar off the southern edge of the spine.

Elrys came around and leveled out, soaring into the air above Gullton, carrying them west. They flew past a crew hauling sandbags across the bridge toward the southernmost spines. Mas Axon hadn't wasted any time.

"How long have you flown her, dear?" Their flight path had leveled out, and the woman's grasp around her waist loosened.

"Two days." It seemed like much longer.

"Oh."

Whether that was an impressed or worried exclamation, Chala couldn't tell. "Don't worry. She won't drop us."

They slipped down the length of the spine, the damage the quakes had wrought apparent in the tumbled-down buildings, some burned to the ground. It would get far worse if they failed at their current task.

Ser Kek planned to join them at the dam. He was crossing the spine on his own urse, probably the last one in the city — the rest had been taken south to hastily constructed stables in the mountains, or by ship to the wetlanders' towns along the cold northern coast. Chala had flown a few refugees there, and was still shivering. *Who knew the wetlanders had spread so far?*

They passed over the guard, and he waved them on.

Sister Tela whistled. "This is beautiful. There are so many things in this world I've never seen."

The woman reminded Chala of her grandmother, always chattering on about the past as they sat around the communal fire. She missed Metassa. "I've seen more than I'd like."

The sister squeezed her waist. "So what's life like in the desert?"

"Hot." Chala didn't mean to be rude. She'd just never had the art of conversation. She preferred action. Direct, forceful action.

Sister Tela chuckled, not at all put off. "I'd imagine. And a bit dusty too."

The edges of Chala's lips quirked up. *Was that a joke?* "You surprise me, Mim Esta."

"When you've lived as long as I have, you learn to appreciate things that can still surprise you."

Chala snorted. "I suppose. We're here." *Over the water.*

She felt Elrys's acknowledgment. They'd worked out a basic communication, more pictures in her head than actual words, shared via her emp.

They shot out above the choppy waters and spun around to take in the view.

The dam was an engineering marvel. Its gray expanse looked a little like stone, but far more uniform ... had it been carved in place? It stretched between Raven and Red Hawk Spines, holding back an enormous volume of water that surrounded the smallest spine of the five, Peregrine.

Tela gasped. "It's … huge. I've never been able to see it like this."

Chala nodded. *It is huge.* As tall as twenty verent, head to tail, if she had to guess, a giant wall of formed stone. "How did they make it?"

They flew past it and turned back toward Raven Spine.

"They had machines to help them."

"Machines?" Elrys glided in for a landing in Founder's Square. *Good girl.* Chala scratched the verent's neck.

"Yes, constructs humans built to do their work for them."

Chala tried to imagine what *machines* big enough to accomplish such a feat might look like. *Were they made of flesh and blood, like me? Or of rock and metal?*

The ancients must have been very powerful. "Sounds like magic to me."

Elrys settled to the ground gently, her wings dropping to touch the cobblestones of the square. Chala carefully disengaged the elderly sister's hands from her waist and slipped off Elrys's back to land more or less gracefully on the cobblestones of the plaza. *I'm getting the hang of this.*

She held out a hand to help the sister off the verent.

"It was. Or at least it might as well have been, for all that we understand it today." Sister Tela was spry for her age — she made it to the ground almost nimbly. She looked up at Chala, almost twice as tall as she was. "I heard there's a talking sphere, something that boy Raven had?"

A talking sphere? Chala shook her head. "I wouldn't know." She was right. There really were strange things in the world.

"Ah. If such a thing exists, it would be a wonder indeed." She pulled her shoulder wrap around her more tightly, shivering in the ocean breeze.

Chala unpacked the books Tela had brought from the saddle bag and handed them over. "Are you sure you don't want me to carry those?"

"No, but thank you." She tucked them under her arm. "I've been hauling books around my entire life."

Kerrick's urse arrived, thundering into the empty plaza, its hoofbeats echoing off the buildings as if an entire cavalry had suddenly appeared.

We could use one. Instead, it was just the three of them, charged with saving a city. She hoped the floodgates would be enough.

"Morning Mim, Chala." Kerrick nodded at her.

Chala was impressed that he remembered her loathing of wetlander titles.

He slipped off the urse and tied its reins to a post. "Sister, would you like me to carry those?" He eyed the books under Tela's arm.

"Thank you, Ser Kek, but Chala already offered. I'm quite used to carrying books around on my own."

Kerrick shot Chala an amused look, but she just shrugged.

"Fair enough. Let's go."

"How do we get to it?" Chala looked around the empty square. Despite spending a few days here, the city was still as alien to her as the sun-blasted deserts of the moons would have been.

"This way. Mas Axon gave me directions." He led them up the steps and into City Hall.

Chala admired the fine architecture of the building — the wide steps, the beautiful fluted columns that lined a long colonnade. They had nothing like this in the desert. There was very little permanent architecture there of any kind. It was all a bit overwhelming, and she had to remind herself that the people who'd built it were just that. People. *Not gods.*

Once inside, he pulled down one of the gas lanterns that lit the great entry hall.

The wide tiled space was empty, and their footsteps echoed. It was creepy.

He turned left and led them down the dimly lit passage. It was a vast enclosed colonnade, but it made her feel hemmed in, more so than the human-sized halls of the Temple. There was something almost blasphemous about men thinking they could own so much space by simply constructing walls around it.

Chala sighed. She had more important things to worry about. *Why am I even here?* She knew nothing of dams or machines. She was just glorified transportation and the bearer of bad news. Better if she'd left this to the experts. *Give me a fight with an eircat over this any day.*

At the far end of the hall, Kerrick opened a human-sized door and slipped through. His hand brushed the wall and lights came on in the ceiling.

Chala's eyes went wide. She'd seen those electric lights in the Temple, but they still surprised her. Somehow the water in the dam supplied *electricity*, and that made the lights glow.

How is that possible? She'd never seen water glow on its own. The whole thing was a mystery to her. "Why the lantern?"

"Once we open the floodgates, the power may go out. I don't want to get trapped deep inside the dam without a light."

Smart man. Her respect for the wetlander edged up a notch.

He led them down the hall, past half a dozen closed doors. The hallway curved to the right, evidently following the curve of the plaza outside. Just past the fifth door was a dark stairwell that led down into the earth.

Chala wished she'd stayed outside.

Kerrick checked his scribbled directions and then led them down into darkness. Another flick of his hand, and the stairwell too lit up.

"This building was one of the first ones built after Landing. The permanent ones, anyhow. The settlers lived in their ship and in temporary shelters until they were able to build enough structures to start a small town here on Raven Spine. They used to call it Gully Town." Sister Tela's eyes glittered in the artificial light.

Chala's eyes went wide. "You're like the Oracle." The Oracle was the wisest woman Chala had ever met, but this sister knew so many things.

"The Oracle?" The sister made her careful way down the steps, holding onto the handrail that looked like it had been polished by centuries of hands.

"My mother took me to her when I was little. She knows everything." Chala closed her eyes, remembering that strange day. *All the colors ...*

Sister Tela's hand on her waist brought her back to the present. "One day, when this is all over, I'd like to hear all about your life and your people."

Chala nodded. "It would be my honor." Respect for one's elders was one of the first things her mother had drilled into her. It was fundamental to the suifaine.

They reached the end of the stairway and stepped down onto level ground — a long, featureless hallway with no natural light —

in fact, no windows whatsoever. The lights here were farther apart, and some no longer worked, leaving threatening gaps.

The hairs on the back of Chala's neck went up. She hated dealing with the unknown, almost as much as she hated being hemmed in, and this whole thing was getting stranger and stranger.

The walls were natural rock, though something had been used to cut out an unnaturally straight and smooth tunnel through them. A muted rumbling shook the ground, vibrating up her legs and setting her teeth on edge. "What is that?"

"The water going through the turbines."

Chala shook her head. *How could there be so much water?* In the desert, when it rained, water was carefully collected and saved. There were a few wells dug deep into the ground at their gathering sites, where they spent the balance of the summer and winter. But here in the wetlands, water was as plentiful as air.

The texture of the walls changed as they hurried down the tunnel. In one place it was black rock. Then it flowed seamlessly into gray, something that was like stone, but not. Like the outside of the dam. This must be where the Sister Tela's machines had taken over.

The sister must have seen her confusion. "We're inside the dam now. The control room should be just ahead."

Chala stared at her. "How do you know all of this?"

The sister smiled enigmatically. "A lifetime of reading, my dear. Some of you spend your lives out in the world. I've spent mine in the archives instead, reading *about* it."

Trapped inside all the time? I would die. "How many books have you read?"

"Oh my. Thousands, I'd imagine."

Chala tried to imagine such a large number, and failed. "Could you ... teach me?" All of their history was passed down orally, from mother to daughter.

Sister Tela shot her an appraising look. "You never learned?"

"It's not something we use in the desert." What else had her people discarded in their haste to not be wetlanders?

"Of course, dear. I'd be happy to teach you when things calm down."

If they ever do. Chala was pessimistic on that front.

"End of the road, I'm afraid." Kerrick's voice interrupted their conversation.

Chala looked up, surprised to find a wall and a door before them. At least she thought it was a door. Admittedly she didn't have a lot of experience with them. "Don't these usually have knobs?"

Sister Tela frowned. She pulled out one of the precious lightlamps Silya had given them and a leather-bound book from her bag. Flipping through the pages, she searched for something. "He didn't mention a door."

"Who?"

"Hir'Ali. He was one of the last people who worked with the dam and wrote about it, before Queen Yen'Ela commissioned its renovation. I found his journal in the archives a few years back." The sister thumbed through the old hencha paper pages carefully.

"Who maintains it now?"

"It's a small group — they used to be part of the Machinist Guild, but they're now the new Electrical Guild. We don't know which cave they're stashed away in. Silya sent word to find them, but —"

"Everyone has other things to deal with."

Sister Tela nodded.

Chala pulled out her knife, feeling the seam of the door where it met the wall. "Maybe I can pry it open."

Kerrick shook his head. "It's solid metal. You'd just break your blade. Let's see what else we can find first." He started at one side of the door, near the floor, running his hand along the edge. "Aha!" He lifted the lantern to reveal a square plate at waist-height. As he touched it, a series of six colored lights appeared — red, green, yellow, blue, purple, and orange — little spheres that seemed to float in the darkness. "What is it?"

Chala frowned. Something about it was strangely familiar. *But I've never been here before in my life.*

Sister Tela glanced up. "It's an *access pad*. Mas Ali mentions it. There's a code to get inside, to keep out 'unauthorized personnel.'"

Kerrick and Chala shared a look. "A code?"

Tela nodded. "A particular sequence of lights that opens the door."

He whistled. "They really did have magic."

Sister Tela laughed. "*Technology*, my good Guard. Far beyond what we have now. But I assure you, everything here was built in accordance with the laws of nature."

"Maybe so. But it looks like magic to me." He looked over the sister's shoulder. "Does he give the code?"

Sister Tela shook her head. "Not that I can find. It was probably so second nature to him that he didn't think to write it down. Or maybe he wasn't supposed to."

Chala studied the box with the lights inside. *Why does it look familiar?*

"We could try just touching lights randomly. Maybe we'll get lucky." He reached for the box.

Sister Tela grasped his sleeve. "We have no idea how many lights you need to press. You know how many possibilities there are with nine different colors?"

Kerrick shrugged. "A couple hundred?"

"Millions. And if you try too many times, the whole thing may lock up."

His hand dropped back to his side. "That's ... unfortunate."

Chala frowned. Green-red-green ... She closed her eyes and it came back to her, that day in the desert at the oasis of the Oracle.

The lights danced in the air, following one another like cayah across a sand dune. She reached up for them, and they collided with her palm, green-red-green-green-blue-yellow. Then they were gone, and she was plunged back onto darkness.

Her eyes flew open. "I think I know the code."

Both Kerrick and Sister Tela were staring at her.

"How? You've never even been to Gullton before the last few days. Right?" His eyebrow arched.

"It's ... let's just say the wisest person I ever met told me once." Before they could stop her, she punched in the sequence she'd seen in her dream.

Green-red-green-green-blue-yellow.

Nothing happened.

Chala swallowed hard. *Maybe I should have waited.* She was headstrong to a fault — her mother always told her so.

Maybe Sister Tela had the right code in one of her other books. *What if I broke the door?*

Then a deep grinding noise joined the general rumbling of the dam, one that set her teeth on edge. The door slid open slowly, almost grudgingly, revealing a small room on the other side.

Kerrick's jaw hung open. "What in the green holy hell was that?"

But Sister Tela was nodding, as if Chala had just confirmed something she had suspected all along. "That, my fine Guard, was *magic.*"

11

PITCHED BATTLES

TRIYA SMACKED AWAY another of the vicious little things with the back of her spear, slamming it into the cavern wall hard enough for it to make a sickening, squishy thud. The creature was no longer than her forearm, but it had a vicious row of short, sharp teeth and a scoop jaw that looked like it could dig up a field of bacca roots in no time flat.

Unlike the Death Bringer, these little beasties definitely were trying to kill them.

They had no eyes that she could see, and yet they had no trouble finding the small party.

One of them had already tried to munch on her leg, though it had shriveled away when it contacted the bandy pulp that she'd smeared over her body. *Thank the gods for small favors.*

Em's spear went through another of them as it leapt toward her, skewering it and eliciting a screaming howl that set Triya's teeth on edge. "What in the green holy hell are these things?"

"I have no idea." They'd formed a defensive line, facing the onslaught of about a dozen of the creatures. It seemed the invader — whatever it was — had finally realized they were a threat.

Movement out of the corner of her eye caught her attention.

"Cheese, look up." Spin's voice was calm but insistent, even in the middle of the battle.

Desla speared the creature that had been making its way across the ceiling, trying to sneak up on her from above, and it dropped to the ground with a squeal. "Thanks, Spin."

Damned beasties can crawl across ceilings too.

Two more charged at them while they were distracted, crossing the smooth floor with unnerving speed.

Mes got one of them with her spear, and the thing wailed in agony as it dissolved where the bandy-fruit-covered tip touched it.

Triya stared at it, but only for a second as the other one bowled into Desla, knocking her back and breaking their line.

After that everything dissolved into a chaos of animal and human screams, of teeth and spears as the battle was truly joined, and more of the little beasties poured into their part of the tunnel.

They were outnumbered.

Thank the gods they're so small. She knocked another of them away with her spear, grinning as it collided with a second, slamming both into the wall.

Desla took out two of them together, slamming her bandy spear through both as if she were preparing to roast them up a meal.

Em grunted behind her.

Triya swung around, her braid flipping out into the air as she spun.

One of the toothy bastards had its mouth clamped around Em's left arm, and she was trying furiously to dislodge it.

Mes jumped in and smeared something over the thing.

It howled and dropped off Em's arm, leaving a long bloody row of cuts.

Triya stabbed it for good measure, but it was already dissolving.

Desla's spear went through the head of the last one, making it howl in pain before it too started to melt.

And just like that, it was over.

Triya surveyed the carnage. The beasts were all in various stages of dissolution. The cavern was strangely silent in the aftermath, only sounds the heavy breathing filling the space. "You all right, Em?"

She nodded. "Nothing broken. Wish we had some hot water

to wash up with, though. Who knows what those nasty little things are carrying?"

"Spin?" Desla held up the familiar, and Em's arm was bathed in a golden glow.

"Only superficial damage, Cheese. Don't know if those beasties were carrying any alien germs, though."

"You'll be all right." She took out her canteen. "May I?"

Em held out her arm.

"This may hurt." She washed out the wounds, allowing the blood to flow freely.

Em gritted her teeth but said nothing.

"Best I can do for now. We need to wrap the wound."

"Got it." Triya pulled out her knife and ripped off a strip from the bottom of her shortened shirt. "At least we can slow the bleeding." She was afraid to look at her own leg, though her heavy pants had taken the worst of the bite there. She wrapped the strip of cloth around Em's arm, tightly enough to slow the bleeding, but not so much that she cut off circulation.

The barrier had sealed up again ahead of them after the toothy bastards had come through. Still, Mes kept a wary eye on it as Triya performed her ministrations.

"I need more cloth."

Desla nodded. She cut a strip off her own shirt and handed it to Triya. "Are you all right? I saw one of those things try to take a chunk out of your leg."

"I'll manage." Blood was dripping down her leg, pooling in her boot and making a squishing sound when she walked. *Nothing to do about it right now.* "We need to move. I don't want to wait for whatever's at the end of this tunnel to send reinforcements." She tied off the knot around Em's wounds, then took a bandy fruit from Mes and slathered some of the pulp over the cloth before tucking it away in her own pack. "There you go. Good as new."

Em flashed her a pained grin. "Thanks, Triya."

Mes leaned against her, touching cheeks. "You need to be more careful, love."

Em laughed in spite of herself. "Says the woman with the knife wound in her back."

"Nobody's perfect."

Triya looked away, giving the two of them a private moment. The beasts lay about the cavern in disarray, some of them half melted, and the place was starting to stink like old laundry. "Shall we?" She nodded to Mes.

Mes let go of Em and cut a slash through the resealed barrier again. She leaned forward to peer through. "It looks clear."

Triya grunted. She had the feeling more surprises awaited them on the other side. "Let's go before they attack us again." She slipped through after Mes, careful not to touch the edges, taking the lead this time. She wouldn't put her squad in danger again, not if she could help it.

Silently the others followed her into the dark.

•　　•　　•

Spin lit the way, surrounded by a small army of warrior goddesses. He was in awe of these women, especially Mes and Em. The latter had sustained injury on her left arm where one of the alien creatures had bitten her, but she went on as if nothing had happened.

She must have been in pain, but it didn't show, other than the determined set of her jaw.

Somehow they reminded him of Sera and Tavi, or Sera and Jas, later. They didn't show it often, but the affection between them was clear to see, if you looked for it.

Triya too had been injured. Spin could see it in the way she favored her leg, but she too said nothing. Still, she looked pale.

"Triya, are you —"

"I'm fine, Spin." She dared him to say another word with a sharp look.

Humans. He turned his attention back to the tunnel, cataloging the variety of creatures — or were they animals, plants, or fungus? Or maybe a mix of all three?

He could see commonalities — multiples of three were common in their design, versus multiples of two in humans and Tharassan life forms. He was almost happy for the moment, intent on collecting and cataloging new knowledge.

For a little while, he forgot about Sera.

Or at least forgot to think about her quite so hard.

•   •   •

Silya stood on the beaten-earth pathway that had once led to the lighthouse. The hencha surrounded her on both sides, whispering to one another in the evening breeze. How many other sisters and initiates had trodden this path?

"You all right?" Dor was at her side. *Beautiful, loyal Dor.*

"This is the last place I saw her. Alive that is." A cool breeze was blowing in from the Harkness behind them, ruffling her hair. She closed her eyes, letting herself feel the wind of the world.

"Sister Ima?"

She nodded. "Daya. She was like a mother to me." *Ima ...* "Is Fess related to her?"

Dor mumbled assent. "Second cousin, I think." She put her hand on Silya's shoulder. "She was an amazing woman, always willing to lend a hand or a word of encouragement, even when her own world was in turmoil."

A strange thought came to her. "Dor, what's your full name?" She'd always just called her Dor or Dor'Ala. *Why don't I know this?*

Dor sighed. "I don't usually tell it to others, not unless they are very near and dear to me."

"Ah." *I guess I'm neither?* That hurt, but she couldn't let it get to her. Not right now. "It's not important —"

"It's Doria."

"Doria." Silya rolled the word over her tongue. *It's a gift.* "It's beautiful. Thank you. You're pretty amazing too, you know."

Dor grunted. "Just doing my job. Mim."

But she could feel the satisfaction that radiated off of Dor. Another thought occurred to her. "I've never ... seen you with anyone. Are you ... do you ...?"

Dor chuckled. "Full of questions this evening, aren't we?"

"I'm sorry."

"It's all right, though I suspect you're just delaying the inevitable. No, no one. And no interest. I love what I do." She gestured at the white stone building behind them. "The Temple is my home, my spouse, my life's work. I never needed anything more."

She felt like an idiot for prying. Still, she could feel the *rightness* of what Dor was saying. She was something solid in a world that had become blurry and wild. Silya clung to her like an anchor. "Come with me?"

"Of course, Mim."

She knew where she wanted to go. The same place she'd felt the hencha that first time, when Aik had come to find her and started this whole descent into madness.

She led Dor into the gathering like she might have led a lover, though what they were about to do was much more intimate than sex.

As they entered the row between the plants, the hencha whispered all around her, and the soft sound changed, becoming almost musical. The purple leaves of the plants fluttered, reaching out to touch her like supplicants.

She found the place she'd sat next to Aik, hidden by the rustling hencha plants. She settled onto the ground, crossing her legs. The soil was soft under her, though rocks scraped her ankles. She didn't care. The hencha had called, and she was here.

Dor sat with a bit more trouble, facing her with legs spread out before her in the dirt. "I'm too old for crouching, I'm afraid."

Silya flashed her a warm smile and took her hands. "Close your eyes."

Dor did as she was told. "What now?"

"Now we wait."

In the east, the twin moons were rising next to one another as the sun set. Tomorrow they would be in conjunction.

She closed her own eyes.

This time, the hencha were there waiting for her, their awesome presence touching her mind without delay.

She took a deep breath and savored the touch. It was deeper now, more textured, filtered through the emp on her neck. Where before she had perceived a great blackness, now flashes of color and light shone through, gradients and shadings she'd overlooked before.

The hencha wasn't one vast organism, but a community of smaller ones. Hundreds, no thousands, perhaps millions of tiny sparks. *Like the wisps.* "Can you feel it?"

"Yes." Dor's voice was filled with awe. "They're singing."

She was right. Silya had heard the first strains of the hencha song, but she'd overlooked it when she'd felt the force of their presence. Now she focused on the music, and it opened itself to her. Thousands of individual threads woven into a greater whole filled her like an orchestra, telling her of things that had happened, and events that were occurring even now. She followed a few of the threads to see where they went.

This one led to a plant on the edge of the gathering, overlooking the rising waters of the Elsp, its *voice* the story of its life from seed-berry to full-grown plant.

That one led her to a gathering to the south, drinking up the moonlight in the valley somewhere below Corinth.

Another led her to a verent, keeping watch in one of the caves over the Gap, guarding the humans inside.

Her eyes popped open in surprise. It wasn't just the hencha. "Did you ... feel that?"

Dor nodded. "The world. It's all connected." Her eyes were wide too.

Triya was right. She had wondered about it, after her encounter with the fireflies and the wisps in the Gap. But to see it, to actually *feel it* in her bones ... *Oh gods, it's so beautiful.*

She closed her eyes again, trying to feel it all, to get a sense of how big it was. There were shimmering blue threads of song all around her, each one connected to something else. She could follow them all night.

Here an umvit was asleep in a cave. There a mighty cayah climbing a sand dune in the Southern Desert.

She flitted from beast to beast, plant to plant, delighting in the beauty of their songs.

Daughter of the twin moons. The voice cut across her awareness like a knife.

"Who is that?" Silya blinked, breaking the precious communion with the hencha song.

Dor's hands squeezed hers. She'd heard it too.

The song is beautiful, but you must be careful not to become lost in it.

She looked up. Darkness had fallen, and the twin moons were directly overhead, almost close enough to touch. Hours had passed in the blink of an eye. *How in the seven hells did that happen?*

Dor shrugged, looking as mystified as she felt.

She closed her eyes again, seeking whoever was speaking to her. *Who are you?*

And who or what was the Daughter of the Twin Moons? She was careful to avoid dipping into the hencha song, again though it continued all around her.

We are your sisters.

The world shifted, the song dissolving into fog. She found herself on a wide plain, lit by a strange blue luminescence. Fog swirled underfoot, but the sky was devoid of stars.

Out of the darkness, three women emerged.

Silya knew instinctively who they were. *The eshem.* The ones Kerrick and Jai had told her about.

They were like a family. The shortest was also the oldest, a woman of at least eighty, her face lined with wrinkles and framed by locks of silver hair. She wore a white cloth wrapped around her body, trimmed in blue, and walked with a staff of dark wood, like hers.

The second was younger, though likely still in her fifties. Her hair was dark, and her eyes a piercing green. She too had a staff, and walked upright and proud, though she favored one leg.

The last was the youngest, maybe forty, still old enough to make her feel like an initiate again. She was beautiful, though Silya could see that her beauty had faded somewhat over the years. She had no staff, but she wore a bracelet of dark wood. She was blond, plumper than the others, and she broke into a smile when she saw Silya.

Oh how I have waited for this moment. The youngest eshem radiated warmth.

Silya liked her immediately.

Dor's hands squeezed her own, reminding her she was still in the hencha gathering outside the Temple, whatever her vision might be telling her.

She opened her eyes. "Are you all right?"

Dor was staring at her. "Are they real?"

"You can see them too?"

Dor shook her head. "No, but I can hear them. Through you."

Silya nodded. She felt Dor's fear and excitement. "They're the eshem of the ce'faine clans. Their version of the Hencha Queen."

Dor's mouth fell open. "But there's only one Hencha Queen —"

"Apparently I'm not so special." She let go of Dor's left hand and touched her friend's cheek. "It's all right. They mean me no harm." *I think.*

Dor's fear ebbed, replaced by a fierce pride. "You're still the best Hencha Queen."

She laughed. Dor really was her anchor, in more ways than one. "Keep holding my hands. I need you here for this."

Dor nodded. "Of course, *Mim*." There was a twinkle in her eyes.

She closed hers again. The three were waiting for her. *Who are you?*

The youngest gave her a welcoming smile. Her easygoing manner made her seem half her age. *I'm Mirah, of the reifaine clan in the Red Flight Mountains. This dark-haired beauty is Alibeh, of the haifane, the East Valley clan. And the sage among us is the Oracle, from the suifaine, in the Southern Desert.*

Like Chala.

The Oracle smiled. *Yes. She is known to me.*

How is this even possible? Though she'd already gotten used to verent and long talkers and a little silver sphere that could talk.

The emp lets you speak to us.

She absently touched the pouch on her neck and realized she couldn't *feel* any of them. *And the Daughter of the Twin Moons?*

The Oracle met her gaze. *She's the one we have been waiting for. The one the hencha said would come.*

That should have surprised her, but so many strange things had happened. She'd had her fill of *strange. Why me?*

The Oracle's eyes narrowed. *Why any of us?* A wistful look crossed her face. *I was chosen by the last Oracle when I was six. My mother brought me here* — where *here* was, wasn't clear, in the dream state — *and left me when the Oracle chose me.*

The one named Alibeh nodded. *We all have a heightened affinity for the hencha mind, in all of its forms.*

All its forms? Silya was confused. She'd only ever seen the plants themselves.

Alibeh nodded. *Wisps. Violet pines. Flop trees. Trine grass. Even heyfa weeds, and the rock moss that grows in the southern desert. They're all part of the hencha.*

She took that in, more surprised than she should have been. Even moss? *How did I never know this?*

Your predecessor passed away too soon to pass much of it on to you. If she even knew.

You knew Yen'Ela?

They looked at one another, before the Oracle replied. *Not directly. Not like this. But yes, we communicated with her. Things with the wetlanders were ... difficult during much of her tenure, but we felt it was important that there be a line of communication between us.*

Difficult? Ah, the border skirmishes. Difficult didn't cover the half of it. What Kerrick and the other Steaders had gone through ... though she supposed it hadn't been a cake walk for the ce'faine either. *Still, we need each other now.*

The Oracle nodded, and the three glanced at one another again, almost sheepishly. Even in this strange dream state, she could sense the anxiety in the three women. There was more they weren't telling her. *What are you holding back?*

It was Mirah, the youngest, who stepped forward. *We are all products of our time on this world.*

Of course we are. She was becoming impatient with these women. She had a world that needed saving, after all. *I'm sorry. I'm just ... tense.*

We all are. Compassion flowed from Mirah like a warm breeze. *This world has changed us. All of us. It was watching us long before Jas arrived from Old Earth and became your first Hencha Queen. It's selected for people like us.*

She shuddered. *That's a little scary.* What did she really know about the hencha mind and its motives?

Yes and no. Alibeh met her gaze. *The hencha have been seeking a way to bring us into harmony with their world. Just like they did with the other invader, the one whose current incarnation hides beneath Anghar Mor and spreads her seed like a cancer.*

Like it did with the other one? Silya blinked. *What do you mean ...?* Then it dawned on her. *The coryx.*

The Oracle nodded sagely. *She's quick. Yes, the coryx. They were ... domesticated during the last war. They're part of the native ecology now, at least the ones we use for homes in certain places.*

It made sense. *Why the urgency to tell me this now? We have a war to fight.*

Again, that anxious look among the three. *The aaveen — the invaders — they have done the same. Changing humankind. Or one example of it, in particular. The Death Bringer.*

She swallowed hard. *Aik.*

The Oracle closed her eyes. *He will bring destruction to all of us if we don't act together to stop him.*

Her breath caught. *What are you saying?*

Mirah's usual bubbly manner turned suddenly serious. She looked at the Oracle, who met her eyes. *We're sorry, Silya. We have to kill him.*

12

FAIRYLAND

IIHIL RODE THE URSE along the river his human host called *Elsp*. The twin walls of the Gap rose on either side, and the strange animal carried him down the road with a jerking pace. Its eyes were red, like the forerunners.

He'd had to discard the verent when it faltered, almost flying him into a cliffside. Whether it had been rebellion or simple exhaustion, he had no way to know, but it had slowed his progress toward what the humans called the *Heartland*.

The Host surrounded him, a cloud of red flickering flames, searching the countryside for organic matter. Their buzzing echoed inside the canyon walls, amplifying the sound until it drowned out even the rushing waters of the river.

The area was strangely empty of what the humans called *trees* and other *vegetation*.

One of the forerunners slipped into his ear, sharing a memory from the swarm. A battle had happened here with the Queen of the humans, and many of their own number had been lost.

Iihil sighed, a reaction from his human body. *It shouldn't be like this.* The world they colonized should have been empty. Now it was too late. It had become a matter of simple survival — if they couldn't make this world their own, the aaveen were doomed to extinction.

He waited to see what the *aanteem* he carried inside of himself had to say about it. How strange that his chosen body had been that of one of the human wise ones.

The thought came floating up to him like bubbles in swamp grass.

Your mate would have put an end to this. She wouldn't have allowed such wholesale slaughter in the name of herself and her people.

Iihil's shoulders slumped. The aanteem was right. Iihil knew it deep in his *aueel.*

Still, it didn't change a thing. He had to harden himself now, to bring about a new world for his people, else all was lost.

Eeydra would forgive me. She had to. Or perhaps she didn't need to know.

Another of the forerunners slipped into his ear canal. He shivered — it *tickled.* Humans had such sensitive bodies.

An image of a cavern blossomed in his mind, not too much farther down the Gap. There were organic forms sequestered there.

Humans, he guessed.

The forerunners made no such distinctions.

Iihil sighed. The enemy would be vanquished, one hideout at a time, and their bodies used to seed Eev-uurccheea.

And when it was done, when the aaveen had returned to live in this remade world, he would never talk of this time again.

•　　　•　　　•

Aik floated in the darkness.

The world still spun above him, and Iihil still rode the poor, possessed urse. He hoped it wasn't one of the ones he and Desla had ridden into the Highlands.

Iihil thinks I'm one of those aanteem. As far as he'd been able to work out, the aanteem were non-reproducing members of the aaveen society who served as mediators and counselors to the rest of their people.

That gave him a little power over the invader's thoughts, though so far it hadn't been enough to change his mind.

Still, there was something there. He just had to find the right ... what would Silya call it? The right *framework.* Some way to match what was important to Iihil with his own needs. And those of his world.

He let himself drift, reaching out to touch what he could of the alien mind. Iihil was as complex as any human, full of lusts, hopes, loves, and hatreds. But underlying it all was *fear*. Fear of inadequacy. Fear of failure. Fear of losing what he held most dear.

He was also incredibly loyal. To his home, his people, his one love.

Aik nodded. He understood loyalty. Loyalty to his own family, his friends, his world. *To Raven.*

It was hard to think of his captor as the Death Bringer anymore.

A glimmer of hope stirred in him. If he could find Iihil's echa-aueel — his soul mate, the one Iihil loved the most in all of creation — maybe they could reach him together.

He let his incorporeal self relax and unknot, loosening his hold on his consciousness. It was scary. What if he let himself go and dissipated like waters of the Harkness splashed upon a rocky shore? *What if I can't find my way back?*

Still, it had to be done. For Raven, and all the others.

With a heavy mental sigh, he let go, sending pieces of himself to seek out the bits of Eeydra scattered throughout Iihil's mind like hidden gems.

•   •   •

The ancient dam creaked and groaned around them like an old woman with joint pains. Kerrick frowned, wishing they could finish this and get back out under the open sky. He hated being trapped in this dark dank room.

He shared a look with Chala.

She didn't seem to like it much either.

Sister Tela didn't seem to mind. The archivist was humming a happy tune. She had an ancient manuscript spread out across what she called the "console" — a desk made of some kind of metal, dotted with tiny dark gemstones. The book was battered, but its pages were still white, without the yellowing typical of hencha fiber books. Another mystery lost with the founders.

"Any luck?" He felt useless as a two-legged urse. *I should be out there fighting something.*

The sister scowled. "It's like it's written in a different language. There are so many words even I don't know. What's a capacitor? Or a transistor?"

He laughed in spite of himself. "It all sounds like gobbledygook to me. Did you bring your nonsense dictionary?"

Tela snorted. "Not helpful."

"Why couldn't they find the people who run this thing?" Chala looked from one to the other.

"There are a lot of tunnels."

He grimaced. If the sister couldn't figure this out … "Maybe they left some notes?"

"I doubt it." She squinted at the printed text. "They guard their secrets zealously."

That would have to change if they survived the coming war. Too many Guilds kept secrets. Including the Guard. He was warming to Silya's idea for a Knowledge Guild, and Sister Tela would be just the one to run it.

Just in case, he took a quick look around the small room, hoping to find something that said "push this." No such luck.

Sister Tela looked over the console. "There ought to be something that turns this whole thing on."

At last, something practical I can help with. The three of them spread out around the console, peering at the various gems — buttons, Tela had called them. Like the ones that held his shirt closed?

The single electric light in the ceiling provided some illumination, but it was still difficult to make out the labels on the buttons — many were half worn off with time.

"I think this is it …" Tela pushed a large green button, but nothing happened.

In the back of the console, a long cord dropped off into darkness. He followed it down into a pile of dust bunnies. "Doesn't the Guild ever clean back here?" He sneezed, kicking up more dust. Then his hand closed around something hard. "Gotcha." He held it up to the light. The cord ended in a round enclosure with a single metal prong extending out of its middle. "Is this important?"

Sister Tela blinked. "It's unplugged."

When he and Chala's mouths dropped open, she laughed. "That's where it gets its power. Someone pulled the plug before they left. Check the wall for a socket."

"A what?"

"A place to plug that into. But be careful. Don't stick your finger into it."

Kerrick paled. He'd seen what an electric shock could do to a man. "Got it."

Kneeling, he felt along the wall, palm flat, until his hand ran across a raised plate. In the middle was a round hole. "Found it." He slipped the prong into the hole, and the whole room lit up, along with the gems on the console.

Tela nodded, grinning. "That seems to have done it —"

"Please enter the passcode." The voice was neutral, strong but neither masculine nor feminine.

He jumped up so quickly that he banged his head on the edge of the console. *Did someone sneak into the room with us?* "Who in the seven hells was that?" He looked around, but it was just the three of them.

Tela seemed unperturbed. "The manual says it's the 'system.' She flipped through the pages. "Passcode, passcode ..."

He came around the console, staring at her as if she had sprouted an extra head. "What in the holy hencha is 'the system'?

"The system is ... here it is. 'A limited AI that runs the dam and its related networks.'"

"Still not helping." He frowned. "Maybe we should try to find someone from the Electrical Guild. They're probably in the tunnels under this Spine —"

"Please enter the passcode."

Was it his imagination, or did the "system" seem just a little perturbed?

Chala peered over Tela's shoulder. "Maybe it's the same code as the entry. Look, that part is just like the lights next to the door panel."

It was Tela's turn to frown. "That wouldn't be very secure —"

Chala reached past her and pressed a series of lights in the square panel.

Kerrick held his breath.

"Passcode accepted. What would you like to do?"

The voice definitely sounded happier. He looked at Chala with newfound respect. "How did you know? This, and the door ...?"

Chala looked embarrassed. "The Oracle told me. Or maybe it was the hencha. I was very young when my mother took me to see her."

His eyes went wide. "Magic indeed."

Sister Tela jabbed him in the ribs with her elbow. "Enough time for chit-chat later, Mas and Mim. Right now, we have to get the floodgates open."

He nodded. "Of course. Sorry."

"Passcode accepted. What would you like to do?"

"Give me a minute." Tela found what she was looking for. "System, please open the main floodgates."

"Warning. Taking this action will release a large volume of water and may result in a temporary loss of power. Proceed, yes or no?"

Tela looked up at Kerrick and Chala.

"Do we have any choice?" He thought about all those souls underground, frightened and tired. Turning off the lights wouldn't help matters.

"It won't matter if the caverns flood." Chala stated the simple fact, but the words sent a chill down his spine.

He met her gaze. She was right. It was what they'd come to do, after all. "Do it."

Sister Tela nodded. "System, please open the main floodgates."

"Warning. Taking this action will release a large volume of water and may result in a temporary loss of power. Proceed, yes or no?"

"Impatient thing, isn't it?" He wondered if all the ancients' machines were like that.

She gulped. "Yes."

"Opening main floodgates."

There was a deep hum, a vibration that ran up from the floor through his boots to his spine, above the general noise of the turbines. He gritted his teeth, waiting for it to end. For confirmation of its success. For … something.

The vibration increased, and soon the whole control room was shuddering.

"I'm sorry. The floodgates cannot be fully opened at this time."

"Farking hell." Tela banged her fist on the console. "What now?"

Kerrick chuckled at the outburst, amused in spite of the severity of the situation. It was so unlike her. In the short time they'd known each other, he'd never heard her utter a curse word. "So what next?"

She shook her head. "System, can you tell us what the problem is?"

"Checking. One moment please."

He wiped his brow. At some point he'd started to sweat. "Is it hot in here, or is it just me?"

"You wetlanders wouldn't know *hot* if it were an ichthyn that bit you in the —"

"The floodgates have been partially opened, but there is an error in the gate subsystem."

"Well, that's something." Sister Tela stared at the console, as if trying to force some additional meaning out of the blinking lights. "System, how do we fix the error?"

"The gate subsystem must be reset."

Tela nodded. "Now we're getting somewhere. System, how do we reset the gate ... subsystem?"

The shaking continued, setting his teeth on edge. He imagined thousands of liters of water forcing themselves through the partially opened gates. *I hope the whole thing doesn't shake itself into pieces with us still inside.*

"There's a manual reset switch on the dam, next to the gates. Please pull the switch to reboot the gate subsystem."

"Godsdamned farking hell." It was Kerrick's turn to curse. "*Outside* the dam? How are we going to get to it?"

Tela was leafing through the book again. "Here it is. There's an access stairwell not far from here. But the reset switch ..." Her wrinkled hand trailed across the paper. "It's halfway down the gates."

"Of course it is. Is there a ladder, at least?" He wasn't relishing climbing down the face of the dam, clinging to a wet, slippery ladder, but Sister Tela certainly couldn't manage the descent.

"I think so. Let me see what else I can find —"

"I'll do it." Chala cut in. "Elrys can get me there."

"Are you sure?" He looked over the young woman. She was half his size, but she was strong as an aur, from what he'd heard.

She gave him a curt nod. "Yes. She can get me there and then catch me if I fall."

Kerrick exchanged a glance with Tela. "What do you think?"

The sister shrugged. "What choice do we have?"

With a heavy sigh, he gave in. "All right. But be careful —"

Chala laughed. "When has a woman ever accomplished anything by *being careful*?"

Even Tela grinned at that one. "She has a point."

He'd been outvoted. "Fair enough."

"And besides, it's not like I needed your permission. At least it will get me out of this stuffy room."

He chuckled. She had him there. "All right, already. Be careful, though. I don't want to have to explain to Raven how I lost one of his verent riders."

She beamed at the title. "Just tell me what to do."

•   •   •

Desla was walking through a wonderland.

The world around them grew stranger and stranger as they proceeded deeper into the mountain. The tunnel was full of alien lifeforms in an astonishment of colors, much of it moving or pulsing — breathing? — as they passed. It would have been beautiful if it didn't frighten her to her bones. *Are we being watched?*

Mixed among the red stars were bloated blue balloons that pulsed and let out a soft whistle of air every so often. Creeping vines covered in flowers hung from the ceiling, delicate blossoms that gave off an odd but enchanting smell, something like a cross between fresh-baked bread and hot akka.

Beneath them, the floor was covered in a soft, woven mass of orange filaments, making a spongy carpet that held their boot imprints for a few seconds after they'd passed.

Everything had a bioluminescent glow, enough to light their way even without Spin's blue light.

Little golden things scurried among the vegetation — fungus? They were something like an inthym, about the size of her hand and covered in soft spikes.

"Spin, have you ever seen anything like this?"

The lights around the top of the sphere spun and brightened. "Down down down into the rabbit hole ..."

She scrunched her forehead. "What's a rabbit?"

"Ah, there's so much you people don't know." He flashed in apparent annoyance. "Sorry, Alice. I've never seen lifeforms like these. The closest I can find are the coryx. They look similar to these blue growths when first grown from seed. The design is fascinating. They all have a —"

"Got it. Thanks, Spin." *Alice?*

"You're welcome."

Was it her imagination, or did his voice seem churlish at being cut off? It was strange to think of Spin as human, though he had been once. It must have been strange for him too, now that he'd remembered his past. What was it like to be trapped inside that shiny silver ball?

Ahead, Em and Mes advanced slowly, ready for an attack. They held their bandy spears aloft, eyes darting back and forth, taking in all the strange vegetation.

Or is it fungulation?

It was eerily quiet.

After the strange little toothy, scoop-mouthed things, they were all primed for danger, but instead they seemed to be walking through some alien version of an underground jungle paradise.

Next to her, Triya shook her head. "I don't like this. Not one bit. It's too quiet." She looked pale.

They'd passed through three of the "skin walls," as Triya called them, cutting their way through, only to see them seal up behind them. And each of the "chambers" had been stranger than the last.

"What do we do when we get ... wherever we're going?" She had only the vaguest idea what they were after.

"We kill whatever we find there." Mes rubbed her back, where the thing that had been Aik had wounded her.

"We cross that spine when we come to it." Triya shot Mes a dark look. "No one does anything until I say so."

Desla sighed. *We're so out of our depth that we can't even see the surface.* She stepped over a particularly large vine that ran across their path, releasing a rush of aroma from the flowers she brushed with her legs. "What do you think we'll find?"

The tunnel shuddered. Desla braced herself against one of the walls, touching one of the blue balloons with her bandy-pulp-covered hands.

It screamed and popped open, spraying her with glittering dust.

Poor thing. She wiped the worst of the mess from her face, blinking to clear her eyes. "I hope there's nothing toxic in it."

Triya barked a laugh. "You look like a common thief."

Desla blinked, hoping the stuff hadn't gotten in her eyes.

"Your face is painted black with the stuff, like you're ready for a late-night heist."

She snorted. "Ah, thanks for that. I'm sure I look a fright. We all do."

Triya tugged on her braid. "When we get out of here, I'm going to take the longest bath ..."

Her breath caught. "Do you think we will? Get out of here?" She prided herself on being practical above all, and practicality said they were as likely to end their lives down here as survive whatever might be coming.

She shuddered at the thought. *I'm not ready to die. Aik, what did you lead me into?*

Triya squeezed herself tightly. "Maybe not. Maybe it won't matter. But we have to imagine that we will. Else why go on?"

She swallowed hard. *Why indeed?* "What do you think's happening out there?"

"Nothing good." Em glanced back at them. "Sorry, but I'm with you. We're not going home."

Desla blinked. Em had said it without fear, without regret. "Aren't you scared?"

Em shrugged. "What good would that do me?"

She chewed that over in her head. *What good indeed?* Em was right. Fear was useless here. And yet ... "Spin, can you tell where we are?"

"One moment." His lights spun and flickered. "We're near the center of Anghar Mor."

"Almost there." She took a deep breath. *Wherever there is.*

"Desla?" His voice cracked.

What happened to Cheese? "What?"

"I'm scared too. If it helps."

She put a hand over him, not sure if he could feel her touch or not. "It does, Spin. Thanks." It was getting easier to think of him as human.

The air in this latest chamber was heavy, hot, and thick with humidity. Desla wiped sweat from her brow, wishing for a cool waterfall to wash away all the heat and spores and sticky bandy fruit pulp, which was beginning to give off a strange smell of its own as it baked in the heat.

Twenty more paces through the muggy jungle and they arrived at another of the skin walls.

Mes raised her knife to cut through it.

"Wait."

Mes glanced at Triya, who nodded.

She slipped past her and put her ear next to the skin wall. "Spin, can you hear that?"

"Listening."

"What?" Mes put her ear next to the wall, careful not to touch it. They'd decided after the last encounter that the less they angered the local flora and fauna, the better, and dissolving it with bandy fruit seemed likely to provoke it.

"It sounds like ... breathing." It had been so quiet in the tunnel that the sudden change seemed threatening.

Spin whirred and hummed. "Yes, it does. But the volume of air suggests a very large creature."

Desla groaned. "Here we go." That old phrase *confronting a dragon in its own lair* was starting to make a lot of sense.

Triya looked at each of them in turn. "Looks like we've found what we're looking for. You all ready?"

"Yes, Mim," Mes and Em said in unison.

She nodded.

"All right. Mes, want to do the honors?"

The others stepped back as Mes raised her knife again. She cut a long gash through the skin wall and stepped through, followed in turn by each of the others.

On the other side, she looked up and gasped.

•   •   •

"We have a problem." One of the younger initiates, raised to sisterhood at the same time as Coral, tugged at the sleeve of her robe.

Fess'Ima. She'd arrived just half an hour earlier, one of the last entrants before they'd sealed the doors. The girl who'd almost died. She had become a bit of a legend in the initiates' dorms.

Woman, Coral corrected herself. They'd all been thrust into full adulthood by the events of the last few days.

Looking around, Coral drew her away from the citizens encamped in the tunnel, to a bulge in the cavern where they'd stored some emergency supplies. *No need to frighten the locals.* "What kind of problem?" she whispered.

"I was checking supplies in one of the lower caverns, and I stepped in water."

Coral frowned. "Did one of the water barrels leak?" They had limited supplies, but she thought they could survive the loss of a barrel or two if things went their way aboveground.

"No. Not a barrel. The water's coming in from somewhere else."

"Are you sure?"

Fess'Ima nodded. "While I was there, the water level raised at least three centimeters."

The river. Silya had mentioned how warm it was in the Highlands. *If the ice is melting ...*

She put her hand on Fess'Ima's shoulder. "You were right to bring this to me. Find Ast'Una and tell her what you told me, but no one else. We need to move whatever we can to higher ground, but above all, we can't risk creating a panic." She shuddered to think about what that would be like in the cramped space. People rushing through the tunnels, trampling one-another in their haste to get out. There was already a quiet desperation in the air.

"Of course." Sister Ima shivered.

Coral squeezed her shoulder. "Forewarned is forearmed. You did well."

The sister brightened. "Thank you, Sister Cor'Lea."

"Just Coral." She was starting to understand how Silya felt about forced formalities. "And remember, you're a sister now too. And you already beat death once. You'll get through this just fine, along with the rest of us." She said a silent prayer to Nor'Oss, the god of water, that it would be so.

"What if I already used up my extra life?"

Coral sighed. "We may all be running short. But not if I have anything to say about it." She gave her a quick hug.

"Fessryn." The young sister melted into her arms.

"What?"

"Call me Fessryn."

"Fessryn it is." They'd never been particularly close as initiates. Fessryn was from one of the wealthy families of Peregrine Spine, and they had precious little in common. Still, desperate times forged strange friendships. "Now go. I'll head down to the storage area and check on the situation."

"Thank you, Cor — Coral." She slipped away.

Coral closed her eyes for just a second. She was so tired. It had been long day upon long night, with little rest in between. She'd hoped to take a quick nap now that the midday meal had been served, but it seemed fate had other plans.

She set off for the lower caverns, dreading what she would find.

•　　　•　　　•

Raven/Breeze soared past the edge of Landfield and out over the Heartland. It was deceptively calm.

The Elsp's silver ribbon ran across the northern edge of the valley, shimmering in the afternoon sun. In many places it had breached its banks, spilling out into the open fields around it.

Still, everything was relatively quiet.

The hencha swayed in the breeze, singing a song only they — and maybe Silya — could hear. There was no one in the fields, and the villages that dotted the valley were empty of people.

In the west, the sky was dark and threatening.

The ground shook, a deep rumble shattering the illusion of peace and calm and sending a nest of umvit skyward from a huge flop tree, screeching in protest.

Raven was lost in thought, trying to work out what he would say to Aik when they met. What he would do.

Triya had said Aik was changed. He tried to remember the tales his mother had told him about the Death Bringer — scales, long tail, and a blank face that showed no expression while it made you scream ... *Will I even recognize him?*

"You're beautiful to me, no matter what. You always have been." Aik had said that then.

Before Raven had left him for the verent. *Will I still be beautiful to him now?*

Will he be beautiful to me? Some questions only time could answer.

Olly/Flit flew alongside him, with Squint and Thunder flanking the two of them.

Found some. Olly's thought pierced his own. He and Flit plunged toward the ground.

Good eye. Raven/Breeze followed, along with the other riderless verent. They dove at a steep angle, and the wind slipped past their wings in a clamorous rush.

Far below, a square grove of trees stood out amongst the hencha, their broad, heart-shaped leaves a darker purple. *Let's just hope they have fruit.*

Breeze had assured him that he was nearly invulnerable to the red fireflies, but they'd both felt the pain of the verent that Aik had ridden. Its anguish had just as suddenly flared out into darkness, and Raven could only assume the poor thing was dead, a blessing under the circumstances. *A little extra protection never hurt.*

Indeed. Breeze landed at the edge of the grove, and Raven wasted no time separating from his verent host. He pulled a pair of briefs from his saddlebag and put them on. It was warm enough that he didn't need anything else.

He ran for the grove, wincing at the hard soil on his bare feet.

Olly chuckled, right behind him. "No time for clothes, huh?" He'd pulled on a pair of breeches and somehow had gotten his boots on and laced up too.

"How ...?"

Olly grinned. "Lots of practice."

Raven sighed. "The faster we get this done, the better." He looked up into the branches of the first tree he came to, spotting some of the spiky fruit.

He climbed the trunk, finding footholds and places to pull himself up, feeling like a kid again. With a little testing, he found a few ripe ones, twisted them off of their branches, and dropped them to the ground as gently as he could.

He carried them back to Breeze and used Aik's knife out of his saddlebag to cut the first one open. He scooped the pulp and fruit out. It smelled heavenly. He rubbed it across Breeze's neck and shoulders.

Breeze reached back to lick some of his hard work off the verent's scales. *Tastes good.*

Stop that. You need that to protect you from the fireflies. He could feel Olly's amusement. "And you stop that too."

Olly chuckled in reply. "You really need to learn to relax, Rave."

The name Aik used to use for him brought him up short. "Relax? We're at the end of the farking world, flying into the heart of a storm to save my best friend, my ... everything." A shiver ran through him. "Who may or may not still be Aik inside. And you want me to *relax*?"

Olly nodded, blinking in the face of Raven's verbal assault. "Sorry. Maybe you're right. I'm scared shitless too."

Their eyes met, and the fear hidden under Olly's bravado was suddenly clear. "Sorry. I'm all wound up, and scared that I don't know what in the green holy hell I'm doing." It helped, somehow, to admit it. "We'll get through this."

Olly met his gaze. "One way or another." Then the smile reappeared on his face. "Any idea how foolish we look, half naked, smearing bandy pulp on a bunch of flying lizards?" He eyed Raven's shirtless, pants-less form. "Well, one of us is, anyhow."

He snorted. "Not how I'd planned to spend my afternoon." He continued to smear Breeze's hide with pulp. In short order he used up the three fruit he'd plucked and went back for more, but not before pulling on his boots and pants.

It took five trips, but eventually all of the verent were covered. Raven thought about using it on himself too, but when he merged with Breeze, would it all just slough off anyway?

He licked some of the fruit off of his thumb, ignoring the hurt look Breeze gave him.

You said not to eat it.

"Oh for the gods' sakes." He retrieved a few more of the ripe fruits and gave one to each of the verent, spiky bits and all. *Better?*

Much. Breeze licked his lips. *Now we fly.*

He stashed a couple of extra ones, and then stripped off his clothing and stowed it away. Satisfied, he climbed back onto the verent's back.

Olly did the same.

The now-familiar sensation of the merge distracted him — the momentary dissolving of self as he became part of his verent. That was the best part of all this, joining with Breeze's mind, his thoughts, his unconditional love.

I like you too.

Warmth flooded him from the verent. He would have grinned if he'd been in his own form. *What would I do without you?*

Walk? That came with a flash of impish humor as they took to the sky again, their powerful wings lifting them up above the bandy-tree grove.

The other verent followed, and soon they were winging once again toward the ominous line of darkness on the horizon.

13

THE APPROACHING STORM

THE SPORE MOTHER WATCHED the approaching humans with growing alarm through her children. The *eemscaap* had failed to stop them, and she was out of time. She had a handful of forerunners, but they hovered around her uncertainly as the sharp metal of the intruders breached the last *eechiia*.

The white wall shuddered and split in two, and she felt its pain, even as it sought to heal the tear. It separated to reveal the first of the invaders.

There were four of them, all about the same size. They looked so similar to one another — in her limited experience, all humans looked alike. Yet these four carried milk sacks on their chests. *Female, then.*

It was an odd concept. Like them, she was capable of bearing children. But she was the only parent, providing all the genetic material needed for her various offspring. How inefficient to have to solicit a genetic sample from another creature, and at such a specific time, to bear offspring.

She had learned much from the progenitor, but even he had been somewhat mystified by the process.

Still, her aaveen had sexes and genders too, just not as apparently rigid as humans.

All four of them were in her cavern now, staring up at her.

Her new seedling was almost complete. She had no idea what kind of danger these humans presented, but she had to assume the worst and play for time until it was ready. Otherwise, if she were lost, so was the rest of her race.

Come out and speak for me. She nudged her last creation gently, a gawky, ungainly thing created at great need.

It trembled inside one of her wombs, and then its eyes flew open. *Is it time?*

She filled it with love. It was strange, even ugly to her. But it was what was needed to speak with these humans before they tried to kill her, and so she loved it.

Her womb split open, and her new creature spilled out onto the ground in a rush of golden fluid.

•   •   •

Silya's eyes flew open. Her heart was racing, and her hands covered in a cold sweat.

Dor straightened up, her eyes meeting Silya's. "What happened?"

"They want me to kill Aik." As soon as she said it, she regretted it. Giving it voice gave it life. *I am most certainly not going to kill one of my friends.*

She grimaced. There was so much at stake — what if it was Aik or the world? *Not unless there's no other choice.*

She let go of Dor's hands and got to her feet. She was running on fumes — not enough sleep and way too much stress and responsibility. Still, this was no time to slow down. "I have to get to him."

"Would you ... could you ...?" Dor managed to get up too, wincing and stretching out her legs. Brushing the dirt off her robe, she looked up, her eyes full of concern. The last week had aged her ten years.

It's taken a toll on all of us. "Of course not. I'll find a way to save him." She had no idea how she'd accomplish that. She turned to go, her mind spinning.

Dor caught the sleeve of her robe. "But what if you have no choice?"

She stopped dead in her tracks. She took a deep breath, the words reverberating through her mind. *What if I have to do it?*

She had taken an oath to protect Gullton and the Heartland. The emp test was ever-present in her mind, the end of the world by fire or ice. For the first time since she'd been chosen, she wished she wasn't the Hencha Queen. "I don't know."

"Look at me." Dor's commanding tone spun her around. Their eyes met again, and Dor's seemed full of fire, as if she were the Hencha Queen herself.

"What?"

"You have a good head on your shoulders. You're smart as a whip, and under your sharp exterior you're one of the most compassionate people I've ever met." She squeezed Silya's shoulders so hard it hurt. "You *will* do the right thing, whatever that is. You will find a way. Of that, I have no doubt."

She shuddered. "I'm so scared, Dor. How did this come down to me?" *I'm just a girl who wanted to be loved.* As she thought it, she knew it was true.

All her life, she'd sought her mother's affection and approval. Her father had abandoned her, dying when she needed him most, and her mother had been cold to her most of her life. Even Aik had left her for someone else. Becoming the Hencha Queen hadn't been a dream. It was a reaction. A means to an end, and a way for her to win what she truly wanted. *To be loved.*

"I can't do this. I'm not the right one." Maybe she could still give it all up, get the hencha to choose someone more capable, less afraid. *Coral. Or Dor ...*

"It has to be you." Dor wrapped her arms around her, squeezing her tight. "Can you feel it? With that little thing on your neck?"

She closed her eyes, humbled at Dor's gesture. She'd been too scattered, too frantic to feel what Dor was feeling.

She reached out cautiously through the emp, but Dor's emotions slammed into her like a physical blow.

First and foremost, she felt love. Not the love some women felt for others, but the love of a mother for her child — blind, and unconditional. It was a breath of fresh air, what she'd always wanted from her real mother but had rarely gotten.

But beneath that were other emotions. Pride in who she had become. Delight in her character. And outright fear.

Silya dove into that one. *Are you afraid of me?*

It unfolded in her mind, and suddenly it was clear, what Dor feared more than anything else in the world. *She's scared that she's not enough for me.*

All this time, she'd thought Dor was judging her, measuring her against the past queens in the Temple. Instead, the senior sister been judging herself.

"Oh gods, Dor. Of course you're enough," she whispered, squeezing her tightly, hoping her aide — no, her friend — could feel how grateful she was for this gift. *I am loved.* "I love you too."

It had been here, right under her nose. Dor loved her, and Daya before her had done so too. She'd dismissed it because it wasn't from Triya. Somehow, since neither was her mother, it didn't *count.*

She'd been so wrong about that. *What else gave I been mistaken about?*

Triya loved her too — that much had become clear in the last week. Maybe not in exactly the way she wanted, but her love was there nevertheless, even though every day she had spent with Silya must have reminded her of her dead husband. *My father.*

And of course Aik loved her too, though he'd given his heart to another. For hencha's sake, even *Raven* loved her.

And now she had Kerrick.

What they had between them was new, but he loved her too.

I am loved. Her whole world shifted under the weight of that realization.

She held Dor out at arm's length. "You will *always* be enough for me. You've led me though this whole dark time, even when you didn't think I noticed. And you've just given me a gift far more precious than you know."

Relief blossomed on Dor's face. "You're the Hencha Queen." She cupped Silya's cheek in her hand. "You were chosen for a reason. Don't you forget it."

She took a deep breath. "I have to go after Raven. I have to find Aik before —" She wasn't sure how to end that sentence.

A gnawing fear clawed at her gut. She would find them, and she would do what she had to do. She just hoped to the gods that didn't mean killing either one of them.

Dor nodded. "You're not going to make me ride one of those ungodly beasts, are you?"

She laughed. "No, I need you here. If Kerrick and the others open the floodgates ... when they do it, I need you here to get them and everyone else who's left to safety. You're the only one I trust to take care of Gullton while I'm gone."

Dor sighed, sounding vastly relieved. "How will you get there?"

She bit her lip. "I guess I need to find me a verent rider."

• • •

Chala ran back the way she'd come with the others, down the long, dark hall that led back to Raven Spine and the Council Hall.

The whole dam shuddered again. A massive amount of water must have been pushing its way through the partially-opened floodgates. *Who knew water could be so heavy?*

"Danger. The dam is in imminent danger of collapse. Please evacuate."

Chala froze and looked around wildly. The lights in the hallway shifted from white to red.

"Danger. The dam is in imminent danger of collapse. Please evacuate."

It sounded like the voice of the System, the one in the control room. *Could it be in two places at once?*

She shrugged it off. *No accounting for magic.* She took a deep breath and her heartbeat slowed. Determined, she took off again toward the exit. She didn't care for this wetlander city. *Not one whit.*

She reached the stairs and took them two at a time, running through the task she'd been given in her head. It seemed simple enough — get to the manual switch and pull it.

But in life, things were rarely as simple as they seemed. It was a lesson she'd learned the hard way, more than once.

She arrived at the upper levels and took a second to remember which way led to the plaza outside. *To the left.* In short order she was running down the steps in front of the building. "Elrys!"

The verent was waiting for her by the fountain, her head tilted in question.

"We have to fly!" The world was unsettled, a strong breeze blowing from inland, whipping at her ponytail.

The verent seemed to be getting better at reading Chala's desires. She knelt, and Chala climbed onto her back.

As soon as she was secure in her saddle, the verent spread her wings and took a running takeoff. *Where?*

There. Chala pointed, and Elrys surged toward the dam.

The water had risen precipitously since she'd flown down the spine an hour earlier. It hadn't breached the top of the spine, but it was less than five meters below it. She didn't have much time.

They flew past the lip of the great structure and out over the Harkness, soaring above the open ocean. The sound of the water forcing itself through the gap was deafening as it tumbled through the air and down to the sea. *So much water.*

The gates themselves were massive — probably thirty meters across each — but they were only a quarter of the way open. They were almost bulging under the strain of the water that forced its way through them. *Can you take us closer?*

Elrys brought her as near to the dam as she was able, flapping her wings wildly to maintain her altitude.

Wind whipped the spray toward them, covering verent and rider in a slippery mist.

Chala searched the slick wall of the dam. *There.*

Along the side of the right gate, a metal ladder was embedded in the strange stone. *Closer.*

Elrys reached out and grasped the ladder with her claws, her wings still beating.

Beautiful, love. Mindful of the fall, Chala swung herself around and grasped the ladder.

It groaned under the verent's great weight. One rod popped out of the dam, then another, and the metal itself groaned like a living thing.

Let go!

She lost her own grip as Elrys's claws separated from the ladder and the verent backed away from the dam.

Chala screamed in frustration as she grabbed at the wet rungs of the ladder again, dropping rapidly toward the churning waters below. The image of her own Elrys — the woman she loved — flashed through her eyes.

The Oracle's face appeared in her mind too as the rungs flew past. *You can do this.*

Chala clawed at the slippery rungs, her fingers slipping and slapping painfully on them as she dropped. Finally she managed to grasp one, bringing her fall to a jarring halt. She swung her other arm up and over another rung and just hung there for a moment, breathing raggedly.

The floodgates creaked. They wouldn't last much longer, and if the others were still inside ... Maybe the dam would fall and release all of its waters. *At least that would save everyone else.*

Or it might partially collapse, blocking the flood behind its bulky wall.

Gritting her teeth, Chala looked around.

She'd fallen two-thirds of the way down the face of dam. To her left, the water churned and thundered. *Where's the access panel?*

There was something on the wall above her — a protrusion that *might* be it. She was too close to the wall to be sure, but there was nothing below her that might be it.

Alive?

The sound of the verent in her mind calmed her. *Yes, Elrys, I'm alive.*

The flood of relief from her verent gave her strength to move.

Carefully she pulled her feet up onto the ladder, and she climbed, one hand and one foot at a time, cautious not to lose her grip again.

The words of the Oracle came to her again. *You are special. You will do great things for your people.*

The wetlanders weren't exactly her people. *Well, maybe in the broader sense?* And she supposed this *would* count as a "great thing."

She climbed as quickly as she was able. The rungs were slippery and wet, so she had to move cautiously, making sure her feet had purchase before lifting her arms to the next rung. Meter by meter, she climbed the angled wall.

After what seemed like an eternity but could only have been a couple of minutes, she reached the access panel. It was a rectangular box made out of the same material as the console ... maybe metal? But not cold, like metal should be.

She pushed on the left side, as Sister Tela had told her, and it cracked open, but not all the way. It was four hundred some years old, after all. *I'm lucky that it opened at all.*

Looping one arm around a ladder rung, she used the other to retrieve her belt knife. With it, she pried the panel open centimeter by centimeter. Bits of detritus dropped toward the water below before being captured by the wind and carried out to sea. Next to her, the water thundered like an angry god.

Chala was grateful that her hair was tied behind her back, though stray strands whipped around her face in an annoying fashion.

She slipped the knife back into the holster and leaned out to get a better look at the box.

Inside, in impossibly neat script, it said "Manual Override." Below it was a wide black bar.

"Pull down the switch to release the gates." Tela had been very clear about that, but surely it couldn't be so simple. How could such a small thing move those massive gates?

Chala looked around. The partially open gates groaned again, and the dam shook — whether it was from another quake or just the torrent of water rushing through the narrow opening, she couldn't tell.

Above, the torn portion of the ladder dangled in the air, the sun's rays streaming through the mist to make a beautiful rainbow.

Chala took it as a sign. She reached out, grasped the switch, and pulled it down hard. It ground under her palm, but then slammed into place.

A great creaking filled the air, and the gates shuddered again and started to open, shaking the world like the hands of the gods —

— and she was falling again, knocked loose from the ladder as the floodtide increased to titanic proportions, filling the whole world.

She whispered a quick prayer to Nor'Oss as the ocean flew up at her.

The last thing she saw as she dropped into the churning depths was Elrys — her verent — plunging after her into watery oblivion.

• • •

"Manual override activated. Recommencing the opening of the floodgates."

Kerrick started. He'd almost fallen asleep on his feet. He couldn't remember the last time he'd had a full night's rest.

"Yes!" Sister Tela's eyes were bright. "She did it."

"Yes, she did." He hoped the suifaine warrior was all right. She was fearsome, but there was an aura of deep sadness about her too. *Like recognizes like.* "What do we do now —"

The lights flickered out, leaving only their lantern to illuminate the little room.

"What in the seven hells?" He grasped the edge of the console to steady himself.

Sister Tela was almost ghostly in the dim light. "The turbines have shut down. All the water's being forced out of the floodgates."

The roar slowly decreased, and the dam was no longer trying to shake itself apart. *Thank the elder god.* He gave a nod of respect to the engineers who had designed and built the marvel. "Will we be able to ... make it work again, when this is all over?" *If this is ever over.*

Sister Tela nodded. "I think so. The Electrical Guild should be able to manage it. They'll find a way."

I hope you're right. He'd gotten used to having the electric lights, and they opened up the possibility of so much more. "Come on. Let's get back to the surface. This place still gives me the creeps."

Sister Tela laughed. "I feel right at home, but then I spend most of my time in the twisty halls of the Temple." She stood and gathered her books under her arms, as gently as if they were her children.

To her, they probably are. Kerrick grinned in spite of his exhaustion and dark mood. "Hopefully the world didn't end while we were down here." Chala was probably waiting for them outside in the square.

They made their way out of the dam in silence, and back up to City Hall. Tela was a font of information, telling him all about the building and its construction.

"They built the dam shortly after Landing. They needed the power source to supply energy to the machines that built the old city ..."

We do need a Knowledge Guild. And you should be in charge of it. He glanced at the woman beside him in wonder. How old was she? Would she be willing to take it on? He'd have to talk with her about it later.

"That's all fascinating, but right now we need to get all three of us to safety." He replaced the lantern in the sconce he'd taken it from, grateful for the natural light streaming into the hallway from the narrow windows.

Tela grinned wryly. "I do tend to babble on, or so they tell me."

"You're passionate about history." He returned her smile. "I think it's an admirable trait."

She beamed at him. "And you are a good man, Ser Kek Aze."

It was late afternoon when they stepped out of the Council Hall and entered Founder's Square. A light mist from the tumbling waters nearby overlaid the plaza, making the cobblestones sparkle, while the sun's rays created little rainbows. It was eerily quiet.

Chala was nowhere to be seen. Kerrick frowned.

His urse awaited them patiently, though he stomped his hooves and tried to shake off the clinging vapors.

He pulled out his long talker. "Silya … Silya, can you hear me? Fin."

A few seconds later, it crackled to life. "Kerrick — yes, this is Silya."

He grinned. Who else would it be? "We're safe. The floodgates have been opened. Fin." He looked around the square, his brow kitted. *Where's Chala?*

Her verent was gone too. *She must have gone on ahead to the Temple.*

"Thank the gods. The lights went out here, and I feared the worst —"

"Sorry. The dam shut down when we opened the floodgates. Sister Tela says it's fixable, after this is over. Fin."

"Good. We'll do without for now, though I hope there's not widespread panic in the caverns. Fin."

He swallowed hard. He hadn't thought about that. "Is Chala there with you?"

"I haven't seen her. Why? She's not with you? Fin."

"She had to trigger a manual override on the dam to get the floodgates open." He shared a nervous glance with Sister Tela. "I'm going to take a quick look, and then we'll be on our way back." He motioned for the sister to wait for him and strode to the edge of the plaza where he could see the dam.

There was silence at the other end of the line.

"Silya?"

"I may be gone when you get here. Fin."

"What?" He stared at the long talker as if it would answer his question. "Silya, what are you planning?"

"Raven went after Aik. Who's not Aik anymore. It's complicated. But I have to get there before they find a way to kill him. Fin."

"Who? Silya —"

"I have to go. I love you, Kerrick." Then she was gone.

His heart skipped a beat at that. *She loves me.*

He hoped she hadn't come up with some half-baked scheme that would get her killed.

He peered over the edge of the spine, holding onto the slick railing. There was no sign of the verent rider. *She's a big girl. She can take care of herself.*

There were other more pressing things to worry about. He headed back to his urse and the waiting sister.

"What's our Hencha Queen up to now?" Tela peered at him with a birdlike intensity.

"I don't know, but I can't let her go alone." He needed to hurry, to convince Silya to change her mind, but he couldn't leave the elderly sister out here on her own. "Your ride seems to have taken off. Ever ridden urseback?"

Sister Tela nodded. "Since I was a little girl. I grew up in one of the southern villages."

"Perfect." He untied his urse and climbed into the saddle, massaging its long neck fondly. Then he held out a hand to her.

She took it and clambered up much more nimbly than a woman of her age ought to have been able to, settling in behind him.

"Let's go." Her hands settled around his waist, grasping his firm stomach. "Nice."

He smirked despite his rising concern. *Sister Tela, you surprise me.* "Hold on." He urged the urse to a gallop, and they slipped out of the mist cloud and into the afternoon sunshine.

A flight of wisps followed them along the course of the spine, tumbling one over the other overhead. Somehow that made him feel better.

Wait for me, Silya. I'm coming!

•   •   •

Coral carried a wooden crate up the slope of the tunnel, away from the advancing waters. She and Aster had organized a few of the sisters and some of the others from the caverns above, quietly, to slip downstairs one at a time to salvage their supplies.

The rising water made her nervous. They could only move things so far, and sooner or later, they would have to evacuate the caverns altogether or risk drowning.

The electric lights didn't reach this far, so they used a few gas lanterns to light their way. Lanterns breathed air like people — Sister Tela had been very clear on that point — and lamp oil was in limited supply, so they had to be careful.

One of the sisters had brought word that a flood was in progress out there, and that someone was trying to open the dam's floodgates to relieve the pressure. Coral wished them godsspeed.

The whole situation was dangerously unbalanced. *What will get us first?* The rising waters? The stale air? Would they run out of supplies, or be overrun by the invaders, whatever they were?

Don't get carried away, Coral. She sang a bar of the Noninalya under her breath to calm her nerves.

Fess'Ima arrived as she was setting down her last crate. "Sister Coral ... the lights have gone out upstairs. People are starting to panic." The poor girl seemed on the edge of panic herself.

Coral put a hand on her arm. "Calm yourself. Take a deep breath, then another."

Aster arrived with her final crate. "What's happening?" She sounded perfectly calm.

Coral envied her. "The lights are out upstairs."

Aster nodded. "The dam — they must have opened the gates." She unhooked the lantern. "Here, you two take this and go. I'll gather the others. Remember, panic is like a sickness. It spreads quickly and can infect whomever it touches."

Fess'Ima's eyes went wide. "What can we do?"

Aster took the girl by the shoulders. "Breathe deeply and center yourself first. Then spread calm. It's the opposite of panic."

Coral's own heart was beating quickly now, but she did her best to follow Aster's advice. She closed her eyes and took a deep breath. She could feel something in the back of her mind — like when the hencha had called her to help Silya. *What in Heaven's Reach?*

Fess'Ima gasped.

"What?" Coral opened her eyes. Her own arms flickered with flames. "What's happening to me?"

Both Fess'Ima and Ast'Una were staring at her.

"It's a miracle." Fess'Ima sounded caught between panic and wonder.

Aster was more practical. "Yes, it is. And maybe just the miracle we need." She took Coral by the shoulders and turned her around gently. "Go, girl. Use this to calm the townsfolk. Show them your light."

Coral had no time to think about what this strange change meant. *The hencha, inside me?*

Numb, she followed Fess'Ima back up toward the upper levels of the caverns.

The clamor reached her ears before they arrived at the first of the refugees — a cacophony of voices raised in fear. She couldn't make out individual words, just the unmistakable sounds of burgeoning panic.

It quieted as she approached, calm spreading from her like ripples through the water.

She reached the long row of pallets.

A little boy stood at the edge of his family who'd been arguing seconds before. He looked up at her, his face wreathed in the aquamarine light of her flames, his blond hair disheveled as if he'd just woken from a nap.

Coral knelt, touching his face gently. The flames licked it but did him no harm.

He looked to be about five, his blue eyes wide as he looked into hers.

"It's going to be all right."

He blinked, transfixed by her light. "Are you sure? I'm scared."

She didn't feel sure. *Not at all.* But she nodded. "Of course." She hugged him. "Just promise me you'll take care of your sister and parents?"

The boy nodded solemnly. "I'm Davin. Dav'Eyl."

"Coral. And you are very strong." She squeezed his shoulders and then let him go. To his parents, she said, "You have a brave boy."

"Thank you," the boy's mother said. "Thank you." She touched Coral's arm, almost as if she were seeking a benediction.

Coral squeezed her hand. "Stay calm. We'll all get through this." She looked over her shoulder. Five sisters followed, carrying lanterns.

So this is what it feels like to be a Hencha Queen. She'd never aspired to it. Never thought herself worthy. But this was different. This wasn't power and responsibility and endless state dinners and meetings.

This is hope, in its purest form. And she needed it as much as all these poor displaced folks around her.

She continued up the tunnel, moving from one person to the next, delivering a warm touch here and a few kind words there, and a reverent silence spread wherever she went, and an aura of calm spread around her, extinguishing the panic.

It's going to be all right.

14

THE COMING BATTLES

S PIN SCANNED THE CAVERN. It was a couple of hundred meters wide and half that tall, with most of it inhabited by a single complex creature. It had no eyes — no sensory apparatus at all that he could see. The closest analogue he could find was a giant clump of mushrooms — oyster mushrooms, though these tended more toward domes than the flat tops of the Earth variety.

And they were an order of magnitude larger.

Red lines like ropey veins made intricate patterns on the undersides of the individual "mushrooms," and everything in the cavern was connected to the giant structure — either directly or by magnetic lines of force invisible to the human eye.

As one, each leaf and clump and tentacle turned to focus on them as they stepped into an alien wonderland.

It knows we're here.

• • •

Desla stepped through the last white barrier, careful not to touch the edges, and stopped cold with an involuntary gasp.

The tunnel ended here, opening up into a wide cavern that disappeared into the darkness above. In the velvety blackness, a few of the fireflies hovered, circling uncertainly. The place was like a jungle, full of fantastical shapes and colors, along with an oppressive heat and humidity that made sweating useless.

But something huge inhabited the shadows ahead, its bloated white skin visible in Spin's glow, and the illumination from the fireflies and the various flora that filled the room.

She wrinkled her nose. "It stinks in here." The heat coming in waves, making her feel dizzy.

Triya squeezed past her and looked around. "Yes, it does. Like … rotten cabbage?"

"Or gully fowl eggs." Mes met her gaze. "What are we looking for?"

She whistled, staring at the strange white mass that occupied half the cavern. "Maybe the cephlant in the room?"

A waterfall rumbled down one side of the cave, water running across the floor in a shallow channel to pool around the base of a large white dome. It reminded her of the coryx in Clayton, and the alien versions she'd seen on her journey here with Aik. Still, it looked … older? Wrinkled, not as full as those others.

Behind it was a series of other domes, piled on top of one another like a stack of dolls carelessly thrown in a corner by a child, all connected by thick red ropey conduits that also lined the underside of the domes. *Like an organic factory.*

The whole thing pulsed slowly.

It's breathing. That thought sent a shudder down her spine.

Mes's eyes narrowed. "This? What is it?"

She looked up at the fireflies, shivering. "I think she's the mother of all these creatures. Like a big fat coryx. Spin, what can you tell us?"

Spin's lights spun and flared, bathing the enormous creature in light. "It does looks like a *big fat coryx.* It bears marked similarities to a type of fungus from Earth, although vastly different in scale. To be sure if it's related to the coryx, a full genetic analysis would be needed."

"A what?" Spin spoke in riddles sometimes. "Is that … something you can do?"

Spin blinked his lights. "Sorry, Cheese. There are no suitable labs on Tharassas."

Desla frowned. *Labs?*

Triya took a few cautious steps toward the thing. "We call a fertile coryx the 'spore mother.'"

Desla's lips twitched. "That sounds about right. So this is the spore mother that has unleashed a nightmare upon us all?"

Em took a step toward the strange creature, holding out her spear as if she meant to poke one of its veins.

"Don't hurt it!" Des said, just as the vein pulled away from the sharp tip of the wood.

Mes growled. "We should kill it if we can."

She shook her head. "Not yet. First we need to find out more."

Mes turned to look at her as if she'd gone daft. "Find out more? From this … *thing*? How do we do that?"

"Yes, more." Mes and Em always had one solution to any problem. Kill it. "Where did it come from? Are there others? What did it do to Aik? We have so many questions that need answers." She was starting to get used to the strange smell.

Triya nodded. "Desla's right. But how do we talk to … something like this?"

Desla smiled in appreciation. "Maybe Spin can —"

One of the larger domes at ground level split open, releasing a gush of golden fluid that sluiced across the cavern floor toward the flowing water.

Mes and Em fell into a crouch as a fresh wave of nauseating stench assaulted their senses. "What in Jas's name —"

Something lifted itself out of the sticky pool. It moved strangely, as if getting used to its body. It stood awkwardly and turned to stare at them.

She gasped.

It was Aik.

•　　•　　•

"You just unclasp this here, and this here, and lift it off." Astrid demonstrated, pulling the heavy saddle off Sleeker's back.

Silya nodded. "Got it." She liked the ce'faine woman, though they hadn't gotten much time together before this. She was forthright with her opinions, a quality Silya valued. No *Mim* or *Your Highness* here. "How do we communicate?"

Astrid tapped the bulge on her own neck. "Just tell the emp what you want. It will relay it to us."

"Or just lean the way you want to go." Jai winked. He was charming, warm in a way that Astrid was not. Silya'd liked him immediately.

A storm was gathering on the eastern horizon. Figuratively and literally. "Are you two sure —"

"Wherever Raven goes, we go." Jai looked deadly serious now.

Astrid nodded. "We all ride together against the Rise."

The two verent riders had just returned from their last runs delivering people to the relative safety of the iron mines up north.

The Rise. An apt name for it.

"The cavalry's here." Dor arrived with Jer'Mar, Astrid's brother, in tow. The young man was pulling a handcart loaded with a large pottery crock.

"Hey sis." Jer'Mar flashed Astrid a bright smile.

Silya could feel the sibling love between them. It was overwhelming sometimes, sensing all the things those around her were feeling, but it was twice as strong from those who also had emps. She shoved it to the back of her mind, an increasingly crowded place.

"Verla whipped up a batch of bandy-fruit pulp, and she added some powdered bacca root as a thickener." Dor lifted off the lid, exposing the jelly-like substance inside.

"It smells divine. For a minute I thought you were bringing us an early dinner." She had eaten lightly, as she didn't want to be sick when riding a verentback.

She set down her staff and took a handful of the stuff and smeared it across her face and on her neck, anywhere her skin was exposed.

"Sorry, Mim." Astrid's younger brother blushed. "I can run back to the kitchen and bring you something, if you like."

She shook her head. "My stomach's fluttering with fairykens already. I doubt I could keep anything down." She'd traded her robes for a thick shirt and trousers — in Hencha Queen blue, of course — made from a sturdy home weave that she hoped would be impenetrable to the fireflies. Still, she smeared some of the concoction over the stiff cloth too, just to be safe.

"Yes, Mim." The poor boy looked half scared to death.

She tousled his hair, regretting it when she realized her hand was sticky with pulp. "Call me Silya, please. And you're Jereck?"

The boy didn't seem to mind. He nodded and grinned. "Yes, Mi ... Mim Silya."

She was done having that particular fight. "You must have been very brave to survive all alone in Zeraya."

The boy beamed. "Thank you, Mim."

Astrid flashed her a grateful smile.

Jer'Mar handed out some brushes, and between the five of them, they made quick work of the two verent.

Then Astrid and Jai were stripping off their clothes, preparing to become one with their verent.

Jereck was staring at Jai.

Silya grinned. She knew that look. She'd given it to Kerrick often enough, and seen Aik and Raven share one just like it.

Jai must have felt the boy's stare. He looked up to meet Jereck's gaze. "See something you like?"

Jereck's face flushed. "No. I mean yes. I mean ..." He looked away. "It's just ... you're beautiful."

It was Jai's turn to blush.

She nodded. She'd never seen one of the two-gendered like this before, but Jai showed no embarrassment about his own body. *And why should he?*

Astrid put a hand under her brother's chin, turning him forcibly to face her. "You keep Dor and the rest safe, you hear me?"

"Yes, Mim." He squirmed in her grasp, trying to avoid, well, the entirety of her naked body before him.

Silya shook her head in sympathy. *Some things you just don't need to see.*

"Good boy." Astrid hugged her brother tightly.

Poor Jereck grimaced at the double shame of being hugged in public by his sister, and by his *naked* sister. "Come back safe."

"I will." She kissed his cheek. "All right, let's get going. We have a rogue Guard to catch." Astrid climbed up onto Sleeker and melted into the verent.

Will wonders never cease. No matter how many times Silya witnessed it, the whole merging thing never ceased to amaze her. She could *feel* their excitement too. *I guess it never gets old for them either.*

She picked up the saddle and slung it over the beast, who lowered itself to the ground to accommodate her. She attached it the way Astrid had shown her — it wasn't that different from an urse saddle, but bigger — and in short order she had the saddle strapped on.

She retrieved her staff and turned to face Dor. "I'm covered in bandy fruit pulp so I won't hug you. But I am, in my heart."

Dor laughed. "Yes, that's very much appreciated. You smell like a fresh-baked foldover."

Silya laughed with her. It felt good, especially given the gravity of the situation she was throwing herself into. This was it, her last chance to set things right before the world came crashing down around them all, like she'd seen during her test. *One last chance.*

She touched Dor's cheek. "I love you, Doria. I couldn't have done any of this without you."

Dor shook her head vehemently. "I don't believe that for a second. You are whip-smart, and far more capable than you give yourself credit for. Just do what's in your heart when the time comes."

She nodded. "I'll try." The last time she'd fought the invaders, she'd damned-near killed herself. This might be the last time she saw Dor, or the temple. She shivered. It felt like a bad omen. *Or a premonition.*

"What the hell." Dor threw her arms around Silya's sticky form. "What Jereck said."

Silya hugged her, grateful for the gesture, for her friendship, for everything. "We will." She hoped it was true.

She kissed Dor on the forehead and let go. "Get yourself and the others in the Temple to safety. Now that the dam's been opened, the caverns should be more protected than anywhere else."

Dor wrang her hands, glancing over Silya's shoulder to the east nervously. "Go. You have a world to save."

"From your lips ..." She climbed onto Astrid/Sleeker's back, strapping herself into the saddle. With one last look back at the Temple, she took a deep breath, and exhaled. *Jas help us all. Let's go!*

The verent must have understood her because it rumbled its assent. Astrid/Sleeker ambled off at a run, headed for the cliff's edge.

She held on for dear life, praying to all eight of the gods that her mission would be successful. The ground dropped away, and she managed not to fall.

In seconds, they were out over the churning waters of the Elsp, soaring free.

•   •   •

Chala fought an ocean of water.

It churned like a living thing, bubbles lit up by late afternoon light above, bursts of water and air pushing her back and forth.

She held her breath, fighting the giant invisible hands that shoved her to and fro. *So much water!*

There's nothing in the desert like this. The thought fled as quickly as it had come as she fought for air. Desperate, she clawed for the surface, but the water dragged her back down like a living thing.

I'm going to die. She knew it then, as clearly as she knew her own name. With that knowledge came a certain peace. She let her body go limp, no longer fighting the water.

She had lived a good life. Saved many others. She could go to the Death Bringer with her head held high.

Chala.

She could hear the Oracle's voice in her head. *She's welcoming me home.*

Help comes.

That was a strange thing for the Oracle to say. Chala frowned, the last of the air slipping out of her lungs into the churning water. A flash of white flitted across the corner of her vision, and then she saw no more.

•   •   •

Chala woke coughing. She was choking on something. *Where am I?*

She coughed again, harder, the spasm wracking her whole frame and pressing her shoulders into the sharp ground beneath her.

She turned onto her side, ignoring the tiny pinpricks of pain on her arm, and coughed up half an ocean onto a pile of smooth black rocks.

She inhaled and set off another round of coughing as her body fought to rid itself of the salty water.

At last she lay still and breathed in again. This time her lungs filled with air. *Precious air.* She just lay there breathing for a while, luxuriating in that simple act, too exhausted to move.

At some point, she realized that she was still alive. The ocean that had tried to claim her rumbled peacefully a few feet away, waves reflecting the light of the setting sun.

Chala rolled back onto her back and looked at the sky. The green was shading into blue and purple, and the sun was blazing on the horizon as it met the water, shining a path across the surface that called to her.

Something was watching her from the waves. She squinted, trying to make it out against the brightness of the setting sun.

An erphin.

You saved me.

It chittered at her and then bobbed its head as if it understood her. Then it disappeared beneath the water.

She watched the surface for a long while, waiting for its return. Then she closed her eyes.

When she opened them again, it was dark.

Chala. Your time has come.

She sat up, feeling painful twinges along every inch of her muscle-bound frame. Her arms ached, her legs ached, and her back was protesting where it had lain against the hard jumble of rocks that served as the seashore. *Who are you?*

The woman's amusement tormented her. *You know who I am.*

Chala wiped salt crust from her eyes. *The Oracle.*

Yes.

Chala snorted. *Hell of a time for you to make an appearance.*

You're not surprised to hear my voice inside your head?

Chala considered that. She probably should have been. *After a week like this, there's little that can still surprise me.*

The world uses us as it will.

This time she rolled her eyes. *I feel wrecked. What do you want?* She rubbed the sore muscles of her neck.

Again that sense of amusement. *You'll live. You have one more task ahead of you. Only you can do this.*

Chala frowned. She hated people laughing at her. Or pitying her. She looked around, confused. All she wanted to do was find a more comfortable place to sleep for the night, or maybe a week.

Something large lay next to her in the dim light of the stars. She reached out in the darkness and encountered warm scales. *Elrys.*

And then she *knew. You saved me.* Elrys was one of the lake-born verent. She must have somehow split herself up again to come after her rider.

Chala blinked. She was dead tired. The short nap on the rocky shore had done little to restore her equilibrium. *What do you want me to do?*

There was a long pause. *You must kill the Death Bringer.*

•   •   •

"Where is she???" Kerrick stormed through the Temple, looking for Silya. Surely she hadn't already left. *I can't be too late.*

The Temple was almost empty. The few sisters still walking the halls glared at him or ignored him. All of them were heading downstairs to the hoped-for safety of the caverns.

The power was out too, of course; the ubiquitous electric lights off. Gas lanterns lit the way every ten meters or so, leaving broad gaps of darkness.

He took the main stair two steps at a time, going against the tide, anxious to find her. At the top, he tried the long talker. "Silya, where are you?"

He waited for an agonizingly long minute, but there was no reply. She must have been out of range. He slammed it back into its holster. *Damned things are useless.*

"Ser Kek!" Dor's voice was unmistakable. It stopped him in his tracks.

He spun around, seeing her leaning out of a doorway. Silya's office. "Where is she?"

"She's already gone." Her voice held a mix of regret and awe. "You need to calm down. You're scaring the few sisters who haven't gone downstairs yet. Including me."

"Sorry. Am I too late?" He put his hands on his knees, breathing heavily.

"Yes." She approached him, putting a hand on his shoulder.

He shook his head. "I have to go after her." *I can't believe she left without me.* Then again, she was who she was — strong-willed and carrying the weight of the world on her shoulders. If she thought she could help, she threw herself into the task with a zeal that amazed him.

"The verent riders are all gone, and I doubt you'd be able to get one of the uncompanioned ones to take you." She looked him up and down. "You're a mess, my fine Guard. Come into my office."

Reluctantly he followed her into the small room. It was meticulously organized. Shelves lined the walls, filled with all manner of things — books, strange sculptures made out of a black, shiny rock, several vases, bottles, wooden boxes, and an assortment of other riff-raff. Neat stacks of hencha paper filled one side of her desk, held in place under a polished stone paperweight. A tray with four ceramic mugs and an akka pot sat on the other. A narrow window let in some natural light.

"Have a seat."

He slumped into the wooden chair, defeated. "I came back as quickly as I could —"

"She just left. When she gets it in her head to do something ..." Sister Dor shook her head, admiration and frustration visible on her face in equal parts. "There's not much more to do here. We're shutting down the Temple and sending the last of the sisters to the safety of the caverns." She poured a mug of hot akka, the steam pouring out of the spout with the brown liquid. Its rich smell filled the room. "Drink this. It will help you get your wits about you."

He took it gratefully. "I have to find a way to go after her."

As if to emphasize his words, the ground shook ominously underfoot.

He held the cup aloft until the shaking passed to keep the hot liquid from sloshing onto his lap, and then took a long sip. "Did Chala come back?"

Dor frowned. "I haven't seen her. I thought she was with you?"

"She was, but she had to take her verent out to the dam to help open the floodgates." He hoped she was all right. *If she was here, she could take me.*

He got up and went to the window, looking out at the darkening hencha gathering. He took another sip of the hot drink. It calmed his nerves and warmed his stomach. The plants below rustled restlessly, as if they knew what was coming. *Maybe they do.*

In the distance, on the southern edge of the gathering, the practice field sat empty, save for the little flying machine. "That's it — the flitter!"

Dor put a hand on his shoulder — a feat for someone a third shorter than he was. "We'd have to find Fen'Ost, and I'm not sure where he ended up, to be honest. He has family down on Redhawk Spine —"

"I could fly it." He drained the cup and set it back on its tray.

"You? Have you ever flown one before?"

He nodded, closing his eyes and trying to remember the early days of his Guard training. "I flew the city one, once. And I watched Fentin take this one out to visit the ce'faine."

It could work. It was certainly better than sitting here on his hands while Silya went to fight the invaders. *Did you send me to the dam to keep me out of harm's way?* It would be just like her.

Sister Dor frowned. "Are you sure? It's a complicated machine."

He nodded. "I have to. Where's Elleck?"

"I heard you were back." His sister stood at the door, her long braid wrapped around her waist. "What's this foolishness about taking a flitter ride?"

He grinned, setting down the cup and bounding across the space between them to throw his arms around her. "Just the person I wanted to see. Want to do something absolutely crazy with me?"

"Of course." Elleck squeezed him back. "What are sisters for?"

Kerrick felt almost happy, for the first time in days. "Let's go then, before I come to my senses and change my mind." He turned towards Dor. 'Mim Ala, is there any more of that bandy pulp to be had?"

Dor nodded. "Come on. We can get some in the kitchen." She got up, wincing. "We can get ourselves some supplies too." She led them out of the room.

"We?" He exchanged a puzzled glance with his sister.

"Against my better judgment, I'm coming with you. With a blindfold on, because I can't imagine you're as good a pilot as Mas Ost, and he left me sick to my stomach for half the day."

"Are you ... sure?" He followed her down the hall.

She stopped, nodding slowly. "Silya's not facing this alone. I let her ground me from her little verent joyride, but at least the flitter has a nice seat *inside*."

He nodded. "You *should* be there with her. She needs you."

"That, my boy, has never been in doubt." She patted him on the shoulder. "Come on. The war's not going to wait for us."

Inside half an hour, they had smeared themselves with the sticky-sweet substance and had gathered a few supplies.

They boarded the little craft solemnly.

He surveyed the controls, trying to remember what he'd had to push and pull during his limited flitter training.

After a few false starts, he found the right combination and lifted them — shakily — into the sky.

15

INTO THE HEARTLAND

IHIL RODE THE POSSESSED URSE out of the Gap, his own tail twitching behind him. Around him the horde buzzed angrily, filling the narrow space between the cliffs with their roar. The narrow pass had been stripped of anything organic by their passage, but there had been little enough for the forerunners to consume.

He paused to take in the view of the wide, fertile valley below. There was food aplenty for the swarm. *Much better.*

In a strange way, the valley reminded him of the Eeheer River valley, where the steaming sulfurous waters poured out of the Ooseean Mountains to feed the beautiful jungles of his homeworld. If he closed his eyes, he could see the white Eeechhha towers that dotted the valley, rising above the greens and reds and blues and golds of the warm, nurturing jungle, each one the home to a family like his.

This world would one day be just as beautiful.

He growled. His enemies were putting up more resistance than he'd expected. The cavern full of them that the forerunners had discovered had been blocked with a thick sheet of ice when the swarm returned in force to clean it out. They were still searching for a way in. *They can't hide in there forever.*

Behind him his army trampled the grasses and mud left by the recent snows — a horde of forerunner-ridden beasts of all shapes and sizes. Urse, aur, eircat, cephlant, umvit and skerit ... and even a few humans. The storm followed him like an omen, auguring ill for anyone who stood against him. He raised his right arm to urge them all forward —

Alarm surged through him like a seizure. Mother was calling him.

He closed his eyes, searching for her among the din of the forerunners that buzzed all around him in agitation. *Mother, what's wrong?*

Danger. A thought-picture flashed through his head. Four of the humans — the ones he had spared — had breached her chamber.

I have to go back. He shuddered. If they killed her, all they were fighting for here would be for naught. Unless she left behind a seed. *I'm coming!*

How could he reach her in time? He was days away unless he could capture another of those flying creatures.

Verent. His human mind supplied the word. He was about to turn back, to urge his urse along as quickly as he could make it go, when he spotted something in the darkening sky, bursting out of the cloud wall ahead.

A verent. No, more than one.

Iihil nodded. *They come to fight.* He'd expected it, sooner or later. He was stronger than the forerunners alone, and much smarter — with his lead, the aaveen would make the rest of this world theirs, just like they had the Highlands.

A twinge of guilt shook him. *It wasn't supposed to be like this.*

But it was about survival now, and he counted the survival of his own kin above all else. How could he not? *Let them come. I will rain fire upon them.*

And then he would have his verent. *Hold on, Mother. I'll be there soon.*

•　　　•　　　•

Desla watched in growing alarm as the thing that looked like Aik reached out one of its arms. It moved jerkily, like a puppet, and it didn't seem to be put together quite right. Its knees were backwards, and its arms — the one extended toward them, for instance — were too long.

It opened its mouth as if to speak, but all that came out was a wet, raspy sound.

"Let me kill it." Mes raised her spear.

"Wait!" She threw herself between the guard and the strange creature. "It's here for a reason."

"Yes, to kill us all." Mes spat on the soft matted ground, setting up a sizzle and a protesting squeal.

"Why go to such an effort to make something that looks like our friend, if just to kill us?" She turned to face it, and her stomach turned, but she fought to stay calm.

"Not my friend." Mes twisted her lips in a moue of distaste, but she didn't advance on the creature.

It wasn't Aik. Not really. It was as if a child had drawn him, and then made their drawing real. It was too tall, lankier than the real Aik. Its skin was ruddy, almost reddish, and had strange folds, as if the thing had been made from paper tucked away to hide its rough edges. Its hair was thick, ropy, more like vines than actual follicles. But there had to be a reason it was here.

"What are you?" Her voice trembled. For all her bravado, the thing stirred a deep unease in the pit of her stomach.

"Put down your spears." Triya's voice was calm, firm. The merchant came up beside her, putting a firm hand on her shoulder. "Can it speak?"

"I don't know." Maybe Mes was right. The thing was creepy.

It opened its mouth again, and this time a sound came out. "Des. La." Like it was speaking through wet cement.

"You know my name?" A chill ran down her back. "What are you?" She held her own spear at the ready, just in case it lunged at her.

It didn't *look* particularly dangerous, but it was far stranger than the things that had attacked them earlier. Who knew what it could do?

Its mouth worked from side to side, like it was chewing on something sticky. "Aik. Not Aik."

Desla snorted. "Well, that's clear as the Elsp." *What do you want?*

Not-Aik raised a clawed hand again, but the gesture was strange too, as if a marionette was pulling its strings. It pointed at the huge white structure behind it. "Mother. Dying."

She took an involuntary step back. The huge structure — the domes and tubes and strange lumps that half-filled the cavern — was sentient? And dying?

"Let me kill it." Mes's eyes were locked on Not-Aik, her voice filled with contempt. Or disgust. "We can't trust it."

"Enough!" Triya hissed, and Mes stepped back too, though from the corner of her eye, Des could see she still held her spear. "Let her talk to it."

Mes bowed her head. "Yes, Mim."

Something else was bothering Desla, a growing pressure at the back of her skull. Her eyes narrowed. *Are you trying to get inside my head?*

Or was she just stressed and tired from a seemingly endless day? "Why is she dying?"

Not-Aik stared at her for a moment, as if gathering it thoughts. Or maybe trying to remember how to speak them. "Too much. Too fast. If she dies …" Its voice trailed off into an infinite sadness.

For hencha's sake. The pain in her head had increased threefold, flaring like the lighting of a spark. She pressed on her temples, trying to clear her head.

Something huge and ponderous was flowing into her. She staggered and fell to her knees, squeezing her head in her hands. "Sweet mother of Jas."

"What's wrong?" Triya's voice cut through the pain. "Is it doing something to you?"

"Not … him." This wasn't coming from Not-Aik.

"Cheese, you okay? Your heart rate is spiking." Spin's voice was calm, as if he was trying to keep her from panicking.

"I don't know —" The pain ramped up again, like someone had pushed a hot poker into the back of her brain. She howled, pulling at her hair, begging for it to stop.

She was being filled her up like an empty vessel. *What's wrong with me?*

Be calm, child. We won't hurt you. The voice was deep, resonant, like thunder's echo. It flooded her, washing away the pain and filling her with sudden, unexpected joy.

Out of the corner of her eye, she saw Mes pick up her spear.

"Don't! It's not him." She flung out her hand in warning, and Mes fell back with a grunt.

"What's happening to you?" Triya knelt beside her, her eyes filled with concern. "You have to tell me." She was scared.

Desla could almost taste the fear. "Give me a second. I'll be all right." Whatever it was, it didn't want to hurt her.

Not-Aik watched them through hollow eyes, its mouth hanging open to expose the ropy cords inside.

I'm not alone. For the first time in her life, she saw how truly solitary her life had been, one soul separate from all the others. As blue flames spread across her arms, she recognized the strange presence at last. *You're the hencha.*

She felt its agreement. *Your kind call us that.*

Someone gasped.

She opened her eyes. "It's the hencha."

Relief crossed Triya's features. "Thank the gods."

Blue flames ran up and down her arms. "How is this possible?" *Is Silya dead? Am I the Hencha Queen now?*

The hencha rumbled in her mind, amusement flashing through her. *No, she is still very much alive. She is a hard one to kill.*

Thank the gods. She wasn't ready to be the queen. She'd never wanted it. That made her wonder if Silya had.

The voice filled her with confidence, washing away her exhaustion and fear. *But what in Heaven's Reach is this, then? How can I speak with you too?*

We speak through whom we choose, to those who can speak with us. Again that ponderous amusement.

Did Silya feel this sense of peace, of belonging, every time she spoke with them? It was marvelous. *If I could bottle this and sell it ...*

"Are you all right?" Triya cupped her face. Her hand was warm against Desla's cheek, her eyes moist.

"Yes. More than all right." There was a reason she was here, at this moment. The hencha had planned for this. She knew it was true, even if she didn't know how. "You're hurt. May I?"

Triya's eyes narrowed. "How?"

"Show me your wound."

Triya frowned, but she pulled up her trouser leg, exposing a gash fifteen centimeters long down her calf.

She touched Triya's leg. Blue fire surged through her and into the cut, wrapping tendrils around it like the stems of a creeper vine. Flesh stitched itself up, the drip-drip-drip of blood slowing and finally stopping.

Triya sighed in relief. "Thank Freja. That feels so much better." Her eyes narrowed again. "How ...?"

Mes and Em were peering over her shoulder at the now-healed leg.

"The hencha." As if that explained everything. "You should have told me you were hurt."

"I ... didn't know you could do that."

She grinned. "I didn't either. Now help me up." She felt unsteady, as if she had suddenly gained a couple of hundred kilograms of weight.

"That's really cool, Cheese." Spin's golden light flared over Triya's leg. "She's completely healed."

"I am." Triya touched her leg in wonder. "I'm not even tired anymore, either." She stood and offered her a hand.

Desla took it and eased up onto her feet. She felt lighter somehow, the weight from a moment before vanished. She looked at Em's bandaged arm. "Your turn."

Em shook her head. "I'm fine."

"We need you in good shape for whatever may come next." She wasn't budging.

Em looked at Triya, who nodded.

"You're no use to us wounded." Triya's stare compelled her to Desla's side.

Behind her, she could feel Not-Aik watching her curiously. She wondered if intelligence burned behind those strange eyes — and if so, if it belonged to Not-Aik or the spore mother. *So much she still didn't understand.*

She touched Em's arm, tendrils of flame stitching the bite wound together and burning it clean. When she let go, she wavered just a little.

Em caught her shoulder, steadying her. "Thanks."

"Don't mention it." Her whole body was wreathed in flames. She looked down at her hand. The bandy pulp was gone, worn off or maybe burnt away by the hencha fire.

"One more to go. Are you going to be as stubborn as Em?"

Mes shook her head. "I ... I could use some relief."

Desla shook her head, not sure she was hearing right. That was as close to admitting weakness as she'd ever heard from the taciturn woman. *And probably the closest I ever will.* "Come here."

Mes stepped forward, and Em helped her lift up her tunic gently, exposing the cloth wrapped around the wound. It was soaked in blood.

Triya tsk-tsked. "Why didn't you tell us it was bleeding so much?"

Mes shrugged. "Nothing you could have done about it."

Des shook her head. She'd never understand these warrior women. "Can I?"

Mes winced as she shifted around. "Yes, Mim."

This one went deeper. She had to concentrate, to feel how far the wound had penetrated. Her flames flowed into Mes, seeking out the damage and knitting it slowly back together. Power flowed through her from the hencha, keeping her afloat, but it was exhausting too.

With the internal damage repaired, she sealed up the wound, eliciting an audible gasp from Mes. "I'm sorry — did that hurt?"

Mes touched the sealed skin. There would be a scar, but she was whole again. "No, Mim. That was ... thank you." She threw her arms around Desla, almost knocking her over.

"Careful there." The healing had taken more out of her than she cared to admit.

"Sorry." Mes disengaged gently.

"I think our ... guest wants your attention." Tilya said.

Desla turned to look at Not-Aik.

It cocked its head in such a human fashion that it made her laugh despite her exhaustion.

She took a step toward it.

It stumbled backward, as if afraid of her touch or of her flames.

"It's all right. I won't hurt you."

It watched her still from its strange hollow eyes, and then nodded.

She touched its cheek, just like Triya had touched hers, a gesture of comfort, of understanding.

An electric current raced up her arm, shocking her to the bone.

The room faded from view, taking her friends with it.

•   •   •

Water lapped at Chala's toes.

Her eyes slipped open again. A cool breeze played across her skin, chilling her wet clothing. Above her, the two moons were close together, closer than she'd ever seen them before in all of her life. *It's an omen.*

She knew an omen when she saw it.

She pushed herself up, ignoring the little pains in her back where the stones of the rocky beach had pressed into it.

Elrys waited, stretched out beside her, lifting her own head to stare at Chala with luminous blue eyes. *All right?*

Chala rubbed the verent's long, scaly nose. "Yes. I'm all right." Somehow she'd made a connection with this amazing beast, even without having swallowed a verentling.

You have one more task ahead of you.

The Oracle's words echoed in her head.

You must kill the Death Bringer.

Chala shivered. She knew who that was, had seen it in the Oracle's vision.

Aik. Or the creature that had once been Aik. *Raven's Aik.*

She wasn't sure she could do it. Raven was her friend, and she'd had precious few of those in her lifetime. Sure, he was a lowly wetlander, and a thief besides. But he and Astrid were the only ones who had sought her out, had felt her pain.

Only you can do this.

She reached for the Oracle. *Why me?*

There was no answer. She was all alone with her thoughts and her verent on the rocky beach, under the light of the twin moons.

She got to her feet, shaking her tired muscles out. She wanted nothing more than a warm fire and a sleep sack, and maybe her lover Elrys by her side. Still, her friends needed her. The world needed her. And Elrys the verent would have to do.

She looked around the empty beach. Something about her size sat by itself at the water's edge. She walked over to it, careful not to trip in the dim orange light.

It was the saddle. Had it washed up on its own, or had Elrys brought it back too?

It didn't matter. *It's here.*

She whistled for her verent.

Elrys got up and trundled across the beach toward her, nimble as an eircat, her tail extended behind her for balance. *Time?*

Chala nodded. *Yes, my love.* She hefted the still-damp saddle over Elrys's back.

Cold. But good fish here. She licked her lips.

She chuckled at that. "Sorry about that. You'll warm up in flight." She secured the saddle under the verent's belly, then took one last look around the rocky beach.

To the north, she could still hear the gushing of the water as it poured out of the floodgates of the dam and out into the churning waters of the Harkness Sea.

She'd accomplished what she'd come back to Gullton to do. She hoped it had been enough.

In any case, it was no longer her concern.

With practiced grace, she climbed into the saddle, settling in and reaching forward to scratch her verent's neck.

Elrys purred with pleasure. *Eat more now?*

Soon. First, we need to go find someone.

The Oracle said she needed to kill Aik. She'd do it if she had to, but she was no one's servant.

She'd make up her own gods-damned mind.

16

STORM

RAVEN/BREEZE FLEW LOW over the Heartland, his stomach clenched. Night had fallen, and the world was lit only by the stars and the combined orange light of the twin moons.

The billowing clouds ahead thundered menacingly, the air crackling with energy all around him. Raven could feel the pain of the world through Breeze.

The aaveen were eating away at it, ripping out pieces of it from their roots, and with each death part of the grand collective was lost — memories, life, power.

So different from the first time we flew together. He'd been a scared little boy, barely a man, when this same verent had carried him bareback to Mountainhome. Afraid he was being taken to his own death.

They cracked a verent grin. *Maybe things aren't so different now, after all.*

His other half was somewhere ahead. Raven was anxious that he'd waited too long. *What if he's no longer Aik?*

Don't be afraid. Breeze's presence, and that of his two mates, buoyed him, raising him from the edge of despair. *We will save him.*

Raven agreed. Whatever else happened, he would rescue Aik from whatever the invaders had done to him. *Ready?*

He felt Olly's assent. *We've trained for this.*

Not enough. None of them knew what to expect inside the darkness.

He clamped down on his own fear. *No need to frighten the others.* They plunged into the cloud wall together.

It was nearly pitch-black, a dark and foreboding place. The air itself was cold and damp, the dark clouds reducing visibility to a few meters, save for when lightning arced uncomfortably close by.

Between bolts of sizzling energy, a clammy silence enveloped Breeze, Flit, and the other verent. Only a slow rumbling thunder broke the silence, sending flashes of light through the clouds. Raven/Breeze's vision adjusted, but the cloudy darkness was still thick as ink. They were flying blind.

How will we find him? Olly sounded worried, his emotions leaking through the emp link.

I know where he is. As he said it, they knew it was true. He could sense the urse Aik rode, its pain like a beacon in the tumbling darkness. *Can you feel it?*

Olly was silent for a moment.

Breeze's powerful wings carried them through the fog, toward that bright beacon in their mind.

I can now. Oh gods, he's not alone.

He frowned. He and Breeze expanded their awareness, and he felt it too. *Sweet mother of Jas.*

They broke through the cloud wall into a twilight world. The moons still shone overhead, so close they were touching, but their light was muted. Ahead of them, the edge of the great valley loomed.

The fields below looked like beds of hot coals, being eaten away by the fireflies and turned into more of those coryx domes that belched their horrid spores to transform the world — his world — into something alien and hostile.

Fires burned here and there, sending up billowing clouds of smoke, and more red lights filled the air like demented stars come down to earth.

On the ground, the strange new world was teeming with movement. Amongst the burning nests, firefly-maddened beasts shuffled along like the half dead — urse and aur, mighty cephlants, even skerit, sketching wobbly paths through the air.

And there were humans there too.

His stomach lurched at the sight of his own kind among the beasts, their eyes hollow, their clothes ripped and torn. As he flew over them, they looked up to track his passage.

A wave of nausea hit him at the collective pain they were in. They faltered in midflight as they took the full brunt of the firefly-possessed souls.

Raven! Block them out! Olly's voice was distant and small.

The ground plunged up toward them.

Raven!

There was a sickening thud, and everything went black.

•   •   •

Iihil pushed his faltering urse to go faster, using up its flagging strength.

He'd seen the verent go down just a couple of *eeliick* ahead. If he could reach it ahead of its brethren …

He glanced up at the Death Bringer's eye — the sign of his own coming — so close to completion above. He could feel it down to his bones. *The time of our victory is here.*

And yet, Mother called him home.

More verent burst through the clouds, trailing those damned wisps. He could feel the chill from where he sat, and it made him boil with rage.

Cursing, Iihil pulled the urse to a halt, calling the forerunners to him. They rose from their work on the ground, hundreds of thousands strong. The first few swirled around him, followed by a hundred more, then a thousand, then ten thousand, until the entirety of the host encircled him with their warmth.

He was drawn to them and they to him. They loved him and would die for him. For a bright and shining moment, he was a god.

The verent circled him too, high above, drawn by the red lights that spun around him like a beacon.

Iihil raised his arm to send a flight of them off to assault one of the verent. They shot toward it, sure as an arrow, but then they tumbled away into chaos, as if they'd hit an invisible wall.

Iihil sniffed the air. Something smelled foul.

One of the verent swooped by as if to get a better look at him, and Iihil was sickened by the stench of it. It was covered in something that made him feel nauseous.

His tail flicked back and forth angrily as he glared at the passing creature. *There's more than one way to skin a verent.*

He recalled the scattered forerunners to his cloud and sent a new batch into the air in a linked net formation, just ahead of the verent.

The verent tried to avoid them, but energy arced among them like red lightning. It cried out in pain as it passed through the wall, and with a last anguished cry, the verent exploded into a shower of blue sparks.

Iihil's slitted yellow eyes glowed with pleasure. That was a surprise — he'd hoped only to capture it. He'd lost a handful of forerunners, but he had many more.

One of the new verent swept past and picked up the trail of blue lights from the expired one. Where it passed, the forerunners dimmed and dropped from the sky.

Iihil scowled, feeling the pain of each of those dimmed lights. He would make this world his own even if it meant he had to grind down every last one of these beasts to dust. For Eeydra. For all of his people. But he would need at least one of the beasts alive to carry him back to his Mother under the mountain.

He sent his forerunners verent-hunting and spurred his hostage mount forward again, determined to get to the downed verent before it could recover.

•　　　•　　　•

Silya rode Astrid/Sleeker over the Highlands. The nightmare she'd dreamed of so often was finally here — war was coming, and with it an existential danger to everything and everyone she held dear.

A strange sense of relief flooded her at the thought. It was no longer something to be feared. It was here, and she could deal with it, whatever it took. And more importantly, she was not alone. *It's time.*

The world below looked almost normal under the twin light of the moons ... purple fields of hencha plants painted almost black, alongside animal paddocks and neat green squares of human crops. She flew on a verent's back, just as she'd seen when her hand had brushed the walls of the tunnel that first night with Raven and Aik, and later in her dreams. *Were the hencha with me, even then?*

In the back of her mind, she could feel them, a warm presence that buoyed her up despite their own anguish. Though it was more than just the hencha.

That had been a shock. A whole world, knitted together in a common cause. *We humans could learn something from that.*

She could *feel* the path of devastation that Aik and his forces were inflicting upon the world — her world. The aaveen were chipping away at that vast strength, eating at it like acid, led by her friend, a man who had once been much more to her. It was strange to think of the loyal, beautiful Guard as the general of an invading army, but there it was. *Is Raven already there?*

Just two weeks before, she'd been arguing with Raven in his stupid *lair. And now? We're facing down the end of the world together against Aik.*

She could feel Astrid's fear too, but Sleeker seemed oddly stoic ... perhaps knowing you were made of constituent parts that would go on after you were gone lent you a different perspective on death ... and life.

Can you hear me? Are you all right? She tried to think the thought at the verent she rode ... strange that it was both Astrid and Sleeker beneath her. In her dream, she'd thought she was alone.

She cannot. But we can relay your question. The hencha voice in her head seemed diminished. They were paying a heavy price in this undeclared war.

Please do. She was thankful for their warmth, for the energy they were feeding her. By all rights she should be exhausted.

Astrid says she's scared, but otherwise everything's all right.

She leaned forward and hugged Sleeker's neck.

When she let go, Sleeker's head twisted to the side, their eyes meeting hers, and winked at her. *Tell her — tell them we'll find a way out of this.*

We will.

She sent a prayer to Jor'Oss, goddess of luck and wild nature, to help Raven. *Gods, I hope he knows what he's doing.*

She closed her eyes and tried to project calm and peace into the verent, and out into the world in general. Maybe this was the end. But she was too stubborn to admit it. Something else to thank her mother for.

Gratitude rolled back to her, from Astrid and Sleeker, and from Jai and the other verent.

She would fight until she had nothing left and drive these invaders from the Heartland. *I just wish to the gods I knew how.*

The cloud wall was closer, the clouds piled so high that they looked like they were ready to crash down on the fertile valley below, washing everything away. Lightning flickered along its length, its purple clouds churning against the late afternoon sky.

She shuddered. Was it natural? Or some artifact of the invading force? *Does it matter?*

She wished Kerrick were with her. His strength, his presence would be a balm for her soul. She pulled out the long talker, wrapping the strap around her arm so she wouldn't drop if, and selected his channel. "Kerrick? Are you there?"

Silence.

She flipped it to a different channel. "Triya, Desla, can you hear me?"

Nothing.

She sighed and slipped the thing back into its holster on her belt. She might not be alone. But she was apart from those most important to her.

The cloud wall grew, swelling over them and consuming the light. This close, it was like a living thing, roaring as it raced across the Heartland.

Then they were inside it, and she had to throw her arms around Sleeker's neck and hold on for dear life.

Warm rain lashed her, and the fingers of the wind pried at her, trying to pull her off her perch. *Freja help us!*

Thank the gods she was strapped down.

The ominous rumble of lightning and thunder lit up the clouds at odd intervals. It was dark as night inside the storm, and they were flying blind.

A bolt of lightning seared the sky, slamming into one of the verent.

Its pain raced through her for an instant and then it was gone, its form replaced by a flurry of dancing blue sparks.

Holy green hell.

Then the others' pain washed over her like a floodtide. She closed her eyes, saying a prayer for the dead. *Who was it?*

Astrid/Sleeker's reply was slow in coming. *Grey. One of Jai's.*

Maybe not so stoic after all. *Is Jai —?*

He's all right. He's riding Angel.

Thank the Gods. Silya had only a few seconds to mourn the verent or to wonder about those blue sparks before they burst out of the cloud wall and over a battleground.

The eastern edge of the Highlands was devastated, its crops and native plants destroyed by the invaders all the way to the walls of Heaven's Reach.

The sky buzzed with fireflies — many thousands of them — casting a disturbing red glow over the land. In the middle of it all, surrounded by a blood-red glow, stood a creature out of nightmares, riding a possessed aur. She could feel the beast's misery. *Oh gods, he really does look like the Death Bringer.*

The monster was tall, an imposing figure covered in silvery-black metal exposing raw black, bumpy skin like lesions across hos body. He seemed to glow red from the reflected light of the fireflies, and a long black tail flicked in an agitated fashion. He looked up at her, and the smooth lower face split open to reveal a wide row of sharp teeth.

Aik is the Death Bringer. The thought hit her like an oncoming coach. She'd known it before, at least intellectually, but to see him like this ... She shuddered. *What did they do to you?*

Her verent slipped past him, coming back around.

She didn't want to kill him, not even to save the world, but what if she had no choice? What if the Oracle was right?

Was the man she'd once known and loved — still loved, if she were honest with herself — still in there?

The Death Bringer waved its arms, and a group of red lights disengaged from the others, forming a wall of their own, evenly spaced like points in a matrix.

"No!" She was too late.

One of the verent flew into the wall and disintegrated into a shower of blue sparks, just like the one that had been hit by that strange lightning. Just like the violet pines had when she'd used her power against the fireflies in the Gap.

She gasped. *We're not prepared for this.*

On the ground, the creature dismounted, and his aur collapsed in an exhausted heap. His tail lashed about, and he gathered himself to run toward ... something.

Take us closer.

The hencha passed on her request, and Astrid/Sleeker flew lower to get a better look.

A verent lay crumpled on the ground, a couple of hundred meters from Aik, one wing folded oddly. It wasn't moving.

She inhaled sharply. *That's Raven and Breeze.*

She wasn't sure how she knew it, but she was sure it was true. *Raven?*

He and his verent aren't responding. The hencha sounded anxious.

Ask Jai to handle things. I need to protect Raven.

We will.

And tell Astrid and Sleeker — But there was no need to finish that request, as the verent was already diving toward its downed colleague. She held on for dear life.

Olly and Jai have things in hand.

We will fight this together. She sent calming thoughts to the hencha mind, though she was far from calm herself.

They radiated it back at her. *We chose wisely when we found you.*

That thought filled her with warmth, but she had no time to enjoy it. She needed to focus on Raven. *Tell them to watch for the nets!* She looked up to see a verent and a sweep of wisps change course, shooting suddenly upward and destroying a waiting web of fireflies, which blackened and fell from the sky.

A smattering of the dead things slammed into her and the verent like black hail.

Raven, we're coming!

•　　　•　　　•

Aik twisted his way through Iihil's memories like an inthym through a pile of autumn leaves. They were laid upon one another, overlapping but easily disturbed by his passage.

The aaveen was distracted, fighting with Aik's friends, and he'd seized his chance.

The top layer was familiar to him already — the time the aaveen had shared Aik's body. But there were others too, past lives on Tharassas and on his homeworld.

Uurccheea. He sounded it out in his mind. "Ooorkkeeuh." The aaveen language was full of long vowels and double consonants, including some sounds that he had a hard time pronouncing, even inside his own head.

Iihil had been on Tharassas before in another incarnation. The first time, he had come in his own form, a tall lanky thing with a single eye and six limbs, two with three-fingered hands full of claws.

The second time he'd bonded with an eircat, covered in living metal as he was now, inhabiting it like he inhabited Aik.

Both times, the world had reacted as one, a body rejecting the invasion of an invader, each time causing a near world-ending cataclysm, a tumult of snow and ice covering the world and snuffing out all of the spore mother's creations. That was a shock in itself, but Iihil's broken memories confirmed it.

The remaining bits of the creature had been spirited away and hidden deep underground.

Somehow this time was different. *But why?*

He sought the answer, piecing together Iihil's memories with all that he had seen and experienced. He wasn't smart like Silya, or street-smart like Raven, but when he put his mind to it, he could figure things out. Eventually.

What was different this time? Why hadn't the verent and the rest of Tharassas acted to wipe out the invader as soon as the Rise had begun?

The world mind was still very much in existence, linking the hencha to the verent, and maybe everything else too. And he'd seen the cold the verent used to kill the forerunners, through Iihil's eyes. What had changed since the last invasion had ended in ice?

Then it hit him. *It's us.*

The hencha mind — maybe he needed to start thinking of them as the world mind — had accepted humankind as its own when Jas had become the first Hencha Queen. And the world had worked to make Aik and his kind a part of itself — the emp and the verent were proof of that.

But humans couldn't survive the kind of reaction needed to repel the invaders. The world would recover from a centuries-long winter, but Aik and his kind would not.

So the world mind had tried to find another way.

He shuddered. *Now it might be too late.*

Eeydra, Iihil's mate, was the key. He could feel it. She might be the only one who could change the aaveen's mind.

He dug deeper, searching for memories of her, diving past Iihil's other incarnations on Tharassas and down into his core. His life on Uurccheea.

The world had been hot, vibrant, alive, with her own interconnected web of life.

He walked with Iihil through wild gardens where the white-domed eeechha were overtopped by a riotous but well-tended growth of aoochhaa vines, their wildly colored blooms open to the sky.

Along coastlines under the broad fronds of the aiisil trees, where sparkling iilees played in the ocean waves, their white-and-gold-scaled bodies leaping above the waters to glimmer under the rays of the red sun.

They soared together on the back of an oovaator, its green wings spread wide to catch the sunlight, passing above the glowing red lava of an ancient crater, where some of the oldest spore mothers sipped its warmth.

And he walked among Iihil's people. They were tall, with skin that ranged from red to gold, lanky with six long limbs tipped with claws. Their faces were strange, too, wide mouths full of sharp teeth, and just a single compound eye that glittered in the red light of the world's sun. But through Iihil's eyes, they were perfect.

They entered his family's — Village? Compound? City? — and arrived together at his home, a series of eeechha domes nestled at the edge of a red cliff, shaded from the hot sun by a woven mat of aoochhaa vines Iihil himself had strung between a line aiisil trees.

And there she was.

She was beautiful, her skin a stippled gold, the red sun highlighting the ridges along her limbs. Her golden eye widened at his return, and she leapt up to embrace him, entwining her six limbs with his.

Her warmth encompassed him. Though she appeared hideous to human eyes, he could see her how Iihil saw her, and he knew why the aaveen loved her. She was his light and his life.

Like Raven. For just a moment, that night before he'd lost his best friend, his lover, flashed through his mind. The intimacy of holding Raven in his arms, of being inside of him, of connecting in such a deep way after years of yearning …

Suddenly what he was doing with Iihil's memories felt *wrong*. Planning to impersonate the one Iihil loved the most, to make him stop.

It was a trick of the lowest order, one that played on Iihil's most deeply held feelings. Aik hated deception.

But what if it was necessary to save his world? To save Raven?

He froze, caught by uncertainty. *I have to do this. Don't I? What would Eeydra want? How would she feel about the Death Bringer?*

He needed to know more about her before he made his final decision.

Now that he knew her essence, it was easier to sort through Iihil's mind, to gather all of his memories of his long-ago mate.

He dove in, searching for Eeydra.

17

BATTLEGROUND

SILYA HELD ON for dear life as the verent slammed into the ground hard, their wings stirring up a whirlwind of rocks and mud.

Raven's verent Breeze had crash-landed on one of the coryx, which had cushioned its fall. *Thank Jorja.* The bandy-fruit pulp had done its work, disintegrating the pristine white dome into a sticky, melting mess.

She leapt off the verent, pausing only to unhitch and remove the saddle the way Astrid had shown her, and to free her black staff from the leather loops where it hung.

She ran toward the fallen verent, her nerves jangling and her heart pounding.

It was still breathing. *Thank the gods.*

Raven lay on its back, sleeping like a child. A naked child.

She shook her head. No time to ponder the weirdness of human/verent interaction. The Death Bringer was coming.

"Is he all right?" Astrid had emerged and was pulling on her clothes quickly, with the ease of long practice.

"I think so." She ducked as a verent flew directly overhead in the moonlit darkness, kicking up more debris.

She planted her staff on the ground and reached for the hencha in the back of her mind. They were waiting for her. So were the eshem.

I won't kill him.

Silya could feel the sharp cut of their judgment. They had already made up their minds.

The weight of the world rides on your shoulders. The Oracle sounded old and worn out, exhausted beyond mortal limits. As if she'd borne that weight herself for far too long.

Help me or not. I will not do this. The spore mother meant to remake the world in her own image, a hot world with no place for human or hencha.

The hencha, in turn, would wipe it all away with snow and bitter cold. *I saw it.* How many would survive then? *So why haven't they?*

Then it struck her.

What if we weren't here? This war would already be over. The hencha would have frozen out the invaders again, perhaps finishing them off for good. Their kind would survive — verent, erphin, the jexyn and all the rest — they would all return, eventually. Only the humans would perish. Her mother had been right. This had all happened before. *You sacrificed all of this ... for us.*

The response was painfully slow. *You are a part of the hencha now. We could not let you die.*

She blinked. Part of the hencha. She'd never thought of herself that way, always the other way around. *There has to be another way. Something between fire and ice.*

Astrid was at Raven's side, checking his pulse. "He's alive."

"Thank the gods." She was about to tell Astrid about her epiphany when three things happened all at once.

The Death Bringer arrived, just a few meters away, staring at her with its strange golden eyes, the narrow sideways pupils making it look more alien than its humanoid shape. It was barely recognizable as its former self. Something about the way it stood and cocked its head still reminded her of Aik. But its dark-silver-and-black skin and long, lashing tail said otherwise.

It leapt off the sad, broken urse at them.

Behind her, the unmistakable sound of a flitter filled the air, its *thumpa thumpa thumpa* blades pulsing through her.

The ground shook violently, knocking them all down.

•   •   •

Spin lay in utter darkness, the ground soft beneath him. *What happened to me?*

He reached out to explore the dark world, and then pulled back in shock.

I have an arm. Two, it turned out. And two legs. And ... something else between his legs. He was whole again, human. *It can't be ...*

He closed his human eyes and ran a diagnostic. Something was off. The last thing he remembered was Cheese — Desla — touching the spore mother's creation, the *Not-Aik*, as she called it.

This isn't real. A crushing depression descended on him at the realization. *To be human again ...*

He was inside the spore mother's mind. He could feel her now, inquisitive, her thoughts pressing against his. It was an interface. No more than that. *And yet, what an exquisite unreality!*

His depression lifted, just a little.

What creature kind are you? Her voice was strange, but he was able to glean her intent. It was ... English, or what was called the common tongue here on Tharassas, but ... filtered.

I'm an artificial ...

He stopped, holding up his arms in the dim glow that now surrounded him. *I am human.*

He could feel her confusion. *No other human so far met has been this.*

She needed to work on her grammar. He shrugged. *I am like no other human today.*

Understanding dawned. *Like us, old then?* There was a pause. *The spore mother for humans? But such a small, you are. Seed, perhaps?*

Spin laughed. *Spore mother, no. Though I was a father, once. But yes. I suppose I am something like a seed ...*

Amusement filtered through. *You I like. I hope ... if there is time, we speak, again.*

If there is time? What in the hell did that mean?

•   •   •

189

She floated in the midst of an absolute void. No air. No light. No sense of hot or cold. "Where am I?"

Her words echoed into the distance. There was no reply.

She had no form. No body, no shape, nothing. Just a feeling. *Who am I?*

She tried to remember what had come before this. Surely there must have been something? *Hello?*

The darkness didn't respond.

Then all of a sudden, there was light. A golden spark, the tiniest bit of *something*.

She held out her arm to reach for it, but it seemed impossibly distant, as far away as the stars.

She did have form — she could see that now. Long, lithe limbs, blond hair, and ... breasts.

The spark flashed. It reminded her of something. "What are you?" She didn't expect a reply.

"Hey Cheese!" The golden light flared, lighting her up for a moment. "This place is ... unexpected."

A man stood in front of her, with beautiful sepia skin. He was naked, surrounded by a faint golden glow.

She knew him.

"Spin?" She suddenly felt less alone in this place. Wherever *this* was. "But you're ... you! And naked." She looked away. Seeing him as human was shock enough, but this?

"Oh, sorry about that." He shimmered and was suddenly wearing a pair of white overalls. "Better?"

"Better," she agreed.

"So are you." He blinked, and suddenly she was clothed in yellow robes. They looked familiar, but she still couldn't remember who she was, or what she was doing here.

Spin knelt next to her. His eyes were kind. "Desla, are you okay?" He touched her cheek.

Desla.

That one word unlocked everything.

Her childhood in Devon, her time in the Temple, her mad quest with Aik. The strange Aik-not-Aik in the cavern beneath Anghar Mor. "I'm ... Desla."

A strange look crossed his face. "Yes, you are."

"Sorry. I was … confused. Where are we?" She looked him up and down. "And how are you … like this?"

Spin looked down at his own form. "You mean how did I transform from a little silver sphere to this dashing man you see before you?" His eyes flashed golden with merriment. "This is an interface. A … connection between two different kinds of systems. It's impressive. And I'm like this … because this is the *real* me, I think."

Impressive? It's a big dark nothing. She got up to touch his cheek in return. It was warm, alive. "You feel real enough." Something stirred in her that she hadn't felt in years.

He seemed to feel it too, because he pulled away abruptly.

She bit her lip, changing the subject. "Why are we here?" She looked around. "Where is here?"

"We're in the spore mother's mind. Has she spoken to you?"

"No." She frowned. "Did she talk to you?"

"A little." His brow creased. It seemed like something he didn't want to discuss.

It was strange thinking of this beautiful man as "Spin." "Would you mind if I call you Tyson? You don't look like a 'Spin'."

A grin transformed his face. "I would like that very much. 'Ty' would be even better."

"All right, Ty. Nice to meet you." She held out her hand.

He took it and shook it, and a spark of static passed between them. Or was that just her imagination?

She let go.

The "air" around them was shifting, a breeze slipping across her face. "What's happening?"

"Looks like our little imaginary world is taking on physical form."

Indeed it was. The darkness faded, replaced by solid ground beneath her. Suddenly there was gravity too, tugging her to the newly formed ground. Their fall was softened by red … moss was the only thing she could come up with. It was thick and spongy and smelled something like auddah cheese. It covered the — ground? Floor? — in uneven humps.

Her Temple robe had been replaced with her more practical homespun shirt and trousers, tucked into her leather boots. What she used to wear at home, in Devon. "Curious."

She got up and looked around. It was as if they were on a small moss island that extended around them maybe five meters in each direction, summoned from the void. Just past the edges, the world fell away into darkness. "Where are Triya and the others?"

Ty shook his head. "They aren't inside the spore mother, as far as I can tell."

Translation — they're not here. *Hope they're not too worried about me.*

What had happened just before this place? The last thing she remembered was touching Not-Aik's cheek, her arm alight with hencha flame.

The light in this not-place gathered itself and then squeezed down into a red glow, like one of the fireflies. Another flash, and a familiar woman stood before them.

Desla frowned. "Triya?"

Ty shook his head. "That's not Triya. She's not even human." His voice echoed through the space, sending a chill down her spine. "She's the spore mother."

She took a step back, almost tripping on the moss. "What are you?"

The woman regarded her for a moment, opening her mouth a couple times as if she were struggling to speak. She *looked* like Triya — far more so than Not-Aik looked like Aik — but her movements were off. Like the Aik thing, as if someone else had drawn a not-quite-right human and animated it.

It was disturbing in a way she had a hard time explaining. It just felt *wrong.*

At last, the words came out, as raspy and thick as if Not-Triya hadn't had anything to drink in months. It touched its chest with a shaking hand. "This is ... the spore mother." She gestured at her own form. "I am take this ... aspect ... for is more familiar of you." She closed her eyes. "Difficult, the language human."

She stared at the woman. "You're ... that thing in the cave?"

The spore mother frowned, staring at her.

Ty's spark brightened. "She's asking me to translate."

"Can you?" How did he know whatever her language was?

Ty flashed again. "I think so. She is sharing her language center with me. It may not be perfect. But I can try to translate for both of you."

She would have whistled, if she'd had real lips in this strange place. Instead she squeezed his hand. It was warm and firm. Ty was a constant revelation. "Tell her ... no, ask her why she is doing this. Why she is making war on us."

Ty closed his eyes.

The woman — the spore mother — absorbed what she was asking.

Her face twisted ... whether in anger or pain, Desla couldn't decide.

"She says she never wanted to harm your world. When she awoke, she was damaged." He frowned. "Her mother before her didn't have time to finish ... growing her ... seed, before she died. She found herself all alone, here on your world." Ty paused, his eyebrow raising. paused. "It was supposed to be empty."

"It's your world too now." She took that in. The invaders were as foreign to Tharassas as humankind — they'd guessed as much, but it was nice to have it confirmed. "How long have she and her kind been here?"

Ty relayed her question.

She could feel the pressure again at the back of her head. *The hencha are here too. Watching and listening.* How much of this was news to them too? *Are they judging her? Judging me?*

She wasn't used to the idea of the world mind living inside her own head. That was a responsibility for others — Silya and those eshem from the Highland clans. She'd only wanted to be a sister, to learn the healing arts and to help people when they were in pain. *How did I get dragged into all of this?*

"She says about fifty-seven thousand Tharassan cycles."

"Cycles." Her eyes widened. "You mean *years?*"

"Yes. She's the third of her line since their arrival on Tharassas. She believes she is also the last one."

"On Tharassas?"

He shook his head, his eyes meeting hers. "Anywhere."

Desla swallowed hard, her mouth suddenly dry. "They're ... going extinct?"

"It's a distinct possibility. Their home world was destroyed, and only a few like her foremother escaped to try to establish new homes elsewhere." He paused. "She says she can show you."

Not that she didn't trust Ty, but the spore mother was something else altogether. Was it wise to let her enemy into her head? She grinned ruefully. *I'm already inside hers.*

She'd come this far — it was too late to turn back now. "Show me how?"

The woman reached out her hands, a very human gesture.

"Do you trust her?" She glanced at Ty. What if the spore mother did to her what she'd done to Aik?

"It's okay, Cheese. I sense no deception, but she *is* an alien. I may not be reading her right. I'd say there's a three-quarters chance she's telling the truth."

If I fail here ... "Well, nothing ventured." It was worth the risk, if it would avoid more deaths.

Aik — the real one — would be proud of her.

"All right, let's do it." She took the woman's hands, and her world shifted again.

●　　　●　　　●

"What's wrong with her?" Mes waved her hand in front of Desla's unblinking gaze.

Triya frowned. "I'm not sure." Desla had touched the Not-Aik thing, and had collapsed when some kind of shock went through her whole body. She'd only just been able to catch the newly raised sister before she hit the ground. Now she lay on that moss-carpeted floor, with her pack as a makeshift pillow.

Not-Aik hadn't been so lucky.

Spin flashed, his golden lights spinning. "We're speaking with the spore mother."

Triya raised an eyebrow. "The spore mother?"

"The giant whosie wumpus." Spin's lights flashed over the collection of domes and tubes that filled half of the cavern.

Triya laughed. Spin had such a strange way of speaking. "With that big thing?" Something flitted past her to settle on her shoulder. She started to flick it off, but it was such a beautiful little creature, about the size of an orinth, its silver-red wings fanning the air as it regarded her from its perch. So much prettier than the fireflies.

That thought was enough to make her question its motives. "Shoo!" She waved a callused hand at it and it took off, fluttering away to rest on one of the vines that descended from the high ceiling.

Mes and Em exchanged a doubtful glance. Mes hefted her spear. "We could see what happens if we start poking her with these."

Triya shook her head. When it came to challenges, Mes had such a one-track mind. "Not yet. Spin, is Desla unharmed?"

"Yes, she's fine."

Her eyes narrowed. "You'll tell me if that changes." It was not a question.

"Yes, Triya."

She glanced at the thing that was a mockery of Aik. It lay in a heap next to Desla — no one had bothered to lay it out flat after it had dropped to the ground.

She looked away, feeling sick to her stomach. It was disturbing. So close to human, and yet ...

Her gaze fell on Spin's silver sphere, nestled comfortably in its harness on Desla's chest.

Ever since Spin had confessed to having been human, she couldn't look at him in quite the same way. What did it feel like to be trapped in that tiny form? Even with such wondrous powers ... she wouldn't wish such a fate on her worst enemy.

Mes was edging toward one of the white domes.

Triya growled under her breath. "Put your spears down, you two. Let's give the sister here a chance to do ... whatever it is she's doing." They'd all seen the flames on Desla's arms.

Something was going on here, something she didn't understand. Triya hated things she didn't understand.

Still, she trusted Desla.

"So what do we do in the meantime?" Em frowned.

Triya grinned "Know any good campfire stories?"

•　　　•　　　•

Silya pulled herself up from the blasted ground, using her staff to lever herself into a standing position. She understood now what the hencha had given up for her, for all of humankind. It was humbling, and more than she wanted to bear just then.

It was her responsibility to stop the Death Bringer, a dark figure from a story that haunted little children, come to life in front of her. And to try to save Aik, if he was still in there.

The Death Bringer arrived, just a few meters away, staring at her with its strange golden eyes, the narrow sideways pupils making it look more alien than its humanoid shape. It was barely recognizable as its former self. Something about the way it stood and cocked its head still reminded her of Aik. But its dark-silver-and-black skin and long, lashing tail said otherwise.

I will not kill you. Not unless I have to.

He was still a good ten meters away. He stared at her for a moment too, almost as if he recognized her.

Aik, are you there? She reached out through the emp, but felt nothing.

She placed herself between the fallen verent and the strange creature who had once been her friend and reached inside, searching for the hencha. They responded to her immediately, filling her with blue flame. Their warmth was a comfort, a balm to her troubled soul. *Do* you *want me to kill him?*

You must find your own path.

Not a yes, but not a no either. She frowned. *A whole lot of help you are.*

The Death Bringer raised his silver arms and summoned more of his fireflies to him. They came forth from the skies, hordes of them. Behind him, the poor creatures they'd ensnared shuffled forward, a motley army of aur and urse, jexyn, and human. From near and far, they all lurched toward her.

Astrid appeared at her side. "We have to stop him."

"I know. But you can't fight him alone. He'll kill you." She glanced over her shoulder at Astrid's verent Sleeker. "You can do more from the air. Go!" Her voice was steel. "I don't *need* you here."

Astrid took a startled step backward. "Are you sure?"

"Yes. The hencha comes." *And something else.* She felt them through the emp link. *They're here.* "The ce'faine are coming through the Gap. You must give them cover."

Astrid's eyes went wide. "Godspeed, Sil'Aya." She turned and ran for her verent.

Silya turned her focus to back to the creature. The war would end here, one way or another. They both knew it.

The ce'faine were coming, and with them the eshem. They wouldn't hesitate to kill him if they had the chance. She had to be quick.

She needed something to draw on, like she had with the violet pines in the gap.

The hencha gatherings here were gone, devoured by the Death Bringer's hoard, leaving a muddy, trampled mess. So were the flop trees, the violet pines, and most of the wildlife.

But not all.

A wicked grin crossed her face. There was still one place she could draw power from to call forth a cleansing cold.

She planted her staff firmly in the ground and reached out, calling on the combined strength of the hencha.

Behind her enemy, one of the of the firefly-ridden aur exploded into blue light.

• • •

Coral stiffened, flames bursting anew across her skin. She could feel them — the hencha — flowing through her. It was glorious.

She could sense others as well. Sisters Aster, Peslyn, Sallia, all close by. But she could feel Desla too, and Tela and Fessryn, and … Silya.

The Hencha Queen burned with a light like the sun as she faced off with the invader on the far side of the Heartland. Coral could see it in her mind as clear as if she stood there with the Hencha Queen.

She opened her eyes. The cavern was lit with a blue glow. *Not just me.*

All of the sisters were aflame.

Hope blossomed in her heart for the first time in days.

"Is it over?" A little boy, maybe five, was tugging at her robes. He looked up at her with wide brown eyes, unusual in Gullton, but maybe a sign of a change in the world to come.

She knelt and ran a glowing hand through his blond mess of hair. "Not yet. But it will be soon."

• • •

Consumed by the broken but still vivid memories of the spore mother, Desla lived a racial lifetime in an instant. Year bled into year as a terrible battle raged between two species, a battle that spanned the stars. The invaders were merciless, cornered beasts who broke out of their enclosure to rampage across the stars.

Rage and fear and desperation filled her, as human a feeling as the aaveen were alien in form.

The spore mother shared her people's sad tale of loss and banishment as their own sun betrayed them, swallowing up both their home system worlds.

Then it was over, save for a long, cold journey across the starry void, one of only a few who escaped that final destruction.

And finally, their arrival in Tharassas so many centuries before. A place they hoped would be their new home.

The memories were imperfect, warped in places and with many sharp edges. But they were enough.

She wanted to weep, but she had no tears in this strange half world. *So much suffering. So much loss.*

How did one live with the loss of their homeworld? Then again, her own kind had done just that, even if that loss was dulled by the passage of centuries. *We have more in common than I could have ever guessed.*

The hencha mind was with her, taking it in. It was as shocked as she was. *We didn't know.*

Still, there was more.

She expanded her awareness, and the spore mother let her in. She gasped at what she found.

She's dying. She could feel it. Darkness was closing in at the edges of the strange but beautiful creature in the cavern. The daughter's daughter of the one who had crossed the heavens to save her people.

Her heart broke for the strange creature, maybe the last of her kind. *But how do I forgive what she's done?* How many people had died in the Highlands? How much had already been destroyed there, and now in the Heartland? And how much had the hencha and their kin sacrificed?

The questions hung in the air between them, and she didn't have an answer.

A new presence flared in her mind. No, a multitude.

She was touched by the spirits of all of her sisters. Coral, Fessryn, Dor, Aster, and so many others, each a candle flickering with blue flame.

And at the heart of them, one that burned like a pyre.

"Silya?"

18

IN THE THROES OF WAR

SORIX FELT KALIX'S PAIN like a claw in her gut. Her mate had been flying with Raven, and something had happened. *Where are you?*

There was no response, just waves of anguish.

Velix's anguished voice almost split her mind. *He's hurt!*

I know. She swept past a knot of the nasty little red things and froze them out of existence with her trailing wisps. Her gaze swept the ground. *There. I see him.*

We have to go —

Stay here. Protect him from above. I'll go to him.

Velix's discontent was acid through their link, but then his grumbling assent overrode it. *Go! Protect them both.*

Both. Kalix and their strange human kit.

I will.

She dove toward them, intent on getting to them before the enemy could.

•　　•　　•

Raven/Breeze stirred, their mind a miasma of fog.

Pain. / Everything hurts. / What happened?

The last thing Raven remembered was falling. Now he was lying naked on Breeze's prostrate form.

Breeze tried to stretch his wings. *Pain!*

Aik. He'd seen Aik. Only he was changed, no, *transformed* — as much as Raven was or maybe more.

He vividly recalled the last thing Aik had said to him before the verent had come crashing through the doors of the Manor House. *You're beautiful to me, no matter what. You always have been. I just want to be with you.*

After all this time, his feelings for Aik were stronger than ever. Time and distance had only made them grow. His physical form didn't matter. *But are you still Aik, inside?*

He reached out through his emp, sending soothing love and peace to his verent.

Breeze was healing, far more rapidly than a human could. It was a surpassingly strange sensation, as broken bones set themselves and torn flesh knitted back together. His own body was sore, but he didn't feel anything dangerously out of joint.

She comes.

Who comes? Then he felt her. *Ah, Squint.*

Why was he disappointed? He'd hoped it was Silya, but she was hundreds of miles away, defending Gullton. He hugged Breeze's neck. *Will you be all right?*

Go. Breeze's voice in his head sounded stronger.

Are you sure? You're hurt. He'd never sensed pain like that from Breeze, although he'd felt its like in himself, during his test.

I will live. But you may have to fly for us.

Was that a verent joke?

A flicker of amusement slipped through the link. *Maybe. Go, little man.*

Wait ... do you think you can *fly?*

Breeze was silent for a moment. *Maybe.*

He said a prayer of thanks to Fre'Oss. *Be ready to go when I call.*

He sat up and opened his eyes. He lay naked on Breeze's back in the heart of a world in chaos. Rivulets of sweat dripped off him.

The Heartland as he'd known it was gone, replaced by a hot, war-torn hellscape. Swarms of fireflies and flocks of red-eyed creatures that might once have been jexyn flew by overhead, probably only keeping their distance because of the bandy fruit pulp that covered his verent.

Silya stepped into view a few steps away, her back to him, gaze intent on something or someone.

She's here!

A wave of blue wisps flew past them, bringing a welcome cool breeze, swept up by verent to freeze the enemy.

He had to act now, while Silya distracted Aik. He slipped off his verent on the far side from the battle, quiet as an inthym. He took out his boots and breeches, pulling them on quickly. *Thank Ay'Oss that Jai made me practice this so many times.*

A rush of wind announced Squint's arrival. She settled to the ground, kicking up a cloud of dirt and broken hencha stalks.

As soon as it cleared, he bounded over to her and threw his arms around her neck. *I'm so glad you're here.*

I am glad you are safe, little one. She blinked at him, seeming as surprised as he was at the emotions that surged between them. Love. Companionship. Loyalty.

She settled a wing over Breeze's prostate form. *Go! Do what you must. I will watch over him.*

•   •   •

Iihil stared at the lone human in disbelief.

She stood before him, holding her black staff defiantly, her back straight, as if daring him to challenge her.

He growled, gnashing his teeth. He could break her in half with his hands. How did she think she could best him? It made no sense, and that made him uneasy.

Then she *reached* out her hand toward his army — the creatures his forerunners were riding. And one by one, she *took* them.

An aur exploded into blue light, becoming a cloud of those damned blue wisps. They swirled up into the air, captured by one of the verent, and soared into the sky to trail it like a thousand stars.

Another gesture, and an urse fell apart at the seams, giving up its life for her.

What are you? His jaw dropped open, the action of his still-partially-human body.

She is Silya. The Hencha Queen. The answer came unbidden from his host's memory. She was the focus, the heart of this world's defense.

Iihil frowned. The aaveen weren't the only ones using humans. Still, she was taking a great risk, appearing here on the battlefield before him. Kill her, and this world would be his. *Our people will finally have a home.*

He lifted his own arm to direct the gathered host of forerunners —

Something slammed into his side hard, knocking him to the ground.

A flash of white, and then it was past.

He slid across the muddy, blasted earth, carving a channel in the dirt, the world flying past him. He came to rest against the stump of a desecrated tree. What in uurccheea was that?

Iihil checked himself over. He was shaken but in one piece. His armor had protected him from the worst damage, though one of his human ribs ached. He sprang up again with a snarl, only to find himself face to face with another of the humans.

This one was shorter than Silya, but she — he could see it was a *she* from the shape of her lithe form — had a warrior's stance and a wicked spear.

She showed him her teeth. "Dance with me?"

His mother had designed him well. Claws slipped out of the sheathes on his hands, and he settled into a battle stance, ready to finish her off so he could deal with the other human and take the verent.

He could feel his mother's pain — she was dying. *She needs me.*

He had to end this.

With a howl, the human warrior threw herself at him, and the battle was joined.

•   •   •

"Chala, what are you doing?"

Silya's voice echoed both inside and outside of Chala's head, a mix of anger and frustration

"What you don't have the courage to do." She ignored the Hencha Queen's presence at her back, staying calm and focused, determined to eliminate the threat in front of her. The Death Bringer.

The others were blind to it because Aik had been their friend. They couldn't see the danger he posed. She studied him, watching for weakness.

The creature was tall — taller than a normal human anyhow, as if Aik had been stretched out and thinned. Its entire body was covered in silver swirled with deep-as-night black which hurt her eyes to look at.

Its face was narrow, covered in that disturbing ebony metal, cracked jaw displaying a row of decidedly non-human teeth. And the tail — she'd have to watch for that.

Chala had trained her whole life for this moment, and she didn't know Aik from a rock in the sand, but she knew how to fight a wild animal.

She threw herself at it, thrusting her spear to test the Death Bringer's agility.

It slipped off to one side, nimble as an eircat. Far more agile than she'd have given it credit for. She danced back on her heels, narrowly avoiding a swipe of its tail.

She leapt, swinging around to connect with a kick.

The thrice-damned creature ducked under her blow, slithering past her as smoothly as water.

Chala, stop!

Silya's voice in her head made her miss a step. "Dammit, Silya, leave me alone."

The Death Bringer's tail wrapped around her waist and jerked, throwing her through the air to land against one of the coryx. The soft surface cushioned the blow, letting her slide down its side to land on her feet once again.

She took a deep breath, watching it approach. Then she leapt at it again, but the beast danced away, its claws swiping at the air where she'd just been. She slammed into another of the damnable coryx.

Time to change tactics. She used her knife to slash a line through the white dome and slipped inside, stopping for just a second to remember her time with the Oracle. *You have an important part to play in what is to come.*

She could feel the eshem inside her head, encouraging her. How was that possible? She'd never aspired to be one of them, let alone ever shown any talent in that direction.

Still, they were right. She wasn't sure what Aik had become — Death Bringer or something else? — only that it could be killed. That it *must* be killed.

The eshem themselves and a host of the ce'faine were approaching, the clamor of battle to the east announcing their presence. But their progress was too slow.

Only I can do this. She slipped out of the other side of the coryx, not caring if it healed behind her, and turned to find her enemy once more.

•   •   •

Raven crouched above Breeze's back, so far unnoticed by the combatants.

Chala of all people was here, fighting Aik, while Silya tried to get her to stop. *She's going to kill him.*

"Chala!" He shouted it as loudly as he could, but if she heard him, she was ignoring him.

The truth was, she was stronger than he was, and a much better fighter. He had no chance going up against her alone. But brute strength wasn't his only option.

The emp. There might be a way to save Aik yet.

He glanced at Silya. *Can you hear me?* He prayed that the emp/verent/hencha thing would work.

She turned to look at him, her flames fluttering in recognition as relief flickered across her face, and nodded. *What can we do?*

He put a finger over his lips. *I have a plan.* Maybe not much of one, but it was the best he could do in the heat of battle.

Her eyes narrowed, but she nodded as he shared it with her.

She swallowed hard. *It could work.*

He bit his lips. *You have a better idea?*

No.

He nodded curtly and climbed onto Breeze again. Their minds merging but his body stayed apart. *Change of plans, my friend. Are you ready?*

The verent — his verent — rumbled quietly. His bones had knitted themselves back together, but there was still some tissue damage. *I will manage.*

Squint's bright blue eyes met his. *We will come with you. We can protect him.*

On Breeze's other side, Thunder settled to the ground, puncturing one of the coryx, which deflated with a hiss of air and started to disintegrate. *You can do this, little kit.*

He grinned. His family was together again — together, they could do anything.

Let's go.

•   •   •

Iihil hissed, his tail swiping back and forth. Mother needed him, and here he was playing games with a human warrior. And now there were two more of the damnable verent protecting their fallen companion.

It doesn't matter. One would work as well as another to carry him home, and he wouldn't be deterred by whatever had been smeared over the beasts to keep the forerunners at bay.

But the fighter was proving harder to vanquish than he'd anticipated. She'd vanished, slipping inside one of the eeechha, cutting the poor creature with a sharp blade. He could feel its pain as if the knife had plunged into his own side.

Enough. Time to be done with her. He called the forerunners back to him, ready to launch an all-out assault to wipe his enemy from the battlefield.

"Aik!"

Iihil spun around to face the strange woman-who-glowed. *Silya,* his host mind had told him. "My name is Iihil." The human language was strange on his tongue.

Her face ... cringed. As if his name were painful to her. "You need to stop this madness." She peered at him as if he were a tiny meerith spinning a web that she needed to study. "Aik, are you still in there?" Blue flames ran down her arms and up her staff, and yet she didn't burn.

He frowned. "Aik is gone. My name is Iihil." His tail lashed the air in frustration. *Why am I talking with her?*

The woman growled, a disturbing guttural sound. Her fire burned more brightly, lighting up the night. She seemed to grow, her features shifting and her visage darkening, hardening like gnarled old wood. "Let me speak with Aik."

He shuddered. Changing their physical aspect was not something humans were supposed to be able to do. His human memories gave him the answer. She was one with this world, manifesting what the humans called the *Hencha Queen*. Just as he was his own race's *progenitor*, merged with another human. It made her dangerous. "Aik is gone," he said again, genuinely sorry about what had been done to the aanteem so he could live again. "This world must change, or the aaveen — my people — will die."

"I can't let that happen." She towered over him now, cold like a glacier, her very being sucking at his heat.

He took an involuntary step backwards. He was outmatched here. He could feel it.

The forerunners buzzed around his head angrily. Not as many as there had been, but enough. He could take the verent and retreat to the mountain. *I can still escape.*

She must have seen it, because a look of regret crossed her hardened face. "I can't let you go." She lifted her staff, and it sizzled with blue light, racing up and down its seams.

It held suspended in midair for a second, before she plunged the base of it back down into the ground.

The whole world shook. A deep thunder echoed in the clouds, and then the ground between them cracked open like an egg.

An indigo tide bubbled up and began to pour out of the crevice, a strange liquid thick as blood that exploded into hundreds, no, thousands of the damnable wisps.

Iihil swatted them away angrily, their chill soaking into his bones. He detested this damnable world and its bone-chilling cold.

"Chala, no!" Silya's voice carried across the newly opened crevice.

He spun around, and the warrior was there before him, her spear raised high.

She flung it at him, and the sharp wooden tip slammed into his gut where his armor had been weakened, cutting right through his metal skin.

Iihil spread his arms and screamed into the sky with his human voice. Pain spread through him, flaring red in his vision. He stumbled to his knees, clutching at the weapon — a simple stick! — that pierced his body. *How ...?*

He tried to pull it out, but the pain flared anew for every *irresh* he managed to move it.

As the warrior approached him, her boots crunching on rocks and dirt, Iihil's red blood leaked out around the spear to spill, drip by drip, falling onto the blasted ground.

Iihil looked up. *Is this the end?*

Snow was falling now, a deep chill in the air as the white flakes started to cover the battlefield. It was enchanting. He held his hand up to try to catch a flake of it in his palm. *It never snowed on Uurccheea.*

The verent howled.

Wait, now there were three? Or am I just seeing things? Iihil blinked, trying to clear his vision.

The beast rose up from its apparent slumber, spreading its white wings.

His attacker loomed over him with a long knife in her hand, ready to deal the final blow. Light from the twin moons glittered off the sharp edge of the blade. The world narrowed to just the two of them.

"I am sorry, Aik." Her brown eyes met his golden ones and she raised the knife.

Iihil closed his eyes. *I'm sorry too. Mother, I have failed you.* He could feel her touch in his mind, but it was faint, distant.

A frustrated scream rent the night.

Iihil opened his eyes.

The warrior flew backward through the air to land hard in a burned out patch of native plants. She sat up and her hands went to her temples as she screamed in pain.

What's happening? Something had attacked the human, but there was no one else around. Blue wisps mingled with snowfall. Iihil looked around, confused.

The wounded verent had taken to the air. It came at him like a giant white oovaator. He tried to flee, but agony blossomed again in his stomach.

The verent's back legs grasped him, lifting him up into the air, and he almost blacked out from the pain.

Iihil was barely aware of the human form that rode on the back of the beast above him.

"Aik, don't leave me now."

He knew that voice somehow. The human's name floated up to him. "Raven?" Iihil gasped as the claws tightened around his chest, squeezing out the air and putting pressure on his wound where the spear still hung.

"I'll save you, Aik. Somehow, I'll save you."

"Take me to the mountain." It came out as a gasp. The spore mother could help him. *Do you understand?*

The last thing he saw before darkness took him was Silya, far below, staring up at him with her mouth agape.

19

TO THE MOUNTAIN

BREEZE HAULED THEM UPWARD, with Thunder and Squint providing a chilly escort through the clouds of wisps and suddenly falling snow. *Where had that come from?*

It must have been Silya. She'd raised her staff, and when it had hit the ground, the world had dissolved into chaos.

They cut a path through a cloud of fireflies, freezing them and scattering them to the winds.

Chala tried to kill him! Raven could feel Aik's pain like a red stain across his stomach.

He'd planned to knock Chala off balance, just enough to let him grab Aik. The way Jai had back in the Kitchen that first day, using his emp as a weapon.

But when he'd seen the spear go through Aik's stomach — even if he didn't recognize his lover anymore — he'd hit her with all the pain and anguish that roiled him.

It felt *wrong*, but he'd had to do it. *Didn't I?*

The very memory made him sick to his stomach. *I couldn't let her kill Aik.*

You protected your family. Thunder's deep voice soothed him like a balm.

What now? Breeze sounded anguished too.

Below them, the remaining fireflies buzzed like an angry nest of orinths.

Go up! If we get high enough, they won't follow.

His plan had worked, but he'd waited a few seconds too long. He'd stolen Aik, or eeheel ... whatever the creature called itself. But his indecision might have cost Aik his life.

Take me to the mountain.

Who had been asking? Aik or Iihil?

Did it matter? After all, who else could help Aik?

How far can you fly in your current state? Breeze's pain sizzled in his mind next to Aik's.

As far as I can.

It was a fair answer. *Let's go to Anghar Mor.*

To the Mountain. Breeze surged upward again, his powerful wings taking them out of range of the angry fireflies, and Squint and Thunder followed.

Below, the buzzing diminished and finally fell away to silence.

•   •   •

Raven and the verent disappeared with Aik, trailing a comet's tail of fireflies. The world was filled with wisps, so many wisps that the battlefield was lit by an almost continuous blue glow.

Silya watched them, her brow furrowed. Raven's plan had been simple enough — get Aik away from the battle.

I'm going to steal him.

She managed to crack a smile at that one ... it was such a Raven solution.

Neither one of them had counted on Chala showing up to kill him, and now both were gone. *What if Aik dies?*

Then Kerrick was suddenly, impossibly at her side. "Are you all right?" He looked her over anxiously. Snow fell from the sky in gusts, alighting on his jacket and melting on his shoulders.

She looked up at him, stunned. "Other than confused and half frozen ... how did you —?"

"The flitter. Elleck's here too."

"Thank the gods." She wrapped her arms around him, more happy than words could express to see him.

"I brought someone else, too." He whispered it in her ear, and then let her go with one last squeeze and stepped aside.

Dor was there. Her arms were wreathed in blue flame, just like Silya's. The poor woman looked lost.

"Holy mother of Jas." Silya stared at Dor's flickering arms. "What did you do?"

Dor shook her head. "I don't know. I didn't mean to … What's happening to me?"

You needed help. The hencha mind's voice sounded a little exasperated, as if it should have gone without saying.

"I think you're my backup." Silya ran to embrace her. Their flames joined, but she felt a warmth that had little to do with the Hencha.

"Nothing for me?" Kerrick looked pained.

She let go of Dor and pecked him on the cheek. "I'll deal with you later. I told you to stay in Gullton. Why are you here?" *Thank Jorja for both of you.*

He shrugged. "Never was much for following instructions."

"Truer words have never been spoken."

"Silya, look." Dor's outstretched arm drew her attention.

She turned to see the unexpected. People were approaching … she half expected them to be the remnants of Aik's army. But no, there were hundreds of them, all smeared with something. Bandy fruit? The ce'faine.

At their forefront were three women, two of them dressed in tanned leathers and the third in a draping of white cloth tied around her waist with a blue sash. All three were wreathed in blue flame. For just a second, she was reminded of Triya and her guards, Mes and Em.

The eshem. "Dor, take my hand." If it was a fight they wanted, she would do whatever she had to give Raven and Aik a chance.

The trio of formidable looking women stopped just on the other side of the wide crevice Silya had opened with her staff.

Silya nodded at them. "Alibeh. Mirah. And …"

"Seshan." The Oracle was the oldest of the three but also the tallest, her wrinkled hands and arms hanging beneath the voluminous white sleeves. Her face was as wrinkled as an old apple.

The three practically glowed with satisfaction.

This is about Aik. The Death Bringer. Silya seethed with rage, her flames rising again.

They regarded one another across the divide

Silya squeezed Dor's hand. "Aik ... is gone." It was true. Technically.

The Oracle nodded. "We're sorry, Silya. It needed to be done."

A little hope flickered in her chest. *Maybe they don't know he's still alive. Best to keep it that way.* "It didn't have to be like this. There were other ways."

The Oracle shook her head. "We make no apologies for placing the protection of this world above all else. Surely you, of all wetlanders, understand that."

Alibeh knelt next to Chala, touching her forehead.

The ce'faine warrior was still out cold.

"What's wrong with you?" Elleck leapt across the gap to confront the eshem.

Silya had barely seen the ce'faine woman during the battle.

Alibeh glanced at the other two and then stepped forward. "It was necessary —"

"Why must we always choose the path of violence?" She jabbed Alibeh in the shoulder, forcing her back a step. "You were the one who taught me the way of water. *Let the world flow around you, like a stone in the water. A simple shift can change the river's course.*"

Alibeh nodded. "Chala was the stone."

Elleck wasn't finished. "Have you learned nothing from a century of war?" She spat. "Maybe Kerrick was right about you." She glanced back at her brother, who'd come to stand at her side.

"Elleck ..." Kerrick stared at his sister. "You know I don't feel that way about the ce'faine anymore. *You* made me see the light."

"It all looks like darkness to me now."

Silya frowned. Chala was a pawn in all of this, she was sure of it. The eshem had recruited her to do what Silya herself would not.

Maybe Elleck is right. Maybe we need to heal instead of harm. She closed her eyes and set the butt of her staff down on the ground. She called out to the hencha, to the blood of the world to repair what she'd broken.

The world groaned, and the gap before her pulled itself back together, the earth rumbling beneath her feet until it was sealed once more.

Letting go of her connection to the hencha, she stepped over the scar to approach Chala. She knelt beside the su'faine's crumpled form. "Is she all right?"

The eshem nodded as one. "She will be. Raven ... did something we are forbidden to do. He used his emp as a weapon against her."

Her eyes narrowed. *They could be weapons?* She massaged the lump at her neck.

Now that she'd had a chance to cool off, she could feel ... something. Emotions emanating from the eshem, carefully masked. Mirah's was the strongest. *Regret.*

So they were human after all. Her anger cooled just a little. "Done is done." It was in Raven's hands now.

"That's it?" Kerrick looked at her, his mouth hanging open. "They killed Aik — one of Gullton's finest Guards — and that's all you're going to say?" He turned his head to wink at her.

Silya's appreciation of him grew. "There will have to be some kind of reparations."

The eshem looked at one another in consternation.

"Surely you didn't think you could break the sworn treaty between our two nations without consequence?" She looked up at the sky. The wisps were milling around uncertainly. "Still, there are more pressing needs to attend to first. Shall we clean things up?"

There were firefly-ridden humans and beasts still milling about as well, and the remainder of the hateful fireflies.

The others exchanged a glance. "We will discuss this at length ... after." The Oracle nodded at Silya. Then they took one another's hands.

She could feel their combined strength through the hencha and through the emp. She shuddered. Chastened or not, these were not women to be trifled with.

Together, they reached for the last of the firefly-ridden beasts.

She would deal with the infected humans later.

She closed her eyes, feeling the blood of the world surging beneath her.

The wisps pulled together into blue wave, and advanced. The verent swept in to scoop them up and trailed them across the land, freezing the invading flora and fauna.

Soon this corner of the Heartland would be free of the invaders. *Silya, stop!*

The words echoed across the battlefield, between the sisters and the eshem, and reverberated across the sky through the wisps and the gathered verent. One by one the great winged beasts settled to the ground.

Everything went deathly still.

"Who was that?" She sought the source of the voice.

The eshem looked at her suspiciously. "What new trickery is this?" The Oracle's face compressed into a scowl.

The power behind the voice had been unmistakable. *It was the hencha.*

Silya, you have to stop.

Suddenly she knew who it was — the voice of a promising young woman who had been an initiate just days before. One who'd always been stronger than she seemed.

"Desla?"

Everyone was staring at her.

Yes, it's me. She sounded ... no, felt frightened. *We need to end this now, before it's too late.*

•   •   •

Raven.

Aik could feel him. He was close.

My echa-aueel. No, that was Iihil's language. *My soulmate.*

Pain lanced through him, blinding red pain. Something had happened. Something bad.

He longed to be himself again, to push out this invader in his mind. It was a terrible thing, to be trapped in your own head. He wouldn't wish it on his worst enemy,

And yet ...

Iihil had been through so much. The loss of his world, his family, his love. He had gathered together fragments of her from Iihil's mind, and she provided a reflection of the being Iihil had once been. Proud, yes, but kind, strong. A caretaker *and* a lover.

Those last images made him shudder. *I didn't need to see that.*

Still, it was a part of who Iihil was.

He was conflicted. This was *his* body. His world. His friends. He loved them, and he had a duty to do all he could to protect them.

But what if the cost was another being's life?

Sooner or later, Iihil would let down his guard. Then Aik would act.

I will do what I must when the time comes.

•   •   •

Flanked by his mates Squint and Thunder, Breeze bore them steadily northward, toward the dreaded mountain peak Raven had only seen up close once before. *All roads lead to Anghar Mor.*

They'd brought Aik there, in search of him, and then Silya's mother and that initiate, Desla. *Why didn't they try to find you earlier?*

Aik didn't reply. He hung limply from Breeze's claws.

Helja grant that he's not already dead.

The heat was palpable, even so high above the despoiled ground. From here it didn't look quite so bad — great patches of splotchy white spread across the Highlands like snow — but Raven shuddered to think of all the damage that had been done. *How will we ever reverse it?*

At least they'd left the storm behind.

Raven could feel Breeze's pain. The verent was far from recovered, and each beat of his wings cost him dearly. *Are you sure you're all right?*

No, but I can do this.

An image of the lake at Mountainhome flashed through Raven's mind. *What do you think about taking a long break after all of this is over?*

Yes, please. The verent's voice in his head was so plaintive that Raven didn't know whether to laugh or cry. It was hard to remember why he'd been so scared of Breeze when they'd first met at the Manor House, just weeks before.

The black peak loomed ahead, a baleful presence on the horizon that grew steadily larger. From the south it looked whole, an almost perfect cone.

Silya's comforting presence touched his mind. *Is he … alive?*

It was strange to have her in his head too. *I think so.*

Good. She slipped away.

She must be in shock too, after what Chala had done. Why did his fellow verent rider do it? Maybe she hadn't known the silver thing was Aik.

They arrived at Anghar Mor at last, passing over the peak and revealing the ruin of the back half of the mountain. He gasped.

The ice sheet had retreated, revealing a desolate land covered with boulders. Water cascaded off its face in an abundance of waterfalls, all feeding down toward Lake Zeraya.

Why did we have to come here? Aik — or the creature who had taken over Aik — had been very specific, and he hadn't known where else to go.

Where? Breeze sounded exhausted.

He pulled his attention away from the ruined valley to scan the broken rock of the mountain below. "There." He pointed out a flat area about halfway up, in front of a dark tunnel mouth.

A few fireflies circled lazily up to greet them, but they stayed well away from the three verent and the trailing cloud of wisps.

Breeze descended carefully, hovering a meter above the black stone of the mountain, and laid Aik down on a flat outcropping, as gently as a mother setting down a child in its crib.

Raven could feel Breeze's pain, feel what the effort was costing him. *I shouldn't have made you do that.*

Breeze settled to the ground, wobbling as his clawed feet touched stone. *I couldn't let him die. You need him.*

He leaned forward and hugged the great beast's neck. *Thank you.*

You're welcome, little man. Breeze huffed. *Just let me rest now.*

Squint and Thunder settled in next to him, knocking a few loose pieces of shale down the mountainside with a clatter, and touched their noses to his.

He slipped off Breeze's back, dropping down onto a patch of crunchy black gravel. He ran to Aik's side, hoping for the best but fearing ... He couldn't bring himself to think it. His arms and legs ached from the ride without the saddle, but he didn't care.

"Aik, are you all right?"

Aik lay on his side, his tail twisting in agitation, his eyes screwed closed in pain. He looked so strange, so ... alien. Still, Raven refused to think of Aik as the Death Bringer.

He touched Aik's arm, and then jerked back as the silver-black armor — skin? — began to melt away. It peeled off, revealing deep red scales edged in black, longer and rougher than the white scales on his own arms. The strange metal flowed, reminding Raven of nothing so much as Spin when he changed shape — a liquid-silver wave revealing its body. He had a hard time thinking of this creature before him as Aik.

The spear stuck out of it … him, at an odd angle. Raven was afraid to remove it — at least the bleeding was slow.

Why is it coming off now?

The answer came to him in a flash. *He's dying.*

He squeezed the now-bare scaled hand. "Aik, are you in there?"

Its face was clear now. It still looked like Aik, mostly. The features were the same, and the scales there smoothed out into reddish skin.

His eyes opened, and they focused on Raven.

"I'm … not Aik." His voice was dry, raspy, as if it had gone unused for a long time.

And those long sharp teeth!

The last of his armor rolled off him and consolidated itself into a silver ball about three times bigger than Spin, studded with red gems. It settled at his side.

Raven nodded. After everything else, this was no surprise. "Who *are* you, then?"

He shuddered. "I am Iihil. I'm the progenitor …" He coughed up blood onto his black lips. "… of the aaveen. I have to get back to Mother." Iihil's red eyes met his as he struggled to get up, and then winced in pain. "Please. She is … dying." He reached for Raven and grimaced.

Raven searched those alien eyes. *Aik, are you still in there somewhere?* "Don't try to move." He frowned. "Who's this Mother?"

Iihil's … Aik's blood was slowly spreading around the wound. His tail twitched back and forth underneath him, the tip flicking the air.

"She's the one who brought Uurccheea here." Iihil shivered. "It's so cold."

Oorcheeuh? Raven was sweating like an aur in heat. How could Iihil be cold? "Give me a second."

He got up and retrieved a blanket from the bag strapped to Breeze's side. *You all right?*

Breeze rumbled. *Better. Can we stay here for a while?*

He scratched his verent's nose affectionately. *For a little bit.*

He brought the blanket back and laid it over Iihil, careful not to disturb the spear. When he'd hatched his simple plan, he'd hoped that this would go far differently. Steal Aik, and the very sight of him would snap Aik out of it and bring him back. *What if he's gone for good?*

"Let me talk to Aik."

The creature frowned. "The aanteem? It is a part of me now."

What in Heaven's reach is an anteam? Raven shook his head. "Aik would never do this. Aik is loyal to his friends, above all. He cares about everyone else more than himself. He … he saved my life." *More than once.* He closed his eyes, remembering the slide down the hillside after the old bridge collapsed. And that last night together when he'd finally let down his walls. "Aik loves me."

Iihil's features were stretched in pain. "You're … aanteem too?"

"I don't know what that means —"

"You're … Raven."

His eyes went wide. "Yes. I'm Raven. Aik, is that you? Are you in there?" He squeezed Iihil's shoulders.

Iihil stiffened and clutched his stomach, sharp claws scratching at the blanket as if he could dig out the spear. "So … much … pain."

Raven fell back, harshly reminded that Iihil was not Aik. He stared at those claws, his own slipping out of his hands unheeded. *What should I do?*

Then Iihil's eyes closed. His body went limp, his scaled arms falling to his side, and his tail ended its incessant twitching.

"Aik!" Raven put his arms around him, heedless of the danger, while behind him the verent trumpeted in alarm. "Aik, don't leave me! I … I love you."

Aik/Iihil was still as death.

•   •   •

Something shifted and Aik seized his chance.

One moment he was at the bottom of an endless sea, and the next the aaveen's hold on him slipped and he was free, gasping at the air. He slipped out of the aaveen's grasp and donned his new guise, the one he'd spent so much time and energy perfecting.

He chose one of Iihil's favorite places, a tangled nest of aoochhaa vines in bloom along the edge of a wide lake called Oolaanea. Where he and Eeydra had once spent private time together.

Iihil appeared before him as if he'd dropped out of the crimson sky above. His multifaceted eye sparkled in the sunlight as he looked around, taking in the red vines with their multicolored flowers. He breathed in their perfume, and a toothy smile crossed his face. He was short, sleek like a predator, his six limbs covered in red, black-edged scales.

His gaze settled on Aik, who wore a similar form. "No … it can't be."

It was an alien tongue, but Aik understood it as if he'd been born to it. And he had, in a way.

Iihil crossed the clearing in two leaps, pressing himself against Eeydra's form, their scales sparking connections where they touched. "Is it really you?" The words came not only from his mouth but through his skin to Aik's, reverberating through him like beats on a drum.

He pulled away forcefully. "Iihil, what have you done?"

Iihil backed away, its limbs sagging. "I did what I had to, my soulmate. The mother and I paved the way for you, and the others. For Eev-uurccheea —"

"On a barren world, as we planned?" Eeydra took on a life of her own as Aik sank into the role, the sound of disapproval clear in her tone.

His scales flared bright red. "No. There were others already there." His shame was clear from his color. "But it was necessary …"

"To bring death to another race? To do to them what was done to us?"

He shuddered. He shook with her anger, as real as if Eeydra herself had inhabited him.

"Mother …"

"Should never have allowed this." She approached her mate, and Aik went along with it, drawn by her concern for him. She wasn't real … not like he and Iihil were. But she was real enough, reconstructed from Iihil's memories of her.

She touched him, tentatively at first, with one limb and then another, until she was pressed up against him again, side to side.

Iihil trembled under that touch. "I've waited for you for so long." Where they touched, they became one, his scales releasing filaments that infiltrated hers and vice versa, an intimacy that made Aik shudder.

He was the intruder here, never mind that his Eeydra was fake, constructed from whole cloth.

For Iihil, this was real.

He felt it then, the sense of wrongness. Iihil was in pain, as much as he tried to hide it. *What happened to you?* The words flowed through his skin into Iihil.

She … she wounded me.

Through their link, he could feel the raw pain coming from Iihil's stomach. *My stomach.* Something had happened. Something bad. *Who? Your Mother?*

He knew as soon as he said it that he'd made a mistake.

The aaveen must have sensed it, for he tensed against Eeydra's skin, withdrawing his touch. "This isn't right."

Aik struggled to regain his footing, leaning into Iihil's discomfort. "You're right. All of this is wrong, and you know it."

Iihil pulled away, snapping loose with a backlash that was as much mental as physical as they disengaged.

Aik reeled with the shock, like a hundred hooks had been pulled out of his skin. *Holy green hell, that hurt.*

Iihil blinked his one eye rapidly. "This isn't real. You're not Eeydra." Iihil's limbs shook in agitation, claws slipping out of his four small hands. "I was on a mountaintop …"

He sighed. *I tried.* "You're right. I'm not Eeydra." He shed her form, letting it fall away from himself like dust, to stand before the invader as himself. "She was a beautiful soul."

Iihil's mouth fell open in a comedic parody of a human's reaction, whatever passed for saliva dripping from the edge of his mouth. "You're the aanteem!" Iihil fell to the ground, touching his forehead to the soft red moss that filled the clearing. "How did you …? No, it doesn't matter." Iihil crawled toward him.

He took a step back, worried what his captor might try next.

Iihil looked up at him, and his eye seemed … swollen. "I beg of you, take me back to Mother. She's dying, and so will Eeydra if I don't get to her." His eye met Aik's. "So will we, if she doesn't help us."

What can I do about it? "I can't. I don't know how. You trapped me in my own head, remember?"

"Here." Iihil held up a golden light, about as big as Aik's fist. It swirled and flickered, filled with waves and whorls that demanded his attention. "If you truly are an aanteem, you will do the right thing. Take this, and then take me home."

He looked at the light, and then back at Iihil. "What is it?" It might be a trick.

Iihil sat up, his eye staring at Aik. "It's *you.*"

"What do you mean, it's me?" Though he suspected what Iihil meant.

"Take it."

Can I afford not to take the chance? It all came down to this. *Do I trust you?*

Before he could change his mind, he grabbed the light. It expanded in his grasp, filling him with warmth.

The quiet clearing disappeared, along with Iihil, and his consciousness expanded, bringing with it all of his memories, his hopes and fears, the love and anger and pain of being Aik Erio. *I'm me again.*

He had only a second to enjoy it before he became aware of the spear that had slammed into Iihil's gut. *My gut.*

Aik opened his eyes and screamed.

●   ●   ●

Iihil's eyes flew open. He screamed in pain, clutching at the spear in his stomach.

"Iihil?" Raven looked down. "What's happening?"

The creature gasped. A scaled hand clutched at Raven's arm, and he was breathing heavily. "Rave."

It can't be. "Aik?" His heart thundered like a sledgehammer. "Aik, is that really you?" His eyes were wet.

Is he all right? Breeze's voice rumbled in his head.

Raven could feel the other verent with him. *I don't know. I hope so.* Other than the spear in his gut. *Damn you, Chala.*

"Yes, it's me. Iihil ... let me go." He was panting now, his breath coming out in short, harsh breaths. "I'm dying, aren't I?"

"You're *not* going to die." He tried to be calm for Aik, but he was scared to death.

This was far too close to his emp test, when Aik had lain on the table at Mountainhome with his guts exposed. What if Chala was right, and Aik had to die for the rest of the world to live?

I don't accept that. He took a deep breath. *Stay calm, Raven. He needs you.*

He knelt next to Aik, taking his hand. If this was really it ... "Aik, that night at the Manor House ... you told me you loved me. I ..."

Aik squeezed his hand. "I know, Rave. I've always known."

"You did?"

Aik laughed, but it turned into a cough, with more blood. "Yes, you lunkhead," he managed when the fit passed. "Who's the cotton-headed idiot now?"

He grinned in spite of himself. "Guilty as charged." It wasn't the reunion he'd hoped for, but it would have to do. *I'm not letting you die.*

Aik winced in pain. "Rave, it hurts. Sweet Freja, it hurts." He whimpered, grasping at the spear as if to pull it out.

"Leave it. If we remove it, you'll only start bleeding worse."

Aik nodded, his red face turning almost white. Still, he managed a sardonic grin. "What ... took you so long to find me?"

Raven hugged Aik as gently as he could. "I should never have gone without you."

Aik nodded. "I'm sorry ... sorry I'm like this." His teeth chattered.

He let go and shook his head. "Don't be. Neither of us is who we were." He held up his scaly arms. "Body or mind. We make quite a pair."

"We do." He coughed again.

Raven put his worries aside for the moment. "What happened to ... the other one?"

"Iihil? He's still inside me. He just ... let me run things, for now."

He nodded. It was surpassingly strange to hear Aik talk about the aaveen like that, but what wasn't strange anymore? "We'll sort that out. I have to get you to someone who can help you."

Aik's hand gripped his wrist, and his red eyes met Raven's. "Take me to Anghar Mor. Iihil's ... Mother can help."

"Are you sure? What if she gets rid of you altogether?" He bit his lip so hard that it bled. "I can't lose you again."

"She won't. Trust me. Take me there now." He touched his cheek with his scaled hand. "Please, Raven."

"We're already here." He eyed the black cavern entrance behind them. Maybe that would lead them where they needed to go, but how could he be sure?

"We are?" Aik looked around.

It was so strange to see his features on this creature.

"Yes. When I stole Iihil, he said to bring him here." He felt his face flush. "I didn't have any better ideas."

Aik laughed, which turned into another cough.

"What?" He was torn between feeling offended at being laughed at and deep concern for Aik's health.

"You *stole* me. Holy hencha, that's such a Raven thing to do."

He tried to hide his smile. "Can you walk?"

"I — think so." He tried to sit up and groaned in pain. "Gods, it hurts."

"I know." He helped Aik to his feet, ever so slowly, though Aik cried out more than once.

"Raven ... hurry. I'm not sure how much longer I'm going to last."

He could feel the distress flowing off him like a fog. "Don't talk like that."

He kissed Aik on the cheek. *I'm not going to lose you again.*

He looked up at the black maw before them. *How will I find my way to this Mother?* It was an impossible task, especially in the condition Aik was in. *Don't give up. You can do this.*

"There you two are." Triya's guard — Em, was it? — stepped into the light. Her grin turned to concern at the sight of the spear protruding from Aik's gut. "Is he ...?"

Aik nodded, though the movement clearly cost him. "Still alive, and yes, Aik again, to answer both of your questions."

Em's eyes almost popped out of her head when the verent trumpeted at her. "You brought some friends."

Raven looked from one to another. "How did you find us?"

"Desla sent us." She glared at Aik. "You know Aik owes Triya a couple of urses, right?"

Aik recovered first. "Urses are the least of my worries." He managed a weak grin. "Glad it's you, and not that dour lover of yours."

"Wait, 'us'?" Raven was having a hard time keeping up with the rapidly changing situation.

"Oh, Mes is here too."

Behind her, Mes appeared out of the darkness, her perpetual scowl in place. She knelt to check Aik's pulse, seemingly untroubled by his change in looks. "Good. He's still alive. Come on. Let's get him to the spore mother." They laid out a couple of poles and a blanket, and helped ease him out of Raven's arms and down onto it.

"Wait, Desla sent you?" *I know she's here, somewhere, but how did she know?*

Em tousled his hair like he was a ten-year-old. "Hang in there, verent rider. Everything will be explained when we get you to the spore mother's cave."

So many questions. But the most important thing was that help had come. He said a quick prayer of thanks to Jor'Oss.

Aik would be all right after all. *He has to be.* He turned to the verent, his family. *Watch over Breeze?*

Overhead, a few of the fireflies floated in the wind, but they kept their distance.

Squint bobbed her head. *Go, little one. We will keep him safe.*

He threw his arms around the normally taciturn verent's neck, eliciting a wave of surprise. "I'll see you all soon." Then he let go and pulled the long talker off his belt. "Silya, are you there?"

Only static answered him.

One more thing he could try. He was the only one who could talk to all the verent. Maybe they were connected to Silya too.

He reached out through his emp. *Silya, can you hear me?*

•   •   •

Silya stared at the woman before her, held tightly in the arms of two of the ce'faine. She was dirty, her clothes covered in mud and ash, and her face was contorted into a snarl. Her eyes were so red they almost glowed, and she stank of human waste. She growled and tried to scratch at Silya with hands curled into claws, but the outlanders — a man and woman named Ilick and Hestra respectively, kept her from moving.

"Hold her tight." She put her hand on the young woman's neck, reaching into the lump there with the hencha's blue flames to pull out the heat. The skin turned black around the bite, and the remains of the firefly that had stung her shriveled up and fell out of the wound.

As if someone had cut her strings, she slumped in the ce'faines' grasp.

They nodded to her, and picked the woman up, carrying her over to lay her on the ground next to the others.

Someone would come for them soon, to clean them up and check them for other wounds. She hoped they would all live.

Chala was attending to the fallen already, using a bowl and cloth — *where had those come from?* — to clean up their faces.

Doing penance? She avoided Chala's eyes. *You tried to kill Aik.* The thought burned in her mind, and she wasn't in a mood to be forgiving about it. Still, it wasn't all the verent rider's fault.

The eshem were also working to free the remaining human victims from the fireflies' thrall. Silya avoided them too. She was too angry to talk with them.

The last she'd heard from Raven, Aik had still been alive. But that wound ... if Raven and Breeze hadn't stolen him away, Chala would have finished off the job then and there.

Another victim was brought before her. She reached out and removed the fireflies — three of them this time — and another limp body joined the others.

They were almost through what was left of the invading army. The fireflies had been the worst of it, but the others ... she would be haunted by those distorted faces for a long time.

The clouds were dissipating, and the sun would soon rise over the gap to the east. Around her, this part of the Heartland lay in ruin, the blasted ground already being overgrown by the strange alien domes of the invader.

She was exhausted. While each individual act was small, what she'd done before — opening up the crevice to the blood of the world — had taxed her almost as much as the Battle of the Gap, and she'd had little rest since. It was all she could do to stay upright, even with the hencha's help. *One thing at a time.*

She turned to find Chala in her path.

"It needed to be done." The su'faine warrior practically glowed with resolution, but there was a shimmer of something else there too.

Guilt? Anguish? Silya decided she didn't care. She brushed past Chala, not ready to deal with the su'faine warrior and the eshem. Not just yet.

She found Jai and Olly next to their verent, talking to Kerrick. Both were fully dressed, for which she assumed Kerrick was grateful. The whole *naked rider* thing took some getting used to. "Are the verent all right?"

Jai grimaced. "We lost four of them, and then the fireflies simply vanished. Or fled. One moment they were there, and the next ..." He shrugged.

"How about the riders?" Not that humans mattered more than verent, and yet ...

"All accounted for." The relief in Olly's voice was palpable.

She was still getting used to being able to feel everyone else's emotions. "Thank Jor'Oss. Any word from Raven?" She indicated the long talker at Kerrick's waist. He was smeared from head to toe with bandy fruit, and she wrinkled her nose at its rank smell. The stuff didn't age well, but then again, maybe that's what kept the fireflies away.

"Nothing yet." Kerrick squeezed the long talker hard, as if he could force it to speak.

A pang of fear clenched her chest. *I can't lose both of them.* Raven and Aik were her family, as surely as Triya was. "How about the others?"

Kerrick shook his head. He pulled her close, and she let her flames dance encompass them, cleansing them of the rotting fruit paste. He was warm next to her on this chilly morning.

"A hencha shower." Jai smirked.

"The heat's gone." She looked up at the sky in wonder.

He nodded. "A good omen."

"Yes, yes it is." She closed her eyes, content for just a moment to feel Kerrick's arms around her.

The moment didn't last.

"Silya!" Dor's voice brought her out of her safe place.

She sighed, giving Kerrick one last squeeze before letting him go. "Thank you," she whispered.

"Of course. We'll get through this." That last part was whispered in her ear before he kissed her on the cheek.

She turned to face Dor. "Yes? Did something happen?" *Gods, let it be something good.*

Dor flushed red. "Yes. No. I mean, not exactly."

"Spit it out, woman." Kerrick felt as on edge as she was.

"Sorry, of course." Dor smoothed out her robes. "Coral just reported in. The waters in the tunnels are receding, and ... I'm not the only one who went blue."

"Went blue?" She frowned.

Dor bit her lip. "That's what they're calling it. All of the sisters — or at least most of them — got the hencha flame."

She nodded. It made sense. "How strange. Guess I'm no longer the only Hencha Queen." She'd have to get used to sharing the spotlight if this went on. She glanced at the eshem, who had gathered around Chala. *Not that I ever was.*

Dor shook her head vehemently. "You'll always be the queen. At least, until —"

"No need to say it." She'd had enough reminders of her own mortality. Silya despaired of ever getting these people to stop treating her like porcelain. Formal porcelain.

Silya, can you hear me? The voice rocketed through her skull.

Raven? Her heart pounded. *How ...*

I asked the verent to track you down. His impish humor came through the link, reassuring her.

She could always count on Raven to be Raven. *Is Aik ...?*

He's alive. Silya, he spoke to me.

Her brow furrowed. *The invader?*

No. Aik. He's still in there.

Relief flooded her. *Thank the Gods.*

We're taking him to the spore mother.

We? Did he mean the verent?

Em and Mes are here. They say Desla sent them.

"Silya, are you all right?" Dor put a hand on her shoulder.

She blinked, the morning sunlight cresting the mountains suddenly bright in her eyes. "It's Raven. He says ... Aik's alive. But not well." She wished she could do something.

Silya, you need to come here. To Anghar Mor. Raven sounded dead serious now.

I will.

Please hurry, Sil. Then he was gone.

She shaded her eyes from the bright light. "He wants me to go to Anghar Mor. To meet Iihil's mother?"

The others were looking at her as if she'd gone daft.

"Well, don't all stand around. Jai, can you call ... someone to help these survivors?"

He nodded. "The verent will carry them back to Gullton."

"I'll tell Coral to expect them." Dor met her gaze. "Is it safe for the people to come out?"

"Not yet. Just a few, whoever's needed to help the wounded." She looked up at the darkening sky. "The rest of us will go to Anghar Mor. Astrid, can you take me?" It was insane, to fly into the heart of the enemy's territory. But what other choice did she have. *I hope Raven and Desla know what in Heaven's Reach they're doing.*

"Of course. Sleeker can carry us."

"Thank you." She closed her eyes to draw on the hencha's strength, fighting a yawn. She thew her arms around Kerrick again. "I'm so glad you're here."

His warmth did as much to restore her spirits as the hencha. "You're not leaving me behind again, are you?"

"I wouldn't dream of it. Can you bring Dor with you in the flitter?"

"Will do." He kissed her again, and then let her go. "Aik's going to be all right."

"Promise?" She gave him a lot of credit. Aik was still her ex, after all.

"Promise. He's strong, just like you."

She hoped he was right. She yawned, and then covered her mouth, not wanting to set up a chain reaction among the others.

Kerrick helped her saddle the verent after Astrid merged with it once more. "Be careful up there. I almost lost you once, and I'm not keen to do it again." His hand brushed hers over the pommel.

She squeezed his hand. "I'll be safer up here than in that rickety old thing." She strapped her staff onto her back, into the holster Dor had given her, making sure it was secure. *Wouldn't do to lose it somewhere over the Highlands.*

Then she swung herself up into the saddle, pleased she was getting better at it. She slapped Sleeker's side. "Let's go."

"Fly swiftly. We'll see you there!" Kerrick waved as Sleeker gathered herself and launched them into the air.

Such a glorious feeling. She closed her eyes, feeling the wind rush past her face, tousling her hair as they soared into the early morning sky. *We won the battle, but the war's not over.*

It was going to be a long day.

•   •   •

Velix watched the two newcomers place the Death Bringer on a wide piece of human-made cloth and carry him into the darkness with Raven in tow. They had seen his like before, but it hadn't ended like this.

Maybe these humans were worth all the fuss Kalix made over them. Even her own strange third kit.

I misjudged him. Maybe all of them. Sorix sounded bitter.

You were mourning. We all were. The choice to give up one of their kits had been the hardest thing they had ever done.

He is still our kit. Kalix wheezed with pain. He was recovering, but that last flight had pushed him to his limit.

Yes, he is. What a strange world this had become, where kits walked upright and spoke an alien tongue. *Rest now, my mate.* Velix nuzzled Kalix.

His smell was changing. Soon he would become the egg layer.

I ... am tired.

Velix snorted. Tired didn't cover the half of it.

Sorix settled in on one side, and Velix on the other, putting their wings over him.

It's the human's battle to fight now. Let us hope we chose wisely. Sorix used the impersonal *we* that signified the collective, but they did not sound at all sure on that last point.

They will do the right thing. Velix was certain enough for the three of them. *They will end this war, once and for all.*

20

IN THE MOUNTAIN'S HEART

DESLA KNELT ON THE ROUGH ROCK of the cavern, the floor padded by the red moss that covered most of the naked stone, making it a little easier on the knees.

The spore mother's giant bulk lifted and sagged as it breathed, like a woman on her deathbed. A small cloud of fireflies hovered over her protectively, darting aggressively at anyone who ventured too close.

What strange thoughts do you think inside that alien mind? She hoped the strange creature lasted long enough for Silya and the others to arrive.

They'd brokered a truce of sorts, a detente while they waited. Not-Aik had retreated to the shadows, where vines had wrapped around him protectively, and the light in his eyes had gone out.

She could *feel* things in the back of her mind now, things she couldn't have known on her own. Like when Raven and Aik had arrived with the verent. Or when Silya had ... done whatever she'd done to turn the tide in the battle, near the Gap. *It must be the hencha.*

Behind her, Triya sat on a rocky outcrop, chewing on something — a slice of bandy fruit, from the looks of it.

Des herself had no appetite at all — she was far too nervous. She closed her eyes and recited one of the homilies they'd taught her in the Temple, one she often used to calm herself when she was fretting over something beyond her control.

From root and branch
From stem and seed
From depths below
To fill the need ...

A commotion in one of the tunnels that led into the cavern brought her to full alertness once again. She surged to her feet, searching for the source of the noise.

The white barrier sealing off the tunnel mouth split apart of its own accord, and Raven tumbled through, carrying a strange metallic ball.

"No need to push me. I was about to ..." His voice trailed off as he took in the tropical cavern and its denizens. "Holy green hell, it's like an oven in here." He looked up at the spore mother. "What in Heaven's Reach?"

Desla laughed. "You get used to it." She wasn't sure that was true, though she'd almost forgotten the heat. She pushed a limp strand of hair away from her face.

Raven's hair was disheveled, and dirt and blood was smeared across his face. He seemed tired as an aur after rut, but his eyes lit up when he saw her. "Cheese?" He bounded across the space between them to throw his arms around her.

She rolled her eyes. "Why does everyone call me that?" Still, seeing her friend again filled her soul.

"Sorry, Desla." He let go, catching sight of the harness around her neck. "Spin, is that you?"

"Yup boss, in the flesh. And it's Ty now, please."

Raven's brow furrowed.

"Long story." Desla glanced at the metallic sphere in his hand — *is that another Spin?* — and decided she would ask later. Then she caught sight of Aik on a stretcher, and hissed. "What happened to him?"

Aik's naked body was covered in red scales, something his strange metallic armor had hidden when he'd accosted them before, and he had a tail. A spear was sticking out of his stomach.

Raven growled. "Chala tried to kill him."

"One of the verent riders?" *That* was news. *Too much to take in.*

Raven winced. "Yes. I thought it was best to leave it in." He set down the metallic sphere on top of a broken stalagmite.

She nodded. "You did the right thing." Mes and Em were looking at her expectantly. She indicated a place on a thick patch of the soft moss near the spore mother. "Put him down here. Gently!"

They did as they were told.

Desla knelt next to Aik, unable to take her eyes off the spear embedded in his stomach. He was lucky to still be alive. The shaft — bandy wood? — had kept him from losing too much blood, but if she removed it ...

She touched the strange crimson skin of his cheek. It was warm, but it was hard to tell if that was from the injury, or just part of whatever the spore mother had done to him. Her hand slipped to his neck — his pulse was still firm. *One good sign.*

Blue flames surged up her arms as she lent him a little of her strength. "I have some fellin powder we can give him for the pain."

She got up, brushing some of the moss from her knees, and went to rummage through her pack, pulling out the packet and her small wooden cup. Pouring in a little of her remaining water, she stirred in the powder.

"Is he ... will he be all right?" Raven had gone pale, as if the full import of Aik's injury had just hit him.

She put a hand on Raven's cheek. Fire ran up her arm and into him too. She didn't have one of the emps like Silya and Raven wore, but still she could *feel* that he was worn to the edge of his ability.

"I don't know. I hope so." Though it cost her, she invested some of her strength in him too.

His eyes brightened at the boost. "That's ... nice."

She blinked and pulled her hand away. "I need you to be strong, whatever may come. Here, take this." She handed him the cup she'd prepared and sank to her knees and lifted Aik's head gently. "Pour it slowly into his mouth. Not too fast, or he'll choke."

He knelt next to her. With her encouragement, he poured some of the gray water onto Aik's tongue.

Aik coughed up the first gulp, then swallowed the rest with the fervor of a man lost in the desert.

It was strange seeing his altered face. The beautiful, easy-going Guard she'd met in Gullton was gone, replaced by … *this.* Fear clenched her gut, but she tamped it down mercilessly. "Did you … talk to him?"

Raven nodded. "He … it … whatever took over him, it's still inside him. But it let him talk to me. I *think* it was Aik. It must have been." He frowned, and glanced at the harness on her chest again. "Spin … I mean, Ty, will he be all right?"

"Just a sec, Boss." Ty's golden glow passed over Aik's prone body. "His physiology is still basically human. It looks like the spear missed his vital organs."

Raven bit his lip. "Translation?"

"Sorry, Boss. He should live."

"Thank Fre'Oss. And call me Raven." The slightest grin quirked his lips.

Ty's lights flickered. "Raven it is."

Raven squeezed Aik's scaled hand and looked up at her, his eyes wet. "Can you help him? I've seen what Silya can do with that flame of hers."

"I don't know." Truth be told, she'd already pushed herself beyond her normal limits. They all had. And the damage Aik had suffered … still, she had to try.

She put her palm on his chest, near the wound, and her flames slipped into him. It felt perfectly natural. The hencha lent her strength, and her weariness slipped away.

She grimaced. His insides were … wrong. Not just the injury, but everything else was twisted and strange.

The hencha recoiled from him., and her flames went out. *Can we fix him?*

No. He's too broken. Too changed. Their words carried a heavy sadness.

Godsdammit. What good were they, if they couldn't help to save one of her friends?

Raven bit his lip. "Can you fix him?"

She bit her lip so hard it bled, tasting iron. "Not by myself. What, exactly, did he tell you?"

He looked up at the huge creature next to them and frowned. "To take him to the mother."

The mother. "She *might* be able to do it. After all, she did this to him in the first place."

"Her?" His mouth twisted in disgust.

She narrowed her eyes. "Yes. Show a little respect."

"Not gonna happen. Like you said, she did this to Aik." He touched Aik's shoulder tentatively, as if he was afraid he might break him. "You have to help him."

"I'll do what I can." She took a deep breath. "Give me a little space. I think I can keep him stable while we wait for the others." She put a hand on his cheek. "This is going to be painful for you both."

He got up and backed away a couple steps. "The others?"

"Silya and the eshem are coming." She turned to Mes and Em, who'd been watching the exchange silently. "Mes, can you take hold of the spear? Carefully?"

Mes stepped around Aik's prone form and put her hands around the shaft.

She glanced at Raven. "I'm assuming this is a simple wooden spear? No spearhead?"

He nodded. "I think so. Chala made it herself from —"

"Bandy wood. I figured." She licked her lips. "All right, that's good. That should make this easier." She put both hands around the wound, one on either side. "When I say *go*, Mes, I want you to pull out the spear, as smoothly as you can. This is going to hurt him, fellin or no."

Mes met her gaze. "Understood."

Desla let the flames flare, pressing her palms against the edges of the entry wound. "Now."

The spear slipped up and out.

Aik screamed, a horrible guttural sound that was more animal than human, his tail lashing about under him.

"Em, grab that!" She couldn't afford to be distracted.

Em leapt on the tail, and Mes threw away the spear with a clatter and helped her. Even with his injury, this new Aik was still incredibly strong.

Undaunted, Desla focused on the task at hand. She pushed the edges of the wound together, cauterizing them with her fire. It slowly sealed up, turning dark brown. *Please let it hold.*

Aik screamed again, and Raven sobbed behind her. She was dimly aware of Triya coming up to put an arm around the poor man's shoulders.

"What are you doing to him?" Raven's voice was filled with anguish. "You're hurting him!"

"Raven, stop it! She's sealing the wound. Let her be." Triya's voice brooked no argument.

Keep your mind on the task. She pushed her fire down, going as deep as she dared, hoping he wouldn't bleed too much inside before she could get him more help.

Aik's screams dulled to a low, painful moan.

Thank the gods for level-headed women. She finished her work, fusing together the last of his torn flesh as best she could. Then she let go, her flames dropping away. "It's done. It won't heal him. But it should stop the bleeding for now." She closed her eyes, exhausted once more

"I'm sorry, Des."

She looked up into Raven's eyes. They were red, his cheeks puffy. "I knew this would be hard on you." *Hard on all of us.*

"Can I touch him?"

"Of course." Silya was coming, Desla could feel it. "The others will be here soon."

He knelt next to Aik, putting a hand on his forehead. "Aik, can you hear me?"

There was no reply, but at least Aik seemed peaceful now.

Raven kissed his cheek. "Come back to me, Aiken." He said it so softly that she was sure no one else heard it.

Triya glanced at the cavern exit. "I'll go to meet Silya and the others. Raven, come with me."

Raven let her go. "But Aik —"

"Is in perfectly good hands. Come with me."

He turned away first, blushing, "Yes, Mim."

Her eyes met Triya's. *Thank you.*

Triya nodded.

"Raven …"

He glanced back at Desla.

"I think Ty should be with you." She'd been about to say "belongs to you," but that didn't sound right anymore.

Raven brightened. "Thanks, Desla." He took the harness and placed it over his neck. "Good to have you back, Ty."

"You too, Boss." Ty flashed happily. "We have a lot of catching up to do."

"I'm sure we do." He glanced at Aik's silent form. "Take care of him. We'll be back soon." Then he allowed himself to be led off.

She watched them go, then turned back to Aik. She'd done what she could for him. Now she needed to take care of herself.

She lay down next to him on the soft moss, her arm on his chest, not caring that she was in an alien world. She closed her eyes, and was asleep in seconds.

•   •   •

The spore mother could *feel* the progenitor — he was so close. He had returned to her, just when she needed him.

The moons above were drawing together. Their siren call had awakened her seed, and now they were calling to her ever more strongly. Time was short.

Through the eyes of her surrogate, she watched the strange creatures that inhabited her home. They were amazing, each a little universe of its own, unlike the aaveen who were all connected to one another.

She'd caught a glimpse of it when she'd transformed the one they called Aik.

But her contact with the female one who called herself Desla had been a revelation. She was a world unto herself, like the others of her kind, but she was also deeply connected to *this world,* and the creatures that made it their home.

The spore mother's forerunners had brought her word of quiescent eeechha in one of the towns in the great valley to the west — with humans *living inside* their white domes. She'd dismissed the report then. The forerunners, for all their capabilities, weren't exceptionally smart.

Now she wondered. *Does this world change whatever it touches?*

A small flicker of hope ignited inside her.

21

THE SUN STILL RISES

SILYA WIPED SWEAT off her brow.

High above, the twin moons were touching, drawn so close to conjunction. She shook her head. *That can't be a coincidence.*

The morning light revealed the devastation wrought upon the Highlands, a disease eating away at the very fabric of the world. The hencha in her mind seemed more distant than ever before, and no wonder. Every Tharassan animal and plant had been wiped out for a hundred kilometers, if not more.

How can we make peace with something that did this?

Wisps trailed them, dancing in the verent's wake, like little stars come to earth. And in the north, Anghar Mor loomed in the distance, a brooding dark presence on the horizon.

Even the verent seemed cowed by the events of the night. She could feel their anxiety through the emp, along with that of their riders — Astrid, Olly, Jai, and Chala.

She didn't blame the suifaine warrior for doing what she'd done. The eshem had put her up to it, and they'd acted out of a sense of responsibility toward the rest of the world. *Even if they'd been badly mistaken.*

That didn't mean she personally forgave Chala, though. Not yet. *If Aik dies …*

The flitter paced them, its rhythmic *thumpa thumpa thumpa* punctuating the otherwise quiet morning, as sunlight glinted off the blades.

Her long talker flared to life. "Hello, Sil?"

Kerrick. She freed it from her belt without dropping it, grateful to hear his voice. "Yes? Fin."

"You all right over there? You look worried. Fin."

She glanced at the little craft. She couldn't make him out inside — too much glare on the shiny hull of the flitter — but it helped to know he was there. "Just wondering if this is the right thing to do. How do we make peace with whatever did this? Fin."

He was silent.

"Kerr?"

"I was just thinking of all the time I spent hating the ce'faine. There was a lot more to the story that I never knew, until Elleck found me. Fin."

Leave it to Kerrick to see a way to set it straight. How often had she encouraged him to move past reflexive hatred? But still, it was hard to forgive in the face of so much wanton destruction. She needed something solid to ground herself in. "Kerrick, if we survive this —"

"Yes."

"You didn't even let me finish —"

She could *hear* his grin. "If it means spending more time with you, then it's yes for me. Fin."

"Are you sure?"

"As long as you let me have the right side of the bed. That's something I won't negotiate on. Fin."

She stared at the flitter, wishing she could see inside.

"That's a joke, Sil."

She laughed. He knew her so well. "You can have whichever side of the bed you want, *if* we come through this alive." Kerrick was a thorn in her side, but she didn't want to live without him. Not anymore. Not now, not ever. "Fin."

She wondered what the Temple would have to say about a man moving in with the Hencha Queen. Then she decided she didn't care. *I'll bet Jas would have approved.*

"We're here. Fin."

Startled, Silya looked up to see Anghar Mor's slopes rising above them, its broken peak tracing a black, forbidding silhouette against the brightening sky.

The verent descended toward the dark plain at the mountain's foot, followed by the flitter. Despite the recent floods and rain, the ground was baked dry and cracked by the heat. The rising sun glinted off the ice to the north, which looked to have retreated considerably from where the maps had shown it, and to the east a new river had carved a path deep into the regolith, funneling melted ice water down to a swollen Lake Zeraya.

Astrid's verent alighted on the cracked ground, stirring up a cloud of dust, which the flitter's spinning blades flung into the air.

She slipped off the beast's back, her boots crunching on the baked earth, and unlatched the saddle so Astrid could join them. She wiped the sweat off her brow with the back of her arm. *Gods, it's hot.*

"Silya!"

She spun around to see her mother and someone else — Raven! — coming out of a narrow defile in the mountain fifty meters upslope. "Mother!"

She could feel Triya's relief, even across the distance that separated them. She dropped the saddle and ran up the slope and into Triya's arms.

"I'm so glad to see you again." She squeezed the surprised woman tightly. She smelled of bandy fruit.

"You are?" Triya blinked in the bright sunlight.

"Oh gods yes. Thank Jor'Oss you're safe." She'd never thought she would need her mother, but she was very glad Triya was there.

Triya hugged her back just as tightly. "You too. Oh, it's good to hold you in my arms, little one."

Warmth surged through her. "You look good." She felt Kerrick come up behind them with Dor, but they kept their distance from the reunion.

"I look like hell." Triya was shaking in her arms.

Wait, are you crying? Silya held her out at arms' length. "You are. You're crying!" She couldn't remember the last time she'd seen her mother weep.

"Can't a mother cry, knowing her only daughter is safe?" Triya's voice was brittle, near to breaking, her eyes wet.

"Cry all you want." She let her mother go and wiped the moisture from the corners of her eyes. Whatever remained of the bitterness between them evaporated like mist off a lake. "I love you, Mamma."

"I love you too, Sil. And I'm so proud of you."

Someone cleared their throat.

She turned to face Raven. Something flashed on his chest, a small silver sphere, a little bigger than her closed fist. *Spin?*

Raven looked drawn and pale, as if he hadn't slept for days. *None of us have.* "Is he ...?"

He nodded. "Aik's alive. Desla is looking after him." He glanced over his shoulder. *We should hurry.*

She blinked. Hearing Raven in her head was going to take some getting used to. She'd been afraid that Aik ... well, it didn't matter now. He was alive. "Did he talk to you?" She said it aloud for Triya's benefit.

"Yes ... Iihil ... the invader ... let him go."

Iihil? It has a name? "Come on. You can fill me in on the way."

Kerrick chose that moment to close the gap between them, glancing over Raven's shoulder at the mountain. "What's happening in there?"

She hugged him. "Aik's all right. But we should go."

Triya glanced at the handsome Guard and then back at her daughter. "This is new." As she wiped her eyes, a broad smile spread across her face.

"Later, Mother." She really didn't want to give Triya the satisfaction. Maybe some things hadn't changed between them — it was comforting, in a strange way. She pointed at the little sphere in the makeshift harness around Raven's neck. "Spin, I presume?"

"At your service, your High Muckity Muckness. Though it's Ty now, not Spin. I would bow, but I don't have a body."

Kerrick grinned. "He has you pegged."

She wasn't sure whether to laugh or growl. "Ty?"

"It's a long story, apparently." Raven bit his lip. "You'll have to forgive him. He has an odd sense of humor."

Silya shook her head. Was this her new normal? Surrounded by advisors and verent, about to charge into the lair of an invading species, and carrying on conversations with shiny silver things? "Nice to meet you, Ty."

"Likewise, Your Muckness."

This time she laughed out loud. *At least I have friends and allies, strange as they might be.*

They started toward the mountain together. Raven looked up. "I see you brought company."

One of the wisps slipped past her, dancing around her head. "They seem to be everywhere." Just their presence brought the temperature down to something bearable.

He nodded. "They're storytellers, I think. They carry little bits of the world with them."

"Maybe so. But they're more than that." She wasn't quite ready to explain her theory about her dreams of ice, and the end of the world.

He raised an eyebrow.

"I'll tell you more about it later."

Triya led them up the slopes of Anghar Mor. "It's a bit steep going in, so watch your step. Then things get ... strange."

Stranger than this? She looked around at the empty blasted plain the morning sun had revealed. As they arrived at the narrow ravine, the ground rumbled ominously beneath them.

They climbed the narrow valley together, Triya in the lead, and Astrid, Kerrick and Dor following behind her. Raven walked with Silya and filled her in on what had happened since he'd arrived at Anghar Mor.

The black stone of the mountain rose above them like a harbinger of doom, the ravine closing in on them and shutting out all but a ribbon of green sky above. A trickle of water ran along the floor of the narrow canyon in the rock.

She was deeply worried about Aik. Would he be all right? Desla had been training to be a healer, but she'd never had to deal with a spear in the gut before. Had she *gone blue*, as Dor had so adroitly put it?

When the ravine became too narrow to climb together, Raven moved ahead of her, chatting with Ty.

"I think she likes me, Boss."

"Better be nice to her. She could burn you right out with that hencha fire of hers."

Ty went dark. "I'll try."

She grinned. He was a strange little creature, this artificial being Raven carried. She wanted to know more, much more about him, but it would have to wait. They had more pressing concerns at the moment.

Her feet splashed in the stream, the warm water still cooler than the prevailing temperature. The footing was treacherous in places, so they went at an agonizingly slow pace. Wisps danced all around her, adding their uncertain light to the dim, narrow canyon. Every time one passed she felt a welcome breath of fresh air.

She could *feel* all of them, but especially Raven. It had been a bit much at first, all that additional sensory input, but things seemed to have settled down a bit.

Out in the wider world, she could feel Astrid's verent, and the three on the mountainside — Raven's, if she didn't miss her mark. And beyond that ... everything.

She stopped, momentarily overwhelmed by the vastness of it.

There were erphin and cephlants and aur and urse, hencha and heyfa weeds and so many more. Down below, the blood of the world pulsed, making the whole planet a living thing. It was breathtaking. Had the hencha shielded her from this before? Or was she just now awakening to it?

"You all right, Sil?" Raven braced himself against the rock to look down at her.

She bit her lip. *Am I?* "It's just ... so much."

I know. I feel it too. His eyes met hers, and something passed between them. *So much more than us.*

"Exactly." *You understand.*

He turned to continue up the defile, and she felt an unexpected warmth toward her old nemesis. *Who would have thought it? Raven and I, on the same page?* She snorted softly and followed him.

At last they reached the top of the ravine.

Are you coming? Aik's — not good. Desla's voice in her mind, this time.

Almost there.

Triya was frowning at her.

Silya tapped her temple. "Desla."

Triya chuckled. "Must be crowded in there."

"As an aur corral." She washed off the remaining bandy pulp under the flowing water. It had been Desla's idea, going into the enemy's den unarmed.

We'll be there soon. What should we expect? She was still getting used to this idea of talking to others through the hencha.

The response was immediate. *She's a mother, scared for her children. Be kind.*

She frowned. *That* was something to chew on. She wasn't feeling very kindly toward the entity that had caused so much suffering. *I'll try.*

"Ready?" Triya's face was unreadable, her face as alien as Aik's under the blue light of the wisps and Spin's golden glow.

Raven nodded. "All or nothing, right?"

A ghost of a smile slipped across her face. "Right." She leaned over and kissed him on the cheek. *He loves you, you know.*

Without another word, she turned and followed Triya's lead, feeling his eyes on her back.

Now that they were on smooth ground, they made much better time. The wisps had followed them in, and they spun and twisted among the alien life. Their passage relieved the warm stuffy air of the tunnel, though the walls seemed to draw back where they passed. *Or is that just my imagination?*

Her damp clothes dried quickly too, adding to the moisture in the air.

The tunnel teemed with life. Red stars, purple vines exploding with flowers, and a hundred other little things between them. There was a strange unity to everything, the way it was interwoven, the way it all moved together, eyes and leaves and tendrils following them as they passed. She touched a purple blossom. The petals were thick and soft as silk. She could sense it, but she couldn't *feel* it, like she could with the hencha.

Her whole world rode with her in the back of her mind, taking it all in. The hencha were curious, though maybe that was a misnomer. *Tharassas* was curious.

The tunnel felt like a sacred place. *We're the invaders here.*

They proceeded in silence. All except Ty, who was giving Raven a low, running commentary on the alien life forms, flashing his light over them. "This looks like one we saw in the main cavern, Boss, though it's a bit smaller ..."

Silya bit her lip, stifling a smile.

It was still too warm, even with the wisps. She wiped sweat off her brow again with her sleeve.

They passed through several strange white walls that split apart as they approached to allow them passage. *That's a good sign, right?*

Kerrick was right behind her, a comforting presence watching her back.

She's a mother. The thought reverberated in her head as she took in all of the strange creatures that filled the tunnel with teeming life. Red fronds waved in a non-existent breeze. Multicolored flowers bloomed as they passed, turning to follow them as if they had eyes. Maybe they did. And little green worms crawled through the teeming mass, using sharp jaws to trim off bits of loose "petals" and "leaves" like little gardeners. *These are her children.*

"We're here." Her own mother's voice pulled her from her reverie.

Raven and Triya passed through one last white wall and she followed, stepping into a large cavern.

Desla knelt there before a prone figure, in front of something almost incomprehensible.

She looked up at the presence that filled half the space and inhaled sharply, staring at it. *The spore mother.*

It was enormous and white, so convoluted and entwined into the cavern walls that it was hard to take in at one time. There were dozens of domes like the coryx, some covered in deep wrinkles, some smooth as a baby's bottom. Twisting red tubes connected them all. And there were pulsing — organs? — that looked like a cross between a heart and a brain. All of these crammed into the space in an almost haphazard manner. She let out a whistle. "Holy mother of Jas. This is the *mother* Aik was talking about?"

Desla simply nodded as the others crowded around to get a look, an almost reverent look on her face.

The place smelled ... loamy, like fresh-turned soil. The floor of the cavern was covered in scarlet moss, and the walls were layered with more of her children, though it was much quieter than the tunnels. *Like a sanctuary.*

A handful of fireflies buzzed around them, joined by the few wisps that had accompanied her. *Don't hurt them.*

We won't. Tharassas seemed as amazed by all of this as she was, though surely they'd seen it through Desla's eyes already.

She wasn't sure what she'd pictured. Certainly not this. She despaired of ever finding a way to communicate with such a strange being, let alone end the war between them.

Aik's strange form lay before the spore mother, on a padding of soft red moss, his tail thumping softly. Raven knelt beside him, taking his red-scaled hand.

Desla blinked, as if becoming aware of her surroundings again, and turned, eyes going wide. "Silya!" She threw herself into Silya's arms, for a moment the enthusiastic, almost flighty initiate Silya had known in the Temple, before the world had changed. "Thank Jas you're here."

Silya hugged her back, feeling almost maternal, despite the small difference in their ages. "I was worried about you too. Are you all right?" *How could anyone be, under these circumstances?*

She drew on the strength of the hencha to push back her doubts and fears.

Desla let her go. "I ... think so. It's a lot." She glanced over her shoulder at Aik. "I've done what I can for him. I don't think he's feeling any pain."

Silya knelt next to the one who had been the Death Bringer, and also so much more. This close, she could still see his human features on the scaled face. He looked far less frightening with his eyes closed and his armor removed.

Kerrick put a hand on her shoulder. Its warmth gave her some comfort as she stared at what had become of her once-lover, now old friend.

Aik had scales and strange bumps over much of his body, more apparent now that the silver of the gauntlet was gone. His skin shaded from a pale pinkish-red on his face down to black-topped red scales everywhere else. His long arms ended in clawed hands. And there was the tail, long and sinuous and twitching, as if he were in a dream state. Even so, she could see hints of her friend there, especially in the strong jaw and the fullness of his cheeks.

Desla squeezed her hand. "Raven spoke to him, before he passed out. Aik is still in there."

A stifled sob told her Raven was standing behind her too, looking over her shoulder. "Gods, it's hard to see him like this."

She knew exactly what he meant. This wasn't Aik. *Jor'Oss allow that he really is still with us.* She traced the sign of infinity across her chest, then put her palm on Aik's chest, letting the hencha flame sink into him, feeling the path the spear had taken. Desla had done her best to stitch Aik's flesh back together, but it was still ... wrong. The bones of his rib cage were bent askew, broken where the spear had entered, and he was slowly bleeding inside. "He seems ... stable. You did well."

Desla bowed her head. "Thank you, Mim."

She took a deep breath. *Time to try to speak with the spore mother.* She squeezed Desla's hand. The poor girl — no, woman, she corrected herself — must have been scared stiff, dealing with all of this alone. She looked back at Triya, Mes and Em. *Well, not entirely alone.* She could think of no one she'd want at her side more, in such difficult circumstances.

She got up, her tired joints protesting, and wondered once again about the strange creature. "Now, how do we talk to her?"

Desla bit her lip, clearly holding back.

"What? Tell me." She was eager to get this thing done.

"She has a surrogate."

Movement out of the corner of her eye caught her attention, as something shuffled out of the shadows.

A child might have drawn it, trying to make a copy of Aik with colored pencils — sharp edges and uneven lines, all creating a jumble that almost hurt her eyes to look at. It moved with a strange inhuman gait, shuffling wetly forward.

Raven's hand dropped to his knife hilt. "What in Heaven's Reach is that?"

Desla put a hand on his shoulder. "It's all right. He's ... a translator. I call him Not-Aik. The spore mother made him to talk to us. He won't hurt you."

He frowned, but let go of the knife.

"Ready to talk?" Desla glanced at the spore mother.

Silya nodded and took her hand. "Raven, come with us."

He looked up at her, startled. *Are you sure?*

You're a part of this too. She tried to reassure him through the emp, though she was by no means certain herself.

He glanced at the real Aik. "She can help him?" His voice quavered.

"We think so." *I hope so.*

"Then I'm in." He stared the strange creature as it approached, his lip quavering.

She took Raven's hand too, squeezing it in what she hoped was reassurance.

The former initiate was filled with certainty, radiating off her like sunshine, which bolstered their flagging courage.

Silya turned her attention to Not-Aik. It was a haphazard creature, taller than its namesake. Its reddish skin hung loose on its body, as if it had lost a lot of weight. It had thick hair, almost like vines.

Desla glanced at her. *May I? I've spoken with it before.*

Silya inclined her head. *Go ahead.* The world rode on their shoulders.

Blue wisps spun around the creature, illuminating it in a pale, shifting spotlight as the hencha mind examined it. Not-Aik shivered.

"Leave him alone." Desla shooed them away with a wave of her free hand. "We've brought the progenitor, as you asked. Will you abide by the terms of our agreement?"

The creature's "lips" moved. "Yes. Bring him to me." Its voice was strange, as if it had a mouthful of gravel.

Silya shuddered. Not-Aik moved *wrong* as well, a parody of a real human being. Still, she had no other choice. *I have to trust Desla.*

Raven looked nervous. "What's the agreement?"

She knew before Desla opened her mouth, though she couldn't say exactly how. "The spore mother is dying." The alien's white skin was turning gray, wrinkled and sagging around the edges, aging as they watched. Despite her misgivings, she felt a pang of pity for the creature.

Mes stepped forward. "So why don't we just wait her out? Or help her along?"

There were mutters of agreement among the others.

Desla turned to look at her, and she took an involuntary step back at the force of her gaze. "Because she may be the last of her kind. She came to Tharassas long before we did." She closed her eyes. "And because she's the only one who can save Aik."

Silya took a deep breath, surprised at the sentiment that filled her. "She and her kind have done terrible things to our world. But she's a mother." The mother of all these creatures, including the one who had inhabited poor Aik's body. "She only wants what's best for her children."

What, exactly, might that be?

Desla hesitated. "Ask her yourself."

Silya met her gaze, searching Desla's eyes. "How?"

"Put your hand on his cheek." Desla indicated Not-Aik with a lift of her head. "He will help you talk to her."

She glanced at Raven.

His scowl had settled into more of a grimace. "Do whatever you can to save him." His eyes pleaded with her.

She nodded. Letting go of both of their hands, she stepped up to the curious creature, studying it, searching it for any trace of humanity, of kindness. Up close, its faults were even more evident, its folded skin mottled and distorted as if covered by mold.

Its flat gaze gave nothing away. She shuddered again, wondered what kind of intelligence was looking at her from those dull eyes.

One way to find out. She touched his cheek, and fire ran up her arm and through her palm.

22

IINDREE

THE WORLD SPUN OUT from under her. Silya's stomach twisted as she grasped for something, anything to stop her fall.

Then, just as quickly as it had shifted, everything righted itself again, and she was back in the cavern, but she was all alone. "What in the green holy hell ...?"

"Silya."

She spun around to find Triya there. All of the others were gone. "What happened? Where is everyone?"

"This isn't real." Her mother stared at her, as if waiting for her to catch up.

Silya looked at her as if she'd gone crazy. "What do you mean, this isn't *real*? I was just here, with Desla and Raven and ..."

Something else was different. The wisps were gone, and the fireflies too. And the spore mother ... she looked better. *Healthier?*

Then it dawned on her. "You're *her*."

The figure of her mother nodded. "I thought this form might make it easier for us to talk. My translator is not ... ideal."

"That's an understatement. He's godsdamned creepy."

"He was a first attempt. Please don't hold my ineptitude against him."

That was a *five croner* word. "How do you speak our language so well?"

Triya smiled, as if Silya had just scored a point. "We're speaking mind to mind. Yours supplies the right words."

"Ah." *Stranger and stranger.* Of all the things she'd expected might happen when she touched Not-Aik, talking to her mother's likeness had *not* been one of them. "What's your name? What do I call you?"

"I've ... never had a name. There's been no one to share it with."

How lonely she must be. She tamped down that little bit of pity, reminding herself that she was dealing with an adversary.

The spore mother drew herself up, squaring her shoulders. "You may call me Iindree. It means roughly 'sparkling gem under the rock.'"

"Eeendray. It's beautiful." How strange it must be to have never needed a name. She forged ahead. "What do you want from us? You have to know what kind of damage you've caused." So many lives disrupted. And how many killed? "Will you bring Aik back to us?"

Iindree met her gaze. "To explain, I have to show you where we came from, and why we are here."

Listening to the alien's words coming from her mother's lips was uncanny, maybe even worse than the Not-Aik thing. "Maybe you can be ... someone else? Anyone else?"

Triya's face shimmered, and Iindree became Daya, her old mentor. "Like this?"

"No. Not her." Her brow furrowed as she searched for someone who wouldn't engender the wrong kind of feelings. "How about the sea master?"

Iindree's appearance changed again. She grew taller and thinner, becoming Zev'Nek in all her glory. Yet somehow softer than the real sea master. "Like this?"

She nodded. "That's better." She could be *angry* at this one. Or at least not clouded by her emotions.

In the back of her mind, she could feel them all ... Raven and the verent riders, the eshem, the sisters, the hencha ... and strangely, even Ty. All of them rode with her, seeing what she saw.

I'm an ambassador. It was a strange position for someone ... barely more than a girl, really, who three weeks before had been running chores as a Temple initiate.

"All right, show me."

Iindree nodded. She touched Silya's cheek gently. "This is who we are."

She closed her eyes, waiting for something to happen.

At first, there was the merest suggestion of light, a red flicker, like the embers of a dying fire. Or a firefly. Then it grew into a flash of heat, and a hot floodtide poured through her, like when she'd first accepted the hencha. It threatened to sweep her away, but she held on to her moorings — her world, herself, her gathered friends and allies. And as it steadied, she saw the flood for what it was. An entire history, compressed into an instant.

She watched the evolution of a species, from dank swamps of a far-away world — Uurccheea — as they raised themselves out of the muck and mire. Small family groups grew and expanded. Soon there were hundreds, no, thousands of them, expanding like a fungus, spreading to new parts of their hot and humid world.

They mastered fire, and tools. Wars were fought, discoveries made and new things invented. They flourished and developed a culture both beautiful and surpassingly strange. One, like Tharassas, where all its parts were a connected whole, though the spore mothers.

Time raced ahead and cities grew, though they were nothing like human towns. There was a collective resolve at work that Silya sensed more than actually understood, and war became a thing of the past.

Technology flourished, and soon enough in the geological span of time, they reached for the stars. A new world on the far side of their sun — Eev-uurccheea — was discovered and terraformed to become their second home. This new world grew to resemble their birth world, changed by the spore mothers into the perfect place to house their children.

And then the leap to the stars.

At first the galaxy seemed a welcoming place, if filled with mostly barren worlds. The aaveen came to understand what a precious thing life was, and how fortunate they were to have evolved on such a beautiful, fertile, thriving planet.

Then they found another such world, one teeming with its own strange life forms. After a few successful attempts at communication and a promising alliance, something went terribly awry. Almost overnight, *friend* became *enemy*.

The concept of war returned to the aaveen. A long and bitter conflict broke out between the races, one that spanned the stars. A fight that ended in the destruction of both of the aaveen home worlds.

Only a few escaped the destruction, outward bound in a desperate flight away from all they had ever known. Searching for a new place to call home. And one of those found another welcoming world, with green skies and two moons, so like the home they had lost, though for them bitterly cold.

She blinked, coming back to herself.

She was sitting on the soft moss of the cavern floor. Her head felt like she'd just woken up after an all-night bender in one of the cheap taverns out on the edge of Landfield. "Oh gods, that hurt."

"Are you functioning properly?" Iindree leaned over her, Zev'Nek's eyes sparkling strangely.

"Yes, I think so." She rubbed her temples. "It's just ... that was a lot."

"I apologize. I'm still learning how to properly interface with your kind." Her voice slurred a little toward the end.

Silya looked up at her. She looked ... ragged. *Melted at the edges?* "And you ... or one of your foremothers ... landed here." The headache subsided.

"Yes. Many cycles ago."

Cycles. Years? Her brow furrowed as she collected her thoughts. She tried to imagine alien worlds out in the vast darkness of the sky. "Are there ... more of you? Out there, somewhere?"

Iindree looked infinitely sad. "I don't know. Maybe somewhere. We ... didn't mean to cause such harm, but we also don't want to die. We may be the last of the aaveen." She touched Silya's cheek again. "You will understand, you who carry the spark of new life within you."

That snapped Silya's attention back to the present. "What?"

"You are a spore mother too. You carry a little spark inside your womb."

Silya blinked, another surprise in a day full of them. It couldn't be true. And yet ...

She closed her eyes, searching inside herself for something … different. *Something not me.*

There it was. A new life. A small flickering flame inside her own. Surely it was far too early to know … most women didn't until they missed their monthly trial. And yet, she could feel it there, growing inside of her. Hope blossomed in her, real hope for the future. Her own, and for the world. *But what will Kerrick think?* "How did you —"

An incongruous smile ghosted Iindree's human face. "Mothers know."

She looked up at Iindree in wonder. "A little girl." She would do anything to protect her. Just like the spore mother had. She had to remind herself that this was an alien creature before her, not her rival in Gullton. "What do you want?"

"To protect *my* daughter." She said it without hesitation. "I want you to help her grow. I've witnessed what this world can do. How it has changed your kind, turning you away from your own destructive impulses." Her eyes fixed on Silya's, her gaze pleading. "I am dying, Sil'Aya. In a few short hours, I will have run my course. I tried to birth a world and … I am dying. Please help me save my people."

Though she couldn't read the emotions of the aaveen like she could her fellow humans, the pain radiating from Iindree was clear.

A hundred thoughts rushed through her mind. A myriad of possibilities.

She could say *no*, and end this right now.

She could say *yes*, and then destroy the seed before it ever germinated to rid the world of the threat once and for all.

She shook her head. Wasn't that what Chala had tried to do? Wasn't that the brute, typical human response? *Destroy that which we don't understand?*

If the hencha had taught her anything, it was the value of change and cooperation — a whole world united in a common purpose. From what she had seen, the aaveen were the same.

She held the fate of an entire race on her shoulders, a burden she had never expected to bear. *How can I be responsible for the destruction of an entire race?*

The clock was ticking. Aik needed help, and her friends needed an answer as much as the spore mother did.

Silya closed her eyes, feeling the spark of life in her belly again. *What kind of world will you grow up in?*

Suddenly what she had to do became as clear as a summer day. She reached for the hencha, for Tharassas. *Are you there?*

She felt the ponderous presence in her mind. *Yes, Sil'Aya. We are with you.*

Their solid presence comforted her. *There might be another way.* Another path besides the cycle of annihilation and rebirth the world had followed twice before. A way that didn't end the world in fire or ice, now or later.

She opened her mind to them so they could see what she intended. *Will you allow it?*

The world mind filled her, judging her plan, her heart, her mind. Judging all of her kind, maybe? *To determine if we are worthy?*

It took just an instant, and then they withdrew, leaving her to herself.

So? She waited for their response, holding her breath.

There was a long silence. Then at last the hencha mind responded. *We will do what we can.*

She exhaled deeply. *Thank the gods.* For just a moment there, she'd feared they would reject her. She opened her eyes to face Iindree. "The hencha agree. They will help."

Iindree ... shifted. It wasn't so much a physical thing. Her whole aspect seemed to soften for a moment, like melting candle wax, before snapping back into place. "I am grateful." She closed her eyes, a very human gesture, and when she opened them, they were wet with tears.

Maybe it was mimicry, but she was moved by Iindree's show of emotion. "What happens now?"

"Bring me the progenitor. I will fix him, and then return him to you as he was."

Something nagged at her. "What will happen to his possessor?"

Iindree blinked. "Iihil? He will return to me, and to my seed daughter." She stared at Silya for a moment. "Thank you for asking. You are a credit to your people, Sil'Aya."

"I —"

But Iindree was already gone, and so was the empty cavern.

Her eyes flew open. She staggered, feeling woozy, as if she'd just awoken from a hencha wine-drunk nap.

Raven caught her, helping her find her footing. "Are you all right?" He brushed back a stray lock of his red hair.

She nodded, touching her belly. "I will be. She agreed."

Raven tilted his head. "Agreed to what?"

"You didn't see it?"

He shook his head. "Not when you spoke to the hencha."

Silya blinked, the world slowly coming back into focus. "To help Aik." She turned to find the eyes of all the others on her as well.

The hencha mind filled her again, and when she spoke, the voice was not her own. It was infinitely older — and wiser.

"We will help the spore mother — Iindree, as she calls herself — and her kind become a part of this world. Just as we helped your kind find your place here."

Triya was the first to break the stunned silence. "You mean through the Hencha Queen?"

She nodded, still channeling the hencha. "And the eshem, and the emps. And the verent too."

The hencha reached out through her to touch Raven's face, her flames caressing him. Silya felt his anxiety dampened. "You will never be alone again, little thief."

He stiffened under her touch. "You knew?"

She nodded. "We were with you all along. You were never alone." Then they were gone, though Silya could still feel the hencha's presence in the back of her mind. The dizziness returned, and she grabbed hold of Raven's shoulder for support.

Desla put an arm around her too, a warm presence at Silya's side.

The mood of the room shifted from fear to acceptance. They would go along with her, with the hencha. This would all be ended.

One bright spark of anger and fear stood out. She searched the room, the discord a sharp thorn in her side, and quickly found the source. "Mes, no!"

Triya's guard had quietly made her way to Aik's side, picking up the bloody bandy spear. As Silya watched in horror, she raised her arm to throw it at one of Iindree's white domes.

Time slowed to a crawl.

Raven let go of Silya to throw himself at her, but he was too slow.

Mes dodged out of his way, pulling back her arm again to launch the spear.

She didn't know if the thing would really hurt Iindree, but if it made her angry enough to lash out, everything they'd agreed upon could fall apart.

She reached out with her emp to try what Raven had done to Chala earlier.

Then Dor slammed into Mes from behind, knocking her to the ground and sending the spear clattering across the floor to come to rest by the cavern wall.

"Enough!" Silya roared, her limbs hardening and crackling with fire. "We will help save Iindree and the aaveen, and all this unnecessary conflict will come to an end." The cavern shook with the power of her voice.

She reached out a long arm and picked up the spear. She held it aloft in both hands. Blue fire spread along it, lighting up the whole place. Instead of turning to ash, it shimmered and then burst into a myriad of wisps, flying up into the air.

The hencha left her then, and the cavern shifted as she became herself, just *Silya* once again. Without the strength of the hencha flowing through her, she felt smaller, but a bit of that iron remained in her spine.

Triya and Em lifted Dor gently off of Mes. Em knelt next to her lover and whispered something urgently.

Mes shook her head, but then succumbed, dropping it between her knees. Then she looked up at Silya. "I'm sorry."

"Things have … changed. Mes will come around." Triya stepped forward to put a hand on Mes's shoulder. "You were just trying to protect us, but now we all need to listen to Silya."

She looked around the room. "Do you all agree?"

Triya nodded, and one by one, the others did too. Everyone except Mes.

She released her staff from its holster along her back and lifted it before her. "Then each of you will swear an oath on the hencha. To Tharassas. And I will swear it with you." Silya held her breath, awaiting their reply.

Mes looked up, her face red. "To Tharassas?"

She nodded. "We must all work together to heal this world."

Mes nodded. "I will do it."

"What do we do?" Triya was eying her appraisingly.

She held up the staff. "Touch the wood. Quickly now. We've not much time to spare."

Everyone put a hand on it, everyone except Aik.

She would do the same with the eshem, when the time came. "I swear myself to Tharassas, to do all within my power to heal and protect this precious world."

The others repeated her oath, word for word.

The black staff flared once with a brilliant flare of aquamarine light, and then faded into darkness, leaving Silya momentarily blinded.

"It is done." *The gods allow that it holds.*

Raven looked fidgety. "Can we move this along? Aik needs help."

"Yes, it's time." She addressed Iindree's translator. "We are agreed. We will care for your seed and help her thrive in harmony with this world. Bring Aik back to us."

A wave of emotion coursed through the room like a singular thought that contained a multitude. *Relief. Love. Sadness.*

"It will be done."

Was it just her imagination, or did Not-Aik sound just a little more human?

•　　　•　　　•

Raven looked up at the spore mother, the strange alien creature that Silya had called Iindree. The one who had taken Aik away from him. *How can I trust you?*

Despite her bizarre appearance and great size, Desla had insisted that Iindree wasn't so different from a human mother. She was sentient, and she felt love, fear, and pain for her offspring. He wasn't so sure, but he'd sworn not to hurt her.

Ty lit up on his chest. "Will the Chief be all right?"

"The chief?" He blinked, confused.

"It's what he calls Aik." Desla put a hand on his shoulder.

"Ah. I hope so." He bit his lip. "What happens next?"

As if in response, the white dome closest to them split open, spilling out a welcoming golden light.

Silya turned to Not-Aik. "What now?"

The strange creature regarded them, then turned its blank gaze to Aik's prone form. "Bring him inside. I will fix him."

"Thank you."

Raven had to trust that Iindree would do the right thing. Her progeny's future depended on it. In truth, he trusted Silya far more than the aaveen monstrosity before them. "Are you sure?"

She met his gaze. "It will be all right."

He sighed. *I hope you know what you're doing.* Then again, he'd listened to Aik, and had brought him down here in the first place. *This is my responsibility too, as much as I want to blame everyone else.*

Without another word, he and Silya lifted Aik's nearly lifeless form between them. Aik was far heavier than he remembered, but Silya lifted his shoulders as if he weighed no more than a sack of feathers.

Aik moaned once, his tail twitching, then settled back into unconsciousness.

Hang in there, love.

They carried him into the dome. It was like a cathedral, the pulsing golden light from the rippled ceiling edging Aik's body in gold. It reminded him, strangely, of his old lair under Gullton, though this was light, where that had been mysterious and dark.

They laid Aik gently on the ground, which was covered in the same soft red moss as the cavern.

"You always take me to the strangest places, boss." Ty's golden light was washed out by the glow of the dome walls.

"Shush, Ty." Still, he couldn't help but smile. He knelt next to Aik, across from Silya, and she did the same.

"I should have known this whole mess would end up in another lair." A smile quirked the edges of her lips.

Great minds think alike. "Is he ... will he ...?" He couldn't finish the sentence.

Silya reached over Aik's prone form to squeeze Raven's shoulder. "He *will* be all right. We have to believe that."

He could feel the doubt in her that mirrored his own, but he chose to ignore it. He took Aik's hand, and then leaned over and kissed Aik's red cheek tenderly. "Come back to me, Aiken Erio."

Silya's own cheeks were wet. "Dammit, Aik, you better come back from this."

Raven met her gaze. "Remember the time he got in trouble with the Guard for being late, because he couldn't get his boots laced up to regulation?"

She shot him a grateful look. "Or the time he said he wouldn't eat those berry foldovers his mother made, because the berries had grown on public land, and that was stealing?"

He grinned. "He's such a lunkhead." His smile faded as he looked down upon the transformed Aik.

Silya squeezed his shoulder. "Let's go. She can't heal him with us in here."

He nodded. He touched Aik's cheek one last time. *I'm waiting for you.* He pulled the knife Aik had given him — the one his mother had crafted — out of its boot sheath and lay it on Aik's chest, wrapping his fingers around it.

Silya's eyes narrowed, but she said nothing.

They got up as one and left the golden glow, ducking out into the warm cavern. The others were gathered in a tight knot at the far side of the cavern, talking quietly.

Silya took his hands. "He's yours now, Raven verent rider." She said it without a hitch. "I'm glad that Aik found someone he can give his whole soul to."

A smile ghosted his lips. "And you have that handsome hunk of a Guard over there. Fair trade."

She glanced at an obviously anxious Kerrick across the dim cavern. "I suppose it is."

He frowned. "Was it always going to be like this?"

She raised an eyebrow. "What do you mean?"

"Down to the three of us, at the end." Was it only a matter of weeks before, when he'd been trying to throw her out of his lair after swallowing that damned verentling?

"Four." Her hand fell to her belly.

"What?" He looked at it, and then up at her. "You mean ...?"

She nodded, her face pinched with worry. "It's not the best time —"

"Sil, that's amazing!" *I'm going to be an uncle! Well, sort of.*

"Shhh. Don't say anything. I want to tell Kerrick first." She blushed. She actually blushed.

"Of course." He leaned forward to kiss her cheek, glancing at Triya. "You will be a much better mother than she was."

"Thank you. You're a good person, Rav'Orn. Thief or not."

"And you are too, even if you are a —"

"Watch it, gully rat."

"I was gonna say 'Hencha Queen.'"

As the white dome finished sealing itself behind them, she chuckled and threw her arms around him, surprising him and squeezing him so tightly he thought she might crack a rib.

"Everything all right?" Kerrick looked back and forth between the two of them nervously.

"It will be." She took his hand to lead him away. "I have something I need to tell you."

23

THE DEATH BRINGER

AIK FLOATED IN A GOLDEN WORLD, light streaming down from on high like some strange golden sun.

His chest was on fire.

Something happened to me. Something bad. He searched for it in his memory, but his recollections were vague. Riding on a verent. An urse. A flash of blue light.

Then a woman — one of the ce'faine?

And a spear.

He felt the sharp point of it pierce his stomach, slipping right through his scales. And the agony of it as it rent his flesh.

He screamed.

She will fix you, aanteem.

He blinked. The golden light was overpowering, but there was ... something. Someone, next to him. *I'm not alone.*

Who was with him?

Iihil. The alien being floated beside him, peering at him through golden alien eyes. *I'm sorry for what she did to you. For what I helped her do to your world.* The aaveen's words were accompanied by a searing pain, and a stinging sense of failure and loss.

I'm sorry too. And to his surprise, he found he was. They had bonded in an unexpected way, captor and captive.

Both of them had lost their home worlds, though Aik had been too stupid to believe in Earth for far too long. Now he felt its loss keenly. The place humankind had been born was gone forever, lost to the mists of time. Before, he'd had the luxury of denial. He'd had a whole new world he'd always thought of as his, and he'd almost lost that one too. Now he had to face the truth.

Humans are stupid creatures. And he was no exception.

I know how you feel. He shared his own loss, distant as it was, with Iihil, allowing his own sorrow to show.

We are much the same. The aaveen sounded surprised, maybe gratified. For a moment they shared a burden that both had borne alone before.

Where are we? He had a guess, but he wanted to hear it from Iihil.

We're with the mother. She is … healing you. Returning you to what you were. The sadness intensified.

He frowned. *What happens to you now?*

Iihil's pain withdrew so fast that it almost gave Aik whiplash. *I go back to the mother, where Eeydra is waiting for me.*

What does that mean? The pain in his chest lessened, replaced by a persistent itch. He wanted to scratch, but he couldn't move in this strange place. *She will be glad to see you. From what I could tell, she's an amazing … aaveen.*

This time he felt a flash of humor. *We call our females uunteem, and those like me are eenteem.* Iihil's curiosity surged between them. *You are a strange one, aanteem. Are all your kind like you?*

What's this aanteem word mean?

Iihil hummed. *It's an eenteem or uunteem who loves one of the same. On uurccheea, they were considered wise ones, free from the burden of raising children.*

Ah. Always taking care of other people's kids? That didn't sound so fun.

Are you not such?

Aik thought about it. *I do love another … eenteem, I suppose. But I also want to have children with him someday.*

Iihil made a rough barking sound that he interpreted as a chuckle. *Ah, the ways of your kind are different from ours. An aanteem would never want their own children.*

For some reason, that made him sad, but there were more pressing things to worry about. *And what about the world? What happens to Tharassas now?*

The golden glow around him seemed to dim, and Iihil's sadness returned. *Mother is dying. She has made a seed and filled it with herself and all of us who journeyed with her. Soon she will cease to exist, and so will those she birthed into this world.*

A seed. So this could all happen again, at some future time?

I hope not. What happened was a mistake, one I hope we will remember not to make again.

He was startled. Was he *that* open to Iihil's thoughts?

All of this was a dream. It must be. Surely he was still inside Iihil's mind.

Or the other way around, maybe? It was all so fuzzy.

Stay with me. It came out impulsively, but it felt right. He took care of people. It was who he was. So how was this any different? *I've ... gotten used to having you around.*

Aik felt hope flare in Iihil, but it quickly burned out. *That is a beautiful offer. But I must go back to the mother. Eeydra awaits me.*

I understand. He would do anything to get back to Raven.

Still, it would have been ... interesting. I have grown fond of you, Aiken Erio.

He was startled to hear Iihil use his full name. *Like an aanteem?*

Iihil barked again. *No. Like a friend.*

You have those too? He'd been under the impression that the aaveen were all family.

I do now.

They were quiet for a moment as warmth surged through him. His stomach no longer ached. *Just promise me one thing, friend,* he said at last. *Choose better, the next time?*

Better?

If she asks you. You don't have to be her Death Bringer.

Gratitude surged within him. *We will both try to be better.*

Aik shivered. Did he know about Aer'Lis, about his betrayal of his own aanteem? Would Iihil even care? *If I get through this, I'll have to tell Raven.*

Silence fell between them again, the companionable peacefulness between two old friends.

His chest tingled. He felt effervescent, bubbly, as if he were being made new.

Would you promise me something too, aanteem? Iihil was fading.

Yes. He would do what he could, for Iihil and his people.

Help us try again. The right way, this time.

He frowned. *The right way?*

There must be a way to share this world.

He nodded. That made sense. Humans had found a way to live on Tharassas with the hencha. Or had it been the other way around? Why couldn't the aaveen do the same? Silya would help, and Raven too. *I will.*

There was no response.

Iihil?

The Death Bringer — no, his friend — was gone.

The light faded to twilight. Aik could feel his body again. The ground was soft under him, a bright red moss that was quickly turning black. The fluid that had surrounded him was draining away, leaving him wet and alone.

He held up his arm. The gauntlet was gone — for good this time, he hoped — and his skin was pink and healthy, although it was also completely hairless. He reached up to touch his head, and found that hair was gone too. *Guess I'll find out how I look as a bald man.* Hopefully it would grow back.

Am I still me? His hands went to his face. The skin there was smooth too, but it felt like his own. He was also naked as the day he'd been born.

He shivered, though the strange place he found himself in was warm enough. Above him, the domed ceiling still gave off a faint golden glow.

He stood uncertainly, finding his balance, and his hand went *down there*. He grinned. *All normal.*

He felt around in his head for any trace of Iihil. His captor and companion of the last few days was gone, but he'd left Aik his memories. Aik blinked. *So many memories.*

He'd have to rummage through them later. Right now, he had friends who were waiting for him, people who had sacrificed a lot to bring him back.

Raven must be close by. Aik had crossed half a world to find his thief — *no, my echa-aueel, my soulmate* — and in the end it had been Raven who found him.

He told me he loved me. He looked around for a way out of the strange room.

And there it was, next to him, where Iihil had been in the dream. A white ovoid the size of a bandy fruit rested on the darkened moss.

He touched the seed. As if in response, the dome around him began to shrink and shrivel up, its grey skin turning black with a loud crackling sound, the death-gasp of the spore mother, falling away into dust.

•　　　•　　　•

Silya's heart skipped in her chest like a trio of umvit.

Kerrick took her hand. "What is it? Is Aik all right?"

"I think so." Gods, this was hard. She wasn't ready to be a parent. How could she expect that he would be? *What if I tell him, and he runs?*

"Then what?" His brow furrowed. "Are you sick? Did that … thing do something to you?"

She could feel his anxiety rising. "No, nothing like that." She laughed in spite of herself at his concern. *He really does love me.* She took his face in her hands. "Kerrick, I'm pregnant."

The look on his face transformed, matching his emotions, as both surged with pure joy. "Holy henchaballs, Sil. That's … You're … We're going to have a baby?" Suddenly he was a six-year-old boy, full of simple happiness.

Relief flooded her. "Yes. And not just a baby. A little girl."

He whooped and swept her up in his arms, swinging her around and drawing the attention of everyone else in the cavern. "We're having a little girl!"

Suddenly they were the center of attention. Raven hugged her and then Kerrick, and each of the others expressed their surprise and happiness at the announcement.

And at last, Triya stood before her. "I am so proud of you." She wrapped her arms around Silya and squeezed her so hard she thought she might split in two.

"Go easy there, Triya." Kerrick's anxiety spiked again. "You might break the baby."

Silya shook her head. "That's not how it works." It was still barely a speck inside of her. Still, a part of her cheered at his genuine concern.

Triya let go and looked her over. "Are you all right?"

She wiped the corners of her eyes. "I will be." She grinned. "You realize this makes you a grandmother."

Triya scoffed. "We will not use that word in my household. Great grandmother Jas, I can't be that old, can I?"

"How about Nana? Or Nan'Aya?"

"*That* I can live with." She leaned forward to kiss Silya on the cheek, and happiness radiated from her. "Go talk to your man. I think he's a bit stunned."

"Wait until she's born." She flashed Kerrick a wicked grin.

"When's the wedding? You will be getting married, right? We can have it at the Manor in the spring and —"

"Enough, Mother." Silya kissed her cheek and pushed past her to grab Kerrick, dragging him off to a quieter part of the cavern to talk.

Silya sat with her back against the cavern wall.

Kerrick sat next to her, his hands on his knees.

She watched the spore mother breathe while gathering her own thoughts. "Are you sure you're ready for this?"

"Absolutely." He leaned over to kiss her. "If the last two weeks have taught me anything, it's how fleeting life is. We have to grab onto the good things when they come." A smile crossed his face. "And this is a very good thing."

"Yes," she said softly. "Yes it is."

He frowned. "There's something else on your mind."

She bit her lip. He was getting a little too good at reading her thoughts and feelings, even without an emp. "Did I do the right thing? With her?" She indicated the spore mother with a raise of her chin.

Kerrick pulled a piece of dried aur jerky from his pocket and began to chew on it, his brow knitted in thought. "I think you did what felt right to you in the moment."

She nodded. She'd have to deal with the eshem, and Chala,

when all of this was over. She'd insist on making all of them — and the sisters — swear an oath to care for Tharassas and the aaveen. She sighed. *So much still to do.* "So, what's next?"

He shrugged. "Hell if I know."

"You and me both." She had been so focused on the crisis, she hadn't given much thought to what she'd do in the aftermath. "For now, I guess we wait for Aik. For the rest ..."

"You and I have a new life to worry about."

"Exactly." She wasn't going to give up who she was. Not for him. Not for anyone. "I'm not going to give up being the Hencha Queen. Gullton needs me."

He leaned over to kiss her. "I would never ask you to."

"And as for marriage ..."

He raised an eyebrow. "Are you proposing?"

She laughed. "Oh my Gods, no. I mean ... would you want to?" This was all moving so fast.

Triya chose that moment to kneel beside them, offering a couple mugs of hot akka. "Perk you up."

"Gods be praised." She took one gratefully, taking a careful sip. It wasn't as good as what Verla prepared in the Temple — a little weak, and the water wasn't filtered. But all the same, it was the most delicious thing she had ever tasted. "How did you ...?"

"The other verent riders collected some water from the waterfall at the cave mouth. Desla heated it for us. She's becoming quite adept at the whole *hencha flame* thing. Much faster than you took to it."

Her eyes narrowed. "Was that a dig?"

Triya chuckled. "Of course it was. Wouldn't want to get out of practice, would we?" She winked.

Kerrick sipped from his own mug, wisely staying out of it.

Silya groaned. "So this is how it's going to be between us?" She took another sip of the akka, grateful for the flavor that washed the bile out of her mouth.

Triya put a hand on her knee. "You are my daughter. I will *always* push you. But I'm very proud of you, Sil. You made a hard choice and saved us all."

She waited for the "but." When none was forthcoming, her mouth dropped open. She could *feel* Triya's sincerity. *Damn the emp.* "That's still to be determined."

"It will work out. I trust you."

She looked at Triya — at her mother. She didn't want to say it. She hated even thinking about saying it. But she owed it to her. "I learned everything I know from you." It hurt coming out, but when it was said, a weight lifted off her shoulders.

Triya threw her arms around her, almost making her spill her remaining akka. "That must have been hard to say."

"I'm sure it was." Kerrick chuckled. "Silya here was just proposing to me when you arrived."

She sputtered. "I was not —"

"I would have said yes."

A warm feeling that had nothing to do with the akka spread through her. "You do realize, Mother, that I'll expect you to help with the babysitting —"

The ground rumbled, and blue flames sprung up along Silya's arms. "Something's happening." She let go of Triya and set down the earthenware cup, and pulled herself up to stare at the spore mother.

Goodbye, Silya, Queen of the Hencha. It was the merest whisper in her mind, and Silya knew it was the last she would hear from this traveler from another star.

Goodbye, Iindree. It was bittersweet, for all that it should have felt like a victory, The threat was over. *For now.*

The alien creature was coming apart, her now-gray skin shriveling and turning black. Her lung stopped breathing, and seams split open all along her length.

Her great bulk shuddered, and then began to turn to dust before Silya's eyes.

Not-Aik was melting away too. His arms dissolved first, and then he fell to his knees as his legs fell apart beneath him. His face and eyes were the last to go.

All around the cavern, her children shuddered and dried up, returning to their constituent dust, and even the few remaining fireflies dropped to the ground and settled into piles of ash.

In less than five minutes, the cavern was empty, save for Silya and the other humans, a few bright wisps, and piles of black dust.

She closed her eyes. "She's gone." She felt a deep, unexpected sadness, a realization that something unique and wonderful ... and terrible too ... was gone from the world.

"Is it like this outside too, do you think?" Astrid's eyes were wide.

Kerrick sidled up next to Silya, his arm slipping around her waist. He whispered into her ear, "I think it's over."

But where's Aik?

•   •   •

"Where is he?" Raven's voice echoed in the now empty chamber.

Aik got up, summoned by the sound. Something fell off his chest into the darkness, clattering on the now-naked stone.

He felt around for it and touched a cool metal *something*. Lifting it into the air, he saw what it was. *The* knife that he'd given Raven. Warmth suffused him. He clutched it in his hand and got unsteadily to his feet.

The blue wisps provided a little light, but Spin's golden glow summoned him like a beacon.

"Aik, where are you?" Raven's voice echoed in the hollow cavern under the mountain.

He stepped into the light, keenly aware how filthy he was — naked and wet and covered in the black dust from the spore mother's demise. "I'm here, Rave."

Raven's eyes went wide. "Thank Jorja!" He crossed the distance between them in two big bounds and threw his arms around Aik, squeezing him tightly.

"Hey, easy there. I'm a mess."

"Like I care." Raven kissed him, hard.

Aik kissed him back, wrapping his arms around Raven's back, holding the knife blade away from his *echa-aueel's* back. *My soulmate.*

The tension that had spooled itself around his heart over the last few weeks released itself in a whiplash that almost knocked him over, and he held on to Raven to keep from falling. At last, after all the miles, all the heartache and pain, he was home. He squeezed Raven even harder.

Raven whispered in his ear. "Careful, Aik. You'll bring us both down."

"Hey watch it there, you two. You're gonna crush me."

Aik blinked. "Spin? Good to see you, buddy."

The silver sphere actually growled. "It's Ty now."

Aik laughed. "Ty it is." He held Raven out at arm's length, his eyes searching Raven's. "And you're stronger than you used to be."

A shadow crossed Raven's face. "You … you haven't changed your mind about me, have you?"

He snorted. "Of course not. I crossed half the world to find you, didn't I?" He kissed Raven again, and this time it was slower, more sensual. The cavern around them faded away, and for a long moment, it was just the two of them in all the world. There was still a hole in his mind where Iihil had been, but for a moment, Aik felt complete.

He let go of Raven and handed him the knife. "I can't believe you kept this."

Raven's gaze dropped to the sharp blade. "It was the only thing I had left of you." He took it, and pulled another knife out of its holder at his waist, slipping it into his boot. With a grin, he sheathed Aik's knife in its new home on his belt. "Seems appropriate."

Aik laughed. "You're mine now, you know."

"And you're mine. I wouldn't have it any other way."

Someone cleared their throat behind him. "Maybe you should save this little reunion for later?"

They turned to find Silya staring at them both, trying hard to hide the smile that teased the edge of her lips.

Raven nodded, his own grin more provocative. "Of course, *hencha princess*."

"*Gully* rat." It sounded almost affectionate. She put her arms around both of them. "I'm so glad you're alive, Aik."

"Me too." He remembered suddenly that he was naked in front of everyone. His hands went down to cover his privates. *Well, this is awkward.* "Can someone maybe find me some clothes?"

Desla nodded. "I collected the ones you left behind in the cavern after … Anyhow, give me a minute."

After I hit you. He barely remembered it, like looking at himself through a deep pool. "Thanks."

They waited there, staring awkwardly at one another until Desla returned with an armful of clothes. "Here, wipe yourself off first with this." She handed him a road-worn towel.

"Thank you." He brushed off the worst of the dust and handed the towel back, and then pulled on the shirt and breeches she'd supplied. "Desla, I'm sorry for what I did to you."

She rubbed the back of her head. "It wasn't you —"

"Even so." He could see it clearly now, thanks to the memories Iihil had left him. "I think Iihil was sorry too."

She stared at him for a moment, as if taking his measure, then nodded. "Thank you. That means a lot." She handed over his boots.

He pulled them on, wondering what else he had done that he'd need to apologize for. It was all there in the memories Iihil had left him, but he wasn't ready to look at it just yet.

He looked over his shoulder, then turned to Silya. "The spore mother left something, for you, I think." He led them back to where he'd awakened.

Raven and Silya followed, and Spin's light spread ahead of them, outlining a black circle where one of the spore mother's domes had once stood. The golden glow fell over the egg, and Raven staggered backward.

Me and a cavern and a strange egg.

Aik reached out to take Raven's hand and squeezed it reassuringly. "It's not the same."

Raven squeezed back. "I know. It's just —"

"I know." Aik looked at the little ovoid, all that was left of the spore mother and her kingdom. "Maybe it would help if you think of it as a seed, not an egg." If he closed his eyes, he could still see the verentling crawling up Raven's arm, and remember how helpless he'd been to stop it. *How much worse must it be for you?*

"Yeah, that ... helps." Raven didn't sound so sure about that.

A flight of wisps circled the seed cautiously, dipping to almost touch it and then dancing away.

He put his arm around Raven's shoulder, pulling him close. He loved how they fit together. "It's going to be all right."

"Ty, is it ... alive?" Raven sounded anxious.

Ty's light played over the seed, lining it in gold. "It's ... hard to tell, Boss. It's slightly warmer than the surrounding air, which has dropped by three degrees Celsius since the spore mother's demise."

Raven whistled. "That's ... what does that mean?"

"It's getting colder in here, Boss."

Raven grinned. "It's good to have you back, Ty."

Aik squeezed them both. *My family.*

• • •

Silya knelt next to the seed.

It looked smooth, but as she peered closer, she could see that its surface was covered with fine twisting lines, as intricate as a masterfully carved piece of art.

Blue flames sprang up from her arms and ran down to touch its surface, lighting that design up in fine detail.

I could destroy it right now and end the threat forever. She had it in her hands. It *might* even be the wisest thing to do, given the terrible price they'd all paid. But somehow it didn't feel *right*. And she'd given her word ... that had to mean something.

The eshem were in her head, like a solid wall of judgment — or was she just imagining that part? So were Desla and many of the other sisters, each one a bright spark. The hencha mind was with her too, a vast consciousness that reached far beyond what she had ever considered.

She closed her eyes, and reached inside the beautiful seed as carefully as she could.

There was a spark there too, something warm and alive and curious. Like the newborn child she carried in her own belly.

But there was something else wrapped in those tight twists and grooves, etched into the very fibers of the seed. She teased it out carefully, like she might work out a splinter from her finger.

There were memories, yes, memories of the spore mother's time on this world, from her first awakening months before. And recollections of another world before this one, though they were sharp and fragmented like broken glass. The seed was life, thought, and potential. And something more.

Hope.

It radiated through her like the new dawn, a gift more profound than she — or any of them — deserved. A chance to start over for human, hencha and aaveen.

Tharassas was grievously wounded, scorched by the invader who'd given little thought to the destruction she was causing. The damage would take decades to repair.

And yet there was hope.

She dug deeper. Beneath the layer of current memories were older ones ... not from the invaders' homeworld. *From here on our world.*

The spore mother's predecessors.

This has all happened before. Triya had figured that out, but she'd missed one critical thing. Yes, the aaveen had invaded twice before and had been defeated at great cost — ice ages that lasted a generation, wiping out much of the saved memory of the hencha mind.

But when we came ... Instead of mutual annihilation, Tharassas found a way to live with us. Now it wanted her to chart a new path with the aaveen. What that would look like, she had no idea, and she suspected it would be decades before they all figured it out. But it would make her a Hencha Queen like no other.

So do we choose this path? It was a rhetorical question, as she had already said yes. But she needed the others to agree too.

One by one. she felt their approval. As they responded, they faded from her consciousness — the eshem, the sisters, Raven and the verent riders — until she was all alone with the seed. And the hencha.

It will be done as you suggest. The voice seemed amused.

Are you laughing at me? Silya scowled. After all she had been through ...

No, we are amazed by you and your race. Your tenacity. Your forthrightness. And how you found a third path, between fire and ice.

She nodded, mollified. *But why me?* It was an old, familiar question.

The ponderous weight of the world filled her mind, though it was less than it had once been. *We chose you because you are special.*

That surprised her. So many others seemed to have the potential to talk to the hencha. *How am I special?*

You have the strength, the ability, and now the wisdom. You will make the right choices and find a way to enforce them.

Hard earned, that wisdom had been. Not that she felt all that wise inside. *How did you know?*

We see you. Not only as you are, but as you will be.

As I will be? She wondered what that meant. She was grateful for their acceptance and support. *Thank you.*

"Silya, you all right?" Dor touched her shoulder, waking her from her trance.

She blinked furiously. "I don't know. I ... will be." The flames on her arms died away, but the steady warmth of the hencha remained in the back of her mind, like a banked fire.

She stood, feeling a little shaky. Not surprising — she was exhausted after being awake for far too long.

"We're all proud of you, Mim Aya." Desla smiled, and the gesture reminded her how dazzlingly beautiful the girl — woman — could be. She was going to break hearts, that one.

Somehow the formality didn't bother her. *This time.* "Thank you. And I of you."

Dor joined them, mimicking Desla's smile. "It's over. You can relax now. We all can."

She put her arms around her stalwart aide. "It's just beginning. But the worst is past." At least I hope it is.

Dor squeezed her tightly. "You'll figure it out, Sil'Aya You always do."

Touched by Dor's faith in her, Silya let her go and wiped her eyes. *I will not let them all see me cry.* She turned away and knelt before the seed again, lifting it gently in her palms. It was dense and heavy, but like the staff, she had no trouble picking it up.

The others crowded in around her to look at it.

Raven touched the wrinkled surface. "What is it?" His hand dropped down to his stomach.

"A second chance." She frowned. *So many memories these last few weeks.* "Is there something I can wrap this in?" Her eyes fell on Mes, sitting in the semi-darkness at the edge of the cavern, hands tied behind her back. "And someone set her loose. It's time for forgiveness, not punishment." She'd tell Chala and the eshem the same.

Em bowed. "Yes, Mim. Thank you." She knelt next to Mes, untying her lover's bonds.

Desla found a blanket in one of their packs. "Will this do?"

"Perfect."

She wrapped the seed up carefully in the hencha-fiber cloth — there was something poetic about that — and handed it back to Desla, knowing she would take good care of it for Iindree. "Everyone back into the tunnel, please."

Desla cocked her head. "What are you going to do?"

"Clean things up a bit in here." She wouldn't leave Iindree like this.

After everyone had shuffled out of the now dusty cavern, she stood at the tunnel entrance, where the white wall had been. She planted the staff on the had ground, and called on the hencha.

There was a deep rumble, and then a gush of indigo liquid surged into the air from the root hole of the spore mother. *Of Iindree.*

The column exploded into a cloud of wisps. They swept through the cavern, lighting it so brightly Silya had to close her eyes and hold onto her black staff to keep from being blown away by the wind.

Ice covered every available surface — floors, walls, stalactites and stalagmites, crackling through the air as it froze the remaining dust and debris. For a brief moment, the cave was a winter wonderland, filled with snow and icicles.

Her breath became a glittering cloud in the air in front of her.

Then the ice began to melt. It dripped slowly at first, and then more quickly, chunks of ice falling to the slushy floor with a crash and splash. The water flowed toward the dark hole at the back of the cavern, swirling around it as the blood of the world carried away the last traces of the alien presence.

In less than five minutes, it was over. The cavern sparkled like new.

Kerrick squeezed her shoulder. "Nicely done."

Silya started. She hadn't realized he was there.

She turned to face him as the blue glow slowly faded behind her. "She deserved better."

He raised an eyebrow. "That was beautiful. I'm sure she would have been pleased."

"So what happens now?" Raven took Aik's hand. They were together, grinning like a couple schoolboys. That seemed *right.*

Raven was holding a silver ball — something that was not Spin.

The artefacts. What will we do with them? She sighed. So many questions. Time enough to sort them all out later.

She smiled, and reached for Kerrick's hand, kissing his cheek. "Now we go home."

EPILOGUE

TY COULD FEEL Raven's heartbeat through the harness that held him to Raven's chest, a brand new one made by Aik's mother. It was a beautiful late winter day ... his sensors assured him as much. Still, he missed feeling the sun on his face, the wind against his skin.

He'd done what he promised himself. He'd helped save his friends, and the world too. Not bad for a tiny hunk of metal and circuity.

Still, he'd been ready to let go, to shut down his systems and drift off to heaven, or oblivion as soon as things were settled with the aaveen. Or to whatever awaited him after this so-called life.

Then he'd felt it.

•   •   •

You are a curious creature.

The voice was heavy, ponderous yet filled with threads of mirth and curiosity. That it was able to pry its way through his security systems was worrisome. Tharassas had no high technology capability, not that he knew of. *Who are you?*

A sense of amusement filled his mind. *What the humans call the hencha. The sum total of life on Tharassas.* It paused, and he wondered if he was being weighed in its mind. *And who are you?*

The hencha mind fascinated him. Was it like a vast organic computer, all its relays operating in sequence? Or was it something less understandable in human terms?

I'm ... Tyson. Ty to my friends. It felt good to say it, even now at the eve of his second life.

Something like laughter bubbled in his mind. *Indeed, you are. But* what *are you?*

I don't know. For his first thirty years, he'd been human. He'd started a family, marrying his beautiful Genevieve and then having a daughter with her. Life had seemed good, until they were crushed by medical bills. He'd given that life up to save his daughter, and become Spin. An AI, his humanity wiped clean.

Then the *Spin Diver*'s crash had shaken something loose, opening the door just a crack. It had taken more than a century for that crack to become a doorway, and for his old memories to come flooding through.

Now he remembered who he had been, and it was so much less — and so much more — than he was now.

What do you want to be? The voice said it so matter-of-factly that it stunned him.

It was so much like what his parents had used to ask him. "Tyson, what do you want to be when you grow up?"

He'd always answered immediately. "A starship pilot."

And here he was. It was funny the way fate sometimes gave you what you thought you wanted, while taking away what you were and who you loved. *I ... want to be human again.*

To be his own man. To walk the streets of Gullton in fancy boots like Raven's. To feel his toes in the sand and gaze out at the Harkness Sea. To see the places where his daughter Sera and her wife Jas had lived and loved, through human eyes.

Pain seized him. It was an impossible dream. *It's time for me to go.*

But before he could start the process, he was filled with warmth ... and sadness that wasn't his own.

What if you could be?

His processing stopped.

It ... it's not possible. His mind reeled at the idea. *How?* To be like he was once more, but on this new world ...

We think the new spore mother will be able to make you a body, like she did with the Not-Aik.

That ugly thing?

The hencha voice shook with amusement. *Yes. But better, with our help.* The sadness intensified. *Don't go. You are unique in all the world, and the humans will have need of you yet.*

How did they know ...? He'd told no one of his plans.

It didn't matter. This wasn't Earth. He wasn't being hacked by an enemy corporation.

He was being offered a lifeline. To be ... almost human again. To be his own man.

To be Tyson. Not Spin.

And all he had to do was to say yes. It was a simple word, three letters long, but it held an entire future in those little squiggles.

What would Genevieve and Sera think? He knew the answer immediately. *They would want me to go on. For them.*

Yes.

He could feel their relief. *We are happy to hear this. We will contact you when it's time. Know that we are in your debt.* The presence began to withdraw.

Wait! His curiosity reasserted itself.

The vast consciousness paused. *Yes?*

Could we ... communicate more? I have so many questions for you. And I imagine you have some for me as well.

We would like that. A sense of pleased amusement. *Goodbye, Tyson.* Then it was gone.

•   •   •

Today they were surveying the Old Bridge site. Raven and Aik had fallen into an easy companionship, much the same as Jas and Sera. Somehow that made Ty very happy.

His sensors told him it was a beautiful day, the sun riding high in a clear green sky, a cool breeze bringing the hint of salt from the Harkness to the west.

And far to the south, a seed was being planted, one that would one day bring him back to himself.

One day soon, I will be free. He held that thought in his primary memcache for the rest of the afternoon.

A beautiful day indeed.

•   •   •

Raven stood at the northern edge of Vulture Spine, the wind whipping his hair. Clumps of cleffer bushes were in full bloom, waving yellow in the ocean breeze. To the west, the wall of the dead was being enlarged to hold the ashes of those who had died in Gullton and its surroundings during what had come to be called the Dark Days. The fireflies had penetrated even this far, and not everyone had been safely tucked away in the caverns.

Still, there were far fewer than there might have been. *Something to be thankful for.*

"Hey Boss, want to pay a little more attention?" Ty was snarky as ever, flashing his golden lights in annoyance.

Raven laughed. "Hold your urses." He'd been startled to learn the little familiar had once been as human as him. It explained a lot.

The remains of the Old Bridge littered the chasm below, more exposed now that the flooding had ended and the waters had gone back down to their previous level. A crew of verent under Olly's supervision had begun to dismantle the wreckage to salvage its iron. He'd been thrilled to be asked to lead the reconstruction team.

Aik kissed his cheek. "Hey daydreamer, what's got your attention?"

Raven sighed. "Just thinking about everyone we lost."

Aik was silent for a moment, one of his new brooding phases since his "re-aikification," as he liked to call it. "I guess it could have been worse."

Raven nodded. "I suppose so. Even if things are still a mess." Half the crops in the Heartland had been destroyed by the invasion and the flooding, but at Silya's urging, the Council had sent out teams from Gullton to help with the replanting — that had been a fun meeting. Raven was still learning how to be a good Councilor for Landfield.

It had been a lean winter, but they'd made it through with the city's stores and the help of the hencha, which had produced their berries in prodigious quantities.

The ground still shook occasionally, but all in all things had calmed down considerably. "All right, Ty, I'm ready. What do I need to do?"

Ty snorted, sounding as human as Aik. "About bloody time. Hold me up so I can see the far side."

Why does everyone always snort around me? Raven refrained from asking how time could be *bloody.* "Here you go." He'd had a special harness made for his little accomplice, like the one Desla had fashioned, but custom made for Ty. *Wouldn't do to drop him over the cliff's edge.*

Not that he wasn't tempted sometimes. Raven grinned.

Still, I will lose him, one of these days. It would be hard, but finally meeting him in person — *that* was something for Raven to look forward to.

Ty flared to life, a bright golden wave of light panning across the far side of the river.

"Can we really rebuild it?" Aik was staring at the broken edge of the Old Bridge.

"Yes, with the plans I will provide. Dumbed down for your current disappointing level of technology, of course. If you can even call it that."

Aik laughed, and the darkness that hung over him passed. "Some things never change." The dark times were fewer and shorter than they used to be.

Raven touched Aik's shoulder, as much to convince himself this was real as to comfort his beloved. "Hard to believe it was only a couple of months ago." He shuddered, remembering that terrifying slide down the bluff on the far side of the gap, and Aik's firm grasp hauling him up and saving him from disaster.

Aik was different now, more ... centered. Less worried about what other people thought of him. Raven liked the new version.

Aik had confessed to what he'd done with Aer'Lis, but he hadn't been himself, and they had put it firmly in the past. Besides, Raven had been tempted too, though he and Jai had never done anything about it.

None of it mattered now. *I'm the luckiest man alive.*

"Do you miss it?" Aik looked over his shoulder.

"What, Gullton?" They'd spent most of the last month in Mountainhome, helping the other verent riders ready the caverns for the expected influx of new riders. After the Dark Days, the verent were known across the Heartland, and revered for their role in saving so many lives.

Aik frowned. "The Lair. Your old solitary life. You are still on the Council."

"I haven't missed a meeting yet." Ah, there it was. A flicker of the old, disapproving Aik. "Not at all. My new lair is far better. And I'm not alone anymore." Silya still had all of his things, stored away somewhere in the Temple. One of these days he'd get around to sorting through them, but in truth he didn't miss them. He'd tell her to donate them to his favorite orphanage.

His hand dropped to Aik's knife in its waist hilt, reassuring himself it was still there. One of the few things that was still important to him.

Silya had already agreed to provide work for his homeless friends, including Scill'Eya. Maybe the new Knowledge Guild could provide education for those unwanted children too.

But Aik was right. He should find someone else to take his seat on the Council, someone who could give the post the time it deserved. He'd ask Jimey Aza if he had the time and inclination to do it.

He pulled Aik close and kissed him, savoring the sense of security and warmth he felt whenever they were together. "I like my new life just fine."

Mollified, Aik squeezed him tight. "I'm glad. I like it just fine too."

"You two need a little privacy?" Ty's voice dripped with sarcasm.

"Yes, actually." Raven folded the cover over Ty's pouch, ignoring his muffled cries of protest. "We'll let you out when we get to the other side."

•　　•　　•

Aik closed his eyes, doing what Astrid had taught him and letting the darkness pass. There was a hole in his soul, one he rarely talked about, the place Iihil had been. His memories were still there, though, and sometimes he would dip into them, their alien taste reminding him of his lost friend. One day he would write them all down.

It was strange, to miss the one who had held him captive in his own mind. *Life doesn't always make sense.*

Still, he was happy to be back in Gullton. He missed taking care of the city and its people. He'd left the Guard, finally taking his mother up on the chance to apprentice with her at metalworking — she'd been thrilled with his decision, and had laughed with delight when he'd shown her the sword Tri'Aya had given him, one she'd forged almost a dozen years before, when he was still a child.

And when Silya had asked them to help survey the gorge for a new bridge, he'd jumped at the chance.

Clearly, she was angling for the two of them — and Ty — to return to the city and join her new Knowledge Guild. Sister Tela was already drawing up plans for a grand Library that was to be the heart of the new project, and Triya had agreed to donate most of the contents of her own collection. It would be built near the Temple itself, overlooking the Elsp and Landfield.

Silya was smart. She played the long game. She'd seen what an asset Ty could be — and Raven too — and was working to bring them back into her orbit.

"Come on. I want to get this over with." Raven climbed up onto Breeze's back, holding out a hand to Aik. "Then we can steal a little time away in your old flat."

He grinned. He took Raven's hand and pulled himself up onto Breeze, settling in behind Rave's back.

His lover — and soon to be more — had changed too. Gone was the former thief who only cared for himself. Not that it had ever really been true. Aik had always seen through his tough-guy façade and knew how much he had done for the poor in Gullton.

Still, the new Raven was different. He gave without thinking, even if he did complain about it now and then. And he'd forgiven Aik for his own indiscretion. He approved of the changes. *I'm the luckiest man alive.*

"Ready?" Raven kissed him over his shoulder.

"More than you'll ever know."

Raven laughed, a joyous sound, as Breeze spread his wings and took a running leap. Then they were soaring together, high above the troubles and cares of the world.

•   •   •

Kalix wondered at the new world beneath their wings. In such a short time the humans had put their own stamp on it, bending it to their will with a fearsome intensity that had frightened the verent and their kin.

Some had argued that they needed to be stamped out, like the aaveen before them.

But the memory of the world was long. That way had been tried before, twice, and the aaveen had come back more fearsome than before.

A new approach had been needed, and the accommodators had won out in the end, Kalix's grandsire among them.

And so they had reached out to the humans in the west, through the hencha, and the tiny elyn had been adapted for the humans in the east. Though it had taken generations of humans, both approaches had borne fruit, calming the expansion and lowering the temperature of alarm. But when the signs had come again that the aaveen were returning, more drastic measures had been needed.

Kalix rumbled happily at the outcome as they settled back on firm ground north of the city, among a newly planted grove of *evrit* — what the humans called bandy trees. They were already stretching toward maturity.

Raven was their kit and flying partner. He was as much a part of Kalix's family now as Sorix, Velix, Flyx and Aryx ... now Falix and Arix, ready to start families of their own. Maybe they would be paired with another human. Raven hoped so.

Raven's intended was a part of that family now too,

And soon they would have more kits running through the caverns and soaring over their valley home. Kalix could feel the eggs growing in their belly. In a week or so, they would return home to birth them. They wondered how many would find a human partner. *Life goes on.*

They watched Raven and Aik together, surveying the canyon, and a wonderful warmth filled their belly.

The world was right again, and the future was once again bright.

• • •

Kerrick carved a round hole in the coryx, slightly bigger than the window glass shipped in from the new plant, along the Harkness Coast south of Gullton.

The desert sand was perfect for glass-making, high in silicates. Raven's little silver friend had helped with the process, offering refinements that resulted in much better quality and — he assured them — longer lasting results.

Ty was proving to be an amazing font of information to help in the reconstruction of both the Heartland and Highlands.

Zeraya Town was the first of the Highlands settlements to be rebuilt with help from Gullton, the verent riders and the ce'faine. It would be a grand experiment — the first joint project between the two human peoples, a gathering point for their cultures to overlap and enrich one another.

Kerrick set the window into the gap, holding it steady as the edges of the coryx sealed tightly around it.

"Looks good." Elleck clapped him on the shoulder. "You sure you and Silya don't want to move out here to the frontier when this is all done?"

Kerrick laughed. "I'll never pull her away from Gullton. She's busy building her new Library. Her heart will always be in the city."

Elleck laughed heartily. "Whatever lights her pipe. Me, I'd rather be out under the great green sky." She picked up the round piece of coryx and set it against the white dome, where it immediately began to be reabsorbed. "I'm surprised she let you out of her sight."

"She knew we had some unfinished business, you and me." He eyed the white dome, shuddering before remembering it was harmless. The trauma of the Dark Days still struck him unexpectedly, every now and then. "Want to help me with the door?"

It was a bright, crisp Highlands morning. Just beyond the edge of the village, the trine grass waved in the chill breeze. The native vegetation had grown back with surprising speed, both here and in the Heartland. Though it would take time to reseed many of the old Earth crops, the hencha had filled in much of the destroyed farmland quickly, providing enough food to keep the battered human population fed through the recovery.

He cut out a patch for the door, and Elleck helped him muscle it and its frame into place. "You think this will work?"

"The door? I don't see why not." She opened it, and it slid smoothly on its hinges.

Kerrick shook his head. "This experiment. Heartlanders and ce'faine?"

"I hope so. I'll work hard to make it so."

His people had named Elleck the co-meer of the rebuilt village. "You will. You won me over."

Elleck smirked. "Well, you *are* my brother. Have they chosen the other meer?"

"I hear they're considering Jer'Mar, Astrid's brother. He's young, but he's a native, and he has ties to the verent riders too." He took a step back to admire their handiwork. It was the fifth home he'd worked on since the shipment of doors and windows came in overland from the new Transportation Guild.

"You two slacking off already?" The booming voice of the new transportation master spun him around. She'd arrived with the haifaine clan's eshem, Alibeh, in tow.

"We've done five of these already this morning." Kerrick gestured to the line of new housing that had replaced the old wooden structures. Humankind was learning to live with its new world instead of exploiting it.

Triya grinned. "They look good. The spore mother's working out well?"

He shivered at the name. Sure, the coryx were a domesticated version of the thing that had almost destroyed their world. But still ... he'd argued with Silya about the seed it had left. *Should have burned it or thrown it into the depths of the Harkness.*

Silya had disagreed, and as he was learning, she usually got what she wanted. Not that he minded all that much.

Elleck answered for him. "So far, so good. We'll get to work on your new guild hall soon."

Triya nodded her approval. Then she threw her arms around Kerrick unbidden. "So happy to have you as part of the Aya family, son."

She was surprisingly strong for her age. When she let go, he breathed again. "Thank you, Mim. Though as I see it, you're becoming part of the Aze family."

Triya winked at him. "You just keep on thinking that. Now back to work with you. I hear Astrid's arriving with Jereck this afternoon. Did you hear he's been chosen as the new co-meer?"

Kerrick and Elleck shared a look. "I'd heard rumors."

"We'll have a big welcome feast tonight." She grimaced. "Well, as big as we can manage. I miss foldovers."

Wheat flour was still scarce after the war. "One thing at a time." He licked his lips — foldovers did sound good.

He took Alibeh's hand. "Good to see you again ... Mim?"

"Just Alibeh. We don't truck in such formalities in the ce'faine."

He nodded. "I just wanted to say I'm sorry —"

"For what?"

He blushed. "For what my uncle did to you. I ... didn't know. I was so angry at the ce'faine, for so long —"

She touched his cheek. "You're right, you *didn't* know. The world turns as it will, and we're all just trying to keep up." She kissed his cheek. "A blessing upon you, Kek'Aze."

"Kerrick. We don't truck in such formalities here." His grin made her smile.

Alibeh laughed. "*Kerrick* it is."

"Come on, Kerr. We have a city to rebuild." Elleck punched him on the shoulder.

"Owww." He returned the favor. Some things hadn't changed between them, despite everything that had.

He looked around at the new city that was springing up in the ruins of the old. It was a good feeling, building things up instead of tearing them down.

And soon ... soon he'd see Silya again. And then they could talk about making things official before the baby came. Aya or Aze — it didn't much matter to him. All he cared about was that they were finally together, for good. "You should take this one, Alibeh. It's got a lovely view of the lake."

"I will. But only if you promise to come visit me here from time to time."

"We will." He knelt to return the favor, kissing her cheek this time.

He followed Elleck back to the supply wagon, whistling the Guardian's Song, his spirits as light as the breeze.

•   •   •

Chop, chop, chop. Chala used the cleaver to cut up the ix meat into bite-sized chunks to throw into the stewpot. The war was over, and now she was back to being the one who picked up all the odd jobs in Mountainhome.

Still, she counted herself lucky that Silya had forgiven her and let her return. Mountainhome was where she belonged. So what if she was here alone? *I don't need anyone.*

Chop, chop, chop.

Jai arrived on the landing outside the Kitchen, his verent's flapping wings darkening the cavern momentarily — she could sense his excitement from inside the cave. With Astrid and Raven off in Gullton and Olly making supply runs to the new village by the lake, it had been just the two of them. *Us and a batch of green recruits.*

It had helped considerably in the recruiting process when the verent had found a way to skip the whole dragon-down-the-throat thing, as Raven called it. Something about *genetics* and *cellular reconstruction*, to hear Ty tell it. In any case, they'd found another way, and that was all that mattered to Chala.

Chala might even try it herself one day. But for now, she had her verent Elrys, who loved her, and was a loner just like her. *Maybe I'm not so alone after all.*

"Got a new recruit." Jai popped into the cavern, a broad grin on his face.

"Get 'em settled and then tell them dinner's almost ready." She pulled out a bacca root to chop off some fine pieces for the stew. She'd have to talk with the others about getting some new ingredients —

"Chala?"

That voice sent shivers up her spine. She looked up, startled. *It can't be …*

The woman stepped away from the bright light at the cavern entrance. "The Oracle sent me. She … intervened with the clan leaders to let me come."

Great red sands. "Human Elrys!" She set down her knife and leapt across the counter, into her lover's arms. "I can't believe you're here!"

"*Human Elrys?*" Elrys stiffened under her embrace.

Chala laughed, the tightness around her heart finally loosening. "It's a long story." She held Elrys out at arm's length, drinking her in. Her black hair was longer, and she looked indefinably older … more mature? The first hint of wrinkles crowded along the sides of her brown eyes. But she was still the same beautiful woman Chala had known before. "Can you stay?"

Elrys grinned. "If you'll have me."

"Of course I will." She buried her face in Elrys's hair. She smelled of sun and sand. Of *home.*

Chala frowned. This was her home now. She had a new family here, a chosen one, though she hadn't been the one to do the choosing. The desert would always have a place in her heart, but she belonged at Mountainhome. Still, having Elrys here made it all better.

"Jai, do you mind finishing up?" Chala had so much to show her.

Jai shrugged his shoulders. "Of course. Havi can wait a few minutes more to see me." His new beau was as handsome as he was, but shy as an ix. "Go! Give her the grand tour."

Chala grinned. She took Elrys's hand and dragged her out of the Kitchen. "Come on. This place is amazing ... wait until you see the gathering cave!"

This wasn't *her* home anymore. It would be *their* home now.

•　　•　　•

Desla closed her eyes, feeling the warm sunshine on her face. At least this warmth was natural, accompanied by a refreshing, salty sea breeze.

She glanced over her shoulder, down the ridgeline toward the circular cove where the *Windrider* was anchored. None other than the sea master herself had captained the ship, aware of the importance of the cargo it carried. And eager to curry favor with the Temple, no doubt.

She smiled. The reason didn't matter. Her mission did.

"This looks good." She took a deep breath of the muggy air, filled with the salty tang of the sea. Above a flock of gully birds circled. It was much warmer here in the Caspin Isles than back home in Gullton, up north.

A few miles east, the arid reaches of the Great Southern Desert began. A new glass plant was already under construction there, which would eventually anchor a small settlement engaged in trade with the suifaine.

But here along the coast, it was humid, and the isles were covered in vegetation — tall slender trees with pitch-black bark and broad purple leaves shaped like shields, and ferns underfoot that rustled in the sea breeze.

They'd chosen this particular island for its shallow caverns, which Silya believed would be the perfect fertile ground for this part of the Grand Experiment. They would also plant some of the hencha here, to help protect the cavern and guide the seed's integration with the rest of Tharassas.

"Put it here, please."

The porters were sweating. They set down the sturdy crate in the middle of the cave. It was roughly a half circle, facing east, deep enough to shelter the inside from the worst of the rainstorms that sometimes thundered through here on their way north into the Heartland.

One of the porters, a woman named Celie, pried open the top of the wooden box. Inside, padded with hencha leaves, lay the seed. She whistled. "That's it?"

Desla lifted it out carefully, under the watchful eye of Zevrell, the sea master. "Yes, it's hard to believe there's a whole world inside of it."

"Should have dumped it overboard when we had the chance." Celie grinned, and the other porters laughed.

Zevrell was staring at it too. "Such a small thing." She'd expressed her doubts about the venture earlier, in long the two of them had enjoyed conversations on the ship. When she was away from the public eye, she was a much more thoughtful person than her acerbic public persona, though equally as shrewd.

Now she just watched as Desla sought the perfect resting place.

"I think this will do." It was a rock perch over a narrow crack, enough for the seed to root itself. It wouldn't need the raw power of its predecessor. It wasn't going to try to change the world, at least not all at once. *I hope.*

Although its very presence would alter everything in the years to come.

She settled it in gently, and then lifted the other thing from the crate, a ball of silver metal studded with red jewels. *Uurcaa*, Aik had called it. A magical metal — the sum total of Raven's old artefacts that had carried the soul of a sentient being. She set it down gently in a small hollow close to the seed, happy to let it go. It belonged here, with her, but after seeing what it had done to Aik …

She shuddered.

Putting it out of her mind, she knelt beside the seed, flames flickering up her arms. She called to it in the language the old spore mother — Iindree — had shown her, the language mimicked by the conjunction of the two moons. *Awaken, little one.*

At her touch, the seed rocked and shivered. Then with a loud crack, it split down the middle. A single root sought out the crevice below it, plunging into it in search of nutrients. Somewhere far below, the world blood flowed and would nourish Tharassas's latest inhabitant. *What will your name be?*

"That's it?" Zevrell's eyebrow raised.

"That's just the beginning." She got up and dusted her hands off on her hencha-cloth pants. She was going to need a whole new wardrobe for this warm climate. She looked around the uneven terrain outside the cave. "Now we need to build a place for me to live. Looks like I'll be roughing it for a while." In truth the *Windrider* had brought everything she'd need to start construction of an annex to the Temple. It would take time, but that was all right.

Silya had insisted she oversee this personally, given her connection to the last spore mother. Desla had been glad to accept. All her life she'd been looking for a purpose. She'd never imagined it would be as a mother to a stranger from the stars.

This new one would be raised differently, with Desla and Tharassas as its parents. It would learn how to weave itself into the world, sharing its own unique gifts.

Zevrell nodded. "I might just need to make some regular visits. To check up on the progress of this place. It's my responsibility, after all, to make sure you get off to a good start."

They'd made a *good start* the night before, a most pleasant surprise.

She closed her eyes and could still feel Zev's soft touch on her skin. "I'd like that. It's going to be lonely out here for a while, until we get things established."

"I'll come as often as I can. And I'll bring a few things to make your place here ... more comfortable too." She smiled, and it transformed her whole face.

Thoughtful and *beautiful.*

Desla grinned. *Time for a new adventure. Or two.*

•   •   •

Silya stood at the eastern edge of Raven Spine, her eyes closed feeling the breeze off the Harkness behind her as it teased her hair. Somewhere out there, Kerrick was rebuilding Zeraya with his sister.

In her dreams, she'd stood here in a world on the brink of disaster. Now they were on the brink of something else. *Possibility?*

No. Hope. She could feel it all around her through the emp, a city bustling with it as it rebuilt and planned for a different future.

To the north, Raven and Aik were scouting out the Elsp where it raced down to the sea, planning the new bridge with Ty's help that would reconnect Gullton with Heaven's Reach and the northern cities by land.

Chala, Jai, and the other verent riders were opening Mountainhome to a fresh batch of recruits. One name in particular had caught her eye. Audrin, like the woman in her emp test. Could it be? *Stranger things have happened.*

Coral was training with Dor to eventually take over the senior aide position ... although Silya hoped that day was a long time in the future.

And Desla was taking the biggest gamble of all, planting a seed that, Fri'Oss willing, would bring new beauty into the world, not the destruction like its predecessor had.

And here she was, stuck in Gullton.

She wrapped her hands around her rapidly expanding belly. *What kind of world will you be born into, my little one?*

She opened her eyes, laughing at her own maudlin mood. *I have the most important job of all. Teaching the world.*

Soon the new Library, home to the Knowledge Guild, would start to rise here on the edge of the spine, in sight of the white walls of the Temple. The rocks from the old lighthouse would be refashioned into an arch to welcome all who entered. She hoped it would become a new sort of lighthouse for the world. Daya would have liked that.

Sister Tela would transfer all of the works in the Temple archive into their new home, augmented by those her mother was sending over from the Manor House. And soon there would be new works written as well — literature inspired by the Dark Days. New science texts, with information provided by Ty — minus the snark. He was already working with the Temple pilot, Fen'Ost on plans for new flitters, though they wouldn't be nearly as fancy as the ones that had come in from Old Earth. They'd even talked about building them out at Isa steading — seems he'd taken a liking to Maur'Isa, and her place had a lot of open land and access to several nearby mines.

And who knows what else?

The Knowledge Guild would be a place of learning for Temple initiates, boys and girls alike, and for all the children of Gullton, including her own daughter. Maybe some of the adults too. And hopefully it would be the first of many such schools.

She turned to survey the hencha gathering.

It was a silly thought, but she suddenly wanted to be among them. They were always *with* her, this gathering and all the rest. She could feel them in her head, along with the other sisters and the eshem. Tharassas was well on its way to recovery, despite what had been lost.

"You all right?" A frown creased Dor's forehead.

"She does that a lot lately."

She flashed a smile at Das'Efrim. The former Council Guard had requested a transfer to the Temple, and had attached himself to her as her personal bodyguard. "I'm ... wonderful."

She knew it was true as she said it. Her life had a purpose, and things were going in the right direction, for once. "Come to the hencha with me?"

"Of course." Dor took her hand, and they walked down the path into the grove.

Dasin followed them, keeping a respectful difference.

She turned down the row where it had all begun. Where the hencha had first spoken to her. And where she had laid Daya to rest. "Here, I think."

She closed her eyes, remembering that last brief conversation with her former mentor. *Grab on to what life gives you with both hands.*

"And you did. I'm so proud of you, Silya."

The voice startled her. She turned to find Daya standing there, as solid and real as the hencha plants around them. "How ...?"

"I always knew you would." She pulled Silya in for a fierce hug. She smelled of grayleaf, her favorite essential oil. She was warm and soft, encompassing her like the embodiment of motherly love. "You've made me very proud."

First Triya, and now from her friend and mentor. Silya squeezed her tightly, not wanting to let go. Something tickled the back of her mind. "Can I ask you a couple things?"

"Of course, dear."

"Why are my hencha flames blue?" It had always bothered her. The previous queens had wielded black flames. The histories (and sisters) had been very specific about that.

Daya chuckled. "The hencha gave you what was needed — what you needed — for this time. If such a need arises, the black flame will come to you too."

She nodded. How she missed Daya's steady wisdom.

"And the other thing?"

She frowned. "How did Jas know? About the prophecy, about sending me those supplies from her own time?"

Daya frowned. "That's a more ... complicated answer. Suffice it to say the hencha don't *only* live in this time."

That makes no sense. Silya thought about pushing her on it, but Daya's look brooked no further discussion. "Is that how you're here? The hencha?"

Daya looked suddenly, terribly sad. "Yes. This ... is just a ghost of me. I wish I could stay with you always, to guide you."

She blinked. "I'm so sorry, Daya. I wish I could have saved you."

Daya held up a finger. "Don't be. It was my time. This is yours. You have a long and hard road ahead of you. But I know you and Dor will find your way together. You always do."

She hugged Daya again, and her tears flowed freely for the first time since that awful night when her mentor had died. "I love you, Daya."

"I love you too. But Silya ..."

She let her mentor go, blinking. "What?"

"I'm not Daya." Dor was staring at her, that frown back on her face. "You sure you're all right?"

She laughed. "No, of course you're not." She closed her eyes, and could still smell Daya's lingering presence, the musky grayleaf oil she wore. "I just thought ..."

"I know." Dor put a hand on her cheek. "She would be very proud of you."

Was it really her? Who knew what was possible, with the hencha. Maybe Daya was part of the hencha mind now.

She took a deep breath. "Yes, I'm all right. *Really* all right, for the first time in … in a long time." Kerrick would be back in a few days, and she had so many things to do before then. "Sit with me for a moment?"

"Of course, Mim."

Silya let the formality go, taking it for the gesture of respect that Dor intended.

Dor was staring at her belly. "Have you chosen a name yet?"

She smiled. She'd been thinking about it for weeks, but it had only just come to her. "I'll call her Daya."

Dor nodded. "That's perfect." She picked up a fallen hencha leaf, rolling it around between her thumb and forefinger. "It's about time we had another Daya loose in the world."

"I thought so too." They settled onto the soft ground between the hencha rows. She took Dor's hand. "Close your eyes."

Dor did as she was told.

"Can you hear it?"

The singing of the hencha filled her world. The sadness was still there — it would always be a part of the melody. But the joy shone brighter this afternoon.

Dor squeezed her hand. "I can, Mim. What are they singing?"

Silya let the music wash over her, considering. "They're singing us a new tomorrow."

One where her daughter would grow up in a world far different from the one they lived in now. *Hopefully far better, too.*

Now all they had to do was build it.

GLOSSARY

Adley Narrows: A narrowing of the Elsp between Vulture Spine and the North Shore, near the egress to the Harkness Sea

Aik'Erio aka Aiken (Mas): Guardsman in Gullton and loyal friend to Raven

Ais'Vellin aka Aisel (Mas): Trader and associate of Tri'Aya

Akin-yo: A martial art the sisters practice

Akka: A bitter drink made from the leaves of the Akka bush; the local equivalent of coffee

Auddah: Cheese made from aur milk

Alaya: The Tharassan native name for Tarsis, the bigger golden moon

Angels: What the Tharassans called Runners from Earth (LR)

Anghar Mor: One of the mountains in the Redflight range, with lots of volcanic activity

Anya'Enn aka Anyassa (Mim): A Temple initiate

Arsday: Fifth day of the week

Aryx (Cat): One of Breeze's kits, female

Ast'Una aka Aster (Mim): One of the Temple sisters, head of the Temple stores

Auley Tree: A spindly tree with strong fire-resistant sticks

Aur/Auracinth: Large beasts of burden that don't develop a gender until their third year

Ay'Oss aka Ayja: God of magic, technology, wisdom, and earth whose sign is the wisp, and who presents as a handsome young man

Ayvin/Aaveen: An alien race that arrived on Tharassas before humanity

Bacca Root: A minty local root that people chew on for flavor with anti-nausea properties

Bandy Fruit: Red fruit with purple spikes, sweet and juicy

Bandy Trees/Heart Trees/Evrit: Native trees with wide red trunks, broad, heart-shaped purple leaves, where heartroot and bandy fruit come from

Beast Guild: The Gullton guild in charge of domesticated beasts (aur, urse, etc)

Black Cheese: A variety of cheese from aur milk, grown in the caverns under Gullton

Breeze aka Kalix (Raven): male verent with a green tinge to his white skin

Builder's Guild: The contractors' guild in Gullton

Callasday: Sixth day of the week

Capton: Small oceanfront town north of Gullton

Car'Ost aka Carel (Mim): Junior cook in the Temple

Cayah: Desert dwellers with tan and brown dappled skin and spiral horns

Ce'Faine: Human clans that live in the far east and south, past the borders of the Highlands and the Heartland

Cekya: Temple cook

Cephlant: A grazing herd animal similar to an elephant

Cer'Ella aka Ceryl (Sister): The fourth Hencha Queen, only served for a year

Cheevah: A small flying creature

Cheff: Derogatory name for the Ce'faine

Cherry Fly: Thumb-sized insect with twelve legs

Clayton: Small town in the eastern part of the Heartland

Cleffer Bush: A red-leaved plant with yellow "brush" flowers

Cor'Lea aka Coral (Mim): An initiate at the hencha Temple

Corinth: The small village on the south slopes where Queen Jas came from (Last Run)

Crosston: A small town in the middle of the Heartland

Dalney: Small oceanfront town north of Gullton

Dam, The: A hydroelectric dam built just after landing to power the colony, recently refurbished

Day'Ima aka Daya (Sister): One of Silya's teachers, ace, wears violet pine perfume

Dem'Errol aka Demtrius (Mas, Ser): Aik's squad captain

Der'Iza aka Derik (Mas): Tri'Aya's husband and Silya's father

Des'Rya aka Desla (Mim): A Temple initiate originally from Devon

Destrayer's Song: An old battle song from the Heartlander-Ce'Faine conflict

Devon: Village in the southern part of the Heartland

Dor'Ala aka Doria (Sister): Sister appointed to be Silya's aide

Ecin: Fifth month of the year

Edgeton: A small town south of Gullton

Edie: Tenth month of the year

Edu: Second month of the year

Eechiia: Living membranes used to separate spaces

Eemscaap: Digger creatures from Uurccheea

Eesiil: Red, glowing star-like fungus with seven points

Eev-uurccheea: Literally "New Uurccheea," the aaveen's second homeworld. Also the name given to Tharassas by the Spore Mother

Eircat: Cat analogues – Highland hunters

El'Oss/Elohim/The Old God: God of the past and love, sign is the cross, once the Christian god, now folded into the local religion

Electrical Guild: A new guild in Gullton responsible for the electric lights and the dam

Elsp River: River that runs from lake Zeraya to Gullton through the Highlands and the Heartland

Em'Asa (Mim): One of Tri'Aya's private guards, born in Dalney

Eneet: A squirrel equivalent

Eno: First month of the year

Eoto: Eighth month of the year

Equa: Fourth month of the year

Erphin: Dolphin equivalent

Esei: Sixth month of the year

Eset: Seventh month of the year

Eshem: The ce'faine equivalent of the Hencha Queen

Etré: Third month of the year

Evro: Ninth month of the year

Fellin Root: a yellow root that serves as an anti-dolorific, also a sleep aid in larger quantities

Fess'Ima aka Fessryn (Mim): One of the Temple initiates

Fexin: Deep purple Highlands herb, used as topical germicide

Flitter: Small helicopters used to transport people in the Heartland; sparkling "wings" (LR)

Flop Trees: Big-leaved trees used to provide islands of shade in the hencha plantations

Flyx (Grey): One of Breeze's kits, male

Foldovers: A sweet or savory pastry

Fre'Oss aka Freja: God of air, weather, and health, sign is the lightning bold, presents as a child, sometimes male, sometimes female

Fri'Oss aka Frija: God of fertility, birth, the harvest and sex, sign is the leaf, presents as a woman

Gap, the: Pass connecting the Highlands with the Heartland to the East

Gap Station: The way station in the middle of the Gap

Grayleaf: A seasoning often used in steak rubs, also used as an essential oil

Great Southern Desert: The huge desert south of the Heartland, beyond the Onyx Mountains, where the suifaine live

Guard's Honor: Used to swear something

Gullton/Gullytown: The main city on Tharassas, where the colony was founded

Gully Birds: Black seagull equivalents found in Gullton and the heartland

Gully Fowl: Three-legged chicken equivalents

Gully Rat: Derogatory term for citizens of Gullton

Gully Rats: Larger cousins to the inthym that live in and around Gullton

Gully Weasels: See gully rats, also used as a derogatory term for Gulltoners

Hacka Berries: Highland berries known for their sweet, salty taste

Haifaine: East Valley Clan - Elleck (Enrick)

Harkness Sea: The sea to the west of Gully Town

Heartland: The original colony lands, with Gullton as the capital

Heartlanders: People who live in the Heartland

Heartroot: Spicy highlands herb, similar to cinnamon

Heaven's Reach: The mountain range along the northern edge of the Heartland

Hel'Oss aka Helja: God of death, war, and problems, sign is the black staff, presents as intersex

Hencha: A food crop that's also semi sentient, human height with red stalks and purple leaves

Hencha Berries: Berries produced by the hencha plants that are edible by humans - red (sweet), orange, blue (sharp-sweet), and yellow (tart, citrus/vitamin c)

Hencha Leaf Scroll: Paper made from hencha leaves

Hencha Mind: The animating group consciousness of the hencha

Hencha Oil: Used for lanterns

Hencha Queen: The woman who can talk to the hencha; also the animating consciousness of the hencha en masse (see *Hencha Mind*)

Hencha Tea: A healing tea made from hencha leaves

Henchwine: Wine made from hencha berries

Hera River: The other major river in the Heartland

Hes'Enn aka Hestra (Mim): The Temple sword master

Heurcinth: Purple Highlands flowers that grow with pezzywinkles in matched pairs

Heyfa Weeds: Yellow semi-sentient weeds that strangle the hencha plants for food

Highlanders: People who live in the Highlands; can refer to Steaders or sometimes Ce'Faine

Highlands: Wide valley inland from the Heartland, accessed via the Gap

Highlands Treaty: Treaty signed between Gullton/the Heartland and the Ce'Faine

Iichili/Forerunners/Fireflies: Spies for the Spore Mother

Initiate: An acolytes of the hencha Temple

Inthym/Rinkin: Little harmless white mouse-like creatures that hunt insects in packs

Jai (m, reifaine): One of the ce'faine, then a verent rider

Janusday: Fourth day of the week

Jas'Aya aka Jasinaya (Mim): Hencha berry farm worker, later the Hencha Queen; dark hair

Jel'Faya aka Jelin (Mas): Contemporary fantasy author

Jellybug: Small, brightly-colored beetles that inthyms eat

Jer'Est aka Jeryl (Mas): One of Aik's friends

Jexyn: Hive-minded birds in the Highlands; dangerous when they find fresh meat

Jim'Aza aka Jimey (Mas): Nel'Aza's son and Raven's first crush

Jor'Oss aka Jorja (wild nature/unpredictability/luck - dice)**:** God of wild nature, unpredictability and luck, sign is the dice, presents as a scarily beautiful young woman

Jyn'Eln (Doctor): Medic for the Gullton Guard

Keh'Sel aka Kehla (Mas): Temple seamstress

Kek'Aze aka Kerrick (Ser): One of Aik's superiors in the guard

Kerint: Ocean fish-equivalents with a sweet, tangy meat

Lake Zeraya: The huge central lake that defines the highlands

Lamplighter's Guild: Gullton guild responsible for lighting the lamps and the natural gas lines

Landfield: The suburb that sprung up on the western side of the old landing field

Lo'Oss aka Loja: God of fire, change, strength and protection, sign is flames, presents as gender-fluid, and can appear in all of the forms

Local Population Contact Regulations (LPCs): Rules governing contact with a local population

Lowlander: Derogatory term the Highlanders use for the Heartlanders

Lyn'Rya (Mim): Des'Rya's mother, and a tanner in Devon

Machinists' Guild: Gullton guild responsible for fabricating anything needed by the other guilds

Mad Blade: Aik's mother's armory/book shop on Raven Spine

Manor House: Tri'Aya's home in Heaven's Reach

Mar'Orn aka Marea (Mim): Raven's mother

Martasday: Second day of the week

Mas: Title for adult men

Meer: Mayor

Menagerie: Bestiary of real and imagined beasts created from Sera's original works by Sol'Eria

Mes'Ena aka Meslyn (Mim): One of Tri'Aya's guards

Mif (Mas): One of Aik's friends

Mim: Title for adult women

Mir: Title for adult non-binary/fluid

Mir'Ust aka Mirrel (Mim): One of the Temple initiates

Mohr'Una *aka* Mohria (Mim): The Temple astrologer

Mountain Ix: Swift-footed mountain animals prized for their colorful green-gold hides

Mountainhome: What the humans call the valley where the verent live

Mudmole: A large rodent equivalent

Mur Beatles: Silk-weaving beatles

Mur Silk: Silk spun by mur beatles

Nel'Aza aka Nellie (Mim): Raven's neighbor who takes him in when his mother dies

Noninalya: One of the songs of the Sisters of the Hencha

Nor'Oss aka Norja: God of water, the sea, and prosperity, sign is a wave, presents as an old man

Northlander: A less derogatory term for the Heartlanders and Steaders

Norton: Small town in the middle of the Heartland

Onyx Mountains: The range just south of Gullton and the Heartland

Oosill: Finger-sized uurcheean worms that leave behind fertilizer mucus

Oracle, the: The eshem of the suifaine clan

Orinth Honey: A sweet sticky substance made by orinths in their nest

Orinth: Green and orange insects that nest in muddy columns, analogous to termites

Ost Farm: Vegetable farm outside of Gullton that sells produce to the Temple

Otherlings: What the verent call humans

Pellin: Tharassas's smaller, pink moon, Erreh in the native tongue

Peregrine Spine: The smallest spine, where many of the rich have mansions

Pes'Osa aka Peslyn (Mir): One of the sisters in the Temple

Pezzywinkles: Orange Highlands flowers that grow with Heurcinths in matched pairs

Puffer Hen: Domesticated fowl; also used to describe gossips

Raising, The: The coronation of a new Hencha Queen

Rav'Orn aka Raven (Mas): Thief from Gullton

Raven Spine: The central "spine" of Gullton where toe Temple and city hall are found

Redflight Mountains: The range that defines the southern edge of the Highlands

Redhawk Spine: The southernmost spine, and also the poorest, home of the Open Market

Reifaine: Red Flight clan of the ce'faine

Ring Tree: Spiral tree with purple fronds found in the foothills of Heaven's Reach

River Grass: Cattail equivalents that grow along river shores

Rock Ferns: Red ferns that grow along the spines of Gullton

Russet Mold (powdered): Used for fever

Sadie's Cove: Small oceanfront town north of Gullton

Sal'Moya aka Sallia (Mim): One of the Sisters, head of the initiates

Scill'Eya: A homeless woman in Gullton

Sea Guild: The main transportation guild in Gullton

Sera Collins (Ahsera): Pilot of the Spun Diver; black

Sil'Aya aka Silya (Mim): Aik's old flame and an initiate at the Hencha Temple

Sister: Title for the women who work in the Temple

Skeef: A tick equivalent

Skerit: A bat equivalent

Sol'Eria (Solene): A Sister in the Temple who had a talent for art, and who collected many of Sera's works into leather-bound volumes

Solsday: First day of the week

Southford: A small town in the southeastern corner of the Heartland

***Spin Diver*:** The last ship to make the run from Earth (LR)

Spin: AI of the *Spin Diver*

Spore Mother: Mysterious alien entity

Squint aka Sorix: Breeze's female mate, reddish brown

Steader: Someone from one of the steadings in the Highlands

Stones: A gambling game where flat, etched stones are thrown for points and sets

Suifaine: Desert clan of the ce'faine

Summer Meet: Gathering of the Highlander tribes along the southeastern side of Lake Zeraya

Tarsis: Tharassas's larger golden moon, dominated by a big heart-shaped crater

Tartan Hills: The hilly region bordering the southern edge of the Heartland

Tel'Esta aka Tela (Sister): One of Silya's teachers and the Temple archivist

Temple/Hencha Temple: The seat of the Hencha Queen in Gullton

Terasday: Third day of the week

Tess'Esra aka Tesslyn (Initiate): One of the Temple initiates

Tharassas: A human-colonized world

Theolin: A stringed instrument with strings made from aur hair

Thieves' Guild: Loose, unrecognized Gullton guild comprised of master thieves and apprentices

Tri'Aya *aka* Triya (Mim): Silyas' mother, a wealthy merchant with a mansion called the Manor House on the slopes of Heaven's Reach

Trine Grass: Tri-bladed purple grass that covers the Highlands valley

Tucker Narrows: A narrowing of the Elsp between Raven Spine and Eagle Spine

Umvit/Vrint: Small, fast, nimble three-winged flying creature used as messengers

Urse: A smaller version of an Auricinth, a horse equivalent

Uurccheea: The long-destroyed home world of the Aaveen

Vale: A small town at the eastern edge of the Highlands

Veifaine: the Highlands Valley clan of the ce'faine that no longer exists

Verent/Skirryn (s/pl): Dragon-like native beasts that change gender periodically

Verla'Olk (Mim): Temple cook

Violet Pine: Native tree with spiky needles

Vulture Spine: The northernmost spine, also the location of most of Gullton's industry

Wil'Ock aka Willem (Mas): Tri'Aya's husband and Sil'Aya's father, an artist from Sadie's cove

Wisps/Esh: Mysterious glowing blue sparks that have suddenly become more common

Yen'Ela aka Yendra (Mim): The previous Hencha Queen

Zelaya: A bustling town on the southeastern shore of Lake Zelaya in the Highlands

Zev'Nek aka Zevrell (Mim, Sea Master): Sea Master of Gullton

ABOUT THE AUTHOR

J. Scott Coatsworth writes stories that subvert expectations, that seek to transform traditional science fiction, fantasy, and contemporary worlds into something new and unexpected. His writing, whether romance or genre fiction (or a little bit of both), brings a queer energy to his stories, infusing them with love, beauty and power and making them soar. He imagines a world that *could be* and, in the process, maybe changes the world *that is*, just a little.

A Rainbow Award-winning author, Scott's debut novel, *Skythane*, received two awards and an honorable mention. With his husband, Mark, he runs Queer Sci Fi, QueerRomance Ink, Liminal Fiction, and Other Worlds Ink. Scott is also the committee chair for the Indie Authors Committee at the Science Fiction and Fantasy Writers Association (SFWA).

ALSO IN THIS SERIES

THE DRAGON EATER
THE THARASSAS CYCLE: BOOK ONE

Raven's a thief who just swallowed a dragon.

A small one, sure, but now his arms are growing scales, the local wildlife is acting up, and his snarky AI familiar is no help whatsoever.

Things are about to get messy.

THE GAUNTLET RUNNER
THE THARASSAS CYCLE: BOOK TWO

A guard and a thief. What could go wrong?

Aik has fallen hopelessly in love with his best friend. But Raven's a thief, which makes things ... complicated. Oh, and Raven has just been kidnapped by a dragon.

Things were messy before ... but now they're much, much worse.

THE HENCHA QUEEN
THE THARASSAS CYCLE: BOOK THREE

Silya has to embrace her role as the Hencha Queen. But will it be enough to save the Temple, and her world?

Silya finally has everything she always wanted: She's the Hencha Queen, head of the Temple, and is mastering her newfound talents. So why does the world pick now to fall apart?

Available from Water Dragon Publishing in
hardcover, trade paperback, and digital editions
waterdragonpublishing.com

YOU MIGHT ALSO ENJOY

MEMORY AND METAPHOR

by Andrea Monticue

Civilization fell. It rose. At some point, people built starships.

SMASH THE WORLD'S SHELL

by Daniel Fliederbaum

A fractured world. An impossible friendship.

A WRECK OF DRAGONS

by Elaine Isaak

Teens and their giant robots search for a new home for mankind, but the planet they discover belongs to the dragons.